JACOB'S DEMON
Originally published as *Jacob's Fire*

"ASTOUNDING! The story's conclusion wowed my socks off. Wow Wow Wow!!! *Jacob's Fire* — A must read.
— Alexis Brown

"A WELL-CRAFTED thought-provoking novel."
— Arline Chase, author of *Ghost Dancer* and *Killraven*.

"IF THE READER EMBRACES a ...challenge and the adrenaline rush of trepidation, this book is for you!"
— Clementine S. Lezon

"I HIGHLY RECOMMEND *JACOB'S FIRE* to readers of all faiths in order to affirm what they believe about their role in this world and eternity."
— Evie Smith

Last of the Wallendas

"...THE GRANDDAUGHTER OF HIGHWIRE WALKER KARL WALLENDA tells the story of her family's ...involvement in circus acrobatics ... a history of this extended family and its unique obsession unfolds [with the]...pungent ambience of circus life."
— *Publishers Weekly* © 1993 Reed Business Information, Inc.

"HIGH-FLYING STORY of the great highwire artists, told by the granddaughter of legendary trapeze-artist KARL WALLENDA and by journalist Nan DeVincentis-Hayes (*People*, *Redbook*, etc.)."
— *Kirkus Reviews*.

TIME

A SEASONAL COLLECTION
OF SHORT STORIES

by Gianni Devincenti Hayes

Cambridge Books

an imprint of

WriteWords, Inc.

CAMBRIDGE, MD 21613

Cambridge Books is a subsidiary of:

Write Words, Inc.
2934 Old Route 50
Cambridge, MD 21613

ISBN 978-1-61386-202-5

Fax: 410-221-7510

Bowker Standard Address Number: 254-0304

Dedication

To all those who weather time

> *The time of trial*
> *the time of love*
> *the time of joy*
> *the time of pain*
> *the time of honor*
> *the time of rain*
> *the time of laughter*
> *and the time of time together*

Contents

PROLOGUE

It's interesting to read snippets of life in short story form, where never is the entire account ever featured. Perhaps it's akin to highlights, or reminiscent of the short accounts in the old magazines that featured something akin to "the story of the month." Whatever it may represent, it is by far, a lie in most cases.

Readers tend to think that what they read is real. Maybe. But usually it is only a modicum of truth, a peek inside a real scene unfolding, or a twist of what may have been true. More often it is what it is — pure fiction, pure-pretense, pure makeup.

Good writers step out of their comfortable shoes and tackle issues that may have unfolded in some way in their lives (but likely not as dramatically), or they take a personal rawness and make it all the more chaffing, or they just design an event that never existed just to explore what may have been or what could have been.

I always find it frustrating that when my college students read short stories — or even novels — they discourse the plot as though it had really happened to the author. This is a huge mistake on any reader's part.

It's important to remember one thing when reading fiction, and to keep this advice always at the top of your mind: Writers lie. It's that simple.

So sit back and enjoy a yarn or two, a fish tale, a pretended event.

Seasons

Autumn to winter, winter into spring,
Spring into summer, summer into fall,
So rolls the changing year, and so we change;
Motion so swift, we know not that we move.
  — Dinah Mulock Craik
    "Immutable"

While the earth remaineth, seedtime and
harvest, and cold and heat, and summer and
winter, and day and night shall not cease.
  — Genesis 8:22

INTRODUCTION

Sitting at the fire or in bed with a good book is always a pleasure and a gift. I write because I have to, an inner part of me forces me to...I'm cursed. But always I hope that whatever I say someone will hear it in words and allow it to strike a chord in them, harmonious or discordant. In reaching inside the readers, I hope that I touch something that will jolt them to life, make them pensive, provoke their emotions, jump for joy, and weep for what was, what is and what should be, and to rejoice in youth reborn and appreciate a future yet to be. These are the times of living, the seasons of being.

Many of my stories were written over a period of time, and many have been published. In them, you can see the changes—like seasons—in my writing; my failings, like leaves dropping from trees; my coveted privacy like snow blanketing the ground; my ups and downs like waves rolling in and out; and my growth like buds on branches.

Nothing offered here is meant to hurt or annoy anyone; rather, it is merely my rendition of life, right or wrong.

To share with you readers, you should be aware of the time, the seasons, as this is what I struggled with the most. It's difficult at times to determine what the time period is in a short story, but my intent was not to give calendar time, but rather internal time, as in spring = the awakening; summer = life's interim; fall = the passing; winter = the settlement.

You, the readers, may read into these stories in any manner you desire, as they are written solely for your entertainment. But they are all written to share the commonalities among us: love, fear, sickness, death, anger, sorrow, helplessness, hope, happiness—feelinsg we all experience, for we all share our humanity.

Part One
Winter

For such a charge, his snow upon the roof,
His icicles along the wall to keep;
And slept. The log that shifted with a jolt
Once in the stove, disturbed him and he shifted,
And eased his heavy breathing, but still slept.
One aged man—one man—can't keep a house,
A farm, a countryside, or if he can,
It's thus he does it on a winter's night."

  "An Old Man's Winter Night"
    — Robert Frost

There's Tomorrow

I'm Gail and I wrote this note:

> *My dear Zach and babies,*
> *I am tired of fighting, tired of living, tired of being a burden on you, and worried about becoming an even bigger yoke on you, and putting you in debt. I love all of you. Forgive me for this.*
> *Love,*
> *Your loving Mommy and wife*

I hurried out of the house to do what I planned before I chickened out.

It's off-season and I easily find a parking space. I sweep and spin the steering wheel to wrestle my husband's ark into a diagonal spot.

Cars to me are cars, but to Zach they're some rare golden gem to be fondled and caressed for years to come.

Zach's always been fanatical about his old Lincoln—my children call it "Daddy Longlegs." I've never liked the stretched black metal because it's old, costly, and too big. Every time he takes it to the shop, it nearly bankrupts us.

Awhile back, we got a $1 thousanf dollar bill from the repair shop just to fix something in the motor. I had said, "Zach, get rid of this money-guzzler. It's costing us a fortune to keep it running. Look at what this rebuilt carburetor costs!"

He cringed the way he does when I misname his car's body parts. Sourly he said, "Transmission, not carburetor or motor.

9

The transmission is like the heart of a car. You put in a new transmission and it becomes born-again."

"More like a renewed demon." I tried a softer approach. "Zach, I know you love this car but do you think it's worthwhile for us to maintain it?"

"Not worthwhile! Do you go around throwing people away when they get old, sick, worn down?"

He was always unreasonable when it came to cars. For our tenth anniversary he gave me his Lincoln. Put a huge red ribbon on it; he blindfolded me and guided me by my arm to the driveway and then into the car. "Oh, honey, this is so sweet of you," I had gushed.

How could I tell him I'd rather have a mink? Or an in-ground pool? Even a vacation? But his old Lincoln I get. And he thought he had offered up his life in sacrifice. He made me promise to take care of it.

I keep my promises. I take good care of his car...but not always of myself.

I suppose I always thought my body was like a car—get behind the wheel, turn the key in the ignition and it runs. But I appreciated that I had to maintain a car in order for it to work well and stay in circulation for years, yet I certainly never thought this principle applied to me.

On days like today, when I would walk the beach, I'd set aside late afternoon to get all the sand out of his car, to restore it thoroughly to its original state. Vacuuming doesn't get it all. Handpicking grains is absurd. So now I always take my shoes off when I walk in the sand, carrying them with me to put back on when I return to the car.

Except for today.

I nonchalantly stretch my arm over my head, take a deep breath, and in one smooth motion, I hurdle my tennis shoes into the frothing water. They jostle in the fast undercurrents, and sink, then go...who knows where.

I have no intention of getting back into my car...ever.

Save for the roaring tide's fizzing as it sprays mist into the biting air, spiraling it into cottony silver, there is silence. I look around as I stand on Ocean City's beach at Tenth Street, in midwinter, thinking about walking into the ocean. Joining my tennis shoes.

I could go on fighting to live, hoping a new heart comes in for me, or I could end it here to avoid the destitute my family will face after my surgery. There is no other alternative. My heart is destined to stop in the near future.

I look around. Seems every year more and more people come to this resort, even in off-season. Clumps of people are scattered behind me on the boardwalk, around me on the beach, bundled up to ward off the cutting ocean gusts. They must do what I do—come here to think, to feel nature's power. But today I'm here for a different reason.

Stinging images of bleak tomorrows fill my head: my husband sitting at the table, running his hand through his graying hair, stammering, "We can't afford groceries this week." Pictures of us selling our furniture piece by piece, our little boat, his Lincoln, our house, while we pick at each other, snarl, cry into our pillows at night, and no longer hold hands, no longer snuggle the children.

This I cannot do to us.

It's windy standing here. I like how the sharp breeze smarts my eyes, making me tear. I kick at the white sand, taking a few more steps towards the water.

I'm thirty-three, but my heart problem started long ago. I guess I was maybe twelve when I woke up that day with soreness in my heel. I had managed to stand, my joints searing, and tried to walk, but my knees buckled, making me crouch at the headboard for support. It was all I could do to lean against the wall, my fist pounding the plaster. I've since had five heart catherizations and each painful one showed the floppy, sloppy valve and damaged muscle.

I never really took this too seriously. How can I when I'm young? I played forbidden sports—dribbling basketballs and jumping for hoops, jogging, bicycling—and I seldom rested. Sometimes I got too busy to remember my meds. But it was okay, I thought.

I'm strong.

Then colds developed into full-blown heart infections— sudden tightness, squeezing in my chest, shoulders, neck, and with constant elevated temperatures—sometimes landing me in the hospital weeks at a time. And the chest pain became

11

more frequent, the medicine less effective. I was tired all the time. I grew so weak that the very thought of having to stand, force my legs to move, made me whimper.

"Mmmm," this big-shot dumpy-looking cardiologist told me when my regular doctor forced me to see him. "My oh my." He pointed to the monitor in the dark room where animated flashes outlined pictures of my heart. "So slow."

"It's beating too slow?" I asked incredulously.

"It's wearing out."

I remember giggling when he said that. Wearing out like car tires. Then, it had seemed so melodramatic. Now it seems so unfortunate.

"This is serious, Mrs. Randall. One day, all too soon, your heart will...stop." In the next breath, he announced, "I'm afraid the only solution is to get a new one."

I thought that funny, like he was telling me to go back to the market and buy a new head of lettuce since the one I had was wilting.

And then it caught up with me. It was akin to laughing and skipping one day, and being pinned under a twenty-ton semi the next.

I gasped for breath with any step I tried to take, like a giant football player bear-hugging me while mercilessly dragging me down field. I was white as whipped cream, except for a pale shade of blue on my lips and nail beds. I knew I was slipping fast.

The sand is cold under my shoeless feet. I make bulldozed paths with my toes. Walk on. Off to my left, maybe eighty-feet is a man, bent over, sitting in the sand, his baggy pants billowing in the sea wind. I wonder what he has on his mind. Is his body failing, too?

In the hospital, I was again told I must have a heart transplant. A transplant...can you believe it? Standing here on the beach it seems so unreal—substituting someone else's vital organ for mine. What does seem real to me right now are the wave's runnelling in and the ocean spitting on my skin. The faulty ticking muscle inside me seems distant and part of some technological fantasy.

From where I stand I can see the man down the beach

struggle to his feet, slog aimlessly around. He's teetering. Maybe he's drunk. He zigzags sluggishly towards the breakers...yet moves faster than my heart can beat.

"Slow beating heart," another doctor confirmed, shaking his head sadly. He gave me an ultimatum when I was in the hospital: "Pacemaker or defibrillator won't help. Get a transplant or go home and die."

"I want to know everything about it," I had demanded. They put me in touch with a Pittsburgh woman who had had a heart transplant.

Here at the beach, with the water's mist on my face, I wonder if talking to that transplant patient was such a good idea. Perhaps the less I had known, the more likely I would have had the surgery instead of standing here on the sand, waiting for my heart to stop.

The Pittsburgh woman had said, "Make sure they tell you everything...especially the side effects. They never went into detail about the depression I would have after surgery. I cried all the time. At times I was suicidal."

She told about the countless visits to the hospital for biopsies to determine the rejection process status—tests that have to be done throughout her entire life because her body will always try to reject her heart.

She said, "The hair on my head thinned, while I grew excess hair on my arms, upper lip, and other body parts. I thought I looked like a gorilla. And the medicine caused me to gain weight."

"Fat and hairy doesn't sound like a great trade-off," I grumbled, discouraged.

"It gets worse," she said. "Because your immunity is depressed you must always be on guard for infections. I was a lab technician but after the transplant, I had to quit. I tried getting work everywhere but no matter where I went, once they found out I was a transplant patient, they said 'You would be a financial nightmare to our company.' Forget lawsuit. HR will just say you don't meet the qualifications for a job with them. Discrimination is hard to prove. You are damaged goods."

I sat clutching the phone, thinking how she put up with all that garbage just to...save her life.

"Last week," she interrupted my thoughts, "we filed for bankruptcy." She was silent a minute, then rushed on: "The total cost involved in the surgery, hospital stays, visits to the doctors, therapy and medicine is just astronomical. The anti-rejection drugs, alone, cost me over $1 thousand dollars every five weeks."

I muttered something unintelligible. "If you have insurance, it'll help, and maybe by now they have less expensive medication, but a transplant is not a cake-walk." I managed to strain to say, "Anything good about the transplant?"

"I'm alive."

But there was no way my family could pay all those expenses. I'd ruin everyone. Even now, Zach was having a hard time making ends meet with all my medical bills and his insurance wouldn't cover me because I have a preexisting condition. The cost of my transplant would destroy him emotionally and monetarily, let alone how it will physically beat him down.

I hung up the phone feeling more determined not to have the surgery. My doctors had discharged me with an impressionable warning: "Without a transplant, we give you three months."

When you start measuring life in lumps of weeks, time sweeps right by.

That was a fortnight ago I had talked to the Pittsburgher, and here I am standing on grainy sand in cold weather, trying to decide what to do with my life. I grow worse every day I let slide by without making a decision. You know, six, seven months ago I ran up and down the stairs of my two-story colonial; now I can't walk a block without stopping three or four times to catch my breath. Just to drive here to the beach was more than I could handle, but I needed to be here, to face the sea that I plan to give my life to.

Suddenly I turn around, look across the mesa of sand to the parking lot, my mind on the Lincoln. How will I get it home if I end my life here? Surely Zach will want it; after all, he says, "You don't throw a car away just because it wears out."

Like my heart.

I can see he would not want me to throw myself away just

14

because my "transmission" is failing.

Yet I feel he and the kids will be better off without me.

I turn back around, plod on toward the thrashing surf. Don't think I'm not scared; I scream from the hurt of paper cuts. If I were running naked on this beach you would easily see the long yellow streak spreading across my back. But the fear of what will become of my family if my surgery makes us penniless is far greater than the fear of my drowning.

It's not that I think we, as a family, aren't close enough to get through any adversity...rather it's the idea of my being so ego-centered to think they should suffer for me at all.

I'm near the edge of the water now; my feet get flooded when the waves swash in. I don't think it'd take much for me to walk a few steps more, into the surging tide. I wonder if I'll struggle as the frigid water ices over me. When will my breathing be totally cut off? When water fills my ears? Nose? Mouth? Lungs?

A pine box...is that what they'll bury me in? Will they miss me? My babies will cry, and my second grader will mope, holding it all in. Zach will withdraw; he's a quiet sort of fellow anyway, relies on me to get things done. But he's strong, so I'm confident he'll go on. My drowning will embarrass him. He likes things to be orderly. If they rule my death as suicide, Zach will be mad because his religion doesn't condone suicide. I better make this look like an accident.

In the long run, my dying now is better for everyone. Bankruptcy is like cancer—eating away at you until you're nothing, like vultures picking clean carcasses. Worse, poverty frays bonds of love. My fight to live is not worth putting my family through such agony.

The water's cold. My teeth chatter as the surf covers the seat of my pants.

There's movement all around me. A scream. I turn. People are running down the beach, into the water. Reaching for something. I crane my neck to see. There's yelling, gesturing. I watch three people pull in a body. I'm not dead already, am I?

Shoes slap sand as crowds jog towards the form being lifted and brought ashore. People everywhere standing, watching.

I wade out of the water and, straining, winded. I tread towards the wide circle. By the time I get there, the crowd has

15

grown quiet, tense. I hear someone say, "It's Cooper, the retired executive turned beach bum. Old man should have known better than to get soused and go near the water."

I'm shivering, standing in the circle of people, watching two men give CPR, others standing nearby looking upset and yet curious.

My stomach somersaults.

Someone else comments, "Yeah, that's Cooper, all right. Always hanging around my shop. His ol' lady'll miss him. Hurt her worse than him."

Muttering all around the circle.

Hurt her worse than him? I guess that makes sense. She's still alive in pain mourning like Zach and the kids would be.

Would my drowning be the easy way out for me? Torture for my family?

I wonder what torture could have caused an executive to resort to a bum's life.

I hear a shop owner announce, "I'll try to get his wife. Poor man."

"Poor?" says another voice in a mocking tone. "Why feel sorry for him? He's a waste. Never did any good. Cheated in real estate."

A lady in the crowd eyes the person who just said that, and scolds, "That's a rumor, Mister! Nobody's life is a waste. I bet if he had a choice, he'd choose to live."

A man dressed like a vacationer calls out, "I'm a doctor! I'm a doctor!" and breaks through the crowd. Checks the drunk over. Shakes his head but says, "Keep compressing until the ambulance arrives."

The rescuer who's pushing on Cooper's chest nods.

Murmuring all around with sounds of sirens in the background. The crowd disperses, leaving the two men and the doctor leaning over the dead form. They're the only ones on the sand. I look around. That could have been me in the water.

Paramedics are loading the body into the back of the wagon; both are laughing over a comical TV program they saw last night. The tall one slams the ambulance door closed, saying, "Boy, was that a funny show. Did you see when—" and the other medic jumps in, reciting the same events in rhythm to the lapping water behind us.

My wet feet pick up sand as I walk, filling the cracks between my toes. Spontaneously I search my soggy pants for my cell phone. Not there, I searched the other pockets; no phone. Wait! Something touches my freezing fingers. It's my wet suicide note I had written but didn't leave at home. Why didn't I do that? That was the whole point of all this.

Thank God I forgot to leave it on the kitchen table. I crinkle it up, throw it into a trash can on the boardwalk.

I spot the Lincoln parked in the near empty lot.

I'll get sand all over my car. Who's going to clean it?

Who cares?

There's tomorrow for me to do it.

CHRISTMAS:
A TIME FOR PAUSE

"Over the hill and through the woods to grandma's house we go..."
A Christmas melody that's familiar to all of us who travel the Interstates and highways to visit relatives for the holidays. This year was no different as we packed big and bigger suitcases to head up to Rochester and Lockport, New York, to visit family.

My husband Larry and our two girls, ages two and four, viewed this mini-vacation as a time to focus and re-center our hectic lives while simultaneously having the opportunity to enjoy the company of parents, siblings, and aunts and uncles. Larry and I, who had taken on a fast pace of life in order to make ends meet, eagerly embraced this getaway since we really needed to spend time together. But who would have thought that being together meant sharing Christmas with 300 strangers?

We began our trek up 1-79 with the sun in front of us and heaps of cars around us. This year was the first time we had elected to travel to New York so late in the holiday week, and I was surprised at the numbers of travelers on the road this Christmas Eve morning. The girls, in a rare angelic moment, had fallen asleep in their car seats before we had crossed the Mt. Nebo Bridge and remained in slumber right up to the most frightening time in our lives. From that moment on, all hell broke loose.

I dozed off somewhere between Meadville and Conneaut while the sun had still been brightly shining, the cat had gotten

18

cozy on Larry's fur cap, and Larry, who began whistling to the Christmas tunes being played by KDKA, had managed to maneuver himself behind the wheel, in his seat belt, puffing on an awful smelling cigar.

Suddenly I popped awake. My innate senses had detected a change from the smooth; humming rhythm of tires at 55 m.p.h. to an agonizingly slow ten m.p.h. Something was wrong. I pulled myself into an upright position while rubbing my eyes awake. "Wow!" I exclaimed when my brain was again capable of registering. "When did this happen?"

"Right before Erie. It got worse when I got on 1-90," Larry muttered while dabbing out his cigar and gripping the steering wheel tightly with both hands. The worry in his voice hadn't escaped me.

The sun had died; cars had slowed before us and the sky, now blackened with swollen moisture, begun dropping bucketfuls of snow in the whirling high winds. I couldn't get over the transformation. Somehow it just didn't seem normal that the sun had been smiling one minute, only to have suddenly and grotesquely metamorphosed into an ugly black mass the next moment. My husband and I discussed the alternative of turning back to Pittsburgh, but we were so near the New York Thruway that we were virtually halfway to Buffalo.

"Maybe it will improve as we drive east," he said as he attempted to hide the frown on his face.

I remained quiet while tuning into a radio station. WTAE and KDKA had long faded and even their weather reports hadn't warned of the blizzard we now faced. After locating a static-filled Erie channel, I knew then we couldn't have turned home even if we had wanted to. Pittsburgh was due to get the same storm. I mumbled, "Weather report says snow for both Pittsburgh and Upstate New York."

Larry looked over at me.

The car crawled at ten m.p.h., then down to five, speeding up at other times, only to slow again, skidding here, sliding everywhere while we held our breaths with each white-out that swerved us off the road. It snowed so hard that the tire tracks of the car ahead of us so quickly filled with snow that not only could we no longer see the tracks, but the car had seemed to drop totally out of sight. Visibility had been limited to the car's hood ornament.

Larry was unable to keep our heavy station wagon, laden with suitcases and boxes of Christmas presents on the road because of wind gusting to 55 m.p.h. The temperature had abruptly and drastically dropped to a minus five degrees, with weather forecasters predicting plummeting to inhumane subzero temperatures before the night was over. With the wind howling ominously, the snow dropping unforgivingly, and the temperatures sinking rapidly, the situation fast became a nightmare.

"There are motels along the way," he tried reassuring me.

I leaned over and whispered to him so the girls, who were now awake and squealing with delight at the rages of the storm, would not hear me: "We'll have to find one soon. If the car gets stuck, we'll freeze to death." It was near noon but with the heavens filled with snow and the sky a pitch black, it looked more like midnight.

"I can't see the edge of the road," said Larry. He was against the steering wheel in attempt to peer out a windshield that was splattered with so much snow-sleet, that the best wiper blades could not keep clean. "Look at that." He was pointing to the side of the road where we could barely make out figures walking the interstate in attempt to guide cars from sliding into the shoulders.

My heart sank. This was no rinky-dink storm we had here. This was a full-blown onslaught of Mother Nature against Man. I lost count of the number of cars skidding into six foot snow drifts, trucks jackknifing off the road right before our eyes, autos buried under mounds of white stuff with people still inside, and travelers, who had already given up hope, hitching along the road in faith of finding shelter before they froze to death. But we were useless to do anything to help anyone as it was doubtful that even we would make it to safety.

"If we're limited to this type of driving, this stopping and starting, we'll run out of gas soon," he said quietly.

Things looked grave.

Forty minutes and two miles later we slid into the parking lot of the first motel. By now there must have been at least five inches of snow and the temperature felt as though they were hugging the minus 20 mark. I was almost blown back against the car door when I stepped out into the gusting winds. When I finally made my way to the motel entrance, I ended at the back of a long line that wove around the lobby, through the hallway, and back to the entrance. I waited an eternity to approach the motel reservationist. I shook my head in disbelief at the long faces of people who sat on the lobby floor, slept in the corridor, or nestled near the fireplace to keep warm—even mothers who openly nursed their infants—so their frozen, numb bodies wouldn't betray them. Seeing all these people, I knew then that we were in trouble.

"Any rooms?" I asked when my turn came. The tiny bit of hope in my voice was quickly shredded when the clerk shook his head without even looking at me.

"Look at this overflow. These people can't get out of the parking lot, and those managing to drive in, like you, find no vacancies. Everyone will be stranded here until the storm dies which will be days because we get the lake effect. And this storm is breaking all the records."

"What are my family and I going to do?"

"I don't know." Still he didn't look me. "We can't feed all the people we have. Try down the road, but I've been told all the lodging places are already full. And now they've closed the Thruway so you're not going too far."

"Closed?" We hadn't heard anything about it on the radio.

For the first time he looked at me, saying, "Sorry, there's no room at this inn."

'No room at the inn at Christmas time,' I thought, as I trudged back to our car which was now being pushed out of the knee-deep, snow-filled parking lot by other travelers in hopes of finding shelter at the motel I had just left.

My husband spontaneously ducked from the blowing snow when I opened the car door. "No luck?" he asked. "I figured as much." He concentrated on getting our tires to tread the parking lot and back on the road. "Honey, we've got to find some kind of shelter. In these frigid temperatures, we'll freeze in no time. And with snow piling, we can't park the car and leave it running to keep us warm because of fumes backing up."

"I know." It was all I could say.

The interstate was worse when we pulled back on it. The next motel, like the one after it, and the one after that one, was so crowded that we couldn't even get our car near their parking lots. Cars pulled off the interstate and slid down ramps to side roads and parked near homes to knock on strangers' doors, with their children in tow and baggage in hand.

"I guess we'll have to do that, too," I muttered, defeated.

"Whatever it takes to keep the girls safe, but there are a couple of truck stops up the road. If we can make it to those, we can sit in one of them and keep warm until they reopen the Thruway. If that doesn't work, we go banging on doors."

After visiting the first truck stop and seeing rows and rows of cars snarled in the parking lot, we headed for the final roadside inn.

Because of the depth of the snow, it took me twenty minutes to plod my way to the front entrance. Inside, people were rushing around, some crying, others cursing the boundless phone and bathroom lines, still others loading up with candies and additional snacks, and more sitting idly in booths or standing zombie-like in hallways—securing their territory for the duration of the storm.

"I have two little kids, babies really, sitting in a freezing car. It's nearly 20 below zero and the wind must be 60 m.p.h. out there!" I pleaded with the cashier who delayed the waiting line, four deep, to talk with me. "All I want is a place to set four human bodies and one tiny cat until this storm quits."

"I know, dear, but there's no room here." She waved her arm around in a circular motion to emphasize the hordes of people.

I turned to leave.

Suddenly she yelled, "Just learned that the civil defense is setting up a shelter in the Heard school building. It's in North East; if you can drive just a couple more miles, you'll get a roof over your head and some food."

I agreed to try to make it to the shelter. Our only other alternative was to sit in the car for however long iwaiting for the storm to end, and chance not becoming hypothermic. Not a very sound plan.

It was the longest two miles in my life. The car spun, stalled, slid, and sputtered, missing telephone poles, hitting ditches, until it collapsed in the parking lot of Heard School. When I got out of the car to trudge into the building, I saw a caravan of cars pulling in behind us. Many at the last truck stop had followed us to this shelter. I laughed with joy on the outside, grateful on the inside to have found four walls with heat.

The girls were crying louder now from the cold, hunger, and the fear they must have sensed in us. The cat whined incessantly as we dragged him along in our trek through the parking lot to the main doors—a trip that seemed more like a mountain climbing excursion rather than a fifteen foot stroll in the parking lot.

We were one of the first handful to arrive at the shelter, and it was only a matter of minutes before our children were settled in and watched over by a young couple while my hubby and I tended to details and helping the shelter managers line the floor with army cots and mats.

Soon the building was filled with local and state police, the civil defense, Salvation Army, National Guard, Red Cross, and an array of paramedics. Down the hall a piece was a small kitchen where the town women set out trays of snacks for us, and begin preparing to cook our daily meals. I watched mesmerized—and at Christmas of all times.

I searched for a phone while taking in the groups, singles, and duets of travelers dragging themselves through the warm schoolhouse, soon to be referred to as "home." An expression of gratitude was etched across each one of their cold-flushed faces as shelter authorities guided them into the gym, carrying their luggage, seating them on a cot or mat, and serving them hot coffee while softly chatting with them to ease their nerves.

Those who arrived with frostbite, shock, or health problems, were immediately cared for by the paramedics who did the best they could since they couldn't get anyone to a hospital. The 50 or 60 travelers who came within the first hour were only a small sample of the hundreds yet to appear.

At the school's reception area, which we later labeled headquarters, stood a man with a walkie-talkie and a wide map laid out on the school counter. "Any phones?" I asked him.

"None that work. Ice froze the lines." He thought for a moment.

"Write down the names and numbers of people you want to call."

I did that as well as jotting a quick message to give them: "Stranded in a shelter in Northeast, Pennsylvania. Will try to be home for Christmas," and left my name.

The man read it. "Hate to tell you but you might not make it home for Christmas, according to the weather report, but miracles can take different forms, especially at Christmas."

"Yeah, sure," I said glumly, already tired of the hundreds in the gym, the inability to find a free bathroom stall when needed, the long lines for food and other necessities. I thanked him and left, wondering how he was going to get through to relatives when phone lines looked like glazed garland. He, like all the other volunteers, stayed with us in the building rather than going home to their families, just to make sure we were fed, kept warm, and felt a sense of "belonging" in a strange place during the most blessed time of the year.

Later that night, sitting on my cot, my husband entertaining our daughters rolling on the mats, I spotted the walkie-talkie man moving around in the gym. I went up to him and asked, "Any word on the weather?"

"I'm afraid you'll spend Christmas Eve here, as well as the next day, and the day after that, and the day after that and—"

"Gee! That means maybe five days here!"

"There's another bad front coming through. The roads are worse now than when you first got here." He was quiet a minute; then: "All of us here have made a pledge not to leave anyone stranded on the roads. We'll get 'em here. There was a woman who skidded into a ten-foot snow drift, and in her cold car, blinded by white all around her, she became hysterical. But we got her out of her freezing car and to a hospital. On this holiest of holiest, we are not gonna let anyone die in the cold."

He winked at me and started towards another direction after telling me that in the kitchen were mothers, grandmothers, daughters and sisters of the shelter authorities who might need an extra hand.

On the way there, I passed by the male shelter authorities. They were heavily into assembling cots and helping carry old canned foods from an archaic civil defense shelter in the basement to the upstairs kitchen. The ladies there were preparing chili for Christmas dinner. Throughout the long ordeal they never uttered a harsh word, never tired of waiting on hundreds of strangers, never complained about spending their Christmas in a cold, austere shelter instead of in their warm, decorated homes. Somehow, they always seemed to miraculously turn one slice of bread into dozens of loaves.

By early evening, over half the gym was filled. "They're expecting close to 300 people by tomorrow," one of the ladies said to me. "All the cots and mats are set up. When this gym fills, they'll start putting people in classrooms."

Before the storm would end, not only did the gym fill to capacity, as well as the classrooms, but a building across the street was opened to cover the overflow. A few families with babies were taken in by some of the townspeople.

Larry came over to me a grin on his face. "Our cat's going crazy. Our new cot-neighbors have an Afghan hound." He laughed. "Worse yet is that there are a few birds up in the ceiling that flew in when people entered. Our cat wants them for fun."

"Or dinner?" I saw out of the corner of my eye, a tiny artificial Christmas tree going up near the gym entrance. Later, another was erected and trimmed in the cafeteria, and a third at the school's main entrance.

Then, suddenly—it seemed—the tree boasted silver, gold, red and green garland, gaily decorated ornaments, and a bright star at the top. The children stared in awe at how the tree seemed to have mysteriously appeared, but yet they understood that Santa wasn't coming to that gym that night.

A little later, a jingling of bells startled the kids who jumped and squealed, knowing that sound by heart. "Santa, Santa!" they cried. And instantly he appeared at the gym entrance. The kids ran to him, stampeding everyone in sight. He was the skinniest Santa I ever saw, but none of our children noticed. Each went to him, crawled up on his lap, told him their names; and Santa, as expected, pulled out from his bulging sack a present for each children (local merchants who had willingly opened their stores that Christmas Eve had reduced prices on toys and games so the PTA could buy a gift for each child.) Every one of our children had been accounted for.

While the kids jumped and screeched with glee, parents watched with smiles on their faces and tears in their eyes. It amazed us how this little town of less than 3000 people could organize themselves so well as to consider such things as our children's feelings, our safety, and our well-being. In the days to follow, the people of this town would make numerous such sacrifices and gestures of kindness.

Our children, big ones, small ones, black and white, American and Asian, went off to the corners and played for hours, sharing with one another in spite of differences in culture, appearance, or income levels. We were all on the same level this singular season in time.

Everyone looked up when three gentlemen appeared out of nowhere, dressed casually, but wearing heavy coats and tromping in high boots. One was the town's 24-year-old mayor, another priest, and the third a minister.

The young priest began, "We were plucked out of the cold and brought here to help you share Christmas. Let's bow our heads in prayer and thank God for your safety."

Jews, Protestants, Catholics, Baptists, Muslims, and even nonbelievers dropped their heads spontaneously and folded their hands. Our children sat perfectly quiet. The only sound that reverberated in that gym was that of our breathing amid the snow and wind pummeling the windows.

The minister said a few words while the mayor gave a slide show of what Christmas was like in his little town. Then he turned to the crowd and said, "Let's try some Christmas carols."

Softly he began "Silent Night." Then shelter authorities, the cooks, and their families joined him. They stood looking at us, smiling, singing to us, and welcoming us into their hearts.

At first only a few of us motorists began singing; then suddenly, song permeated the entire gym. When we had finished, waves of applause and handshaking punctuated the room as cooks passed around trays of homemade cookies. We were all brothers and sisters that night.

Like the gales gusting outside, a whirlwind of activity spun through the gym over the next few days. Motorists continued to arrive in droves, substitutes replaced weary cooks, kitchen help, and exhausted shelter authorities. New National Guard, police, firefighters and paramedics succeeded the exhausted ones. Meal lines wrapped endlessly around the gym; cots and mats were aligned, rearranged, and realigned to get that one more person in.

Birds, ferrets, and even skunks were added to the already saturated menagerie of pet land while some animals became sick or whiny. Children grew tired and bored, travelers became homesick, privacy evaporated, bathroom facilities filled, sitting room was nonexistent, and space at a premium. Showering and changing clothes were idealistic.

While food supplies started dwindling, people lined the halls and slept against the walls. Anxiety heightened. We had been cut off from the outside world.

Those who tried walking the two blocks to the main street in hopes of locating a working phone, not only found lines downed, but also returned with frostbite. Fretting over perishables in our cars, or the engines freezing, along with a host of other worries began overtaking our thoughts. Were we ever going to get out?

As soon as we noticed another getting depressed, we'd try cheering them up. There was too much to lose if just one of us becomes incapable. Townspeople brought in jigsaw puzzles, playing cards, black & white TVs, board games, and magazines and books. When weary of these, we struck up a choral ensemble. Many college students lugged their guitars into the gym from their cars to sit around the dining area, the gym, hallways, or bathrooms, and play for us.

When we would start to feel sorry for ourselves, someone would remind us of our blessings. Soon we would be back to chatting, drinking pounds of coffee, eating infinite numbers of always available Christmas cookies, singing and playing games, or telling jokes.

During a Christmas Day dinner of chicken soup, a woman visiting the States from London had said, "You Americans are a bloody lot of nice people."

27

Later that night, we motorists from all points of the globe managed to pull together over $700.00 for the cooks and shelter authorities, who turned right around and weathered the ongoing storm to buy more food for us.

Then came the announcement: "Friends, crews are still out trying to clear the roads," bellowed the shelter manager, "but I must tell you that they are preparing to give it up. It's impossible out there. The wind's beating so hard that the snow whirls right back on the road as soon as it's been cleared. Temperatures are inhumane, so road crews are going home."

We tried not to groan.

He added, "And weather forecasters say there's yet another storm coming on the heels of this one. Right now, it's twenty below zero, and there's over a foot of snow. But we must continue to do our best in here."

At the end of his announcement, he pleaded for continued hope and patience, and for prayers for those still stranded on the roads, ending with, "If you have extra blankets, coats, clothing here or, in your cars, please loan them to those coming in who have none and no place to sleep."

In groups, we approached him, handing over extra blankets, coats, clothing. Accolades must go out to 300-plus strangers who seldom complained, who gave what they could, who took things in stride, and hoped for the best. During our stay there, not one item was reported stolen, not one fight broke out, not one nasty word or angry look was exchanged. The Spirit of Christmas reigned; the spirit of humanity prevailed.

The next day, word had reached us that it would be New Year's before we got out of the shelter and back on the cleared Thruway. Downhearted, we retired to our cots early that evening. We understood that not only would our spirits be put to the test but so would our food and drink supplies.

My husband and I tucked our daughters in, fed the cat, and then lay side by side.

"Think we'll see the family for New Year's?" I whispered to him who was watching a bird fly across the gym ceiling. "Doesn't sound like it. I bet they're all home in Lockport and Rochester (New York) wondering where we are. We never did get a phone call into them." He looked at me. "We'll do okay, honey; we have each other and the kids."

"And God," I softly added.

He kissed me good night and was asleep in seconds, leaving me wide awake to listen to the sounds of strangers whispering, snoring, or moving about. My thoughts roamed to Christmas of last year, when we had spent time with loving family. Holidays were always 'special' to us because it was the only time we could renew distant relationships of close relatives. I wondered what this year was going to be like without not being able to see them, to share that holiday warmth.

One night, I couldn't sleep at all, and when I finally did doze off, I was nearly instantly jolted awake by a voice shouting, "Look! Look!" I lifted my head off my cot to see what all the fuss was about. The gym was pitch black. Standing over me was another female traveler who I had talked with many times over the last few days.

"Look outside," she urged.

Getting up from my cot and making my way across hundreds of sleeping bodies, seas of suitcases, and countless animals, I finally arrived at one of the small gym windows.

"What do you see?" she pressed, her voice filled with excitement.

I stood on my tiptoes and peered out. Before me was the brightest star I had ever seen. "A star," I mumbled. "In the northeast." The irony caught me off guard.

"A star, yes!" she squealed. "A star smiling down upon us from a bright clear sky...an early morning where no wind blows the snow."

I turned and looked at her.

"It's time to go home:" she cried. "The Lord has filled the North East with a bright, shining star to guide our way."

I moved so fast that I could have been Peter Pan flying over the gym as I raced to my husband to tell him the good news. He was already up and packing when I reached him, as were many other travelers who had heard the word-of-mouth bulletin. No one could understand how the weather could change so quickly and so unpredictably. A miracle had happened. Within two hours the gym had emptied of its hundreds of ever-grateful travelers.

As my husband packed the car with suitcases, boxes, cat, and kids, I watched the shelter authorities disassemble cots, fold blankets, clean the kitchen, and mop the floors. The gentleman in charge, the one with the walkie-talkie and who made all the announcements, walked around the vacant gym that was once our home. I watched him.

"Good job," I said, smiling, as he neared my direction.

"I guess those relatives of yours will be glad to see you," he said, remembering I was the first to ask him to make a call for me.

"But how would they know? You said the phone lines were down."

"What I did for you and everyone else here who asked, was to contact ham operators in the towns of the relatives and had them make the calls for you. Your relatives got the message. All in all, a couple hundred ham operators got involved and formed a network."

I shook my head in disbelief, amazed at the power of humanity. "Thank you," I whispered.

"Gives us pause, doesn't it? Certainly puts things into perspective. Makes us stop and wonder why things, gifts, become more important than people, why money is more powerful than love, why our jobs are more essential than family." He was looking around the gym, not really seeing me, but mentally recalling the space filled with people.

I nodded. "Guess it makes us grateful for what we do have rather than for what we don't have," I muttered.

He walked over to the skimpy Christmas tree and, with one hand, lifted it off the floor to haul it out. "Yep," he said again, "gives us pause." He turned back to me and, grinning, said, "Christmas is that pause in our lives."

"Merry Christmas." I smiled a grateful thank you.

"Merry Christmas," he called back. Winking, he added before leaving, "A darn good pause in life."

There I stood, in a huge lifeless gym that once was so animated, so warm, so joyful—all served on tumbling mats and rickety cots.

Empty now, the gym was. I was alone. Just pausing.

Merry Christmas.

But a Moment in Time

I'm sitting here thinking about an Augenblick. Do you know what it is? Well, I discovered it unwittingly.

It's a string discovery, or, at least for me, it was.

The second we become truly aware of ourselves, we lose the opportunity for what writer Annie Dillard calls an Augenblick—a moment of stark "elsewhereness" that can't be defined in words.

When I look out the same window every day, I see essentially the same scenery. I mean, try it. Do you see anything differently today than you did yesterday?

You can do that every day of your life until—that one day you look out and your eye catches something not seen before. You're suddenly given an entirely different insight. This is an Augenblick.

It could be the way a swatch of light shines across your child's face one sunny day or even the way your friend moves her hand at a certain moment—things done hundreds of times before until this one particular second when you sense everything poles apart.

In my experience, I've learned that existence seldom offers an Augenblick; instead, we have only life's circularity: birth, death, and a rebirth, like a chalkboard that's written on, washed off, and written on again. Everywhere we see life's cycle: In the thirteen-year cicadas, the passing of seasons, the waters rushing out to new ground only to cycle back again. From where we start, we return.

To me, our cyclical lives are but flashes in time; so, in the overall scheme, we live but a moment. Yet during this moment, we might be fortunate enough to experience an Augenblick when our sensibilities are totally caught up in the instant and yet we're moving on to something beyond our consciousness. When that happens, we've achieved something few others are aware of. In that spark, we are suddenly brought closer to knowing who we are and where we come from and where we'll go. This knowing isn't factual or absolute; it's mere insight, as though seeing everything in the dark when lightning lights up a black sky.

When have you experienced this? The day your child was born? The day you said "I do"? The day that rainbow encompassed your home, your family? The day you startled deeply over an unexpected cat's meow? Can you pick it out? I doubt it.

But I had one.

For me, my Augenblick came abruptly and explosively.

My father lay in bed, his eyes unseeing yet moving wildly back and forth in his head. I discerned then that he was never to see me graduate from high school, watch my brother play football, or smell lilacs in spring, or touch my mother whose softness he loved. This is the moment when I lost my innocence, and realization thundered and I understood there was no reply to the falling tree in the uninhabited forest. Daddy was forty-seven; I was all of sixteen.

And Death came and took him away.

Before word of his fate was colored in the cosmos, he'd annoy me with, "If something happens to me..." and then a sequence of directions would follow: "take care of your mother, spend little on my funeral...." I would snap back, "Don't talk like that!" He'd smile and say, "We'll all die someday."

That we had never gotten along until his end seems hard for me to believe today, knowing what I know now about living. He was verbal, strict, and headstrong; I was stubborn, determined, and rebellious. I thought he wanted perfection: "Always do your best; don't take on anything you can't give 100 percent to," he'd emphasize whenever I'd say I was taking up trumpet in band, trying out for the school play, or decorating for the prom.

The entry "failure" had been snipped from his dictionary. He made me think blundering was as shameful as a lisp or holey socks.

When I was eight I was scheduled to go on a Brownie camping trip but my older brother had terrorized me all night with Hook Man stories. The next morning as Mom checked my duffle bag and Daddy drank his coffee, I announced I wasn't going camping:

"I'm scared of the Hook Man."

I heard my dad set his cup on the saucer and saw him throw me "that look" with his specially made eyes that turned coal black. He could even move them like those darting pupils behind portraits in too many slapstick comedies.

"You will go to that camp!" he ordered. "If you're scared, too bad. Learn to do things in life that you don't want to do."

* * *

In the few years that I got to know my father, I never saw him cry, or heard him say he was afraid or couldn't go through with something. Always he was brave, held his head high even to the very end. The end, however, is the memory that is most vivid to me, even all these years later.

And Death came and took him away.

When I force myself to remember what he was like, I get confused because I know how unreliable memory is, and how it's not to be recorded as fact. When someone asks me something like, "Tell me what happened," I give only highlights—montages popping on the screen of my brain. Scenes of my father are fragmented and buried deep in the layers of my mind where at certain times they surface, distorted and as reliable as a mother laying her hand across her child's forehead to check body temperature.

One scene I recall is of Daddy sitting on my bed late one night asking why I was crying into my pillow. I told him all the girls at school got invited to a slumber party but me. He stroked my curls, whispering, "That's okay, you're a unique kid."

"How?" I asked through sniffles.

He pushed his dark hair back with a stroke of his hand, saying, "You like playing alone, making up tiny dinosaurs with your thumb, forefinger, and index finger, and you draw and write so well. And I love that you see the days of the week in color." He made me laugh; I didn't think he knew that.

He smiled, added, "Other little girls aren't as creative. I bet if you had a party you would outdo them." I nodded, blew my nose into his hanky.

"Then you go right ahead and plan it, and when you're ready, we'll send out invitations."

Years later he would not be so willing for me to make friends or attend parties. He was worried about my dignity with boys, as if my mother hadn't preached enough about sex, always ending her "chats" with "Something that good Catholic girls don't do." I've since come to believe that my father feared for me what other parents feared of him when he was a teen.

Once, I had a party in our finished basement; my mother decked me out in a peach colored A-line. I remember how Joey Brown—tall and lanky with fluffy hair then; fat and bald now—showered attention on me. That night, Daddy went out to water the lawn while my mother played server and animal keeper to forty adolescents who ran up and down the basement steps. Joey and I danced most of the evening, shuffling our feet to some early Seventies beat. He towered over me, so he had to bend down in order to place his cheek against mine in a slow dance where I closed my eyes dreamily, never seeing my father peering in through the basement windows.

But after the party, when everyone had gone, my father made me sit on the couch and listen to his haranguing: "That dirty dance," he said. "I saw you through the windows, letting him run his hands up and down in front of you."

And Death came and took him away.

I looked down to my chest, trying to envision Joey doing that. Inside me, I went hysterical; outside I remained silent. I was cool to my father for weeks after.

And Death came and took him away.

Yet another time, when I had broken off with Charlie—my "steady" (a word my father hated)—Daddy said to me one night, "You know, dear ol' dad has a moth-bitten tux up in the attic; I'll put it on and proudly escort you to the prom." I leaned over and kissed him, but I didn't take him up on the offer.

When I think of good incidents, my mind tricks me, drives me back to one particular episode that will forever bear-hold me through my life. It's an event that I put into other stories, as if telling it enough times on paper in make-believe worlds will somehow erase it in my own. I was seven; Daddy had gone out to mow the lawn. Interested in how the round, sharp, metal disk chopped off blades of grass, I tagged along. Because he never let me get close to the mower, I often found my attention diverted. On that day I was drawn to a nest of moles scurrying in and out of tiny holes underneath our porch slab. When I got close enough, I saw they were blind, and heard their funny squeaks made with near-missing mouths hidden in purplish, streamlined bodies. They made the hair on my neck stand up. My mother came, screamed like a crazy woman. I ran to Daddy. He waved me off a number of times but I was determined to have him gallantly save Mother.

It seemed like hours before the mower stopped. As he approached me, mumbling "out of gas," I dashed up to him, bubbling about the "damned stinkin' moles," as my mother had christened them. I saw one climb up his leg, making him hop around, and then he slammed his hand down on his thigh, and the flattened rodent dropped out of his pant-leg with a thud. Wildly he rammed a shovel down on those little things, slicing them in half, their screeches ricocheting in my ears. When done, he stood leaning on the shovel, panting, his black hair shiny with sweat and falling off his face. "They multiply," he said to me.

"Wow!" I gasped, wondering if they could add and subtract too. Muttering that he had to finish the lawn, he went off to the garage to get the gasoline.

"Hush," he had said to me, still breathless and rubbing his thigh through his pants. I wanted to know what it felt like to split each one. "Not nice," he grumbled, and then asked me to please let him work. But I kept asking questions, some which I repeated, and as he was pouring gas into the mower, he stood up and rasped, "If I had a match, I'd pour this all over you and light it." Those were his words, forever etched into my brain.

I froze. Just looked at him, trying to first picture the words he used, and then imagining him doing it. Slowly I backed away from him, shell-shocked, backed right up to the car and stayed behind it. My mother must have been standing near because I heard her confirm how serious an offense he had committed: "My god Howard!"

He just stood shaking his head, mechanically tipping the gas can, letting the liquid overflow onto the mower, over his pants, down into his socks.

* * *

I was afraid of him for awhile after that, and I feared even more that he hated me. I knew he was sorry for uttering those words, but somehow his sorry didn't wash clean his mistake. And Death came and took him away.

Growing up with Daddy could only be described as a "challenging;" As volatile as his temper was, he could be equally tranquil and steady; as much as he swore when angry, he could usher out gentle, reassuring words. If I sassed him, I was certain to be punished, but if I said those same words in a teasing manner, I knew I'd get a laugh; if one day he told me I was too young to go someplace with him, the next day he'd take me somewhere nearly as provocative. When I aced most of my tests up to middle school, he applauded and fussed over me, but when I purposely failed my exams in junior high, he said nothing. Always he demanded that I display proper respect.

"Remember," he used to say, "you stand up for older people, say yessir and no ma'am; you help the elderly, and be careful not to embarrass people or hurt their feelings unless they really have it coming to them."

Yet, he didn't mind being joked with or even laughed at. He was a reservoir of self-confidence which he tried to pass on to me. Never was he predictable, and always I was consumed with a rash of emotions about him. The only certainty I had was that he was my father, and for that reason alone I loved him.

When I turned sixteen and hit double-dating age, our disagreements worsened. I could only date certain boys, with certain couples, and had to be in at a certain time. He drove me nuts. Because he dreaded this age in me, he wanted to forever protect me from boys, from myself, from life in general; he was always on edge, and I became self-conscious when I was in the room with him for longer than fifteen minutes. He checked out my hair, clothes, makeup, worried about my homework, what colleges I would go to, what I was saying or not saying on the phone. I just wanted him to leave me be. I wonder if my regrettable inner thoughts, *I wish he were dead,* had made it happen. Constantly I carry this guilt.

And Death came and took him away.

Somewhere around a year before the fateful call came, I discovered buried in him a soft spot. When I found it, I tried visualizing where it was located in his anatomy, and what it would take for me to press the right button to turn it on. Soon after, I could get around him with a particular grin or a sugary voice. My mother said it was disgraceful how he always gave into his little girl. I started joining him in watching Steeler games, accompanying him to garage sales, walking with him in the park in Pittsburgh arm in arm, even meeting him for a lunch. I gave him a pet name, "Poppy-Dop," and he loved it.

Having just got in the door from school one day, I stuck my arm into a cookie jar, hoping to snack before dinner while my mother was outside hanging clothes. The Oreo was up to my mouth when the phone rang. The doctor on the other end said, "Your father in?"

"He's at work. I'll have him call as soon as he gets in."

I knew something was wrong. When I told my father later, he gave a slight nod and headed out the door to his Buick. I wanted to go with him. At first he refused. We spoke little on the way to the doctor's and not at all on the way back. I remember how I stole glances at him in the car, his face set straight ahead, lips turned slightly down, eyes clouded over. He could have been anybody's father at that second, but I knew how unlikely it would have been for someone else's dad to be sitting behind the wheel driving home, driving onwards towards his death. I tried seeing through him, as if the football-sized tumor in his lung would loom forward at the passing of my gaze.

After the exploratory, the doctor said "a year"; he lived six months. During that time, I struggled with accepting his death sentence. I didn't understand that unlike his Buick, a living thing doesn't go into reverse once the process of decay has started. Whenever I'd hear my mother say, "He's dying," it'd take my brain seconds to fade in a picture of my dad. The words "dying" imply a process that will go until its end, ravaging the host while doing so. Then, I couldn't see that the bad cells had broken off and travelled to his legs, his lymph system, into his back, to finally consume his brain. That he lost weight, moved and breathed in racking pain, grew paler by the day, did not come as evidence to me of his "failing." I had never seen him fail; how was I to gauge it?

By the fourth month I was spending nights awake and days asleep, dozing off even in school. He'd want company in the middle of the umbra, perhaps afraid of shutting his eyes for the last time with no one by his side. After midnight he'd wake me, ask me to make hot chocolate, sit and talk with him, so that his hours of pain would pass more sanely, if only for a moment in time. We talked as equals, and he told me of his hopes—hopes for my and my brother's future; he revealed his weaknesses and I loved him even more for letting me in on them.

During these times he'd ask how he had done as a parent. I'd tell him; he'd laugh sometimes, other times he looked rueful. I never brought up the lawn mower incident lest he left this world thinking I never forgave him for his one slip of the lips.

And Death came and took him away.

We had to get my brother released from the Navy, as he would be the only man in the family. I called town leaders, representatives, the Navy, filled out forms to have him released. After a seemingly long wait, he came home to be with his mother and sister, and to say good-bye to our father.

Daddy wanted to die at home, with his family, in a landscape still a part of his identity; he lay flat on his back New Year's Day. I could see him losing ground with loved ones who seemed destined to go on without him. Tears filled his eyes, seemed to stay there like morning dew droplets. Only once he asked me to close off his misery. And I failed him in this.

When the end arrived, out of his mouth came groans and a sound I didn't recognize until I asked an adult. "It's rales," an aunt said, who stayed with him hour after hour, kneeling at his side, murmuring the rosary from start to finish, caressing

each bead, her head bobbing up and down. "What does that mean?" I asked. She looked straight at me. "Your daddy's lungs are filling up with fluid. He's drowning."
I turned and walked out of the room.
Sitting on the sofa, trying to imagine someone I loved drowning...in himself...I must have dozed. I might have stayed that way for days—chin fallen, lids tightly closed—if it hadn't been for the howls. I jolted awake, sat trembling. When I focused, I saw my older brother sitting opposite me on the edge of a chair, his eyes big. Via some evolutionary gift gene-marked only in siblings, I saw in my head the exclamation point he put at the end of "He's dead!" He jumped up, ran to my father's bedroom. I remained sitting, hanging back. When at last I could move, I skulked into Daddy's room, as though badly wanting to see the monster in the horror movie yet too frightened to look.
At his side, my brother stood and cried—an act my father wouldn't have liked but would have understood. I stared from the doorway. He looked the same, my father; only his chest did not rise and fall rhythmically. Around me, everyone sobbed: my mother, relatives, and my brother
I am told, for here my mind has no record, that I walked up to the bed, climbed on it and crawled over to my father, and then collapsed atop his dead form, bawling, "Daddy! Daddy!" My brother says when he lifted me off my father and held me, my face was completely dry, and inside my eyes, I looked vacant. The gap in my mind had already been cordoned off and closed up, much like nailing up boards on vacant homes.
And Death came and took him away.
Over the years, I have thought about that vacancy. What happened during that gap, that split second when I walked in and stared at my father to when I momentarily lost touch with reality, I cannot say exactly; I can only guess that it was the moment of my innocence lost, my Augenblick—a crack of a second when some part of me experienced a truth—a truth not mathematical or cerebral, but a truth a priori, a truth empirical, based upon something encoded within man's germplasma that lies dormant until the right moment appears when it pulsates and surges, heaves with some raw power,

some unharnessed energy, only to burst forth, stream past so quickly that we can never catch it, hardly even glimpse it, but yet sense it only long enough to come to a veiled awareness. Somewhere primitive in my mind is a remembrance of what passed in that space of seconds when I stood staring while others went from one embrace to another, wailing. For an immeasurably brief instant, a part of me transcended the moment, went beyond the bedroom smelling of decay, beyond human sounds of sorrow, beyond the reality of a loved figure lying in a bed that my mother was to never again sleep in. That transcendental part of me experienced so intense an insight in so short a time that words haven't yet been invented to describe it. It was as though the wind had been knocked out of me, and in the second I had caught my breath, it was over, but in between, my mind went elsewhere, coming close to connecting with this "something," yet not close enough to grab it and hold it in my hands and name it.

And Death came and took him away.

I've never shared this moment with another, perhaps out of worry of being ridiculed, or maybe out of fear of fear itself. Had I harnessed "it" long enough to peer at it, fondle it, shake it and put it up against my ear, it might have stayed. But then, perhaps I wouldn't be here, for it is a realm not meant to be understood, not even meant to be peeked into by humans...by the living.

The only certainty I feel inside me is that at the second of my discovery, my father's soul passed me.

BALTHAZAR:
MAGICAL REALISM

If anything has ever been said about Balthazar, it is that his creativity was one of genius. Since I have been elected to write this sketch, I can only tell about him through observable data that has come my way after having met him that one day last week.

As a hardworking biographer who has sketched the lives of Meursault, Dmitri Karamozov, and Cinderella, I had gone to Macondo that day for a brief R and R. But it rained the second my boat hit the shoreline (Macondo's literature fails to mention monsoons that last eleven of the twelve months, as Macondoians don't put time into usable chunks like the rest of us). I moored my boat, shuffled up the shore, climbed over the dunes, across the marsh line, stumbling twice, and finally onto the town's wooden streets, where stores were beginning to close up one by one.

"Hey!" came a voice from inside a barn where a horse with wings of Pegasus was tied up. "You're wet. And sand's stuck to your ass. Don't you know we don't swim in the rain? We have lakes and rivers for that."

"No pools?" I doubt he detected my sarcasm.

I looked around the barn, then glanced outside and back to him. "Why's everyone closing up their businesses? It's dead here."

"Of course."

I stared at him. "Of course," I mocked, hugging my arms to my chest in hopes of warming up. It was December. "Shouldn't people be Christmas shopping or something?"

"They're at a picnic, on the west shore."

"Picnic in winter? In rain? Sleet?"

He mumbled and went back to polishing what looked like a huge golden cage big enough to put that horse in it. "That for troupials?" I ventured.

"Gerimmpys."

"But I heard no one's ever caught one. Maybe they're not even real."

"Y-y-y-ep. They're stupid enough to be caught."

"Then why doesn't anyone have one?"

He rolled his eyes at me.

"Well, okay then who's the stupid one to have ordered a cage to put it in? Have you made other cages? And where can I go to see a gerrimmppy in it?"

"You can't order gerrimmpys. You have to catch one, he said."

"Then, who is the cage for?"

"A boy. Sez he's gonna get one and make it a pet."

Balthazar explained that Gerimmpppys are like castrated capons, but bigger, 12.9 times bigger, and they have no feathers, for there are no wings, but the appendages they do have are like hands extended where wings would be. Rumor has it that a gerrimmppy can quickly, and in one smooth motion, reach out, grasp a person's neck and squeeze until the Adam's apple pops out through the ear canal.

Gerimmpppys' faces contain the eyes of a timid doe and the frown of a Richard Nixon. Because of the horror they convey to the man who looks at their chins, gerrimmpppys are usually shot on sight, providing the shooter gets his gun up in time and a round off before either the stench of the animal or the hands of the beast don't get him first. However, extinction is hoped for by the year 4003, as the animals are slow to multiply because of their Richard Nixon frown.

Yet, if they ever did proliferate to their standard size of a mammoth yak—which would make them the meanest suckers outside of man—what we will have on our hands then is man-in-animal, or something like that.

So you can see why it has been said that here on this island hidden in the tunnels of the marshes are creatures—

gerrimmppy—so awful that even Christ can't love them, creatures that have gone from one form to another, crossed over somehow, transmutated, transformed into another type of creature with the eyes of the timid doe and the frown of Richard Nixon, and the fingers, where feathers should be, of a Boston Strangler, but also the chest of a Hercules, the legs of a gorilla, and the smell of spoiled salami—half-man half-monsters who rides the winged horses when the eclipse happens. They are said to be no more than legend.

Rumor has it that those who have been unfortunate enough to have witnessed the occurrence of a gerrimmppy's coming out is immediately turned to stone the second they spot it leaping off the back of a Pegasus and running towards him with their chins stuck out.

His words broke into my thoughts. "Who you here to do bio-graphery on?"

"You, but when I go back I have to cover Don Quixote, and I'm not up for that without a little rest."

"You loco."

"You think I'm crazy! You're the one with a winged horse!"

"And a cage, but horse is special. Didn't get them out of no Sear's catalogue like everyone else here who wanted one."

My head spun. I cleared my throat and tried again. "Only Perseus wanted a winged horse. He was a legend...just a legend."

"I don't know no Perseus; I jist know winged horses and gerimmppys. My goal is to catch one, and I think I'm close to doing that?

"How? Why?"

Baltazar looked at me, stood up and straightened his back, while saying, "Because, like I sez, one has to come to you."

"None of this makes sense. Look, I'm freezing here. Do you have a place I can get a cup of coffee to warm up?"

"We ain't got that kind of drink or food here in Macondo."

"Then what do all of you eat or drink?"

"What nature supplies." He studied me, and then turned to polish and buff up the cage he created. "So if you hurry, you make the picnic. I'm going there."

"But it's raining out!"

"When else you have a picnic?" He looked at me, shook his

head, loaded his huge cage on a rolling cart, like a truck flatbed. He was less than middle-aged and about the size of a Don Rickles and a humor by far better. He carried the general expression of a wired Einstein-boy. His paunch made his bald round head look ever more like a shinny bowling ball which I was told that the children of Macondo used bowling balls as hockey putts. His yellow shorts stopped at his crotch, and the sleeves of his collarless shirt with its one button hung down past his bloated belly to his ankles. He didn't seem at all cold.

"Then what you want in Macondo?" He didn't even look up from the cage when he asked that.

"As you know, I'm a biographer." I looked over and studied the winged horse, wondering why it wasn't tied. Then I emotionally slapped my face, saying, 'What the hell.... a winged horse! I am losing it'. "I told you I came here to interview you for my editor."

He said he was interested in past lives while I said I was interested in the living who I can only get to from the past. But he started to tell me his story, so I found a pile of straw, sat on it, rubbing my hands to ward off the cold. I heard him ramble, his voice soothing like the rumble of a train on a track where the passenger can throw his head back against the seat and rest his eyes—eyes not big and round and timid like a doe's—and let the bump-bump of the metal wheels against the steel tracks roll in rhythm to his breathing.

"I was born in poverty—still am poor—in Macondo—this sleepy coastal town that needs tourists like you to stay alive, yet in the end you take all its residents captive."

"What tourists? I'm the only one here."

Balthazar went on, saying he had always dreamed of becoming as rich as Jose Montiel, whose son ordered the making of the cage. Balthazar—the only cage maker in Macondo (maybe even worldwide) claims he got his expertise from his father who was born of a phoenix while his mother, an archeologist, came from Venus As Balthazar was getting ready to hand-deliver the cage to Montiel's home, he had chattered senselessly, his voice droning.

Finally, reaching the western shore, we both looked at the drenched "picnickers" who had evidently somehow heard about the cage and broke up their party to run towards us. They began clustering around, oohing and aaahing over the cage, many of whom were children. So much of a fuss did they create that Balthazar had to try shooing them away to the chanting of "Balty. Balty."

Balthazar asked me, "What you think I ought to charge?" He stood back after buffing up the gold for the twelfth time.

"Well, now, I don't rightly know." I scratched my head. "Is it made of good materials?"

"The best and finest metal you can find."

"And it is pretty big."

"Big enough for a gerrimmppy. Maybe two."

I nodded. How would I know? I never saw one.

"It's gold, too," he said.

I shot him a look.

"It is," he said.

"That would make it worth a fortune."

He shrugged. "All of our buildings are made of gold—foundations, thresholds, windowsills, anvils."

I laughed.

"And so are our faucets, toilet bases, too. And it paves the roads here in Macondo."

"The roads are wooden," I reminded him.

"Underneath. Underneath. Don't you know you're s'posed to save the good stuff?"

"Then that makes the cage worthless."

"But my time and talent are worth something." He patted his belly. "So? What you think? How much?"

A woman, who I later learned was named Ursula popped up her head in the crowd. Before she could say anything, I offered, "Look, Balt, it is a nice cage. Let me take it off your hands."

He looked at his hands. I looked at them, too, hands that had hair layered so closely together that if you took a quick look, they'd seem to be gorilla-like; his face, too, was full of hair, bristly hair, but none on his head.

"I promised it to Pepe Montiel."

"How much do you want for it?" I persisted, more admiring of it the longer I looked at it because it seemed to portend marvelous things as it sat there, all shiny and big.

"Thirty pesoliryen," said Ursula.

"What?" I asked.

"Thirty pesoliryan?"

"Don't you know nuthin, stranger?" Balthazar shook his head. "Our money is pesoliryan; it's like a peso, a liar and a yen. The really big bills are dolurules—dollars, Euros and rubles, but neither denomination is like any others anywhere." He paused. "Yes," that's what I'll charge Mr. Pepe Montiel and hope for twenty pesoliryens."

"Twenty! But you've said you've lost a lot of sleep in these last two weeks, and you've not done your regular carpentry work, and you left the place a mess. Besides, the cage is rather large; I think it's the biggest one I've ever seen. So you can get rid of it by selling it to me."

"Gerrimmppy's are big, you know."

"How big?

He studied my form, his eyes moving up and down me.

"Maybe yer size when babies."

"Look," I urged, seeing more and more fantastic qualities in the cage as he guarded over it, resting on the sandy wooden street. "Forty! I'll give you forty for it." I was betting money that I had no idea of its value. "Forty pesoliryans."

"Fifty dolurules," said Balthazar.

"Wait, you changed the denomination."

"But, Senor, do you not see the specialness of the cage?"

"This is certainly a flight of imagination." I ran my hands over the double port-a-potty sized, piled three high, domed cage. "Okay, fifty dolurules." I thought a moment. "Where do I get this denomination of money?"

"At the bar, but Pepe Montiel will be upset that I not give it to him and instead sell to you. But it okay. I always wanted one."

"Wanted one?"

"I tol' you—at least *one* gerimmppy."

I wasn't going to argue with him. "But you did say that this cage wouldn't be right for troupials, didn't you?" I bit my lip. "What is a troupial, anyway?"

"Eiyiyi. It is me a troupial and everyone in Macondo."

"But not me?"

47

"You are something else." He and everyone in the crowd laughed, and I joined in, just glad that I was going to get this amazing cage. He hedged, "I calculated the measurements perfectly. It's the strongest wire you can find, and each joint is soldered outside and in; gerrimmppys will not fly away."

"You contradict yourself. We're agreed on fifty dolurules, right?"

"Two-hundred, it so good." He smirked. "Why would you want this, stranger? And I can't sell you something that's already promised."

"A hundred! No! I'll make it a hundred and fufty dolurules" Balthazar smiled. "Come, you can walk to the bar with me to get your money." He rolled the cage-throwing a massive sheet around it—on that platform with wheels. It trailed behind him as he huffed and puffed, a cigar hanging from the corner of his mouth, his massive pot belly propelling him forward.

When we got outside the bar, I saw that Balt was smiling. "What're you laughing at?" I'm pretty mad, considering I offered a hundred-and-fifty dolurules for it and you still haven't given it to me."

"You'll get it soon enough. Celebrate, I say."

"Celebrate what?"

"I have a person for the cage."

"But it isn't me. And I offered to buy it!"

Someone at the bar shouted to Balt as gossip seemed to take wings like that Pegasus and fly all over the town, "So someone gave you a hundred-and-fifty dolurules for the cage, huh?"

"Two hundred," Balt boasted.

I cut my eyes towards him.

"Score one for you," someone else said. "You're the only one who has managed to get such a pile of money out of someone and have a person for the cage."

Balthazar was completely drunk by dusk when he was telling me about a fabulous project of five-thousand cages at three-hundred pesoliryens each, and then a million cages, until he had five-hundred-million doluruples. "We have to make a lot of cages to sell to the rich before they die," he said, blind drunk. "All of them are sick, and they're going to die, them rich people."

Hours later, he was still in the pool hall with lipstick slapped on his cheeks, and two women kissing his hairy face and his eyes. He said to me, "You bought my cage and I got a person. A double win for me."

"What do you mean? I am the person who bought the cage." Right before my eyes, his features seemed to be transmutating, his eyes becoming shy—like and his smile turning upside down. God, I've drunk too much.

Suddenly everything in the room went stark black. When I came to, blurriness watered my entire vision until it cleared enough for me to see everyone standing around me. I felt the knot on my head. I thought the bars in my eyes were from my concussion until I realized they were the wires of the cage.

"Balthazar!" I screamed. "What are you doing! Let me out!"

The crowd backed away and there I saw him lying spread-eagled in the saloon pretty much looking dead, his hairy hands now like wings, his unmoving eyes wide open and doe-like, and his Richard Nixon frown pasted on his head that shone like a bowling ball.

"Is he dead! Is he dead!" I was screeching.

Ursula pronounced, "He is metamorphosizing." She held up a mirror to me where I stood locked in the cage. In the glass reflection, I saw a man with the wide eyes of a timid doe and a frown of a Richard Nixon. I guess Balthazar did "catch" me as he believed. "You two become a gerimmppy."

This, then, is my recall of Balthazar, and my memory of my last day of freedom as a human.

AND MILES TO
GO BEFORE I SLEEP

Spooky; her nickname, was something she had acquired after pulling off an eerie near-miracle that saved several lives. In turn, one was due her.

Her long wavy tresses got lopped short once medical wonders destroyed them—wonders that made her normally steady hands move to a beat of an elusive butterfly; her eyes, bright and laughing, turned dark and shadowed.

She, Arline and I were thought of as the triumvirate. It seemed only fitting the three of us should be together when the spindly fingers of death reached out and wrapped around our throats to squeeze off our breaths.

I was the naive one—the only one—who refused to believe that Spooky wouldn't get that miracle, especially when she was so close to being accepted into a program that offered hope. And somehow I thought that if people were in the hospital preparing to vacate the mortal world they looked like they were ready to tip over the edge. But with Spooky, she stayed uncannily together, making it all the more difficult for me to grapple with the eating-away of her lungs.

It started out with my entering the white antiseptic smelling hospital room; I teased her, "Get back to writing."

As artists, Spooky, Arline and I shared a world different from most. I remember how we'd sneak private glances at writers' and critics' circles and authors' meetings; Spooky usually rolled her eyes. Our time was spent exchanging manuscripts and scribbling helpful or nasty, and sometimes funny, comments in red felt pen on crisp, nicely typed white paper; and the lunches we shared where I'd spill drinks over manuscripts or photographs, making her shake her head, look hopelessly at me. Endlessly the three of us talked about writing, about paper-people and pulp-style crises. I liked how we, game-style, debated the merits of an Updike over a Sheldon.

Too, there were long talks about her illness, and how she decided to opt out of life if it got really bad. Forever we bantered the existence of God, her premise that He did not exist, mine a Pascalian Wager. She'd snap back with ' That's a cop-out" each time I'd offer the standby argument that it was safer to believe than not to. That she was opinionated, stubborn, egotistical, and abrasive is only half true, as her whole was greater than any of her parts.

She overlooked my grumpiness when I was sick with mono or tired from long nights of checking ill-written college essays passed off as glossy literature; she was honest about my writing, often making me stretch for bigger and better things, with her famous words echoing in my head. "I can't see your images! Make pictures."

I liked best how she'd throw her head back, white teeth showing, and laugh—laughter like a shish of scalding water on ice cubes—sharp, caustic, a laugh that made my sometimes ridiculous perceptions seem even more absurd, or my most serious behavior turn light and relaxed.

I leaned over the bed rail. "I got a sitter tonight, and I can at last be alone." I remember how she smiled, weakly joked about my husband's and my activities while on a mini-vacation. It felt wrong leaving her. Polk, her husband, insisted I go, said that he'd call if he needed me.

At the resort, the ocean spray felt refreshing; tension seeped from my muscles; my overworked mind mellowed. For the first time in months I wasn't tormented with plot-making, fact-checking, or yelling children, and jingling phones. Still, flashes of Spooky lying in the hospital zipped constantly through my head.

When I returned home Sunday the sitter greeted me at the front door. "Your friend's husband called from the hospital several times. He wants you to call him immediately."

My fingers twittered as I dialed. "Polky? What's wrong?" Over the phone his voice quivered: "Come right away." My husband and I rushed to the hospital.

I couldn't believe it. There my friend, at 33, a year older than I lay peacefully, a grin on her face. I said to her after my husband left with Spooky's daughter, "You're not sick. I worried about you the whole time I was gone so I hurried over here...and look at you lying there smiling."

Polk winked. When he looked down at his wife I saw a shiny water drop slip out from the corner of his eye. He patted my hand, then followed his mother-in-law out the door.

I sat on the edge of the hospital bed, noting that the color of Spooky's face was no different than that of the sheet she lay on. "Want me to read?" She pointed to Amelia in the stack of books. "Your story in this issue?" I asked, rising and going for it.

She shook her head. Mumbled: "I won't be alive for it."

"You're gonna out-live me," I snapped back.

A nurse and technician came in. Sweat ran down the sides of their faces as they pushed-pulled, fingers shaking, a long needle in-out of Spooky's tender swollen veins.

"No more," she cried. "Let me go in peace!" She looked at me with her sad, brown eyes. "Tell them to catheterize me."

When the nurse returned with the catheter, I rose to leave. Spooky yanked on my arm, wanting me to stay, share in her utter privacy. I wet my lips, listening in agony as she screamed each time the nurse tried repeatedly to run the catheter into her bladder. After the torturer had gone, I asked Spooky if she wanted me to call our other writer friends. "Sharon? JoAnna? Chris?" I knew Arline, the tip of our triangle, would be along soon.

She shook her head. Beckoned for me to tilt my ear against her oxygen mask where she struggled to say, "I don't want them to see me weak like this."

During that long morning, I managed to sneak out into the hall and sit in the lobby with Spooky's mother, Gloria, who sat rigid, weeping convulsively into a crinkled blue tissue. I looked at Gloria's red, swollen eyes, said, "Spooky's gotten through rough times before. She'll make this."

Gloria rasped in her Cuban accent, "No oxygen left."
I pulled back, stared at her. Was that possible? To lose oxygen like air seeping out of a balloon? "What...does that mean?" Gloria held my hand tightly. "You, my daughter, so young." She shook her head. I felt like I was five years old, not understanding what this woman knew that I didn't. She wiped her runny nose, wailed, "Her lungs are not making oxygen."
"Not making oxygen?" I asked dumbly.
"The doctors say...24 hours."
I remember the day, its unfolding a constant ache in my body. Through the long hours I read short stories and poetry to Spooky, one of her favorites being Frost's "Nothing Gold Can Stay":

> *Nature's first green is gold,*
> *Her hardest hue to hold...*
> *Then leaf subsides to leaf.*
> *Nothing gold can stay.*

"I'm gold," she huffed-puffed through the foggedover wide plastic mask 'Nothing gold can stay.'"
I kidded, "You're more like coal...."
She winked; and shortly dozed off, sweetly asleep. 'Nothing gold can stay.' Polky brought his guitar in and played folk songs. Spooky's fingers curled around my thumb; I sang to her. Poorly. I saw Polk swallow hard, quickly swipe at his watery pink eyes. A lump rubbed raw my throat. Tears washed my cheeks. Spooky mumbled something. I didn't need to ask her to repeat it; I knew she didn't want us to cry.
Polky sang, "If you miss the train I'm on...."
My scratchy voice tried: "...know that I am gone." And I saw her grin, laughing at us. I laughed, too. She squeezed my hand. I nodded, unable to stop my tears from dropping onto her puffy porcelain-white fingers. Polky turned and faced the window, sniffling. I grabbed a poem, stared at the black print, unable to do anything more superior. My peripheral vision saw coming down the long hallway the third of our triad.
In the corridor I said to Arline, "I've been trying to get you!"
Arline hugged me, sobbed, "This is the end, then."
I broke the embrace. "The end? No. She'll make it."

Around six that night, Arline and I went to the airport to pick up Spooky's sister and father; he said, "How is she?"

"Okay," I answered right away. Arline shot me a look.

We returned to Spooky trying to scribble a note: "A good time was had by all." Arline and I glanced at each other. By the penmanship, we could see the ongoing nerve damage.

For the next nine hours we sat with Spooky, talking to her even when we knew she couldn't hear because her mind would drift into some unknown realm. Our rest periods consisted of sitting out in the hallway lobby, staring at the ceiling, floors; sometimes telling stories to keep our minds off what was going on inside the room a few feet away.

* * *

By 2:30 am, my body gave out. My eye sockets burned and my mind cried for sleep. "I've got to get some sleep, Ar," I said. "And Spooky's daughter stayed overnight at my house. I have to get her and my kids up in a few hours for school."

We drove the short piece to my house where we collapsed into a restless sleep.

It was about seven in the morning when Arline had gone back home to Cambridge, 30 minutes away, to take care of her ill sister-in-law. I remember I was standing in the doorway checking my pockets for car keys when Spooky's nine-year-old asked, "How's my mom?"

I thought about it.

My head filled with snapshots of how Spooky had looked earlier, before I had left her—her face more flushed with color than it had been, looking pleased that her parents and sister and husband, and two best friends were gathered around her. I answered, "She looks better."

The little girl's eyes lit up as she jumped into the air, her fingers closed into a victory fist. For a fleeting second I wondered if I had misled her, then I remembered Spooky was going to make it.

Spooky was drowsing when I got to the hospital, slipping in and out of the dimension holding the brink of elsewhere. When she awakened, I read to her:

I wandered lonely as a cloud....

When all at once I saw a crowd,
A host of golden daffodils

By her smile I could picture how she might have mentally painted a blue sky with wisps of white smoky clouds capping fields of green-stemmed yellow blossoms.

I distinctly recall it was noon when she said, her breathing labored, "This isn't fun anymore." Her exact words.

Arline and I believed she would do it one day because she had vowed that when the pain got too bad, she'd quit. Through thick vocal cords, she whispered: "Morphine." She closed her eyes; breathed hard, quick; said, "Lethal dose."

Spooky's mother cried, "No!"

Polky eyed the nurse.

I grabbed Spooky's hand, leaned over her, said into her ear, "No, Spook. It's not time." She looked up at me, my face over hers. Her tears didn't go unnoticed.

The doctor appeared soon after.

How strange it is that I recall his floundering phrases, and searching eyes. Clearing a deep voice, reminding me of a slow-speaking athlete, he said, "Morphine. Fine. Slow drip...we'll start slow. Is that what you want? Or fast? Let's start slow; we'll increase it when you want. That's what you want?" He played with a pen in the pocket of his long white smock.

I stood to the side of him, my hands behind my back, against the wall. I watched him fidget with his mustache, shift his stance. Listened to him trip over his words.

Spooky's mother said, "Pain medication is good; relax her."

This time it was I who knew what Gloria didn't. Morphine would only reduce Spooky's respiration. Was this her plan?

The doctor turned on his heels, clicking the pen rhythmically in his hand while saying, "Three bags. We'll hang three bags."

"Three bagsful,..yessir, yessir, three bagsful," just like in the nursery rhyme.

An Episcopalian priest entered. Lingered. Tried talking to Spooky. Saving her? She ignored him. He asked, "Can I pray for you?" She pointed to the doorway, he left. Then she turned to me, rasped, "William Carlos Williams."

What shall I say, because talk I must? That I have
found a cure...for the sick?

I paused, looked into her eyes. She had that silly grin on her face, teasing. Her fingers motioned me on.

*I will teach you my townspeople how to perform a
funeral.*

I closed the book. "I can't read this!" She was enjoying my wretchedness. And I could tell by the crinkles around her shadowed eyes, how she had enjoyed the priest's and my anguish over her soul.

* * *

She dozed; the morphine had begun to work.

A few hours later I left her to make family dinner.

JoAnna, another writer, appeared unexpectedly while I sat having coffee. "What are you doing here?" I asked.

"I stopped in to see Spooky first. Are you all right?"

I rubbed my eyes. "How was she when you left her?"

JoAnna's gaze lowered. "We kidded with her a little."

"I told everyone she'd make it! I just knew it!"

JoAnna frowned. "I don't know. She's in pain."

"But she's going to be fine. Spooky's a fighter." I rose to leave for the hospital. JoAnna got in step with me.

We walked down the hospital hallway, our sneakers noiseless against the tiled floor, each to our own thoughts. Out of nowhere, an aged bony-patient popped out of his room, dashed down the hall, his gown flying open in the back, exposing his rear, the wheeled IV stand and the sole wisp of hair on his head chasing after him.

JoAnna and I looked at each other out of the corner of our eyes and burst into laughter. Uncontrollable, inappropriate loud laughter. The more we looked at one another, the louder we howled. To this day neither of us can forget how we behaved, and how, in a way, nature had set us up as we entered Spooky's room still giggling. I had expected her to be lying there relaxed, a smile playing around her mouth, hearing us carrying on out in the hallway like two snickering kids in church.

I liked best was how she'd throw her head back, white teeth showing, and laugh, starting first with a snicker. Even when she laughed hard, it was still soft. Tonight, it was entirely different.

Instead, the second I stepped across the threshold, a brick wall slammed into me. I inhaled sharply, gasped for breath. The room's perfect silence slashed into my nerves. My survey swept in the faces of gloom—her whole family was assembled statue-like—then my gaze settled on Spooky.

She lay there unseeing; I'm sure, as her clouded, hazy eyes darted chaotically back and forth in her head. Her body heaved grotesquely with each respiration. "She's worse," I mumbled, afraid to admit it out loud. Polk's gaze caught mine. "What happened?" I whispered, but I think everyone heard me.

Massaging his wife's legs, Polky choked, "She was in pain. Wanted more morphine."

A shock went through my soft tissues like a high-voltage electrical current. I swallowed, consciously forcing the lump down my throat. For some reason I stood awhile with my hands pressing against my temples. Then slowly I walked up to the side of the bed, leaned over, kissed her clammy forehead.

"Spook?" My voice cracked. I cleared my throat. Mesmerized with fright, I watched her eyes shoot left and right...once beautiful eyes that were now thin and nearly opaque with Death's breath on them. "Want me to read? Spook?"

I was shaking, I know it. I remember standing there, knees bowed and vibrating, hands trembling. This couldn't be happening. "Want me to read Frost?" I could have sworn, just a wee bit, she moved her head. No one else saw it, but I'm sure it happened, just as sure as I heard the sound of gurgling rails, smelled the sewer-like odor of decay, felt the gritty fear of Life's End reaching out, touching.

I saw the unplanned positioning of her loved ones: her husband at the right side of her, holding her left hand; I at the opposite side holding her right hand; her parents at the foot of the bed, her sister near me. JoAnna stood in the doorway, halfway in and halfway out, but I could feel her eyes on me.

"Frost. I'll read Frost." It was so quiet, deadly quiet, in the room, that my voice muffled and muted seemed stuck on the ceiling.

Tears poured out of Polk's eyes. He tried turning his mouth upward in a smile for me but his lips trembled and he brushed his face with the back of his big hand.

"Arline should be here, too." I think I whined it. We all knew the triangle was incomplete in its final seconds. I picked up the book I had left on the hospital stand; read: "'Whose woods these are I think I know....'." I looked up from the page. Spooky was the same; I read some more:

These woods are lovely, dark and deep,
But I have promises to keep,
And miles to go before I sleep...

I took in a deep ragged breath. Saw my tears wet the print, and did nothing to hide them.

Then her eyes stopped moving. Fixed.

Polk and I glanced at one another. I turned, headed for the nurses' station, passing JoAnna. Later she told me I had said, "I don't believe this. She's dying and I'm reading poetry here." I have no memory of this but I believe JoAnna, for she did the sane thing—wrote everything down as it happened. It took me three months before I could again write.

The nurse looked up when I said, "We need you in there." I returned to Spooky's silent room where everyone stood mute, exactly the same way I had left them.

Two nurses entered after me, checked her IV, her pulse, and then positioned themselves around the bed. Waiting.

I was holding Spooky's hand, listening to Polk say, '1 don't understand. Her eyes have stopped moving. What does this mean? Is she in a coma now?" His tone was sharp and brittle with a fear ready to shatter into a million pieces, the same fear that suffocated all of us.

The nurse near him said, "This is the natural order."

"I don't understand!" His voice shattered.

"This is how it is to be," she said softly.

"What does it mean? What does it mean?" Then suddenly he leaned over his wife's head to grab my arm, cried, "What does it mean, Nan? What does it mean! Is she dying?"

Everlastingly I will remember those words.

I may have nodded; I'm not sure. I was trying to concentrate on stopping my tears from sopping her hair, on how strangely her rib cage contracted, as if her chest were sucked back to her spine, then released and immediately repeated. She made noises, an almost cyclic sighing. I squeezed her hand. Counted her breaths.

One
Two
Three
And she stopped. Completely.

We all stood freeze-frame still, glued to our spots. A nurse passed a flashlight across Spooky's glass-like eyes, then shook her head and shut off the machines.

It was the sister who screamed first. Threw her body over Spooky. The mother's flat palm smacked a wall over and over again, her high-pitched voice screeching, "Oh God, oh God!" The father turned, turned his face away from me, all, his shoulders rocking.

JoAnna darted out into the hall.

Polky hugged me, wept. I remember thinking his large form would protect me from this suctioning of my beating heart out of its cavity.

The nurses tried to calm the sister who was pointing at Spooky, screaming, "Close her eyes! For God's sake, close her eyes!"

We cried and moaned, went from one person's arms into another's. The nurses began shepherding us through the doors, but Polky and I lingered.

As if in step with marching caissons, we walked to her bed, he to one side, I to the other. Across her unmoving chest, we clasped hands.

I whispered to her, "You're done with your miles, and I'll miss you." Everywhere through me shot vice-like pain. Polk and I stood staring at her for a long time saying nothing. Then I left, giving him privacy with the woman he had held in his arms for fifteen years.

Polky, Spooky's family, and I agreed there would be no church service, for Spooky had no God. Instead, we planned a "healing" where we would read her poetry and that of her favorite poets.

* * *

On the night of the healing I wore my beret and dated bell-bottom blue jeans that Spooky had always termed outrageous but befitting an artist. I remember standing in the small kitchen helping Arline uncover the catered food to be set out buffet-style. I glanced up each time friends, family, and other artists came trooping in, hour after hour, until it seemed mourners, like goo, would seep through the building's seams.

* * *

Ice snapped in buckets, glasses clinked, voices came strong and loud, weak and muffled, music played her favorites while over and over again I answered to prodding questions, "No funeral service; this is her way of saying good-bye."

It was time for the readings. As if a shot went through the room thick with people, the chattering instantly stopped. My eyes panned the room quickly, seeing the older adults seated on the couches, the younger ones leaning against walls and door frames. Movement came to a halt. I wrack my brain to recall who read first. Arline or me? I don't know. Vaguely I remember saying to the crowd that I had a poem to read to Polky, written by his wife for him.

Polk sat next to me. I said to the mourners, "I once asked Spooky why she always wrote about death. She answered, 'I don't write about death; I write about life.'" My voice wobbled when I began:

This night of pain,
morphine doesn't dull the prickly sense of fate.
He rubs me down to quiet my groans
so I will not waken our daughter...
And l accept...t he firm strokes of his hand
as assurance...my family will go on without me.
The whole world is not sick and dying.
Only me.

I looked up from the pages, saw old ladies shake their heads, trying to shape their tear-drenched faces into stoic masks, heard men honk loudly into hankies, saw young people cover their eyes with spread fingers, and I knew how pleased Spooky would be that her creation had affected each life in that room, in her death.

What happened from then on for months after reminds me of sitting in an old theater watching montages of represent-ations of life. To me, it seemed nothing would ever occur again with any thread of cohesiveness.

She has left much besides her writing: the philosophy to live life every minute, and to be in control in writing, in living, in pain, and in sorrow.

I understand the mourning process for me may never be over.

I have those miles to go before I sleep.

Note: *After Spooky's death, her father committed suicide .*

INSIDE ME

A part of me is shut off from others; a part that has become cold, frozen; and although it is fragile, it, nonetheless, manages through its own internal tug-of-war to stop the sea from gushing out, from letting loose the torrents of all that I fear and hate, hide and protect.

Certain writers I read are able to zero in on my vulnerability, to sneak unwanted photographs into my head in order to make me aware of life's peculiarities and how I'm affected by them. And like these writers, I too have been called intense, temperamental, even rebellious, because of my insistence on doing something right or not doing it at all and my resulting frustration in not always getting it right. So, I will attempt to get it right here, too.

* * *

What it is that I'm trying to perfect is the momentarily unleashing of my soul, a flashing and unheralded revealing of myself, of uncovering my sores.

Allow me to start by saying that distinctly I remember when I turned old enough to vote and my father sent me off to register, throwing his arm around my shoulder, saying, "Now don't forget, we come from a proud line of Democrats." I registered Republican, then refused to join any party support group: Daughters of American Revolution, The Republican Club, and The League of Women Voters.

I hate exposing my inner core like this, but for you—just this one time—I will do it. I'd rather remain private, so as not to be judged, unlike others who willingly hold themselves up to scrutiny so that some invisible ax will start picking away. Where do I go from here, in my lost sanity to bear my nature? For one thing, I hate being dictated to, or interpreted, especially by those so-called analysis experts. For example, many of those old asinine tests like the "Stanford-Binet Intelligence Test" or the "Iowa Test" ushered out reports that even today I share only with deep reservation. The "Kuder Preference Record" and the "Strong Vocational Interest Blank" stick in my mind. When I got to be "grown-up" they let me read the comments on me by these "interpreters":

> *'Student is withdrawn, though has ability and talent to achieve success; separates self from other children; will use gregariousness to hide shyness. Her "dazed" states are indicative of deep-rooted psychological problems that are most likely a result of the mother's periodic chain-smoking. Years of counseling might alleviate her inattentiveness to the external environment.'*

It gets worse:

> *'Child tests well-above average in I.Q. but her choice of answers yields little direction her talents should be steered in. Her scores for creativity are the highest, suggesting such careers as painting, music, and writing/poetry. Scores also show scientific/math potential and this should be encouraged. Prohibit student's insistence on doodling on homework and test papers; prohibit her "day-dreaming" through scolding, written punishment, or by compelling her to share with entire class her "dream" contents as a technique of embarrassment and hopeful cessation. Teachers should maintain records indicating the number of times per class per day student tends to bore and become inattentive. Under no circumstances should teachers encourage the child to continue writing the items she refers to as "stories," as these fairyland accounts only promote escapism.'*

* * *

I saw my high school algebra teacher this past summer (I loved algebra; it had absolutes that simplified life, unlike art). I asked her if she was surprised I had become a professor and writer. She said, "I had you pegged as an artist with all those stick figures you used to draw on your papers. But I always felt you would have made a wonderful mathematician." I reassured her that writing was a legitimate career. "You never did work up to your potential," she announced as she got into her car.

Periodically I must make a point of reassuring myself that I'm okay in spite of my inability to remember my children's birthdays or something that was said to me not more than a day or so ago; despite my having to be told that a group in a club's membership is attempting to usurp my presidency because I forget to show at meetings; or in spite of my having to appear in court on a certain day for balling up a ticket I got doing 65 in a 35 mile zone and then throwing the crinkled wad at the officer. "I don't understand you!" my husband lectured me in the car on the way home that day. "One minute you're revolutionist Jane Fonda, the next you're withdrawn and 'mentally off' somewhere. Normal people don't throw speeding tickets at the arresting officer!"

It cost me $200 in fines, and never mind the points.

What is it I think of when I'm "off," my husband wants to know, demanding that I be specific—as specific as his computers are. "Maybe you should talk to someone—other writers—about these "dazes" you have. You're living life on the surface and your writing makes you moody and intense. Have some fun. It'll be good for you."

I don't bother to tell him that he goes "off" about his modems and motherboards. In fact, exasperating is what he is when he rambles on in computerese. The difference is that I keep my passion inside whereas he can't. I'd love to crawl into a corner with paper and pen and be left alone until the end.

I wonder, is it normal for people—especially artists—to look deep inside ourselves, only to turn and run away when we get too close to the core of the volcano? Is it just as normal for artists to be sick all the time? Sick from chemicals like drugs and alcohol? Sick from organic diseases caused by years of bodily abuse?

For me, it's earaches—the kind that throb and demoralize because they rob me of all hearing in one ear. "What? What?" I go around saying all day. Noises are foreign and disoriented since they're no longer stereophonic, words are garbled, and headaches always follow. I cannot conduct daily affairs, let alone give a reading or teach a class; I can't even write because sounds in my made-up world become inaudible to me; and I can't hold up my end of dinner conversation with my family who is usually a heartbeat ahead of me on my good days. Driving is impossibility, as is listening to classical music. When as a student, I used to doodle even more during these times because I couldn't hear the teacher or fellow students.

It takes days for the medication to work. When I sense an ear ache coming on, I pump up on the antibiotics and anti-histamines. It comes anyway. "Probably forever," says my ENT doctor in response to how long I have to put up with this. "It's one of those things that got damaged from rheumatic fever." The other is my heart.

Thirteen catherizations, three episodes of pericarditis, a pacemaker, endocarditis, open heart surgery and many periods of hospitalizations have yielded the inevitable: a sloppy floppy valve coupled with an irregular beat that would drive a drummer crazy. On my really bad days, my joints hurt so much that I can't even get out of bed and my glands swell as though I have Bubonic Plague. But why bother to tell others? They cannot change the course I'm on. Why let the world know of my anguish, because, like with my ear aches, life pushes forward in its cycles, with or without me.

What I haven't told you is that I have some pre-, pseudo-, mis-, quasi-diagnosed immunological disease. My examination is a diagnostician's orgasm: pulmonary function tests, CAT-scans, gland biopsies, bone marrows. And in the end, it's always the same: "You have what we believe is chronic adult rheumatic fever, though there is some chance it's leukemia."

Why am I telling you what I'm trying to hide somewhere in the attic of my mind?

I'm so vulnerable, so flawed, that if I don't at least write about it this once, I'm certain to someday just permanently hibernate in that attic. Besides, you should be made aware of just how wrong all these so-called faultless experts (doctors, politicians, academicians) are, for there's this part of me that boils with contempt for any form of bureaucracy and all its made-up numbers and charts and graphs used to back up the nonsense or the misinformation giving or the information being hidden. These are things that get at me because they're out of my control to change them. It all seems so unfair from my angle.

I hate unfairness and injustice, from something as minor as a kid lying about "who started the fight" to as serious as the mistreatment of humankind. The first time I was called "dago," I ran home and asked my father what it meant; the next time someone screamed it at me, I walked away, fuming inside but determined not to dignify the remark. Walking away emotionless is a good method, providing your eyes don't give you away.

My father, being an immigrant himself, had a curious concern for minorities. On the Christmas he moved us to the suburbs where families had surnames like Jones, Wilson, Carver and Smith; he decided to put up blinking lights, red and green decorations, and a worn nativity scene. He spent days intently making a star which he nailed to the peak of the roof and lighted like a neon billboard. None of the neighbors talked to us after that. He kept saying, "Whatever did we do to them?" The kids at school would look at me and giggle. It wasn't until a man pulled into our driveway, saying: "I'm Rabbi Rosen and I know this is none of my business but you really ought to decide which you want to honor: Christmas or Hanukkah." My mother gasped. "But we're Roman Catholics!" The Rabbi smiled: "You have a six-pointed star out there shining like the Northern Lights." My father took down the nativity scene and let the neighbors gossip even more. It took them six months before they bothered to say hello again.

Because my parents were bilingual (and my father had put up the six-pointed star, I've always had an interest in foreign worlds. In grad school, I had a close friend who was raised on a Kibbutz, which seemed to me wild and wonderful. Twice a week he gave me Hebrew lessons; taught me how to read and write the 26 consonants and vowel points; tutored me in Judaic ways of life; explained the difference between being Hadassah and modern Orthodox, Reform, or Conservative, or a variety thereof; told me interesting tidbits: how Yiddish came out of Italian, Hebrew, French, and Aramaic, how Christianity came out of Judaism; took me to Jewish weddings, to Bar and Bat Mitzvahs; taught me the difference between those "holidays" Christians always screw up: Rosh Hashanah, Yom Kippur, Passover, Shabuoth, Sukkoth, Hanukkah, and Purim.

One Easter I went home, said to my mother, "I learned Hebrew." She looked at me, asked while basting a ham. "Why didn't you take up Italian?" I shrugged. "I already know some Italian." She shut the oven door, then turned to me, and smiled while ordering, "So speak to me in Jewish." I rolled my eyes and walked out of the kitchen. Later, she went around telling our relatives that I "knew Jewish." My need to consume everything I could on Judaism reminds me of just how neurotic I am.

By my own admission, I'm not a spontaneous person. I design my writing to be exact—like surveyors and geometrists—in order to give the impression of one body of thought; yet, I also enjoy mazes and abstract paintings. I fool people into thinking that the final form of a play I produce or a story I write comes together naturally, without my behind the scenes strategizing and laboring, and yet I'm open to randomness—so much so that often I depend on it to alter my otherwise routine day.

And while the precision of science and math doesn't turn me on, new snow and old movies do. Not the slushy-mushy city snow but the pristine falling flakes that land haphazardly to give, in the end, the overall forms and patterns of man's existence. When it's the right kind of snowfall, where tree branches and lawn lanterns glaze over, I want to run outside with my arms open and scoop it all up to make it "mine."

Old movies, too, touch me, placing me inside a story. I can feel myself crawling into the television set, putting my foot on a snow-covered (of course) cobblestone street, circa early 1900s, and walking along the antiquated shops with rustic street lamps, enjoying the night, not worrying about AIDS, or some war, nuclear weapons, or running out of resources, or a lunatic releasing plutonium on the earth, terrorists blowing up the next plane or building, or someone kidnapping my kids. I would take my make-believe apartment steps two-at-a-time and cloister myself in my pretend room overlooking the lamp-lit avenue below where people, dressed in mufflers and hats window-shop and greet one another. There, in that old-fashioned apartment, I would write until I dropped. No one would say "Where's dinner?", or "Mummie, you color with me now?" No one would expect errands to have been run, dishes and laundry to have been washed, or groceries to have been bought. My naiveté serves to retard my having to face today and certainly tomorrow.

And while I try to be fastidious about my writing, which is my life, chaos of any sort animates me. I prefer to live quietly, but if something is going to "break" lose, (backed-up sewer in the basement; trimmed Christmas tree collapsing; street pipes freezing, then bursting; tornado ripping through; spaceship crashing) then let all hell erupt in that one quick shattering second. When it's over, the shape of a vestal life will have unfolded, the parts will have gone back together to form a new whole, so that like the Phoenix arising out of the ashes, I too can start afresh. It can be seen, then, that while others make a point of distancing themselves from chaos, I try to get close enough to feel it, smell it, inhale it.

I'm a survivor of life because I resign myself to believing that everything comes to an end—that backed-up sewer, the tornado, the freezing pipes—and whatever the end brings is the beginning of the next event that will also come to an end. It is the valley in between the peaks that I like. The chaos does not scare me; it just momentarily diverts my writing. My fear is only that in the end, there is no end.

* * *

Of all the things that pick away inside me until what left is raw and pure, is that I represent—or at least I think I do—what is the epitome of existence in modernity. My worldview is one of the pointlessness of life; of our alienation and despair over the disintegration of ourselves; over the estrangement of our unconscious world and empty existence; over the annihilation of our once moral and tranquil humanity that has since become amoral and battle-stricken. Simply put, I have trouble existing; for me, it's ineptness at tolerating the waste and falsity of life. Any kind of meaningfulness, to me, comes only from what's inside a person and not what's external with all its trappings.

Being angst-ridden has little, if any, benefit, especially in a period of the 21st century. Am I living in the wrong period? ...Or just living wrong...period?

* * *

Now you know something about me. Does it help you in anyway? For me, it's perhaps a purging, but like the repeated ear aches and joint pains that return, this too will come again. But next time there will be no telling about it, no talking it out. How can I play the silent, suffering, sulking martyr if I go around unloading my burden to anyone who will listen?

Put the ax back down. I prefer to suffer alone in my cushioned mind.

BLUE BLOOD CHRISTMAS

January 1978

Charlotte Taylor wiped sweat from her brow. She hated being a hospital housekeeper, working until she was ready to drop while her friend and boss, Lenore, had a husband who also had a salary; Char's had died of cancer right after Vicki was born.

She punched out, washed her hands in the cubby-hole stained sink and turned to leave. Lenore came up behind her. "Char," Four-oh-one was just discharged. Would you handle it?"

"I just punched out."

"Time and-a-half."

Charlotte nodded; she needed the money. "Tell me, why don't you ever complain? Even though you're the boss, your salary's not much more than mine and I can barely make ends meet."

Lenore shrugged. "I look at it this way: my job's just that—a job. I measure wealth by having good health and a loving family. In that sense, I'm rich. You know, here we are...what? Fifty of us working in this hospital? Every day we see things that make us grateful for what we do have, like that pale little seven-year-old who's dying of leukemia; or old man Greiger who's so senile he can't even wash himself. And how about that gal on three who made a living as a seamstress and lost her hand from diabetic gangrene?" Lenore shook her head. Returning to her seat behind the gray metal desk, she added, "Money can't buy health and love. Trust me; I know what I'm saying."

"All flowery talk. Gratefulness don't pay the bills."

"But in the overall scheme of life, those aren't important."
Char spun around. "No? Tell that to my landlord, to the
college my daughter wants to attend."

"What good is money if you're too sick to appreciate it? What
do you want out of life, Char?"

"Money. And lots of it. Enough to buy anything I want."

"That's it? What about your daughter?"

"That's a given."

Lenore chuckled. "Nothing in life is 'a given.' Money? You
better play the lottery."

"I've done it every week for the last five years," Char called
back, heading upstairs. She pushed her cleaning cart onto the
elevator, thinking, Lenore's soft in the head.

March

Saturday morning broke with sunburst, spring smells and
birds swooping and singing. Char rose and joined her daughter
for breakfast in their three-room apartment. Immediately Vicki
pressed, "Mom, what about my going to Vassar?"

"I'm proud you got accepted to Vassar but unless you get a
scholarship, you can't go. I'm not even sure I can send you to
the community college here."

"Great. Just great." Vicki lowered her eyes. "Community
college! Vassar is special, Mother."

Char shook her head. "I just don't have the money."

Vicki jumped up, shoved her plate hard. "Why do we have
to be poor!" She ran to her room.

Stooping, picking up spilled food scraps, Char mumbled,
"I'd give anything to be rich."

Later that day, as Char prepared to go into town, Vicki came
downstairs. "Mom, I just wanted to tell you I'm sorry about
this morning. I know you don't have the money."

Smiling, Char said, "I'm sorry too." She kissed Vicki on the
forehead. "Someday we'll be so rich and we'll have everything
we want." Char winked, then left for her usual trek to the local
drug store to buy the paper and her lottery ticket.

Neither said much the next morning as they read the Sunday
paper, lingering over house decorating ideas, and store fliers.

Char sipped her coffee, and then reached behind the spice rack to produce last night's lottery ticket. She leafed through the paper to the page with the lottery numbers while mumbling, "Let's see how many millions of dollars I won this time."

Vicki rolled her eyes, returned to reading the fashion page.

Sounds of newspapers shuffling and coffee cups tapping against the Formica table top lingered in the silence.

Suddenly Char whooped. "Ohmigawd!" She felt Vicki's eyes on her. "Look here! The newspaper! My ticket!"

Vicki was on her feet, at her mother's side. "Let me see!

Char's hand trembled when she gave Vicki the newspaper.

Their heads came together and they read aloud the numbers over and over, mechanically repeating: "40, 17, 67...."

Char dropped into a ripped kitchen chair trying to catch her breath. "We won. Really hit, after all these years."

"How much? How much?"

"If there are no other winners... about four million." Char shook her head with disbelief and again rechecked the numbers. Then she leaped out of her seat, grasped Vicki's arms, and danced around the kitchen with her, laughing, singing, squealing.

Late October 1980

Cool fall winds picked up leaves and tossed them around the yard, across the wooden veranda. Char sat on the porch glider sipping Asti Spumante out of fine crystal. She pressed the intercom button and asked Robert to come out.

"Yes, Mrs. Taylor?"

"What's on tomorrow's schedule?"

"You're leaving for Paris to shop."

"Is Vicki going?"

"She's leaving in the morning to ski in Switzerland."

"Can't that kid ever spend time with me? She's either at Vassar or off somewhere!"

"She says the same of you, Mrs. Taylor."

Char grumbled. "Send her down, Robert."

"Yes, ma'am. Is there anything else?"

"Have Carl bring the limo around."

"Very well." He paused.

"What is it?" Agitation colored her voice.

"The staff, Mrs. Taylor. They're complaining of being overworked and underpaid."

Char shot him a look. Don't they know how to be properly grateful for what they have? "They can look elsewhere for work."

"But, Mrs. Taylor—"

"Get Vicki." She shooed him away with the flip of her hand. Several minutes later Vicki walked out to where Char sat on the wrap-around veranda.

Char said, "You're looking grumpy today."

Vicki sat on the glider near Char. "What do you want Mom?"

"What do you want Mom?" mocked Char. "That's all you have to say? I haven't seen you since you came home from school for the weekend. Aren't I important enough to you?"

"I didn't think it mattered to you. You're always going somewhere doing something entertaining at all hours."

"What about you?" Char set her tulip shaped glass on the wicker table.

"I go to college. But you...you really went overboard with this money thing. Ever since we got rich, you changed."

"All my life I've been poor. Don't tell me how to live now that I have money."

Vicki grumbled. "I give up." She started for the door, turned and said, "What's happened between us, Ma? We used to be so close, nothing could come between us."

"I don't hear you complaining about all the nice things the money got you."

Vicki sighed. "I'm sorry I even came home."

"Then leave," Char said, throwing her hands up in the air.

"I am. Switzerland, first thing in the morning." Vicki stomped off, slamming the door.

Early November

Carl rushed the limo through heavy traffic. Char had to get home immediately. "Come on, Carl!" she yelled on the intercom.

"I'm rushing, Mrs. Taylor."

How could he drive so slowly when she was urgently called

home? Char sank down in her seat, scanned the people outside the car window hustling to and fro from everywhere. *How can they look so caught up in their lives when something terrible has happened?* The start-stopping of the car in city streets frazzled Char. She clenched her fists against the seat. In the circular driveway, Carl shifted into park at the house's doubled-door front entrance. He said as he held open the door for her, "Looks like Dr. MacGuire's car is here."

Hurrying into the foyer, Char dropped her coat into Robert's hands while asking her friend, "What's wrong; one of the staff?"

"Let's sit down, Char." Mary led the way to the parlor. "Vicki's been in a skiing accident and is in the hospital."

Char held her breath, her muscles going tight as a rubber band. The hysteria began building inside her, pushing itself to the top. "And? And?"

"Damaged spinal cord."

"She's paralyzed?" Her voice cracked.

MacGuire nodded solemnly. "I talked to her Swiss doctors; they said it might be temporary; there's hope. They've immobilized her and are sending her here to our hospital."

Char's voice sounded as though it would shatter the second she opened her mouth. "Paralyzed? Her legs?"

"From her neck down."

Sweat sneaked out at Char's temples, hands and knees rocked, light grew dim. She felt MacGuire walking towards her. The silence seemed so long that she thought she could count it the way she did with thunder years ago as a child.

MacGuire cleared her throat, went on, "Her spinal cord injuries may have caused brain damage; she's still unconscious."

"A coma?" Char's eyes got big, her heart beat fast; she had to suck for air. Blackness swooped down on her quietly, swiftly.

* * *

Outside the hospital window the wind whistled and slammed against the panes. Below, city storefronts boasted hanging turkeys or pointed Pilgrim hats. Snow blanketed sidewalks and car roofs, reflecting the street lamps' yellow glow. What a Thanksgiving, sighed Char. Two weeks, and still her daughter had not spoken or even curled a toe. Char couldn't resign herself to having a rag as a substitute for her once vibrant child whose only dream in life had been to attend Vassar. Char had a dream once too—to become so rich she would never want for anything.

Walking back to the hospital bed, she placed her hand on Vicki's forehead. "Come on, sweetheart, talk to me. Open your eyes; move your fingers. Just a little, baby. Do it for Mama."

Char shook her head, waited. Still no response. What had she done to deserve this? Please, God, anything! I'll do anything to get my baby back; make me paralyzed instead! She touched Vicki's upper arm. It felt cold, inanimate; her cheeks: white like whipping cream. Was she even alive? The rhythmic hiss of the respirator offered no comfort. Char ran her hand through her hair. Make things go back to the way they used to be even if it means being poor again. She studied her baby.

No movement

It was no use; Vicki was paralyzed for life. Char rested her head on her arms at the bedrails. What will I do without her silly grin? Bright blue eyes? She stared unblinking at the small form that was made of her flesh, her soul. She sensed someone next to her and she looked up. "Lenore!" Without thinking, Char jumped up and threw her arms around the woman she had tossed off as her friend three years ago. Char liked the feel of Lenore's comforting embrace. "I thought I'd never see you again after the way I treated you and everyone when I—"

"Became rich and thought you were better than us?"

Char winced.

"Friendship is one of those riches you can't buy." Lenore walked over to Vicki's bed. "Not even a little bit better?"

Char shook her head.

"As soon as you came through emergency, the staff knew about it; I would've come sooner but I stayed with my sick mother for two weeks; my prayers were with you. All of us feel real bad about it, especially since we've known you and Vicki for years."

"I don't deserve your prayers." Char reached for Lenore's hand. "It's something...my getting my start here in this hospital twenty years ago and now in this same place my whole world's collapsing. What a life." Char shook her head.

"She's young, Char; strong."

"You were right; nothing in life is a given." Char returned to the window, peered outside. How could everyone seem so holiday-happy when her daughter was fading? "I look back now and see that I was so preoccupied with wanting things, I was not properly grateful for what I had." She rubbed her eyes, then looked at Lenore. "You were right: money can't buy health or love. I really messed up."

Lenore said nothing.

"This is my fault! If I hadn't been so greedy, this wouldn't have happened. No matter what I had, I wanted more." Char returned to the sole bedside chair.

Minutes passed before Lenore said, "If you believe Vicki's paralysis comes from owning material goods, comes from your greed, then get rid of them. The Lord loves us so much that if we gave away all our possessions, he'd still take care of us."

"You always were a dreamer." Char sniffled, pulled her shoulders back, dabbed at her eyes.

"A few weeks to Christmas. Miracles do happen."

Char shook her head. "I think my baby will be like this the rest of her life. And it's my fault."

Hours later, red-eyed, exhausted, Char slipped into the limo Carl drove to the hospital curve.

"How is she?" He looked into his rearview mirror. Then, pulling the long black car away from the curb, he asked louder, "You'll return again in a short while as usual?"

She said nothing, just looked out the window at a Santa standing on a street corner ringing a bell over a large pot, hoping to collect money for the needy. Needy. She repeated the word in her head. What had Lenore said? 'If you think Vicki's paralysis is your punishment for being so greedy, then get rid of all your wealth. At that very second, compulsion hit Char. She picked up the limo's phone intercom: "You like this car, Carl?"

"Yes, ma'am," he whistled.

"It's yours; happy holidays." She heard him gasp.

Near Hell's Kitchen she made Carl pull to the curb, double-parking. "Wait here," she ordered while climbing out of the car. Reading a sign—BRETHREN HOUSE—over a paint-chipped, crooked door, Char entered. Ten minutes later she returned to the limo, got in the front seat with Carl who looked aghast at her.

Shocked, he muttered, "Are you all right?"

She nodded.

He maneuvered the limo into holiday traffic. "This is a seedy place, Mrs. Taylor. If I'm not prying, ma'am, may I ask what we're doing in this part of town?"

Her profile forward, Char said dryly, "Giving away my money. Brethren House is a shelter for the homeless."

If she had recorded the entire forty-eight hours after she left the hospital, had written it all down in a log or a journal, she could prove to the Guiness people she did it all in record time. To prove what, she didn't know. Surely it wouldn't return Vicki to her normal self. But the very act of undoing what she did by giving away her possessions made Char somehow feel purged.

December

Arctic gusts sliced deep into Char's raw nerves. She lowered her head, her body leaning into the wind to ward off its biting edge. Walking the streets, she realized that her recent generosity had done little to change her daughter's state. Where was this God anyway? It's been almost a month. When is she going to jerk a finger? Blink an eye?

She spotted a soup wagon and headed for it to get her day's meal. Christmas was less than three weeks away, making Char wonder where would she spend it; on the streets the way she spent the last two weeks after she had given away her furniture, antiques, coats, even her house with salary on Robert, Carl, and all the help? She had an attorney sign over half of her monthly lottery payments to a national spinal cord research center; some went to the cleaning ladies at the hospital where it was divided into monthly bonuses, the rest went to orphans' homes, shelters, and friends at her old neighborhood, while all her stocks and bonds and other values were transferred to the hospital where Vicki still lay lifeless. When she had walked out the door of her mansion at the end of the forty-eight hours, she owned nothing except for a few undergarments, a couple of blouses and slacks, and the coat The Salvation Army had given her.

After eating a sandwich, she returned to the hospital where she heard nurses and others whisper, "There goes Crazy Charlotte Taylor, the cleaning lady turned rich woman turned bag lady."

As usual, that night she sat at Vicki's bedside and told a story. "How about 'A Christmas Carol'; you always loved Scrooge." Char smiled, thinking how contradictory that was to her daughter's personality.

What personality? Gone.

Moisture filled her eyes as she stared at Vicki lying rigid.

Char glanced up when Lenore entered the room carrying a small silver artificial Christmas tree and a box of ornaments. "Merry Christmas," she sang, handing Char the box. "Decorate it, then set it on Vicki's bed stand.

"Throw the tree away," snapped Char, and yet she absently hung a pink bulb on it, then she stood back and stared. Suddenly she backed away, putting her hands to her face, her body rocking. "Look at what I've done to my little girl—I've given her money to go anywhere, do anything—everything but my time. How do I make it like it used to be?"

"I don't think it's in your hands."

Char wiped her face with a handkerchief and blew her nose.

"My house is open to you, you know that. Even with four kids, a husband, dog, cat, and a mother-in-law, I'd find a bed for you and Vicki." Giving Char a quick squeeze, Lenore left.

Char returned to mindlessly trimming the tree, listening to Christmas tunes drift from down the hall, thinking about how she would give up living if she never got her girl back. The holiday music reminded Char of Vicki's seventh Christmas when they were so poor that only three presents sat out. But still Vicki cheerfully placed icicles one at a time on their crooked, wilting tree while gay yuletide tunes played on the old radio.

"The third present," Char said aloud to Vicki. "The third present was your gift to me. Remember that, honey?"

No answer

Char went on. "On Christmas morning, you jumped up and down in your Dr. Dentons, squealing, 'Open it Mummy open it!' How I cried when I saw it. Such a beautiful present—a sheet of red construction paper bordered by green strips with a stick figure of Santa in the center. You had smudged it with excess glue, and on the bottom you scrawled in crayon, 'Mummy, I luv you I yam happy yore my mummy. Mary krismess.' Blubbering, I said, 'You couldn't even spell back then but the note was beautiful!' and I grabbed you and smothered you with wet kisses."

She looked over at Vicki. Nothing.

"Remember how we sat in the middle of the floor holding each other? I said 'As long as I have you, I don't need anything else' and you started singing your favorite Christmas song: 'I wish you a Merry Christmas.'" Mindlessly fondling a blue bulb, Char turned back to Vicki.

No movement

"You remember the song, baby?" Char started humming lowly, then words came out strong and solid, so loud that people passing in the hall looked in. Her body prickled with excitement as she leaned over Vicki and sang deep from her heart. Her tears wet Vicki's face as she sang, "I wish you a Merry Christmas. I wish you a Merry Christmas..." She squeezed her daughter's hand.

Vicki didn't squeeze back.

"Come on, baby, please. *Please!*" Char closed her eyes. Seconds later she tried again, her notes off key, her voice shaky: "I wish you a Merry Christmas. I wish you a Merry Christmas." Hardly aware that onlookers stood nearby, Char's voice reached the top of the scale as she pitched out the words.

Still nothing.

She rested her head on the cold bedrails, feeling drained. Please, God. Make her say something. Again she sang, this time in hushed tones as though she had somehow lost her voice: "I wish you a...." She waited; no response. Defeated, Char lowered her head to her lap and wailed.

A slight rustling noise and then a groan. So weak a sound.

Slowly Char pulled her head up. Suddenly her heart felt stilled, like it had been held in midair and pinched.

Vicki's eyes fluttered.

Char screamed, hit the nurse's intercom, screeching, "Get Dr. MacGuire!" Instantly she was cradling Vicki, alternating between sobbing uncontrollably and laughing hysterically.

* * *

Sitting in the hospital room while Vicki was at physical therapy, Char felt depressed. Oh sure, Vicki had made great progress: she limped with a cane now and had only minimal brain damage—certainly Char had a lot to be grateful for. The only problem was that Vicki was almost ready to go home but Char had no house. She rubbed her eyes, exhausted from walking here and there, calling this agency and that, talking to this or that person—all in attempt to get back some of what she had given away so that she might be able to support Vicki. She had first gone to the mansion she had given away in those quick forty-eight hours where a young man stood at the door apologizing.

"I wish I could help, Mrs. Taylor. I am indebted to you for pulling my wife and me out of shelters but my wife's mother and sisters are here; our baby is due and there's no room. I could loan Robert to you. You did pay his salary in advance for us."

Char laughed. "And put him on the streets with me? I shoulda never come back; this house is my past."

Then she had gone to Carl to ask for help, but Carl had sold the limo and was running his own furniture store. Next she tried the homeless shelters, the orphanage, the hospital, but none were able to help without first going through administrative channels. Next she went door to door in her old community where Char had freely given each of her former neighbors' money as well as freezers to store all the food she bought them. Still no room.

No room at the inn. At Christmas time.

Char rose and walked over to the window. Thanksgiving had come and gone and Christmas was at the doorstep. She had to find a place to live. She wanted to avoid going to a shelter—that was no place for a kid at Christmas, especially a crippled one.

Mary MacGuire entered the room, her mouth drawn tight like a line across the horizon. "Soon Vicki will be discharged—insurance rules—so you must find a place. And according to our records, your coverage is due to run out; if you let this premium lapse, you won't be able to get or afford another carrier."

"I don't have money to pay for insurance. I can't even put a roof over my kid's head."

"I wish I could help but I can't let you stay at my house because I always rent it out while I'm gone over the holidays."

Char bit down on her lip, stared into space. Then she rose, and dreading to do so, she asked, "And if I can't?"

"Vicki's only seventeen, a minor; child welfare wants—"

"How soon?" Char wrung her hands, looked out the window.

"The surgeons have set her discharge for a week from today—Christmas Eve morning, sometime after lunch."

Christmas Eve: 8 a.m. 1980

Having sneaked into a hotel lobby bathroom, Char washed, tidied herself and then set out for the hospital. It was a cold snowy morning and the thin coat did little to keep her warm. She tugged it close to her to walk the five blocks to the hospital. Will they release my baby to me? My whole plan backfired. Not only do I own nothing now, but I can't even get my daughter back.

The shelters Char went to denied her access. "Worst time to try to get in is during the holidays, especially Christmas," one shelter manager told her.

At the hospital Vicki lay in bed crying. "Mommy!" she wailed. "The neurologist said I can't leave with you; he's going to call child welfare, and they'll split us up!"

"It's still early. I'll figure something out."

"Miracles don't just happen! I don't want to leave you!"

"It's Christmas. Miracles do happen." She wondered if she really believed that. She cleared her throat. "I'll be back."

* * *

At four o'clock Char gave up. The people she needed to see were off for the holidays and those who were in had shuffled her from office to office. In the end the answer was the same: "Your insurance will no longer cover your daughter's stay; sorry." Char felt failure the way she felt a kick to the head; couldn't provide her daughter with a home or even one measly Christmas gift. If she didn't return to Vicki's room, they'd have to keep her one more day since Child Welfare was closed; at least her daughter would then be fed and kept warm.

The cold smacked Char's face as she walked the streets, her eyes lowered, body stooped in defeat. Beaten, she climbed the snow-covered steps to a church; perhaps it would be open and she could hide inside awhile, thawing herself before she was discovered and made to leave. She tried the door. Locked. She turned to leave. But then, for no reason, she spun back around and tried the other door. It gusted open.

Char closed her eyes. The sweet smell of incense embraced her as she huddled in a front pew. She unflapped her coat in the warmth of the lighted candles. Head leaning against the pew's back, eyes closed, she felt peaceful for the first time in months. Her taut muscles loosened as she silently pleaded, "Please Lord, help me; make it right again. You taught me a good lesson but please don't take it out on Vicki. I've prayed my heart out to you and now I'm too weary to go on. I put it all into your hands. If I can't have her, give her a nice home with a loving family." She shut her eyes and soon she reached some plateau distant from her earthly plane, letting the silence and heat envelops her, the serenity soothes her.

Suddenly she shot straight up. She had to say good-bye to Vicki before they sent her somewhere! Had to tell her that no matter where she was, Mama loved her. Char scrambled down the snowy church steps, ran down the sidewalk, her breath coming out in popcorn puffs, the chill bringing tears to her eyes. Faster she raced down the street, slipping, falling, and struggling back up.

In the hospital, people stopped, looked at her. A guard pulled her aside in the corridor. "Something the matter, lady? The hospital don't allow no bums in no matter how cold it is."

Her lips quivered as he stared at her eyes, mouth. "I beg

you; I'll only be a minute. Please!" Her whisper sounded so frantic that he looked stunned when he let her go.

Huffing and puffing, she scurried up two flights of steps, her face shining red and wet from snow and perspiration. Her body heaved as she panted. Need to tell my little girl I love her, that no matter where she is, Mama will always love her.

Up another flight of stairs, down the hall, into Vicki's room where in one quick movement she scooped her child into her arms. "Oh, baby. I love you I love you."

"Please Mama don't let them take me away from you!"

Char nuzzled her face against Vicki's, their tears intermixing, "I'll always love you no matter where you are." The two remained holding each other, bawling.

"Charlotte? I've been looking for you. I think I found you a place," Lenore said, then turned towards Vicki, "And you, get dressed. Someone will be along."

Char and Vicki exchanged looks as Char followed Lenore, grumbling, "What's going on? I've got to get back to Vicki."

"Trust me, okay?" Lenore guided Char to the parking lot. "You need a good coat; what you're wearing is flimsy."

"I need a place to live, too."

Neither said anything in the car.

Twenty minutes later, Char protested, "You've brought me to my old neighborhood. I told you I can't get my apartment back."

"Another one has been made available."

"How?"

Lenore smiled. "The miracle of Christmas."

Char stared, her mouth open, as Lenore opened an apartment door. Inside stood a group.

Char went rigid when she saw all the faces; her eyes fell first on Carl.

"Hi, Mrs. Taylor," he said. "I couldn't get the limo back you gave me but I can do this for you." His arms swept in five rooms completely furnished with chairs, end tables, curtains, beds, appliances. "Merry Christmas."

Lenore handed Char an envelope. "Housekeeping collected it remembering how much you used to do for us when you worked there and then when you gave us all those bonuses.

We paid for six months rent too. There's a thousand dollars in this envelope to get you started. Oh, and you're hired back — that's the hospital's present to you, and since you donated so much to it, the brass said they'll cover the bills."

Char gasped, her knees trembled. Someone was leading her to a soft chair. She looked up. Robert stood over her. She tried smiling but her mouth twisted and her lower lip quivered.

He kneeled alongside her, softly saying, "I'm a gift from the young couple you gave your house to. I'll take care of Vicki while you're at work, make sure her therapy is done daily. And I'll cook, do laundry, whatever you want."

"But that's not your job," Char choked out.

"I know," he grinned. "That's my gift to you."

Char heaved, her chest filling with pressure; she kept swallowing but the wad only cramped more in her throat.

A woman approached her. "Do you remember me, Mrs. Taylor? I'm the state orphanage director. Our children wanted to thank you for your generous contribution." She signaled to a child who immediately came forward carrying a bushel packed with gaily wrapped presents. "Some gifts are hand-made," continued the director. "Others were purchased with the children's allowances or chore monies. I know a few of the gifts are gloves, scarves for you and your daughter." Smiling, she added, "God bless you."

The knot rubbed Char's larynx. Unable to say or do anything, she nodded and nodded, like a wind-up doll.

Another unfamiliar face came forward. He held a wide box covered with a large clean white towel, saying, "I'm head of the association for the homeless and because you gave so much to our shelters, the residents wanted to return your kindness." He pulled back the towel and placed the box in her lap.

Char's hands flew to her mouth, a squeal escaping. Inside the box lay dozens and dozens of cookies, cakes, fruits, rolls. She looked up at him, saw him motioning to another person who walked towards Char holding yet another box, this one filled with steaming casseroles, hams, vegetable dishes, and quiches. "Ohmy ohmy ohmy!" gasped Char, finding it hard to refrain from folding like an accordion and crying her heart out until it hurt so much, she couldn't ever again move. Instead, she watched as the two men headed for the kitchen where they opened the new refrigerator.

Silence fell over the room. The sound of "Joy to the World" could be heard coming from the apartment next door.

Char got to her feet, feeling her body tremble. Her voice wobbled out, "Thank you. Thank you." She saw her tears mirrored in their eyes. A few looked away, had grins on their faces.

Footsteps out in the hall. She looked in their direction.

Dr. MacGuire was helping Vicki into the room, guiding her to a corner to set the small artificial Christmas tree on the top of the television. Vicki looked at her mother. "I couldn't leave it, Ma. It needed a home, too."

Feeling ragged, Char choked up, pulled Vicki to her.

"Break it up," Mary teased. "I have something for you."

"More?" Char heard her voice sounding high and screechy. Please, God, let me have some control. And then she smiled at everyone, allowing her tears to flow unchecked.

Mary handed her a key. "This is for that car sitting out there. It's not new but it sure works well. It's been all checked out. There's a full tank, and the first year's insurance has been paid for. All the doctors and nurses chipped in. Merry Christmas." Mary winked.

Motion at the back entrance caught Char's attention. She spun around as the door opened.

A former neighbor stood outside, wind blowing his beard. His hands full, he held the door open with his foot while saying to Char and Vicki, "Merry Christmas, friends; welcome home. We haven't forgotten what you've done for us." He nodded to someone behind him and in single file they came. Twenty or so, men and women, boys and girls, carrying boxes of clothes and much needed items like silverware, pots and pans; others brought food. Each walked to the door, smiled, and then set their offerings inside the threshold. Then one by one, they walked away.

Char laughed and cried, dancing from one person to the next, embracing them, and thanking them. To Carl she said, "Always you were there for me," and pecked him on the cheek. She threw her arms around Robert. "Thank you so much for putting up with me." To Mary, she cried, "You're a wonderful doctor" and then she hugged her. She turned to embrace Lenore, but Lenore was already in her arms. "You deserve better than me," Char said; she blew her nose, looked around the room at her friends, studied each face, and thought, It is the miracle of Christmas.

Over the next hour the room emptied, leaving Char and Vicki alone. They walked over to the little Christmas tree, looked at its ornaments and glowing lights.

"This is the best Christmas I ever had." Char squeezed her daughter's hand.

This time Vicki returned the squeeze. "It's the richest."

Both laughed.

Char said, "You're my Christmas miracle, baby."

Vicki looked up at her mother. Softly she sang, "I wish you a merry Christmas."

Part Two:
Spring

> *The budding twigs spread out their fan; to catch the breezy air; and I must think, do all I can, that there was pleasure there.*
> *"Lines Written In Early Spring"*
> *— William Wordsworth*

ODE

Naked I live alone and there are no visitors to my place.

Before you label me as a recluse, try to understand the conditions under which I live:

This is a place much like a towering apartment complex, except here there are only two rooms. One is huge and all encompassing while the other is tiny and sheltered. I live in the sheltered compartment while my landlady lives in the other.

It was not my choice to live here but rather circumstances forced my presence. Because of this, I have opted for a month to month contract.

The roof of my building is about twenty-five years old and composite material with dark brown standing out as its main hue. It appears to be a strong cover but powerful blows may incur its destruction even if it does seem capable of weathering the rages of the elements. My landlady complains that occasionally a shingle or two is lost or discolored, causing her to run to the repairer as soon as this occurs, as she is fanatical about her structure's outside appearance.

The front of this structure sports two curved skylights that protrude over a small single dormer. Below the dormer is a wide, griddled bow window that opens or shuts out external light into my apartment. I've never been up to this area but I understand my landlady does much of her thinking here. She is a caring woman, a little young and naive, but attentive all the same. I am bothered by the way she hovers over me, as if to say that she doesn't trust my ability to take care of my apartment or myself.

The building's foundation is constituted of two medium sized footers with long flexible reinforcement rods running vertically into the region of the bottom, or what she calls "the basement." Directly above this basement area is my one-room efficiency, or what I intimately refer to as "My cell."

My apartment is such a tight fit that once I'm out of here, there is no way I could ever again get back in. You grow with this place and outgrow it. As my landlady reminds me all the time, "It's temporary, darling. Be cool. It's not forever." My chamber is ovoid with the rear of the apartment being slightly larger than its front and sides, and it's protected by sturdy but breakable walls. In its own way, it has individual artistic appeal with colorful networks of irreproducible mottled patterns.

It reminds me of red and blue spider webs pulsating with each capture made by the arachnid. The color is mediocre, but what bothers me more is the lack of space. I often wonder how more than one person can fit in here but I am told it has been done.

Since there really are no windows here I refuse to wear clothes. I receive no visitors and I have yet to meet face to face with my landlady. To get her attention I bang on the walls or kick around in my apartment. This unnerves her, but sometimes I think she likes it; I try not to damage anything because I have heard stories about poor, innocent tenants getting evicted without warrant.

I frequently sense some eavesdropping, as though eager ears were placed against my walls. When I suspect that someone is listening in, I am perfectly still. As soon as the ears pull away, I go back to banging on the walls. I can only imagine my landlady's frustration, but it sure passes time for me. I am in a holding pattern until I can get out of here, so I have to find ways to entertain myself. In this cell, opportunities are limited.

The interior of my dwelling is always damp—at least I can't complain about not having running water—and pitch black because she doesn't offer me lighting. There's no furnace in my apartment because she says I have to share her utilities. I don't mind the sharing but I hate her controlling when and where I get to use the lights and heat. Of course, I shouldn't complain—she pays the bills.

Because I am alone I pass my time sleeping, dancing...I don't bother anyone but rather just bide my time. Sometimes I just sit quietly, taking in my environment...waiting. When I'm quiet for long stretches of time, my landlady panics, thinking that I may have left or even died. Since she can't get into my apartment she really has no way of knowing. She should have a key, don't you think?

My landlady—sweet 'ol gal—can be a might bit reckless, drinking and smoking to excess sometimes. Lately, though, she's been heeding her diet, but I wish the walls were more impenetrable so that cigarette smoke wouldn't filter down into my place and smell up my room. I have never smoked and I don't think it's fair that she subjects me to such harmful elements. I guess I'm just not a 'good egg,' as some of you say. But the noise is worse! Unbearable. Loud music, traffic...and I can hear my lady argue with that chap she goes around with. I don't know him but I have a feeling that he thinks he is obligated to look out after her—and even me—because my landlady has me in her residence.

I have to be honest and tell you there have been times during my months here when my landlady has gone out of her way to make life comfortable for me. She is concerned about my welfare, doesn't really bug me—except to demand that I keep my place in good shape for future occupants—and does address me with endearing pet names. She has even gone out and bought me clothes and some neat items. Actually, she uses them as a bribe, telling me that if I leave this room, she'll give me all these wonderful things. Why would she want me out in the cold?

Rumor has it that when I leave here next month she plans on reducing the size of this apartment. I ask you, how much can a place shrink? The woman needs her head examined.

But I have a surprise for her!

I'm not staying until next month as she expects, instead I'm leaving this month, in the eighth month of my contract I wonder she she'll take that.

And when I slip out the basement door (maybe not slip but wrestle out) I'll open my blue eyes and face my lady for the first time. With a smile on my face and love in my heart, I'll tell her I love her the only way a newborn knows how. Thanks, Ma.

Sunset

Schuyler "Sky" Hall and her friend, Nina, crossed the wheat field, their high school less than 200 feet in sight. The pulsing red sun played hide-and-seek with cottony clouds as it gravitated towards the horizon.

The spring breeze lifted Sky's hair at her neck, signaling that winter was but a breath away when the fields would be filled with snow instead of corn and alfalfa. She hated the idea of crops, cattle, and silos. There were other things in life she wanted to do, to be. Throughout her school years, she worked hard at making As to get into Carnegie-Mellon University—top-rated for drama, among other majors.

She remembered how she jumped up and down, banged pots and pans together, squealing, when the letter came in announcing the scholarship. She had danced her mother around the country kitchen and hugged her father who said, "I don't know why you want to be an actress when we got a good farm."

She knew why; being an actress allowed her to be a thief one day, a college president the next; a spy another time, or a hobo after that. The scholarship not only meant she would receive the finest education, but that she would also get to leave Granite, Iowa, to live in a spirited metropolis where operas, ballets, and musicals played to packed houses; massive department stores towered over specialty delis; subways and trolleys shuttled urbanites up and down streets.

All those years of intensely studying served as her passport to an exciting future. The anemic life of the Midwest bored her, especially all those goody-goody two-shoes in small towns.

She and Nina continued walking across the field. Sky wondered what they would do with their time; just as important, she wondered what she'd do the rest of the summer until she got to leave the town and move on in the world.

"Gosh, no one's here," Nina said.

Sky turned to her as they reached the schoolyard. "It's evening. I don't know why we came. Nothing's going on. None of the team's out practicing."

Their shoes kicked up dust as they plodded across the meadow to the paved drive circling the newly built brick high school set in the middle of a table land.

Sky grinned as she realized this rural life would all be behind her and instead city neon lights would beckon to her and open up a whole new existence. She only wished Nina would go away, too.

"I think you oughta go to college too, Nina. I've told you that before." Sky reached down, grabbed a reed and stuck it between her teeth.

"You're the smart one, Sky; you're gonna be a star. I just wanna get married and have babies."

"You know, there are scholarships available if you don't have the money. That's how I'm going."

Nina shrugged.

Feeling uncomfortable in the silence, Sky shouted out, "Hey! Isn't that Donny Stanwick in his Chevy?" Sky cocked her head to look as Nina squinted to make out the driver. The car speed around the school a couple of times, as if doing laps at the Indy 500.

"Why's he going so fast?" Sky's eye widened.

She and Nina reached the school driveway. They stood waiting for the Chevrolet to come around again. "Look at him; he's like out of it," Sky chided.

Nina ventured, "Probably he's drunk or drugged. Let's head back."

"Wait and see what he's up to."

"Donny's bad news, Sky."

"Just when I get up for a good time, you put a damper on everything. So what if we spend ten minutes talking to Donny before heading back home. Maybe he'll even give us a quick spin."

She and Nina walked up to the driver's side of the car, and Donny rolled down the window. Right off, Sky noticed how red and watery his eyes looked.

"See," hissed Nina in a whisper. "He's high...as usual."

Sky waved her off with her hand, and got closer to the car to hear Downy slur, "Wanna ride?"

"Don't, Sky!"

"Do not get into the car with him,"

"Right," Donny laughed. "Don't get into the car; get on the hood."

"The hood?" Sky stared. Sitting there would be like the Queen waving from a carriage.

"Don't!" Nina grabbed Sky's arm.

"You're a spoilsport, Nin."

Donny laid on the horn. "I'm revved up here. You better hop on or I'll pull out."

Schuyler hunched her shoulders, turned to Nina. "Coming?"

"Schuyler, don't!"

But Schuyler had already vaulted onto the midnight blue hood and sat on the edge.

Nina called between cupped hands, "Hold on!" as the engine revved.

Schuyler lay prone and reached for the windshield wipers to brace herself. In that position, she could look into the glass and see Donny's face. His smirk contorted into a sinister frown. She grasped the wipers tighter. Maybe it's not too late to jump off.

Donny pulled out slowly—so leisurely that Sky raised her head to see if they were moving at all. The tarmac beneath passed by sluggishly. She moved her eyes from the pavement to the windshield; Donny waved.

She released her death grip on the wipers and sat up straight. If he was going to drive like an old lady, she'd at least sit and enjoy the sights. She swirled around on the waxed hood, and crossed her legs. With her hands at her lap, she sat like the First Lady. On her left were the recently installed tennis courts; a few more yards away was the track circle.

What's Nina worried about anyway? Donny's driving like a perfect gentleman—cautious almost to a fault. What kind of joy ride is this, anyway?

They passed the football field, muddy from a recent storm. Three-quarters of the way around the school, Sky spotted the faculty parking lot. She relished the cool wind blowing, her long tresses flying her face, and the large orange orb setting for the day. She would miss Iowa's glorious sunsets. God did something special with them.

But she wanted to make it big in acting, send her parents all kind of money, and buy them everything: New home, better car, a long cruise. She'd live in New York or Hollywood and fly them and her sister in for visits.

Minutes later, the Chevy neared its starting point, and Sky saw Nina standing where they had left her, her hand on her brow as if searching for them. Schuyler waved at her; then she turned and looked at Donny through the window.

A chill zapped down her spine.

His eyes glazed over, moisture swelled in its sockets. His mouth hung open in a twisted sneer.

Oh God! Hold on! She scrambled into the prone position to grab the wipers. Suddenly the car shot out like a ball out of cannon.

Donny held up both hands, releasing the steering wheel, to form the number eight, his grin drooling.

"Oh No! Eighty miles an hour!" She gripped the wipers harder and tighter.

The car shuddered underneath her as it surged from five mph to eighty. Her stomach somersaulted. She fumbled to grip the vent on the hood while squeezing her body against the car's metal.

She pitched forward, flying through the air, thudding hard against the concrete road. When she hit, it sounded as though her organs squashed the way a pumpkin splatters when thrown on the ground. Her body went numb.

For a second her eyes opened to see Nina running towards her, Donny at the wheel—laughing as he aimed the car at her; and that crimson sun lowering behind the skyline, giving way to darkness.

DOMINICA'S DAVIDO

Dominica Santiago saw her mother's unhappy face. In fact, everyone in her little town of Davido, Peru, on the East coast of South America, was sad. Her father, too, seemed sorrowful the other day when he came home from work and announced, "I've lost my job. They're closing the mines." Steadily, Davido was losing its people because of unemployment.

Dominica, with her brown skin, cropped black hair and short legs, watched her mother hang the clothes she had washed by hand, on the line stretched across the kitchen. In Davido, no one put anything outside they didn't want ruined by the guano from the seabirds in the area. And if the gulls weren't dropping their dung, then they were eating planted seeds. The birds were part—if not all—of Davido's problem.

"Mama," began Dominica, "I heard Daddy say that a big shot man wanted to buy our town. Wouldn't that be good? He would give everyone jobs, and people would come back here to live."

Dominica's mother shook her head, her mouth holding a clothes clip. "That man—Señor Malhombre—would own us then. We would have to work when he wanted us to, eat what he made available to us, act the way he wanted us to act. No one wants to be owned, Dommie. Poppa will just have to find a job elsewhere."

"You mean move...I'll miss everyone here, especially my friends," she wailed. "We're like a big family here in this village, Mama!"

Mrs. Santiago shrugged, said to her nine-year-old daughter,
"Pray; it works. But we'll have no other choice but to move if your poppa can't find another job here."

* * *

Dominica and her girlfriend, Carmen sat on the sand's edge, dangling their feet in the South Pacific's low tide. "My mama says Davido will become a ghost town." Carmen, with bronze-skinned framed by cascading dark hair, grew lanky for a child her age. "And it's such a pretty little village." Dominica looked behind her at sand layered and formed small dunes, and beyond that layered bright, lush green grass in between acres of white, nitrogenous fields. She looked back to the ocean. "I like the brownish sand set off by emerald green grass and white fields. I will miss it."

"When did you become so poetic?"

They giggled.

Dominica added, "I'll really miss not having a chance to ring the borough's bell. I always wanted to do that since it's never been rung in my life. I thought as long as I kept living here, there might come a day when I'll be able to strike it."

The village bell was a large gong hanging in an arched stone threshold near the town's church. It was rung by a resident only in times of emergency or urgency. There had never been a need to strike it in the last fifteen years, so Dommie had no idea what it sounded like. Everyone in town, though, knew she wanted to ring it because many times the villagers had caught her staring at it or stroking it.

"The bell, like the grass, has dung on it," said Carmen. "We can thank the birds for that. But my mama tells me there are places in this world where everything is brown and dry because there's no way to fertilize the lands because it costs too much. Yet here, we have hundreds of fields with bird droppings, making the land look like snow."

Dominica piped in. "Ha! We ought to fly our birds to dry towns. We can call them 'snow birds.'"

They chuckled, picturing their gulls and pigeons soaring to other places to do their business and then flying back.

Suddenly Dominica burst out: "I've got an idea!!"

"Like what?"

Holding up three fingers, Dommie ticked off: "My plan has three parts: First, we get containers, dirt, and seeds; secondly, we nurture, coax, and cultivate; and thirdly, we write, sell, and fill. Let's go!"

"What!" Carmen exclaimed, "Ooooh, I know what you're gonna do, Dommie. You're going to catch our seabirds, feed them seeds, and train them to make droppings in other towns that will pay us for their use," Carmen ran after Dommie.

"You'll see," Dominica hollered over the roar of waves, as she sprinted across the sand to home.

* * *

Over the next several days, Dominica and Carmen went from neighbor to neighbor, collecting old pans, crocks, urns and vases, pots, and various other containers. Then they went to the local mercantile.

"Mr. Pesado," Dominica began, watching him pull his inventory inside the store from a stand outside. "Will you seeds for my bag?" she turned to Carmen to hold up the empty plastic bag.

Mr. Pesado glanced at Dommie's dark hair, saw bows in her pigtails, and the jacks in her little hand. "What does it matter, Dominica; my store is failing anyway, and soon I'll have to close. Sure, take a bag of seeds. Take some corn, too, and flowers and herb seeds as well."

She thanked him, and loaded her wagon with as many bags of seeds as it would hold.

Then, they went from house to house gathering soil from neighbors' yards to fill the pots, vases, crocks and cans with the guana she and Carmen had collected from the ballpark, school yard, church sanctuary, and anywhere they could get samples.

While Carmen began losing interest in the project, Dominica only pushed harder. It took her nearly a week to do this, all the while battling the birds for the earth, and fighting the smell of their droppings.

She toted the dirt-filled containers into her father's old, weather-beaten, wooden shed behind the house. She set each up, and planted the seeds in them. Every day she went out and watered them, checking each for any sign of growth.

Then she started over, spending weeks visiting neighbors for containers, the fields for guano, Mr. Pesado for more seeds.

She had done this so many times that soon the entire town was talking about her project, and jokingly calling her "The Little Sprout."

Some nights Dominica was so exhausted that it was all Mrs. Santiago could do to get the child into a tub full of water and shove a washcloth into her hands. "You can't go through life smelling like bird dung. For sure you'll have no friends then," her mother would say.

"Carmen smells just like me... when she helps me."

"The two of you deserve each other." Mrs. Santiago would hand her daughter a bar of soap and a capful of shampoo.

Day after day, Dominica worked on her project, enduring the heat, the bending and lifting, and the town's teasing. "Well, how's our little sprout today?" Another would remark, "Aaaah look, she's growing!" Or she would hear, "Look at that child, playing in bird manure. What's the matter with good ol' mud pies?" And everyone would laugh. Dommie's cheeks would redden, her eyes water, and her chin would stick out, but still she wouldn't give up on her idea.

One day when Dominica was at the library researching areas around her region that were arid and crop less, she saw a tall, mustached man in an ivory suit with white shoes and white cane, enter the one-room building, and nearly fly around the stacks of books in his hurry to get in and get out. He snapped his fingers and a group of men appeared, looked around the library, took notes, discussed among themselves. Sitting there, reading a children's encyclopedia, she heard the man say, "The library, like the town, is not much. I'll offer even less for all of it." Then they, headed for the building that served as police station, city hall, and court house.

"I've got to get my project moving before papers are signed and this Señor Malhombre owns all of us," she thought.

* * *

"Wow!" Carmen whispered when she popped into the old shed where Dominica stood watering her greenery."They grew so fast!" Her eyes took in the tall tomato, corn, herbal, and flowering plants.

"My idea's working."

"Yes but it smells rotten in here."

"And so do I." Dominica giggled. Her eyes fell on Carmen's hand. "No mail?"

Carmen shook her head back and forth. "Don't give up, Dommie. We'll keep sending out letters."

"But I don't know how much longer I can afford postage or the film to take pictures of our plants to include them with the letters." Dominica plopped on the floor of the shed, her back against the splintered wall, pouting. "I used up all my savings and my weekly allowances just for this." She waved her arm at the plants.

That night, in the tub, she had decided to give up her project. "Just a kid's stupid plan," she told herself. "Whatever made me think I could make a difference, that I could help my family and my village?" She threw the washrag on the floor, her tears dropping in the tub of water.

At dinner, Mrs. Santiago said, "Eat, Dommie. You're losing weight."

"Eat good now, child," her father agreed, a grim look on his face. "I have no job yet, and today I heard that Señor Malhombre will be back in a few days to sign papers to buy our town."

Dominica stared at him.

"Besides," he added, "this project you've been working on seems to require much of your time and energy. You need food to sustain you."

Dommie shook her head. "I'm ready to give up, Papa."

"*Que lastima!* Give up?" His eyes got big. "We Santiagos never give up. Besides, child, you have the three elements it takes for success: Cleverness, determination, and the materials to pull off the job."

She studied her father. He, too, was meeting a challenge and doing his best to get through it. Just yesterday he had a job interview in Chincha Alta—a town near them—and though he too didn't want to move, she knew he would do whatever it took to take care of his family. He looked so worried that she wanted to reach out and make things better. "Maybe I will go back to my project just one more time before I give up," she looked at her parents, said, "I do have Papa's three elements."

100

She remembered other past struggles she had faced but pushed forward anyway. Besides, the worst that could happen would be that she would fail, which would be a situation no more dire than it was now. Yes! She would keep trying. She nodded to herself, now more determined than before.

For the next few days, Dominica went around the town and collected more containers, gathered mounds of dirt, bags of seed, and spent hour after hour planting those seeds into the guano-filled dirt. Then she watered and re-watered each vessel, and talked to each of the seeds, cooing at them, caressing them. At night, after her bath, she sat writing batches of letters to places where crops couldn't be grown. This, and licking stamps on envelopes, she did into the wee hours of the morning, falling asleep.

* * *

On Friday—the day Señor Malhombre had arrived in Davido and stood at city hall waiting to sign papers—Carmen had gone to the post office and asked for mail for Dominica. Through the streets, across meadows, past the shore, over the hills, she sprinted, screaming, "Dommie! Dommie! Dominica!" The townsfolk stopped what they were doing and watched Carmen dash at breakneck speed, waving her arm holding envelopes high above her head.

When she reached Dommie's shed, she flung open the door, and squealed, "We have tons of letters!"

The girls ripped into the mail, tearing open envelopes, watching checks flitter to the floor. "They're buying our soil, Carmen! They want lots of it! You did it!"

Dominica whooped so loudly that her parents charged out of their home and into the shed, seeing its floor lined with hundreds of checks.

"Oh Dommie! Papa and I love you so much! Gracias!

"Now, my child, run to the town center to ring that bell to call our friends together." Her father's fingers nuzzled each of her cheeks. Turning to his wife, he said, "Never have I seen so many checks!"

* * *

101

Dominica and Carmen scuttled to the town center, with Dommie's parents behind them. Pasted on Dommie's face was a smile as wide as an ocean as she and Carmen struggled to pull the rope connected to the clapper. So little, they needed help, and by this time word had reached the town, so men and women and the girls' friends crowded around and helped Dommie and Carmen pull the rope. Dommie jumped up and down, screaming with delight. Townspeople jabbered in excitement.

When everyone had paused in their excitement, her father explained his daughter's project and how hard she had worked, with Carmen assistance. Then he held up wads of checks, and everyone hooted and applauded, calling out, "Dommie, Dommie! Hooray! Ring the bell, Dominica! Again and again and again!"

With the crowd's help, Dommie scrambled up on the bell's top so she could be seen by everyone. "Do you know what this means?" she asked the people who had seen her brought into the world, who had watched her grow up, and had even helped raise her. "Our village—we—all of us—can go into the business of supplying guano as fertilizer to all these places and others."

"Yes! Of course!" called out the mayor who had left Señor Malhombre standing on the porch steps of City Hall the second he heard the gong sound in Davido's town center. "We could use our trucks and ships for transportation, and—"

"We can employ ourselves as shovelers, vendors, and caretakers of the lands," interrupted another villager.

"And we women can help advertise, write letters, take pictures—just like Dominica did," cried out a mother with a child playing at her ankles.

"We'll all have jobs and work together. Our town will survive on its own, run by all of us and not by one individual," shouted an elderly villager.

Everyone started to clap again, shout, and whistle. Some even cried with happiness while many ran into their small homes, only to come running back out with accordions, banjos, cymbals, and other instruments. Soon the town was filled with singing and dancing, cheers and tears.

Without realizing what was happening, Dominica was

picked up, set on someone's shoulders, and carried around the center by a herd of men as everyone sang, "For she's a jolly good fellow." She laughed and squealed with delight.

Quiet fell upon the joyful when Senor Malhombre made his way into the crowd and over to the mayor, gnawing on a cigar. Said the mayor, "I'm sorry, Señor, but the deal is off. No contract has been finalized. We don't want a dictator. We'll go down fighting in bird manure before we give up our freedom. Adios."

Grumbling, Señor Malhombre shook his cane at the mayor, and then left with his attendants.

As the night grew long, and the festivities raged on, the village's dirt-lined streets glowed with lit torches, where Davido residents—with women attired in their simple garb of peasant dresses and aprons, and men in overalls and sombreros—hugged one another, ate and drank, sang and danced. And in the distance, rang the periodic sound of a large gong resonating in the air at the whim of a little girl.

LOOK WHAT THEY'VE DONE

I'm a mother and I'm hurting inside. I had a son, but they killed him...mercilessly, violently.

A mother always worries about her children: if they'll fall and cut themselves, if they'll get lost, have friends, do well in their studies. But a mother doesn't think, or doesn't want to think, that someone will deliberately hurt her child. But they hurt my son; they murdered him.

I know my son was different but he was kind. Unlike the other fellows his age, he didn't care about having the latest in fashion, or the most impressive girl, or being popular with his peers. I'm not saying he was a perfect child. Heaven knows, he wasn't, but he was a loving son.

In my heart, I knew my son's differences would someday cause him harm, but when it came, it was ugly, painful, unbearable.

It happened awhile back when mankind wanted more but did less; when government was against the people, instead of for; and when society had no morals or mores. It was a time when I was very young, very quiet, and very pregnant—a young lady living in a Jewish neighborhood with strong beliefs and an identifiable culture.

I was engaged to a hard-working man who eagerly counted the minutes to our wedding—until he discovered I was pregnant and he was not the father of my child. His immediate reaction was to privately send me away; especially when the priests condemned me. But something overcame him and convinced him that it was all right to marry me and adopt my child. He became a good provider and a fine father to all of our kids.

My husband moved us around a few times to settle in a small town in the east, where the people were ordinary and industrious, much like me, but disillusioned about their lives and future. Our government was apathetic towards us—the middle class. It seemed it forgot that we farmers, businessmen, ranchers, fishermen, and merchants, were its backbone, yet it relied heavily on our products, wanting them at absurd prices. Those with more riches, the upper class, ridiculed our commonness; we became tired of it and fought back.

Soon everyone was involved in the rebellions: politicians, the religious, brothers and sisters, husbands and wives. Robbery, gambling, drunkenness, vandalism, sexual pervasion, prostitution became the norm. Looking back now, I realize it was a turning point in history.

I now understand that things were that way back then for setting the stage for my son who opposed the rich and the government, so much so that he carried on in streets about the injustice. I am proud that he stood-up for his beliefs, proud that he tried to make an impact on society, but how does a mother deal with such a blow? How do I forgive those who tortured and killed my son just because he was different, because he didn't agree with them? How do I forget my son's look before he yielded to death? I am asked if I have forgotten; I say 'no.' I am asked if I have forgiven; I say 'yes'—because it is how my son would have wanted it.

My son was a good boy, never ashamed to say he was Jewish, so our neighborhood thought of him as just another kid. He seldom had to be reprimanded for not studying or completing chores; even as a child he helped my husband, though, like any kid, he sometimes wondered off. He was the kind of son every mother wants—polite yet not timid, gentle but determined.

Because of his distaste of government, I never thought he would become a politician or even a tradesman-businessman, like my husband, but I did think he would become a dearly loved minister. Instead, he died.

To me, as he grew up, he became a handsome young man— a fine jaw sporting a thin beard and with his long hair. He was what people today call an 'activist,' a 'hippie.' It was his appearance that people resented first, his philosophy second. Intelligent and persuasive, he could gear his message to the cerebral as well as to the slow-minded. He truly believed that his purpose in life was to show man how to live peacefully and eliminate poverty, corruption, irreligious priests, and dishonest politicians. He wanted everyone to believe in his message, and to love one another no matter who they were or what they did. I guess he was an idealist.

Unfortunately, he did not have enough believers.

Spending time thinking about how he could be more effective, my son told my husband and me that he should become a rabbi, believing this was the way to make the world a better place and to bring peace to all. So he studied hard for the ministry.

When at last he felt competent enough to share our Jewish faith with others, he went out among the people and talked to them. He eschewed many of the traditions, refusing to wear clerical garments, ignoring many of the established customs and laws. For this he was cruelly criticized; yet, even as a liberal, there was no one who believed more in God's way than my son.

He was accused of persuading people to perform unorthodox rituals, of forming a cult initially of a handful who in turn recruited hundreds, encouraging people to disclaim the state as being greater than the church.

He was called a fanatic, an opportunist, but worse, he was called 'son of Satan.' People, resenting the fact that my son made a living by traveling and lecturing instead of working the soil or helping my husband; they accused him of getting rich off the gullible and frightening children with concocted stories about their future. The religious leaders, jealous of all the attention my son was receiving, and envious of the crowds he was attracting, publicly came out against him, scoffing at his demeanor, denouncing his beliefs, marking him with heresy.

"What kind of rabbi is he?" they would mumble in our Jewish community, huddled in corners in buildings and on streets, laughing among themselves.

On trumped-up charges arranged by his enemies, my son was tried for attempting to overthrow the government...a traitor. How I remember the day of his trial—the kangaroo court! When my son remained quiet and cooperative with all the judges' questions, the people demanded his execution. My son looked so alone standing there in front of the judge.

And so it was. The court bailiffs quickly removed him to prepare him for his execution on the charge of betraying our religion and our government. They called him a double-crosser, a disgrace as a minister and as a Messenger of God. The burden of the charges they placed against him made me weak and sick. I bawled day after day.

But my son never cried as he walked to his death; never turned on those who deceived him, who hated him, who sentenced him to die and called out for the death sentence.

With his sweet lips pressed tightly together and the sweat running down his face, he paused only once—to look at me, his love flowing into my heart. The look in his eyes made me wail, pull at my hair; the agony, the heaviness inside, crushed me, punched at my heart.

The blood splattered from his hands and skull.

Then he was up! His head hung low and his body went limp.

It seemed like an eternity before it was over as he whispered, "It is finished. Father, I commend my spirit into your hands."

'56

Here I sit, fortyish, on the edge of the bed, thinking back. The acne-faced fellow next to me reminds me of an event that sticks clean and sharp in my brain.

* * *

It happened mid-spring of my senior year in high school when my daily functions centered on Courtney Collins. She headlined dinner conversation that one night.

I began, "Excuse me." I didn't call him anything because I wasn't sure if it should have been `Harry' or `Dad 'or variations of those. I coughed a little like clearing phlegm from my throat.

"Yes, son?" Harry said.

I hated when he called me that.

"Can I borrow your '56?" I asked sourly.

He was big, from Macon. But soft-bodied with a round face. It had surprised me when my city-slickin' Yankee mom upped and married him, but there he sat, across from me at the dinner table.

He wasn't a bad guy, just not a great father—stepped into instant papa-hood when my dad died.

Harry was what I called a nerd. It came as no surprise he hadn't been married before or been around kids much. He was so god-awful twerpy. He wrote technical manuals for a living—got off on bizarre-sounding terminology and colorful computer-generated graphs. Harry and Mom had been married about eight months, yet they walked around like they'd been groping through cobwebs in a dark attic.

I had answered, "Friday's our senior prom and it took a lot to get Courtney Collins to go with me and I don't want to take her in Mom's beat-up jalopy."

He laughed a little and my lips went straight as a horizon. "My car? You've got to be kidding." He checked his tie—always wore a tie—for any signs of food spatters. I called his car the "BVM" for Blessed Virgin Mother because she had to be the best mother around. It was a wide sucker, white top, green bottom, with white vinyl seats, and tailfins that reminded me of sharks. Harry claimed it was a real antique. I claimed it had enough room for my first lay. Seventeen was too old to still have been a virgin. Maybe I was the nerd?

"So? You gonna give me your car or not?" I pressed Harry, knowing he tended to forget what was said seconds after you said it.

"No. You won't take care of it."

"I will! Look, if I promise to be extra careful, would you let me have it? Come on...man to man...."

He stared at me and I could tell I hit a soft spot. He had been trying to make "friends" since he first met me. But maybe he figured the BVM was too high a price to pay for my friendship. God, I would have given anything to get behind the wheel of that baby. Harry seldom drove it, saying cars like that were for parades and shows.

His mouth was stuffed full of meat as he looked from Mom to me, then said, "If this girl likes you for you, it won't matter to her what kind of car you drive."

His words, "matter to her," sounded like "Matta ta ha," in his country southern drawl. He added, "People should like each other for whom they are and not for what they have."

"Man," I whined. "You living in the dark ages or something?"

Mom cut me a dirty look.

I sighed for effect. She had wanted me and the Georgian dude to get on well, yet she had no idea how different we were. He was huge and manly, where I barely topped five-two and was skinnier that a sheet of paper. My face looked like a war zone with all the pimples and pus popping out, and my voice chirped high and feminine-like. Had I been chubby, I could have been Truman Capote's brother.

"Is it certain she's going out with you?" Instead of looking at me when Mom said that, she concentrated on her plate of beef.

I said, "Just because I don't get lots of dates doesn't mean I'm a liar."

Flustered, she attempted: "Oh, Alex, honey, I didn't mean it that way."

"You know," I began smartly, "you two don't understand anything today." I jumped up, left the kitchen, heard Harry yell, "Alex, come back here. Your mother and I have not ended this conversation."

It bugged the hell out of me when he acted so damn authoritative. I was halfway in the door's threshold when Mom called pleadingly, "Alex, come back here, please. You're going to put everyone in a bad mood."

Me?

"Come on now," Mom sang. "Harry's trying."

Harry's trying, the voice in my head mimicked her. "Shit!" I kicked my bedroom door and returned to the kitchen, flopped into the vinyl chair, crossed my arms at my chest, stared at the wall.

"Don't be so disrespectful." Harry pointed his fork at me. "Let's just see how much of a man you are. You can use my '56, but know that your maturity rests on this."

"My maturity?" I wasn't even sure what he meant.

"Show us how grown-up you are, how you can keep your word. Agreed?" He set his fork across his place.

I stared long at him, and then nodded.

"Say it out loud, Alex. 'I agree to act maturely when I get the car.' Go on, Alex. Say it. Give us your word."

"Oh cripes." I sank down in the chair.

"You want the car; give your word. I put a lot of integrity on someone's word." He jammed the fork into his salad.

I said it, word for word.

He chomped on a roll. "And you must do chores." He pointed at me for emphasis as if there were twenty other fellows in the room.

"Chores?" I'd have climbed the Empire State Building blindfolded. "Like what?"

Mom counted off on her fingers: "Take the garbage out, clean the garage, pick up in your room and the basem—"

Harry cut in: "Cut the grass, and wash and polish the '56 before and after you use it."

"That's slavery!" I yelled. Harry made a face like he was going to change his mind, so I quickly said, "Okay, okay," then muttered under my breath, "You're never gonna make a good father."

* * *

Well, Friday came. I hurt all over from doing all those chores, all the bending, pulling, lifting, and lugging and tugging. When Harry handed me the car keys, he spewed a litany of orders: "Don't speed don't show-off don't be a wise guy don't drink and drive don't spill anything on the seat covers don't dragr ace don't blast the radio. And don't screw in the car. Do put gas in the car do park far away from other cars so no one bangs into the doors do keep your eyes on the road and hands on the wheel, do not talk on your cell phone while driving and do have my car back home and in the garage by midnight."

The midnight thing threw me. "Things don't get going until one or so, then breakfast at dawn."

He stood firm. "Midnight's your curfew. If you want some extra time with Courtney, drive her here and your mom or I will take her home."

"But this is our prom."

He shrugged.

"How about if I bring your car back before midnight and then borrow Mom's Chevette?" My voice cracked just saying the word 'Chevette'—the basic, no-frills, middle-class clunker. Imagine me taking a girl out in that.

"Midnight, Alex. There's lots of crazies out—"

"And there's some in here."

"You know what I mean...all the foolishness that goes on around prom time."

"Like you would know!" I shook my head, stomped up to my room to shower and put my tux on.

A knock at my bedroom door. Mom peaked in. "Sweetie, you look so handsome in that tux."

"Why'd you marry such a dope, Ma?"

Injured, she said, "I happen to love him."

"How can you love someone eight years younger than you? Cripes, Ma, he's only thirty-two. He could be my older brother.

No wonder he's not a good father." My fingers fiddled with the bow tie.

"He's trying hard to be your friend."

I said nothing.

"He believes in you enough, Alex, to let you have his most treasured possession."

"You're supposed to be his most treasured possession." She shoved her hands on her hips, stood in the doorway, and said, "A lot you know about love."

I thought that was an odd comment. But then again, what *did* I know about love? Ha!

After Harry made me stand next to Mom so he could snap the camera, I got in the BVM. I had to give old Harry credit—he put lots of money into his baby. She purred so soothingly it could've put me right to sleep. In my hands, the steering wheel felt solid, yet obedient. Everything was perfect!

The back seat looked wide enough for me to work my way into Courtney's heart...and then into her crotch.

Initially, I wasn't sure I'd get the date because she was the hottest thing at school. In the gym locker room, I told my two pals, Bubba and Luke, that I would take the risk and ask her out.

Luke yelled to all the guys to circle around me. When their hot, sweaty bodies had crowded in, Luke said, "Let's bet on Alex's odds." He put up ten dollars and Bubba a ten, the highest both could count, then turned to me and teased, "If you screw her, we'll give the money to you," and then he and the guys plummeted into laughter.

"Maybe I just want to have fun with her and maybe I don't wanna screw her."

They howled so loudly that I thought the gym teacher was going to come out.

"Such a wauss."

"Nerd, geek, idiot. Ass." They were still laughing when they left.

How I got Courtney to go out with me was by telling a little white lie. You see, as the new girl in town, she didn't know I was a shy zit-faced virgin. So I figured she might accept a date from me strictly on the basis that I hadn't chased her like all the other guys.

Days after the locker room fiasco, about three weeks before the prom, I had been walking to the cafeteria when I spotted Courtney at a water fountain. I said, "I know you probably got a date, but I, uh, was wondering—"

"For the prom?" She stood staring at me, a cute smile on her face. "You're Alexander Wharton?"

I waited for her to throw up in my face. Instead, she kept staring, checking me out. "Like, my mom's famous, an actress, and she buys me lots of things: pool, quarter horses, cars, like the '56.... and she's really cool and hip."

She giggled and a flush rushed through me. I nervously glanced around the hall.

She said, "I'd love to go to the prom with you."

*I'd love to...*rang in my head a long time. Why did she agree to go with me, of all people, who's anemic-looking and clumsy. She probably hadn't gotten the scoop yet on who was popular and who wasn't.

I ran into Luke the night she accepted my invitation. "We already know, man," he said when I told him. I looked at him, wondering how he knew.

* * *

Weeks later, prom night arrived. I reached her house, and pulled the car into the wide circular driveway, saw her standing by the window, smiling across the huge fancy room at what must have been her parents taking pictures of her. I sucked in air. Jeez! She was she forever beautiful!

She hung onto my arm, glowing, as I guided her to the '56 and closed her door, then walked around to my side. Her dark hair was up on her head, making her dimples more noticeable. Slender but meaty, she reminded me of the kind of girl every mother wanted her son to marry.

"You look nice," she said.

My grin stayed stuck on my face. I felt so jittery I thought for sure I would pee all over the seat—like Mom's French poodle did.

We talked...about everything: graduation, college. I didn't want to go into the gym when we got to school. She'd say something, commenting or making an observation on life, and then she'd laugh at what she said. And I laughed with her.

I craved being with her, bathing in her warmth and charm, swimming in female scent, her melodious voice, the way she grinned, touched my hands. Was this what love was all about? I couldn't name any other time in my life when I'd been that content—not in a hurry for anything, just wanting the moment to go on and on.

"I guess we ought to go in, Alexander. Everyone's already in there. We've sat out here talking too long." She reached for the door handle, tossing her head to move a strand of hair from her eyes.

I leaned over and gently removed her fingers from the handle. "Let's...let's talk some more."

"Alex."

"Look," I began. "I...I have to be honest, tell you something." All I wanted was for us to have gone on forever sitting in the '56, with the car windows down, a breeze teasing our hair, and voices from inside the gym sailing out to us.

"Honest about what?" She glanced outside, then at me, and back outside again.

I looked out, too; saw nothing. "Why're you so skittish?"

"Oh, you mean being honest about the lies you told? I already know about that."

I wondered why she was going out with me when she knew all along I wasn't special.

* * *

Inside the gym with too many streamers and painted cardboards, everyone circled her, oooohed and aaaahed over her hairdo, gown, the way she smelled so wonderfully of a mixture of fresh air and Irish Spring soap. Guys kept trying to take her away from me. Luke and Bubba gravitated to her, mouthing words into her ear. Were they jealous of me being with her? To me, she seemed to be the only breathing soul in the entire damned palm-decorated gymnasium.

I walked her around the gym, showing her off like she was an Oscar, and told everyone, "She's my girl."

Luke smirked when I said that to him.

"You jealous, farthead?" I flipped him the bird. Courtney walked away from me.

Bubba got a silly grin on his mug when I met him at the punch table. He leaned forward and whispered, "The bet the guys ran in the locker room pooled a hundred big ones. It could be all yours, Alex."

I looked at him like he was slime while thinking a hundred greenbacks was nothing to pass off, either.

He added, "Luke and I put a bottle of Jack Daniels under the 56's driver's seat to give you courage."

"Shove it up your ass, Bubba. Courtney's a sweet girl."

He hooted, covered his mouth with his big hand.

"It's 11:30, Alexander," Courtney said softly, coming up behind Bubba and me.

Had to get the BVM home. Yet I didn't mind because it meant being alone again with Courtney. But $100 dollar bills danced in my head. So, what was wrong with screwing her? I didn't want to be a nerd forever, and it would stop the guys from harassing me. It had to be done eventually. So why not the '56? It would be ceremonial. Years from now I could tell my son about my first sexual experience in the BVM...why, his mind would be spellbound with admiration.

I got Courtney, said our goodbyes to our friends.

How scared I felt, walking her across the gym floor, out to my car. So much rested on my making love to her: Not only my first lay, and my son's heritage, but also the hundred smackarooes.

In the car I groped for the bottle underneath the seat and, sliding it out, I said, "Sip?"

"I don't drink." She gazed forward.

Just my rotten luck. I glanced at her. She looked sad. I must have really messed up her evening. "Look, I'll see if Mom or Harry will bring us back to the gym, okay?"

She just fluffed her long dark hair off her face.

I brushed my lips against hers.

She pulled back, stiffening.

What did I do wrong? I looked out at the gym's front doors, thinking that inside some of the guys were making better time than I was. But I wouldn't push her...I was too much in love with her to make it dirty...money or not.

Again I put my lips to hers, shut my eyes, let my tongue

probe her mouth while my hands moved up and down her gown. When I opened my eyes, I saw her staring wide-eyed at me.

She grabbed the Jack Daniels off the seat, threw her head back, and chug-a-lugged while making a face.

I took the bottle from her. "Hey! What're you trying to prove? You'll get sick."

"It'll numb me."

I put my arm around her shoulder. "Your first time, too, huh? I'm a little scared, myself."

She passed her hand across her mouth, as if wiping off a grin.

I trembled as I stuck my tongue inside her mouth and clumsily swished it around. I felt hot and moist in my pants— or had I spilled whiskey down them?

She squeezed her eyes closed and shoved her hand inside my tux pants.

Hurriedly I yanked down my zipper, pushed aside the cloth to my briefs, sweating at my neck, temples, between my legs. I could hear her pant, feel her smooth skin. I kissed her on her breast and Goosebumps crawled across my scalp.

"Oh oh oh quickquickquick!" I cried out. My pants and shorts came down, my wiener went up. It was unreal what my body went through—tightening, squeezing, my heart's beating like fast-moving hummingbird wings. It felt like my ticker would just stop and I would die...happily."

The faster she pumped, the faster my heart pounded. I slipped my hand under her gown, felt her legs, ran my fingers up the inside of her thighs...in her middle. She felt like velvet. Oh god, man! "Come on, baby! *Now!*" I groaned, writhed.

Suddenly, outside my car, dozens of heads popped up around us. Laughter everywhere. Bubba was stooped at the waist, laughing so hard he couldn't get his breath. Howling, Luke pointed at me, and all the guys and girls screamed uproariously.

Hurriedly I tried pulling my pants up. Next to me sat Courtney, her eyes filled with moisture.

Gingerly I touched my hand to her arm. "Don't cry."

When she turned to me I simultaneously saw the tears and heard her snickering. She covered her hands with her mouth, her muffled voice mocking, "Oh quick, quick, quick!" Her laugh came in snorts as she held her stomach; she almost fell out of the car.

I watched her step out, still snickering, and go stand between Luke and Bubba. Between titters, Luke managed: "Get your pants up, ol' man, before you try screwing the glove compartment."

My face burned hot. If I had had magical powers, I would have buried me and the '56, in a hole. I started the engine and peeled out of the parking lot.

How could she hurt me like that when I loved her so much? Like Mom had said, a lot I knew about love.

The wind spun through the '56's open windows, cooling my fiery cheeks. I went into my house, threw the car keys on the kitchen table and, without acknowledging Mom or Harry, I went up to my bedroom.

"Alex?" came his voice from my bedroom doorway. "Go away!" I buried my face in my pillow.

Harry's big slippered feet whisshed across the room to my bed. "What's wrong?"

No answer.

"You can tell me, Alex. Maybe I can help you."

"What do you know about helping me? You're not even a father. You've probably never even dated."

"There'll be other girls." He stuck his hands into the robe's pockets.

"They made a fool of me." I sat up on the bed. "I...I was...making love to her. Everyone, Bubba, Luke, others, had sneaked out of the gym, hid around the car...and just when I...she...." I stopped, wondering why I would share a story with him. Worse, I had just admitted I tried making love in his car.

"And they jumped up and surprised you, right?"

"I was never so embarrassed in my whole life." I shook my head. "And I was stupid enough to want to win the bet."

"God, I did that once, too...made a bet that I could screw some girl in the gym. Well, I did...with the usual groaning and panting. But I hadn't known that the guys opened the intercom. Picture the kids walking down the halls, in classrooms, falling over with laughter. Worse, picture the female principal and teachers."

I looked at him, broke into a grin.

"You liked her, huh?" He took his hands out of the robe pockets.

I shrugged my shoulders.

"Don't give up just because of one girl, who's not worthy of you anyway."

I ran my hand through my hair, trying to put things into perspective. "I'm sorry about the car. I know you said no screwing in it. I let you down. Guess I wasn't too mature."

He stood. Crossed his arms at his chest. "What happened doesn't exactly qualify as screwing." He placed his palm on my shoulder. "Look, Alex, I know how rotten you feel but what you have to do now is go back to that dance, laugh about it with them, pretend like it's no big deal, and show that Courtney how cool you are."

My mouth dropped open. "You've got to be kidding! Go back? See her? Them? Again? And Bubba and Luke?"

He nodded, tossed me the car keys.

"The '56!"

"A cool guy has to have a cool car." He turned and walked out of my bedroom, saying over his shoulder, "You have a good time now, you hear," his drawl coming to me like an old friend. "Take good care of our car."

Impulsively I shouted to him, "Thanks!" He was all right for a father. I guess he wasn't such a dope after all.

* * *

I turn to the pimply-faced kid sitting on the bed. "You see what I mean, Brian?"

He looks at me. "You mean you and Grandpa Harry have been humiliated before too?"

"When it comes to women, no man's immune."

He lifts his short body off the bed, grins at me, and says, "You aren't too bad, Dad, for a middle-aged father."

I guess I'm not such a nerd after all.

PEGGY

While my boyfriend Wuzzle—real name Walter—is outside the Ellen's house leaning over the engine of Mr. Ellen's car to fix it when he couldn't even identify one part of it. My friend Shelby, along with Mr. and Mrs. Ellen, look out the window with me (Mr. and Mrs. Ellen are an elderly black, cultured and educated senior couple—everything I am not. I've been living with them until dorm space frees up; I'm crazy about them, so I kind of don't want the college to find dorm space for me).

Mrs. Ellen mentioned that she wanted to buy a new car.

"What would you do with the car you have now?" I asked all too eagerly.

"Sell it, I suppose," she said.

I jumped right up. "I'll buy it!" Everyone turned and looked at me.

"Why, Peggy, you don't even drive," Missus Ellen said.

"I'll teach her," Shelby volunteered.

"Over my dead body," said Missus. "I'll teach her."

"No," Mr. Ellen interjected, "I'll teach her."

"Oh Martin." Missus started cleaning the sink after him. "You don't have enough patience to teach a bird to sing, let alone a teenager to drive."

"I know what I'm doing, Doris; I'll show you. Peggy, get behind the wheel."

Shelby groaned.

"What car? Yours is all apart. Wuzzle has the parts all over the ground out there." I was still staring out the window at all the blackened engine things lying on the grass.

Mr. Ellen looked stymied a minute.

"Just forget it, Martin." Missus was shaking the contents of a can of cleanser into the stainless steel double-sink. "Do it when you're calm, not angry with Walter...or me, for that matter."

"I'm always angry with you, Doris. If we wait that long, Peggy will be fifty before she learns how to drive." Mr. Ellen glanced out the window with me. Slowly our heads turned to look at each other, the idea coming to us at the same time. "Let's go," he said, but I was already on my way out the door.

"Where?" "How?" the Missus and Shelby said in unison.

"Walter's car," Mr. Ellen said over his shoulder.

I heard Shelby say "I've got to see this" as she came running out the door.

Wuzzle went down fighting and screaming, not wanting to give up his wheels. Mr. Ellen threatened to take the motor out of Wuz's car and drop it into the reservoir if he didn't give in like a man. Pouting, Wuzzle got into the back seat of his Bug with Shelby while Mr. Ellen climbed in the front. Fearing for her life, Missus stayed home. Maybe she was going to grab a bottle of wine just to prepare herself, even though she didn't drink.

Just as I started the motor and put the gear stick into reverse, Mr. Ellen screamed, "Don't floor it or you'll back into the Hildebrand's pool!"

At the same time, Mrs. Ellen leaned out the kitchen window, calling, "What about your Spanish, girls? I was going to teach you conjugation today."

* * *

I felt like I was undergoing a test to determine how sane I was because only crazies would let Mr. Ellen teach them to drive. He yelled the whole time: "Down is for the left signal, right is for up, I mean, up is for right...Watch out! Don't hit that crossing guard!" His foot slammed the floor on the passenger side more than mine on the brake. It wasn't like I was a complete idiot behind the wheel; my friends back home let me try out their wheels—some stick shifts, too—on rare occasions, and if anyone can drive the hills in Pittsburgh, they can drive anything anywhere.

"We should have gone on the back roads," Mr. Ellen was mumbling to himself, yet being answered by Wuzzle's endless moans and Shelby's repetitive, "Oh man, Peg's gonna hit the medial stri..."

"Now, Peg," Mr. Ellen said, his voice noticeably shaky, his hand trembling as he shoved his gray hair back from his face. "See that light in front of us? It's going to turn red and—"

"I can make the yellow."

"NO!" they all screamed at once.

"Come to a nice slow stop, Peg," Mr. Ellen said, his one hand holding on to the dash, his other gripping the handle above the door. "You do that by anticipating the light turning red, and pumping your brakes...now, Peg, pump. Pump, Peg! Pump! Hit the brakes!"

I slammed them. The bug screeched to a halt; tires squealed all the way to the light, smoke smoldering off them, billowing past the rear window.

"You almost put Mr. El through the windshield!" Shelby sounded breathless.

"Aw, man, like I shoulda never got into this car," Wuzzle was saying as Mr. Ellen tried ungluing his fingers stuck on the handle and dashboard.

Horns blared all around me.

"Go, Peggy. You can't sit at the light all day. It's green now." Mr. Ellen looked out his window and made a motion as though he were cutting his throat; the guy in the car next to us smiled and gave him a friendly wave.

"What'll I do?" I cried.

"What do you mean, *what'll you* do? Take your foot off the brake, shift gears, and step on the gas!"

The car behind us laid on his horn.

"Look!" he yelled. "You've got a line of irate drivers behind us. Hit the gas!"

"Oh no!" Shelby groaned and covered her eyes with her hands.

I did what he said—hit the gas pedal.

We shot out like a ball blown out of a cannon.

"Nooooo!" screamed Mr. Ellen.

I jumped the brakes. Everyone, including myself, pitched forward.

Horns screamed at us from everywhere.

"You just can't stop in the middle of the road like this; someone will cream us from behind!" Mr. Ellen screamed. I floored it. We zoomed forward, stopped dead, then lurched ahead, and stopped, repeating the process over and over again. "I'm getting sea-sick," Shelby said, as the car sped, stopped, sped, stopped.

"We're gonna die." Wuzzle cried into Shelby's shoulder.

"Stop it, you two!" Mr. Ellen looked at them and then realizing he had taken his eyes off the road, he jerked his head back towards me; I heard the pop in his neck. "Oh no oh no, I got a stiff neck, oh no...Look Out!"

The curb should have never been that close to the road.

With the big tires Wuzzle had on his Bug, the car climbed right up over the yellow curb, under a swing set, through a bush, and landed squat in the middle of a park fountain. Water spurted into the open windows. I looked over at Mister. His hair was soaked through, flat on his head, and water gushed up through his plaid shirt. Wuzzle had his mouth open like he was trying to drown himself as water shot upward, and Shelby kept saying, "My hair's gonna frizz."

People gathered around us. Laughing. Pointing.

Five guys easily picked up the Bug and set it on the road where traffic had stopped as rubberneckers watched. Mister and I checked out the fountain, which was still spewing water but now at the speed of an erupting volcano. Shelby and Wuzzle sat on a park bench where it looked like Shelby was shaking Wuzzle as if to bring him around or maybe she was just angry with his whining. I got behind the wheel again and the crowd began dispersing.

"I'll drive," said Mr. Ellen, pointing to himself while Shelby and Wuzzle climbed back in; actually, I saw Shelby push Wuzzle into the car.

"No, no. I started and I'll finish," I said.

We argued. But when Mr. Ellen saw that I was already in gear, he stopped debating with me and instead said, "Pull into the side road on the left."

I turned the wheel.

"Left!"

I turned it the other way.

His fingers went to his mouth where he gnawed on them. "Now watch the barricades up front," he said. "See, Peggy, two horses—"

"Horses! Where?" I forgot what I was doing and turned, looking for them.

"The barricades, Peggy! The barricades!"

I slammed on the brakes, missed the barricades but hit the hole they were blocking off.

"There goes the guts of my car." Wuzzle shook his head and, like a dog, splattered water on everyone.

"I told you to watch the horses!" Mister opened the door to check out the car.

I got out my side. "I didn't see any horses," I shouted back.

"Didn't see them! You dang near made them your hood ornaments." He pointed to the wooden barricades. "Those horses!"

"Oh."

He drove home.

NOTE: *This story is excerpted from the author's published novel,* 22 Friar Street.

IRRESPONSIBILITY

Why is it when we're younger we think we can break the rules, even when we know that death as a consequence always hangs in the air, hovering, ready to charge? Under-age drinking breaks the rules, for a teenager playing with alcohol is like a toddler hot-potatoing a live grenade. I know; I was one of those teens.

Whenever I'm asked if I'm handicapped, I lie and always say "no," simply because I want no one's pity, and no labels.

How I took all this ranks with getting a root canal; when I learned of my fate, I tuned everyone out.

I can't help but wonder if my temperament is the result of my head being smashed against an all steel dashboard when we hit and severed a telephone pole—or did it happen on the second impact when we broad-sided the school's brick wall, slamming me head-first through the windshield? I still hear the sound of glass shattering into thousands of tiny little puzzle-like pieces that went gracefully flying into the air, into my eyes.

Two, ten, a hundred times a month images of the accident will cut through my everyday thoughts, making me wonder if it is the cause of my loneliness. "No brain damage," all my doctors said; but what if the destruction is buried between the atoms that form the organic brain tissue and simply can't be seen? I try not to dwell on it. But remembering supposedly helps purge the soul, helps forget what you don't want to recall. In my case, forgetting is not likely to happen.

It's strange that I can't recall who I was pre-accident. I do know my writing was important back then but not as foremost as graduating and breaking loose into a world that was eagerly awaiting my emergence. Whenever I see any "Josephites" who taught me, they put reminders out: that never was I nun-material, that I had liked "boys" too much, had stuffed the covers and crawled out of the window one too many times, had caused Sister Borgia to break her leg in the last fire drill I faked. I want to prod their memories to learn if I was as dreamy in those days as I am today, but I don't, lest they say no.

The nuns didn't know about the impending party. A gang of us—all under-age—had collected money and rented some hall, maybe the K of C's or something, and our contributions paid for several kegs and some cheap quarts of Boone's Farm Apple Wine and Thunderbird—brands that have since been banned by the FDA.

It's odd that I can still recall what Dave looked like. Back then I thought he was a "looker"—big at 6'4", wide shoulders, thick legs, muscles that rippled when he reached, breathed. I liked most his pumpkin-orange hair and neat matching fluffy mustache. That he worked full time and could afford the luxuries most school girls panted for was a real plus; one of those gifts was an expensive blue metallic motorcycle helmet he bought me. I had asked him if we were buzzing over to the party on his bike.

He looked at it thoughtfully, then shrugged.

An intuition—something—told me not to get on that bike.

"No. Let's not."

"Well, I bought you an expensive helmet." He paused. "Okay. We'll take the Chevy.'"

When I look back on this chapter in my life, embarrassment consumes me. How could I have been so naive to give cause to the re-shaping of my face...of my life? Over sixteen reconstructive facial surgeries still have not perfected my face, not returned it to how God made it. I cannot offer excuses (that I was childish, thrilled, and filled with the freedom that comes when shedding adolescence and beginning adulthood), for I understood well the risks of irresponsible drinking. But I believed, like all foolish youth, that those things happen to others. I can also give some lie that might redeem both David and me, but I won't bother...the damage cannot be undone.

David and I had entered the hall and split, only to bump laughingly into one another now and then. My relationship with him swung on a manic-depressive basis, with the down periods being some of our better times. I liked that we never put pressure on each other; I was into my writing anyway while working to help pay tuition. That night at the party marked five months he and I had dated, five months after a two-year relationship with a Pika (Phi Kappa Alpha fraternity) who had "pinned" me, and five months during which Dave neglected to tell me he was married.

"Cripes, you're drunk," he had said near the end of the evening when I ran into him at the bar. I giggled and he slid another drink towards me. "It's a damn good thing I'm driving."

I hiccupped. "Ken'u d...dddr...ive?"

"Canoe dive?" He tossed his keys into the air and held out his hand to catch them. They landed in his glass, sloshing beer all over him; I remember laughing so hard that I wet my pants. I could hear him swearing as I dashed off to the ladies' room.

Once I start reliving this, I remember too many details because scenes have replayed tnemselves so many times in my head that I can almost see the colors, as though I'm standing in an art gallery studying a painting and the longer I stare, the more I find. I force myself to picture getting into his antique Chevy—pre-seat belts, pre shatterproof glass, pre-padded dash, pre-safety locks, and then—I force myself even more to recall—that as he had started the engine, one of the other girls from my dorm came running over asking for a ride for her and her date.

All this info has been gleaned from police reports, insurance forms, doctors' charts, and family members. What is in my mind—primitive in some form—is that I turned towards the girl and her date in the back seat. But how can I ever be sure what those little incidents were before the crash—incidents that forever changed my life?

This next part is blurry: how I started coming out of that layered drowse where time and space had no dimension, finding myself alone in the car. This I wished I could forget. The blackness I saw when I tried opening my eyes always stays with me; how pressure inside my skull built up so fast I thought I was having a stroke; sparks and flashes zipped through my

126

brain. I could hear voices crying, "Get out of the car!" Glass smashed near me and hands reached in and touched my shoulder, yanking it. Everything was blurry, like swimming under water so long that when you surface, figures blend into rainbow auras.

Nothing made sense: People screaming at me in the dense blackness, hands pulling, tugging; snatches of shouts and screams: "Get the jaws! Bust this door off its hinges!" It was only when the rescue squad had broken open the car door and tried pulling me out that I realized how trapped I was. The impact had jammed the engine up through the floorboards under my feet, and it sucked me in all the way to my thigh.

Someone said, "Oh God, what if we have to amputate!"

Once, I had gotten brave enough to ask a doctor, "How bad am I?"

He shrugged. "Lucky. Must have had God riding on your shoulder. You oughta be dead." He closed my chart with a snap and stuck it under his arm and went on his way.

I never cried that night in the car, even when they talked about cutting off my leg right there, in the darkness outside of me, in the darkness inside my head. But when my hand moved up to my face to push the hair out of my eyes, then came away wet and gooey, and yet the blood thin and runny, I knew what happened, and I made deep throaty sounds. With disbelief I demanded my fingers to run over my forehead, eyes, cheek, mouth, lips; touch my face, search for structures intact. No framework.

I sat perfectly still, both hands in my lap.

The bones in the right side of my face had been crushed. I must have given up right then and there, eyes unseeing, and willingly, I let the blackness slip over me, suffocating me again, hoping never to surface again. How does a disfigured female exist in a world of emphasized beauty? How does a blind writer write? Does this not seem ironical? A cruel joke of force that plays ad infinitum to remind me who's in control of my destiny? Or does it seem just plain old bad luck coupled with carelessness and stupidity?

I lay on an emergency room gurney with dozens of hands touching me and a myriad of voices going at once, none aware that I was in and out of my fog. "She wearing ID? Where's the kid who was driving? He know who she is?" Another voice: "BP's shocky." All of it ran together like a discordant combo. "ID says she's a contact wearer. She got 'em in?" How well I remember someone answering: "Her face is crushed; orbit's shot. She's gonna be blind anyway. I doubt if she'll make it before morning."

My date, David, ended up getting six stitches in his hand; he really never bothered with me again after that. The two students in the back seat were found in shock along the road.

Even now, all these years later, I press myself to learn how I feel about the man who carelessly undid what God gave me, who has never picked up the phone to ask if I've regained my complete eyesight or if any of the many surgeries have given me back the mischievous smile I once had or the opportunity to run and jump like I used to. Nor has he ever called to ask if I hate him.

I remember precisely the fast gurney ride from the emergency room to surgery, where the nuns, my mother and brother, and a priest, solemnly waited. I felt their wet kisses and hand-holding as I was whisked by them. As the anesthesia took hold, I fondled in my mind the words to the Last Rites Father had given me. I weaved in and out of consciousness.

I woke up to my mother's hysterical crying outside ICU, refusing to come back in to see me. A house-mother had gotten the nurses' permission to visit. "It's Mrs. Thompson" sang the old lady, only inches from me. "My God, it looks like your face went through a meat-grinder."

The first operation left me badly scarred, with bandages around my eyes. What sickened me most was how I depended on "see-ers" to guide me in a world where objects no longer had pictures. I toyed with changing careers—one that did not stipulate high cheek bones, a winning smile, or acute vision.

But it did not take a long time for me to decide that if I could not write, I could not go on, and I would simply end it quickly and painlessly. The thought preoccupied me all my time.

Weeks later, the nuns and my family returned to the hospital where they all sat biting their nails while a doctor cut bandages away from my eyes. It was so quiet I felt like I was at a funeral.

I heard the Sisters mumbling under their breaths—praying?— while my brother's inspirations got ragged and short; he had helped all he could as my father's proxy.

My mother, I thought, had stopped breathing altogether; the first layer of bandages fell off at the snip of the scissors. "Do you see any light?" asked the doctor.

I shook my head. Wet my lips.

Off came the next layer. "Do you see now?"

Again I said no.

The last tier of bandages dropped off; I heard my mother's voice snag deep within her.

"Keep your eyes closed," ordered the doctor. "When I count to three I want you to open them slowly. Wait a sec, and try to focus before saying anything. Okay?"

I was never so scared in my life. If I failed, who would feel the worst over my flunking—me or everyone in the room?

"One"

I wanted to upchuck on the spot, and the quivering in my fingers paid no heed to my ordering them to be still.

"Two."

I sucked in my breath and started talking to myself—no matter what happens, I remember thinking, I would not cry in front of this group who was there to root for me.

"And three. Open your eyes. Slowly."

They flew open.

"Easy now. Don't panic. Sometimes in trauma like this they take a long time to readjust...."

I understood he was rambling for my benefit.

"What do you see?" he asked over my mother's voice screeching, "Can you see! Can you see!"

A lighter blackness shone through but darkness all the same. It was so quiet in the room I could hear my heart beating.

"Sometimes," the doctor went on, his voice noticeably weaker, "these things take longer."

I heard my mother sniffle, pictured her putting tissue to her nose; I recognized my brother's shoes hitting the tile floor, the sound then getting farther away. By the nun's silence, I imagined them standing, hands folded under their long black dresses.

"Don't give up." I could hear the surgeon say as he clicked open my metal chart. "Writers can make a living with Braille...."

"Misty." My voice sounded as though I had just awakened.

"You see light?" He set the chart down on the bed.

"Just now. A sliver. But it's all misty." By the time my mother and the nuns moved, talked at the same time, the blur was almost gone, reminding me of how a window smears in the rain but goes sharp after the wipers run a little. "I can't see; my peripheral vision is—"

The room went silent again dead, cold silence.

* * *

The following twelve plastic surgeries rebuilt my eye socket, formed a cheekbone and forehead, but never gave me back the vision I lost. Wires instead of bone mold the right side of my face which in size and shape is slightly off from its once matching left side; nerves around my lips are permanently damaged giving limited mobility; scars from hundreds of stitches have faded, yet on close examination they are as visible as thumbprints on a photo; an artificial tear duct inserted years ago has never worked right. Blood clots still remain under my skin, and resulting dental problems plague me today.

Sometimes when the weather is damp and cold, I limp or my hand aches—the same hand that touched my face and found no form. And all over me are those tell-tales of a trauma that has taken hold and never fully let go, never fully given itself up, as though it must remind its owner of a debt that has never fully been paid.

After the accident my roommate visited me in the hospital, "Man, what a bummer—get your face messed up, miss graduation; shit, I would have given up long ago. Had you been in a newer car, you know, you would have never gotten hurt that bad."

"But I could have been on a motorcycle."

Constant reconstructive surgeries over years, from one hospital to the next, still have not given me back the face the Lord blessed me with. But now when I look in the mirror, there's a glimmer of hope.

Sometimes, though, I wish I could get a partial lobotomy and remove that one center in my brain where this memory kicks off at its own free will. But then I think that my remembering reminds all of us that with irresponsibility comes payment due.

Note: Since this account was written, I have had numerous facial reconstructive surgeries, and my face has improved, but as I age, I lose more bone mass in the traumatized facial areas.

WAITING

A sign over the door: ONCOLOGY DEPARTMENT. Fancy word for leukemia. I enter the sterile white room filled with plastic—plastic seats, plastic plants—and cross to the hospital window where outside cars and trucks putt-putt past. Life goes on routinely while I await the verdict. Will they tell me to begin slotting my time, like sorting mail into cubby holes? Twenty years ago and 400 miles away, I stood before a hospital window, waiting, too, but only then I wasn't the direct target.

* * *

It had been late May in Pittsburgh's Allegheny General and I sat on a green vinyl chair, eyes fixed on the floor. Opposite me sat my mother blowing her nose with a chalk-blue tissue. She mumbled, "Who would have ever thought..."

I stood, paced. My mind filtered background noises: a gurney's metal wheels squealing across cold tile floors, sirens in the distance, the PA system barking out doctors' names. A whiff of ether caught my attention and I stopped moving back and forth to stare out a rusted window. From that height I could see the wedge-shaped Golden Triangle, cranes erecting the U.S. Steel building, and Mt. Washington miles ahead. Below me, walkers looked miniature-sized and in rapid movement, and where the Monongahela meets the Allegheny to form the Ohio, boaters frolicked around the point. Why couldn't I have been playing too instead of waiting?

Behind me Mom said, "It's not good, I know it, and he's so young."

So young...and I had just turned seventeen. I remember standing there, looking out that window when my mind

132

recalled another birthday—my seventh: Daddy had come down with strep throat, and Mom constantly went in and out of the bedroom carrying hot chicken soup, blankets which she put on, took off. I grabbed her arm, asked, "Will Daddy be okay? He promised me a clown!" She shrugged. "Don't count on it. We may have to call your friends today and tell them the party's off."

I peeped through the crack of his bedroom door, heard every few seconds "oh shit" and "damnitdamnit

!" It was then I learned you could be sick and mad at the same time. As though analyzing a specimen under a microscope, I tried making out his form in the dim room. "Monica? Come here to Daddy," he called to me.

Sheepishly I opened the door, walked up to the bed and stood next to him. His eyes—normally the color of my mother's fake emerald ring—were red and watery—and his face was unshaven yet clean. He winced when he tried speaking. "Moni, you'll have your party."

I wanted to say to him "It's okay, I know you're sick and I understand" but my child's "me want" curse ruled and I did nothing more than nod. When I stood on my tip-toes and nuzzled his face, he managed a wink. I left knowing he meant what he said but yet believed somewhere deep inside my little kid's head that he would never be well again and I would turn eighty and still not have that party.

He had been the sweatiest and reddest-faced clown I had ever seen. Mom had later told me his fever was high when he put on the rented clown's suit.

* * *

Years ago, that was. Now I wait again, but this time for my verdict. ONCOLOGY: such a strange name for so dire a state. Where is my doctor? The waiting is the worst part because I have all this time to think. In my head I can see my doctor's grim Asian face, hear words that easily and naturally roll off her tongue that might change my life. I pace from the window to the doorway, hoping to catch her, and then pace again back to the window.

* * *

The waiting was no easier that day at the hospital with my mother sniffling into her blue tissue and I looking at nothing out the hospital window. Biting my nails, I asked, "How long has it been?" I turned from the window to look at her.
She rummaged through her purse and found her watch tucked deep inside. "Forty-five minutes. The doctor said about an hour. We should be hearing something anytime now."
And what is it we want to hear, I had wanted to ask her. That it was a heart attack modern medicine couldn't repair in an era when serious-faced Walter Cronkite told viewers that Martin Luther King had been killed.
I wanted to give Mom hope, but as a teen then, the most sophisticated technique I possessed was imagination. "When Daddy's out of the hospital, we can go on a vacation...to Disney or Europe."
She shot me a look.

* * *

ONCOLOGY...a Latin word, you think? Where the hell is my doctor? She told me to be here now. Why can't she plan better? She reminds me of my parents who seldom planned well, either, especially when it came time for summer vacations which never came off as scheduled. I've always intended to write a piece on "How I Lived through Another One of my Parents' Harebrain Vacations." The one we had taken when I was ten was worth an Oscar.

* * *

Mom had decided we'd go to Jersey to see old relatives. Directions were one of life's necessities she couldn't handle. Daddy said we'd go via the turnpike; my mother countered with, "No; I-79 North to Erie then across New York state, and over to 88." Even I in my limited map reading skills could see that the Pennsy Turnpike offered the better route. It amazed me my mother could be so authoritative about it when she didn't even drive.
Resigned,
Daddy went north with Mom reading the map, telling him where to turn, estimating according to her fingernail's length

how many miles we had to go. From where I sat in the back seat I heard her say, "I don't understand. There was a road here." When we neared the Peace Bridge, she said, "We're in Canada! They must have given us a bad map."

A masochist, Daddy, months later, allowed Mom another stab at navigating. En route to D.C., my mother traced a "blue line" on the map that she said had quit and hence there were no more highways. "Now how can that be, Anne, when our car is still going down this road that you tell me isn't here," argued my father. Shouting back while pointing at the map, Mom insisted, "No blue line, no road!"

"And the nation's capital just fell off the Earth?" He shook his head, and with one hand still on the wheel, his other reaching over towards Mom, he flipped the map and, *Voile!*, there was the "blue line." He sighed, "I don't know how you got this far in life! What would you do if something happened to me?"

* * *

...If something happened to me... The words ricochet around in my head as I wait in this hospital for my doctor. If I have leukemia, how will I deal with it? And how long will I be given to deal with it? I've heard months are all you get. For my dad, it was only a matter of months, too. I can still remember that warm May morning in the hospital with my mother, waiting then, too.

"I'm sorry for all the times I got mad at him," I mumbled to my mother who was pulling out another tissue. "To be honest, sometimes I wanted something to happen to him because he bullies me a lot, always tells me what to do, doesn't trust me, thinks I'm doing something wrong...."

"Don't talk like that; he's your father. It's his job to do that."

To my mom, everything was either black or white, though I know that sometimes even to her it seemed as if he was penalizing me over trivial things. He doled out punishment the way he dealt gin rummy.

I left my post at the window in Allegheny General and went and sat by my mother. "Ma, you remember when I was in second or third grade and I used the bricks on our house as a canvas?"

She nodded, sniffled louder, her eyes darting towards any sound made out in the hospital hallway.

I recalled how I had found a gallon of lemon yellow paint in the basement, and spending an hour working at getting the lid off, I climbed the cellar steps carrying the can with two hands, sloshing yellow over the risers, onto the slate foyer, and headed outside. With wide sweeps I outlined the round head of what was to be Jesus on the Cross, which I had just learned in religion class, then I centered a dot inside the circle—Jesus's nose. With my tongue sticking out the side of my mouth, I brought the wide brush straight down and then across to make the crucifix. I stood back, studied my work. Something was wrong. Jesus should have looked sad—not like he had just eaten a Klondike.

Out of nowhere, Mrs. Dina, in her old black dress and black babushka, a rosary hanging from her age-riddled fingers that twittered as though affected with St. Vitas dance, screamed at me, "Sacrilege!" Wagging a crooked finger at me, she added, "Badbadbad!"

My mother emerged from inside the house, no doubt hearing Mrs. Dina's hysteria. To this day I can picture how Mom threw her arms up in the air, smacked her forehead, saying, "Sonovabitch!" She shepherded me into the house by my collar, yelling, "Sacrilege! Sacrilege—she's right! That's what that is! Why, Lord, must I have a child who cuts out my heart and tromps on it! Wait 'til your father comes home!"

I kept hoping Daddy would like my drawing on his newly sandblasted bricks, but when he stepped into the house yelling "Who the hell did that to my house!" I knew I was in big trouble. Seconds later he stood leaning against my bedroom door, one hand rubbing his chin like he often did when he meant business. He said, "I see you've been painting again." He straightened, crossed his arms at his chest. "So maybe you'll be an artist when you grow up, but right now you'll be punished."

Spankings rated high in my father's repertoire of inhuman and prolonged suffering. "You have a choice. A good spanking or a twenty page written explanation for your behavior. And no printing, either. Only babies print. Every single word must be absolutely perfect, no spelling errors, and if just one letter isn't legible, you have to start over." Twenty pages would take weeks, a spanking only minutes. But Daddy had wicked hands. This had to be thought out.

"Well?" he asked.

"I'll do the twenty pages." I planned on writing big.

"And tomorrow you'll get a bucket and wash off that stick figure. If it doesn't come out and I have to call someone in to do it right, you'll not see your allowance until you're forty. Got it?" He turned to leave, paused, and then asked, "Why Jesus?"

"I couldn't draw Pontius Pirate."

"Pilate."

I caught the smile on his face when he left.

Later, when I became a young mother, all the doctors and experts and child books said not to damage your child's psyche. I don't think my father cared about my psyche; he only wanted me to grow up, become something, model good behavior, be productive and useful in society and to care for others. It was a tall order, as they say, but my dad never said the word 'can't' or 'failure.'

He believed that a swift kick in the bum or a slap across the bottom did wonders for one's 'psyche,' caught your attention and was then stored in your brain so as not to do it again. He was a logical, pragmatic man who left the daily dealing with the kids to my mother, and the disciplining to him.

* * *

Even as I sit here thinking about diagnoses and hospitals while staring at the "Oncology" sign bolted to the wall above the door, I remember how Daddy ended up at the hospital that day—a hospital where my mother and I sat and waited—like I'm doing now, without either of my parents at my side, without even wanting my husband here.

I need to face this alone at first. Just as I'm holding on to the hope that I won't have the Big-C, I held on to hope that day thirty years ago that my father hadn't had a heart attack.

Back then, my mother said between sniffles: "Can you believe it? A heart attack." She dabbed Kleenex at her eyes.

"The doctors said they're not sure; maybe it's just indigestion. Besides, if it is a heart attack, there are lots they can do to make him better." Tired of pacing the hospital halls, I had sunk into a chair watching her put make-up on her nose where it shined red. An act as simple as powdering her nose suddenly seemed out of place on this day when that bond holding our lives together dissolved molecule by molecule. And earlier had been normal, beginning with Mom waking and getting Daddy's coffee going, bacon sizzling in the frying pan. At my bedroom, she hit the ceiling light, and sing-sang, "Moni, get up." Kissing me, she said. "You look cute asleep." Another weekend had begun.

On Saturdays, Daddy cut the grass. In the early morning breeze he had gone out to mow our stamp-size Oakland lawn. I picked up a rake. Tipping the gas can's spout into the mower's tank, he yanked the starter cord a couple of times to fire it. I noticed him stopping often to run a red hanky across his face and inhale deeply, then he'd go on mowing.

Enrapt in the idea of going to Buhl Planetarium, I didn't investigate why he labored over such a mindless job that he had done dozens of times without even a grunt. I wanted him to hurry and finish so that we could get on with our plans. He and Mom were to drop my girlfriend and me off at Saks while they did some errands around town. I wanted to know how much longer he would be. Walking over to him, my recently polished white sneakers staining green from freshly mowed grass, I got close enough to motion to cut the engine—close enough to see dark shadows under his eyes, his lips a slight blue-grey color, his skin white as my tennis shoes, and sweat dribbling down his face.

Not more than minutes after he had wheeled the mower into the garage—his face drawn tight, lips still blue—he went into the house, the screen door slamming behind him, and climbed into the shower. The water ran maybe ten minutes, and then struggling out of the shower with a towel around him, he winced, "My heart my heart!"

The ambulance came, whisked him off to the hospital where emergency room personnel scurried about, stuck tubes into him, ran him through a boot camp of tests, and then wheeled him into the CCU.

Over the long hours, my mother and I walked the halls, switched seats in the waiting room, dozed off, mindlessly read magazines, and walked some more.

* * *

I take my eyes off the "Oncology" sign and instead pick up a magazine, reading the same words over and over, and none of them sticking in my brain. I hate waiting, and waiting in hospitals seems to be some kind of punishment God has designed to get my attention. I've skimmed over at least a half-dozen articles and paced this room countless times. I peek out the door; only a janitor mopping the floor is visible. Maybe my doctor has the results but is too busy having coffee at the nurses' station to walk out and tell me. Or maybe she's just trying to put off what has to be said. I remember with my father's doctor there was no preparation for what he told my mother and me.

* * *

That day, down the corridor of old Allegheny General, I saw green scrubs nearing the room where Mom and I agonizingly waited.

Head bowed, the surgeon said, "Let's sit." My big brother should have been there with us instead of in the Navy. I needed his strength.

I saw Mom's eyes grow big and doe-like with fear. My heart flip-flopped. I listened to the tone of his voice, studied his eyes, watched the muscles flex in his face when he addressed my mother: "You know when your husband was brought in and we ran the cardiogram and tested him, we told you that it might not be a heart attack?"

My hands balled into a fist.

"Well, it's not." The doctor paused, wet his lips. "More tests and his last set of X-rays show a mass in his chest that we thought was an infection, even TB." He ran his hand through his hair, the strings of his mask still tied around his neck. "Now we know it's a tumor. Must have been there weeks, months."

Mom squealed, "Take it out!"

The doctor shook his head. "It's pressing on his heart; it's what caused his pain." The doctor cleared his throat. "It's malignant...spreading."

139

My mother screamed, her eyes fluttered, and she went cotton white. I felt sweat spread across my forehead the way his tumor spread throughout his body; my hands shook, and in a wobbly voice I asked, "How long?"

The doctor stood, surveyed my mother who sat moaning, her head against the back of the seat. He looked at me, pronounced my father's sentence, "No more than eight months." Even at seventeen when time seems like forever, the doctor's words had an impact on me—eight months meant Daddy wouldn't be alive for Christmas.

"Eight months," I repeated to my mother as I drove home. She remained silent, not talking about my father's cancer, as if not saying it aloud wouldn't make it real. When I pulled into our driveway, I went straight to my bedroom and prayed hard for Daddy.

* * *

I'm praying the same way for myself now, in this waiting room of the ONCOLOGY DEPARTMENT—a word I've come to hate. I've been praying since I first suspected, then prayed even harder after the procedure was done, prayed more when the doctor's office phoned and said to go to the hospital to talk with her. Now I just want to know the results. The not knowing, the anticipation, the waiting, is hell. But then when I am told, maybe I'll feel as though I wished I had never known to begin with.

* * *

All those years ago when my dad was discharged from the hospital, we pretended happiness. When school was out for the summer, I drove him to his radiation trips to Allegheny General. He made an adventure out of our hour drive; sometimes he'd sidetrack us, like visiting different Nationality Rooms in the Cathedral of Learning; another time we toured Phipps; and we made a couple of tours to the Strip District.

The last time, we went to the Point where we sat and watched the boats on the three rivers. That day, sitting on the concrete bulkhead, he played a game: "Worth ten points...which river flows backwards?" I answered, "None. Just looks that way." "Good girl!" he said.

"My turn," I said; he nodded, listened closely. I posed, "How many bridges?" He snapped back, "Seven-hundred and twenty with all but two in disrepair." We laughed. I continued excitedly, "The color of the inclines?" He creased his forehead in thought as though this were a question worthy of an answer, and said, "Shit brown." He laughed louder, then stood and said, "C'mon, let's go see what how bad they'll burn me today" and off we went to the radiation department at Allegheny General. Over the many trips I drove him to and back to the hospital, the worst part was having to stop on the way home— after radiation and chemotherapy—so he could barf. Tears stung my eyes.

* * *

Will I be as accepting of my fate as my father was of his? The longer I wait, the surer I am that the news is bad. Will I turn into mush if my doctor says the ugly word? How will I tell my husband? How will I keep it secret from my kids? Maybe the explanation for the bruising is one I don't want to hear. I understand that leukemia had no radiation therapy, no cure.

* * *

This one time, when my father returned from his treatment, he showed me his chest with his skin seared, blistering and purplish-red in color from the radiation, but he didn't complain. On our way home, we stopped so he could upchuck. It wasn't until I pulled over near a park that he started feeling better; then, he made comments on how the Democrats had laid the country's foundation and how important the work ethic was. He talked a lot but he never talked about his dying. And today I am a Republican.

Days later, back at the hospital, we sat in West Park on a bench passing time until he was to have his treatment. I liked how the wind cut across our faces, tousling his once thick rich black hair that now, gray and thin, sported bald spots. Of all the fears I had about his cancer, his going bald was the greatest. I know for myself, I'm not above refusing treatment for that very reason. Isn't that stupid on my part?

In the park that autumn day with Daddy, something in the air made me feel alive, as though the death of the leaves on the

141

trees signified nothing to me. I turned to Daddy and said, "Isn't fall great?"

He gave me a look. "What, great? Fall means dying." He held my hand for the first time in years. "How come you're not like other kids, huh?"

To this day I don't know if he was praising me. We sat for a long time, laughing about the bums snoring on benches and how the pigeons kamikazied passersby's heads. Then, while walking the cement path with him, he bumped into some guy he had known before my time; he stopped, chatted, and turning to me, still holding my hand, he announced, "This is my little girl," and he pecked me on the forehead.

I blushed. Still his "little girl" at my age? Neither of us said anything for a long time; we kept on walking but I felt him glancing at me. Finally, I met his eyes. Shaking a finger, he said, "Don't you quit after. I believe in you. You keep at it, you hear?"

My windpipe knotted. I did not want to cry in front of him, this man who lived each second in unbearable agony.

Amid the sounds of cars whizzing by, trolleys clanging, street vendors barking, he stopped walking, stared at me, saying, "Promise me you won't quit." It was the last time he ever asked anything of me.

June fifth began as a bright sunny day. My father limped into the living room, his once muscular legs now struggling to carry the same weight it had done for decades—as high school quarterback, in WWII infantry as a Merrill's Marauder, at the steel mill, or when lifting his little girl. He sat down with me, watching the black and white picture, and then pointed to the figure on the screen.

He's going to make as good a president as his brother." I studied the fluffy-haired guy smiling a wide-toothed grin. My father and I heard the shots, saw Bobby Kennedy slump to the floor. When I looked over at Daddy, he blinked fast to hide moisture puddling in his eyes. It was the only time I've ever seen him teary....

Autumn went fast, Daddy's treatments stopped and he grew worse. Towards the end, he'd awake in the middle of the night and hobble into my bedroom, shake me saying, "The pain, my legs; I can't sleep. Please sit with me." And he and I would

pass hours away at the kitchen table with hot chocolate before us, talking, listening to birds chirping the arrival of dawn.
It was when my father began fading that my mother came down with the Hong Kong flu. All she kept saying was "Put me away somewhere so your father doesn't get sick!"

Christmas morning, in so much pain he slept his days away under sedation, his eyes opened to my watching him, studying his face, seeing lines where none used to be; I listened to his in-out rhythmic life sounds and tried absorbing a future without him. Seeing me staring, he said, "Help me to sit up." He patted his legs. "On my lap."

"I can't do that!"

"You no longer my baby?"

"I'm too heavy." The hurt in his eyes made me climb on the bed, position myself on his useless legs as lightly as possible. He never flinched.

He said, breathing hard, "You are never to forget that I've always loved you." He rested his face with its day-old growth against my smooth skin and sucked in air. It was then that I had heard the rales in his breath.

"I won't forget, Daddy; honest." I felt my own lungs squeezing; I looked up at the ceiling in hopes he wouldn't see my lips quiver. He groaned a little and I slid off his lap, asking, "Do you want something for pain?" I repositioned him. "Want some morphine?" I heard down the street the bells of St. Paul Cathedral announce Christ's birthday.

He said, "Give me enough to end it now." He was forty-eight.

* * *

Now, years later, here I wait in a hospital, reading over and over the word ONCOLOGY, as though the word will give meaning to all that has happened in my life. The death of my father is a pain that will never ease.

Pain—needle through my bone into my marrow, a gland sliced off. Ways to predict my lifespan. Throw the dice...fifty-fifty. Dealer takes all.

I see the dark hair of my *Philippina* doctor; sh e walks towards me with her head slightly bowed. Always her voice is soft, inside or outside, life or death. What will she tell me? I stand, chew on my thumbnail.

But I remember the promise I made to Daddy years ago— the last time he had asked anything of me. No matter what the verdict, I won't quit.

Part Three: Summer

WATERMAN

Dorian. It meant "the sea." He hated his name almost as much as he hated living here in this village surrounded by water. But that would soon change, for he was going away to college in a few weeks.

From downstairs his grandmother's voice rang out. "Out of bed and wash for breakfast. Your grandfather's waiting for you."

Sighing, he threw his leg over the side of the sagging mattress and headed for the bathroom.

As usual for early August, the bathroom was hot and smelly, like a dog had dropped a pile or two; and the flies were everywhere. Thank God soon he would be back in the city where he was born and raised—until last year. His parents had died then.

Dorian never did understand the details—both gunned down by hoodlums as they stood behind the counter working. He hadn't been at the store then but later he was told that his mom had been cleaning the glass counters and his dad had been at the cash register.

Like his parents, Dorian had been happy living in the city. He remembered those Christmases when his mother sang "Deck the Halls" while helping him trim the tree, and his dad sat square in his favorite chair with a spiked eggnog in one hand and tangled tree lights in the other. His father had always talked about how Boston "lent itself perfectly to the Christmas atmosphere" and then Dad would add, "Wish my parents would leave the village and come here for the holidays." Dad would chug-a-lug the spiked egg-nog, fiddle with the tree lights while commenting, "God, I'm glad I made the decision to move to the city to start my seafood business instead of staying on the shore." The shore, actually a peninsula, was a fisherman's haven, offering up crabs and oysters, and many villagers had made a fine living working its water. But Dorian's father hadn't had any desire to become a fisherman...or 'waterman,' as Gramps called it.

Once Dorian's dad explained the gap by muttering, "Your grandfather never understood that I needed to live a different life. I thought my owning a big business would make him happy but I don't think he ever forgave me for going away to college and never going back home."

Dorian had never known the difference between city life and water-life until his grandparents sent for him after the shooting. They settled his parents' estate, setting up a trust in Dorian's name, then had him packed and on the shore within a week. Dorian had never really stayed on the shore before, save for that yearly visit he made with his parents. Oh sure, Dad had periodically called his parents, mailed them presents, even sent money, but he just couldn't ever bring himself to go back to his native town, except for that one trip made every Easter out of respect for his parents' devout religious beliefs. For Dorian even all this visit was difficult, as there were no other relatives on either Mom or Dad's side. He had just his grandparents...and the water.

Dorian leaned over the old pedestal sink that was cracking at the sides, breaking loose at the base, and streaking orange inside the basin. He had once heard that fishermen made good money; he wondered why Gramps hadn't bought a fancy house like Dorian's parents had owned in Boston. Thinking about it for a second, he decided that Gramps had no appreciation for the "good things" in life. It didn't matter...soon he'd be leaving.

He stopped washing and looked into the small square mirror over the sink. Things were so different. Back in the city he would be with friends traveling to Patriot or Red Sox games on his fat allowance, or riding around in sports cars and in subways. But here there was only the water and Gramps's old boat. Gramps had said it was not so old...mostly a boat he used for pleasure fishing, not like the big one he owned before he retired. Retired?

Not his feisty grumpy Gramps! He'd never quit; he was going to live on forever, much to Dorian's dismay.

"Hurry up, boy." The voice had its ordinary gruffness.

"Coming, Gramps." He grabbed for the grease-stained towel. Another argument was likely, even though he'd given up arguing with his grandfather.

Entering the kitchen he kissed his grandmother. "Morn'n, Gramma." Then nodded to his grandfather: "Gramps." The beard, snow-tipped in places, was more scraggly than ever. And Gramps looked thinner. Much 'tireder' than usual.

"I told you, Dorian, I don't like that name. Down here, we call grandfathers 'Pop-pop, and grandmothers-"

"Hick sounding names." Dorian eyes dropped to the floor. "Sorry, Gramps...er...Grandfather."

"Maybe it don't bother your grandmother none that you talk that city language, call her 'Gramma' and me 'Gramps' but here—"

"Zeb!"

Dorian glanced at his grandmother; she was giving Gramps that look again. Gramps shut up.

Finishing grace, Dorian's grandfather stabbed a pile of hotcakes with his fork and slapped them down on his plate while remarking, "Outside's a might bit breezy now but nice day for the water."

"Water...always the water, thought Dorian.

"Lunch is packed, Zeb."

Dorian saw Gramps smile at Gramma while murmuring thanks; he was amazed at how his Gramma endured. What was even more amazing was that she had finally agreed to let him attend the University of Massachusetts, Dad's *alma mater*— money in escrow for a four-year education. His grandparents had fought him all the way on this 'college thing', as they referred to it, claiming they felt it safer if Dorian stayed with them. After all, Boston was a big strange city, where things happened that people like his grandparents had no idea humans could do.

But Dorian kept throwing his dad's will up to them, and in concession, Gramma reluctantly told Dorian, "Go, providing you come home every holiday and summer...and weekends and—"

"Gramma, I'll be home more than I'll be at college." He winked at her, and she melted.

Gramps was still holding out, grumbling, "Just like your father...gotta run off. You belong here, boy. The waters need fishin' and ain't nobody gonna do that but us watermen." Gramps must have thought all the males on the shore had to grow up to be watermen, like their fathers before them.

So with Gramma's approval Dorian was college-bound. He didn't want to hurt his grandfather, but knowing he had to be degreed to become a business lawyer, Dorian had made the decision to go against his stubborn, unloving gramps who would never forgive him...just like he never had forgiven Dad.

This morning, like all mornings, Dorian tried chatting with Gramps over the breakfast table. "Going shrimping today, Gramps?"

His grandfather said nothing.

Dorian asked again.

"We don't shrimp here. When you gonna learn? Had you cared two bits about being a waterman, you'd known better." Here his grandfather leaned forward over his plate of pancakes, his eyes level with Dorian's, and said, "If you took some interest in my livelihood like you want me to with yours, you'd know that!"

Dorian shook his head; this was the price he'd pay for wanting to leave.

His grandfather's voice softened. "Dorian, I do what my pa did and what his pa done before that. I'm darn proud of that. I ain't ashamed, like your pa was of me." Gramps looked away for a second; a frown formed on his creased face signaling his inadequate search for words. Then he turned back to Dorian. "I don't blame you none for not understanding the water yet, but there ain't no shame in what I do for a living."

Dorian bowed his head. After living in Boston for seventeen years, everything about this world seemed embarrassing. He understood how his dad must have felt.

"I made your lunch, too, Dorian."

He looked up when Gramma broke into his thoughts. "My lunch? For what?" Oh damn! No doubt the old man told Gramma to pack two lunches for an all-day fishing affair. Dorian was ashamed that he hated the water—hated it because it terrified him...the way guns terrified him, the way the idea of never leaving this shore terrified him. He didn't understand why God had cursed him with this fear of water when it was He who took his parents away and shoved him into a water-centered world with Gramps and Gramma.

"Stop your whining, boy." Rising, his grandfather pushed his plate away. "Get your boots. You still got them?"

Of course Dorian still had them. Gramps had bought them when Dorian first came here—high boots three times too big, but the boots were supposedly symbolic of the waterman's future, and heaven help Dorian had he tossed them into the trash. The last time he used them was ten, eleven months ago when Gramps convinced him to go out on the water; the boots were too big even then and they had vomit all over because Dorian couldn't control his queasy stomach. It was then that he swore he'd never go out on the boat again!

"Gramps, I was going to drive over to the mainland. The mall has some things that I need for school."

"You can't use the car today, Dorian. Besides, I done spent enough on you already."

"But I have the Trust-"

"You think I can't take care of you, boy? You save that money. What you need, Dorian is a haircut instead!"

"I wasn't asking you to buy me anything, Gramps; I know you take care of me, but I saved some money from cutting lawns and I planned to buy notebooks and stuff for college."

"You'd rather do that than spend the day with your grandfather?"

Dorian rose to meet Gramps's eyes. "We've been out on the water together once before. What's so important that I have to do it today?

His grandfather's normally rough tone deepened. "I know as sure as I stand here, the boy going to that city college ain't gonna ever come back again." Then Gramps said no more but turned and walked out the door.

Quickly Gramma called out, "Be careful, Zebulon. There's small-craft warnings out for later in the day. High winds..." Her voice trailed off.

* * *

Huddled at the bow wrapped in an old woolen blanket that smelled of rotted fish, Dorian shivered again, his teeth chattering every time the wind cut through him. Gramps had said little the whole time they had been out but Dorian could tell he had a lot on his mind. Damn, it was cold! "Gramps, it's freezing. When are we going in? It's getting rough out here."

"You sound like a sissy." Zeb walked aft.

Staggering towards his grandfather, his voice sounding thick: "Gramps, I'm sick to my stomach. And cold. The sun's gone behind the clouds and the temperature's dropped, and the wind's picked up. What if we get a Nor'easter?"

Zeb lurched forward, the white caps slamming against his boat. "Getting a li'l rough, I s'pose. Yep, storm's comin' from the Nor'eas'." Gramps was quiet, but Dorian could feel the old rheumy eyes absorbing him. Out of nowhere, Gramps said, "I guess you are learning something about the water." Then Gramps smiled.

Dorian beamed.

They stared, grinning at one another. Dorian heard the cry of the sea gulls, the hiss of the wind at his back, felt the water spray cold in his face, and smelled the atmosphere's ozone—dense like it always was before a storm. He looked out at the waves. How threatening they seemed, while inside the boat there was temporary safety...and Gramps was smiling.

"Gramps?" Dorian started. "Has it been a good year?"

Zeb shook his head. "Worse every year. The water's so polluted the crabs and oysters are hard to get; you can't make a livin' at it these days."

A long silence.

Dorian's gaze returned to the water; it was rougher now...much rougher, and the sky was blacker. Hadn't Gramps, a seasoned waterman, noticed? "Gramps, don't you think we oughta go in? It's pretty choppy out here."

For a space of seconds Gramps studied Dorian, then said, "All right, boy. Hit the winch and pull the anchor up."

Seconds later, more relaxed, Dorian watched his grandfather's deft hands move the wheel in sweeping notches to buffet the building waves licking at the boat.

At once fear drained him—fear of being sea-sick in front of

Gramps, fear of the waves' up-down movement tossing him overboard, fear of...drowning. Ever since he was almost sucked underwater by the rushing currents at Cape Cod that one windy Sunday afternoon many years ago, Dorian had feared the water. He remembered his dad running fast across the sand to reach down under the water, grab him, and yank him up into big arms. Dorian couldn't breathe and he panicked. In his dad's arms, between sobs, he spat awful-tasting salt water and sand. After that, Dorian had no desire to be near water.

And now his gramps expected him to become a fisherman.

Dorian turned back to Gramps who was saying abstractedly, "Nope, fishin' ain't like it used to be; can't make a good livelihood at it no more."

Zeb went about his business of collecting gear to call it a day. He seemed preoccupied. Suddenly he stopped as if in revelation and turned to Dorian, announcing matter-of-factly, "Maybe you do belong in college." He said no more.

Surprised grabbed Dorian and he remained mute.

Zeb grasped for the boat's side to steady himself as a wave washed over deck. "Gettin' rough right quick out here."

Then it sunk in! Dorian's eyes grew wide; he yelled, "You mean it, Gramps?"

"If you're gonna be a good lawyer, I mean it." He turned around, faced Dorian. "I don't want you to go, that's true. But now I see that you got to move on in life. I'm not sure there's much here to offer a city boy like yourself; I doubt if you'd ever be happy. I guess everyone's got to move on. Your pa saw that before I did." His shoulders lifted in a conciliatory manner.

The sea gulls called and swooped over the boat in their occasional dive for food. "Gramps?" Dorian's voice cracked when his grandfather looked over. Clearing his throat, Dorian said, "I'm not ashamed."

"Sure you are," Zeb's regard made Dorian wince. "But it's okay. It's okay. I understand now. You got to be happy doing what you want to do so when the Good Lord calls you, you'll go up with a smile."

"But I'm not ashamed of you...Pop-Pop. I want you to know that." His voice faded. Turning his back to Gramps, Dorian sat quietly, feeling green eyes search him.

The old man said "Dorian," and Dorian turned around to see Gramps cock his head and smile.

Dorian was pleased Gramps heard him say 'Pop-Pop.'

Then Gramps looked absently out at the water, as if seeing nothing but the images inside his head. Absorbed in his reverie, he mumbled, "Your grandmother's ailing, you know that."

Dorian nodded; Gramma had licked it for so long he momentarily forgot she was still sick.

"I'd be alone then. Could be soon."

The silence was thick, thick like the growing wall of water.

"I'd come back...for awhile...stay with you."

Above the roar of the wind, Zeb challenged, "And her? You'd come back for her? If something happened to me?"

For the first time in a while, Dorian laughed, his eyes twinkling. "Aw, Gramps. Nothing's gonna ever happen to you. You're too tough."

"You'd be all she had...until her time was up."

Dorian grabbed for the side of the boat, his stomach rolling. He struggled to speak. "I'd come back, get a job, keep her, just like you'd want."

Zebulon said nothing for a long second, then nodded. "Then, boy, you go to that Boston school with my blessin's. I'm letting go of you."

If his intestines weren't in his mouth, Dorian would have screamed with joy. Everything was going to be fine. Life went on and he was Boston bound!

"I'll make you proud, Gramps."

Zeb was silent, staring.

Dorian watched the old man cast a glance out at the swollen waves, the water splashing the silver-tinged beard; almost in slow-motion, Gramps turned back to look at Dorian. And he winked at him.

Dorian broke into a wide grin, goose bumps flushing him. Swallowing hard, he rasped, "You're okay, Pop-Pop. I was wrong...about you." He went silent lest tears give him away.

"Be happy, boy," Gramps's voice cooed softly.

"You're happy, aren't you? Working the water. Even in weather like this?"

"Even in weather like this," The old man grew quiet again. When he spoke, it was in uncharacteristic weak tones: "I wanted your pa to be happy doing this, too..." here, Gramps's voice got shaky. "When I knew you were coming to live with us, I thought the Good Lord gave me a second chance at raising a son."

Dorian's throat tightened. "You're doing okay at it."

"Nope. I don't change none."

"But you're happy, Gramps. Aren't you? You said so."

"That I am. Happy, with my life, with my boat, with your grandmother." Zeb stroked his beard, and stared at Dorian. "And happy with you, Son."

Dorian's grin radiated the dark sky. At that minute he felt like running across the deck to hug the old man; instead, he grabbed his heaving stomach. *Please, God, not now. Don't let me be sea-sick now.*

"You're lookin' green at the gills, boy. You get puke on them boots again and we're gonna drop them down to the fish."

Dorian attempted a chuckle.

Seemingly pleased with making Dorian feel better, Gramps added, "Or we could go grab some crabs from the bushel baskets and stuff them in your boots and give them to your grandmother as a present." His head was tilted toward the pots in the back. "You wanne dump that last pot into the basket?"

Dorian's head turned toward the direction of the crab pots stacked at the stern, opposite Gramps's makeshift chrome chair with the uncomfortable plastic seat. 'Pots,' thought Dorian, returning to his survey of the water from his position in the bow while holding the blanket near his mouth. 'Pots' to Dorian looked like metal rat cages. Gramps had immediately trained him not to say 'cages.' Dorian was thinking about how many pots Gramps said he used to have on his workboat years ago when he fished full time—a big boat, Gramps had said, with hydraulic machinery and what not. What'd Gramps call it? A trawler? Now he had a smaller boat to go fishing for his enjoyment, and hopefully snag some crabs for Gramma and the neighbors, and even few more to sell. But what he did now that he was older was less than half what he had done a decade or so ago.

Dorian spun around to ask Gramps bout the pots when suddenly his stomach contents gushed upward, filling his mouth cavity to flood the blanket and overflow onto the boat's deck. "Jeesh!" His grandfather's tone would have sounded uglier had the wind not robbed it of its smack. The gusts whipped in, twirling the boat, ramming it against the waves. Lightning cracked, zig-zagging through the ink-colored sky with swollen grayish black clouds above the roaring, spitting swells. Thunder crashed like huge mortars exploding.

The boat rocked and swung. Dorian slumped to the deck. Lying flat on the floor, he could feel the water rumble underneath him; then he heard the crab pots farther astern crashing to the deck or flying overboard, splashing into the bubbling angry water. He tried to stand.

"Hold on, Dorian! Get low or the waves'll toss you out."

Dorian's head pounded up and down against the deck with the thrust of each wave. His stomach squeezed and grinded. He tried to pull himself up but the water's thrashing and the boat's spinning pulled him downward. His dizziness worsened as the boat twirled frenziedly, swashing into tidal-like waves.

At last he made it to his knees and then he raised his legs so that he could cross over to the old man to feel safe.

Out of the corner of his eye he saw Gramps's high boots step gingerly towards him—one foot, then the other, testing its way while looking back at the bow.

"Dorian! Lay down! CRAWL, damnit! I can't let go of the wheel! Dorian! Get in the hatch or you'll be thrown out!"

The boat yawed and pitched with each gush of white foamy suds, throwing Gramps off balance and hurtling him against the boat's sides.

Through half-mast eyes, Dorian took in his grandfather shaking his head as if to clear it, then pushing his bulk forward into the wind to charge bull-like. "Gramps...you okay?" It sounded muffled and retched.

"Please, son. Go down! For god's sake!" Gramps's voice was sucked up by the crash of the water. Fishing rods snapped and whipped in the surge.

If Dorian stood upright, he could be thrown over; but what about Gramps? He was standing, trying to control the boat...for both of them.

Dorian pulled himself up, only to fold at the waist, his control entirely gone.

Zeb went for Dorian."Boy, keep that life jacket on and get down into the hatch!"

Dorian hit the deck again, gulping water that slammed onto the wood. His knees bent to crawl but he couldn't even see the hatch's opening.

Captainless, the boat slashed amuck in the torrents.

From water-filled eyes, Dorian glimpsed his grandfather grip the boat's gunwale for support as he fought his way over to secure Dorian.

Again Gramps yelled, "Go down, Dorian. Now!"

Dorian heard his grandfather huffing and puffing. The wind and water thinned Gramp's labored breaths as he neared the stern and reached towards Dorian. With one swift movement and a long strong arm, he grabbed Dorian, pulled him up to his shins but the next tsunami-like crash made Dorian fall limp, collapsing into rushing furious waters swallowing the deck.

Breathing harder, Gramps dragged, tugged on and lugged Dorian with one hand, while holding on to the gunwale with his other, to inch the boy across the sopping deck toward the hatch.

But the crushing whitecaps clobbered the boat's side, forcing Gramps to let go of Dorian who was crawling to the hatch on his stomach on the flooded wood.

Dorian glimpsed Gramps working his way toward to the wheel, knowing if he didn't do something, he and Gramps would go down.

"Dorian, get into the hatch! Damnit!"

Pain zinged Dorian and sapped of strength. He did nothing but fall forward in a heap at the hatch.

"Dorian!" His grandfather grabbed the wheel again while eyeing the teen. "Get into the hatch!" He screamed it so loud that Dorian heard it sharply in spite of the booming thunder, moaning high winds and roaring gush.

The boy peeped at his sopping wet grandfather who turned from the wheel, skid toward Dorian's weak form, and pushed him half-way into the hatch as the rest of the stacked crab pots flew into the violent surf.

"Dorian. I gotta get to the wheel! Pull yourself all the way into the hatch!" Gramps spun back around and forcefully closed his hands around the wet sturdy chrome braces of the makeshift chair. "Get below, and don't you come out for no reason. You hear!"

Dorian hung on; he felt his grandfather eye him to make sure his hands still clenching the hatch's framework.

"Boy, you pull yourself in that hatch right now!"

Torrents and surges drenched both of them, pounding their bodies; lightning and thunder cracked all around them.

Gramps nodded to the water, grinned, and again wrestled with the wheel.

Riding the bronco waves, a crab pot tumbled down on Dorian and grazed Dorian's cheek, breaking skin; blood trickled into a widening pool. He flinched and squeezed his hands tighter heave around the jamb while straining to look sideways: Gramps had not yet made it the few steps remaining to the wheel. *Come on, Gramps!*

The wind howled and the rain rushed out of the sky. Waves stampeded the still unmanned boat like a cyclone attacking a doll house.

Then it happened.

One powerful burst of a brutal swell, a vortex-like twister, slammed the matchstick boat, heaving it up in the air.

* * *

Their talking, even solemn and low-pitched, made him uncomfortable. He hated viewings. And he hated the after-funeral even worse because people came calling with foods and drinks, saying over and over again how sorry they were. He wondered why they had to apologize.

Across from him sat spinster Meg Berkshire—nosey and usually loud, save for today when she was as solemn as the minister had been standing over the grave. She gave him one of those droopy sad expressions while mouthing something like, "Wanna talk about it? Make you feel better inside."

No, he didn't want to talk about it; he was to live it...the rest of his life. He rose, throwing her a look, then glanced around the dim room with its other somber visitors. He shook his head and went quietly out the screen door to stand on the small square porch.

Outside, on the stoop he touched his hand to his cheek. The bandage was gone; the wound had dried and scabbed but the hurt was raw and throbbing. He looked up at the sun. It was warm, calm, bright--so unlike a few days ago when the wind howled and beat his body as the sky blackened, and the cold froze his blood.

Or was it fear that froze him? They wrote "death due to drowning" on the death certificate. He thought it was more like "death due to fear." His fear...not Gramps's.

Dorian sat down on the cracked cement step, half listening to the sober tones inside the house, half-listening to the cries inside his head...his grandfather's cries that brought it all back too vividly.

When the giant wave battered the boat, Dorian, already prone on the deck with his hands tightly clutching the braces, watched through water-blurred eyes his grandfather fall hard against the wheel, then slide, slide into the rabid brew—a brew that ate him. With the next huge wave, the boat's bottom smacked the water, landing it upright. Up and down the boat went. Dorian's eyes had remained closed and his hand still grasped the brace as he screamed, "Gramps. Pop-Pop!"

He remembered he was so frightened he hadn't bothered to release his lifesaving grip to work his way around to the side of the boat to look over for his grandfather, and he most certainly hadn't plunged into the ebony wet abyss in search of his father's father.

What he had done was wet his pants; peed out of sheer fear. And then he cried. He wailed hauntingly right into the late dark afternoon as the squalls blew over and the water calmed. He hung on until the Coast Guard brought him in.

Now, days later, sitting on the steps, he could replay the scene over and over in his head, second-guessing his actions, asking himself 'what if?'; What if he and Gramps had held on together—would they have made it in the end? What if Gramps had decided to let go so he wouldn't pull Dorian down with him? Inhaling a jagged breath, Dorian ran his hands through his hair, his vision turning misty.

The shrill sound of the phone's ringing inside the hallway brought him back. He heard his grandmother speak softly into the phone. He wondered about her future. Mostly he wondered about his. He turned when he heard the screen door creak open. She looked so small standing there, her eyes puffy and red.

"You coming in, Dorian?" Her voice sounded weak and weary.

He shook his head. He could feel her moving towards him, and in the next instant she was sitting at his side, on the stoop. "Dorian, look at me."

He did so. Her rough calloused hands cupped his face. A long bony finger touched his swollen eyes. He blubbered, "Gramma, I'm so so sorry. I'll stay with you. I'll take Gramps's place and I'll never leave you-"

"Shhh," she soothed; he felt her hand stroke the nape of his neck, pat down his hair. "T'weren't your fault. Meant to be. Just as it's meant to be for you to go to that college; it's time for you to move on, like it was time for your grandfather to move on."

He buried his head in his hands and whimpered. "I can't leave you; I promised."

"You got your whole life ahead of you; you got to do what makes you happy, Dorian."

"Gramps said that too."

"I know. I learned it from him." She tried for a smile but instead, she suddenly in one quick movement turned fully to Dorian, grabbed him by his shoulders, and wept into his chest.

Dorian's voice trembled. "Gramps was happy, Gram. He told me so...on the boat. He was happy." He pulled back to look at her. He saw for the first time the once dancing mouth now lined with age, the eyes of wisdom now hazed with sadness, and he wanted to make everything all right for her.

Dorian choke, "I never understood it before, Gramma, that Gramps loved the water and wanted everyone to love it with him, and that he was rich in his own way and wanted others to share in his riches. And he loved...loved so much he gave up his own life."

She nodded. "That's all he ever wanted, was for you to understand."

"He gave up his life for me. He loved me." Dorian blinked. "Me," he repeated, his hand against his chest. A tear rolled down his cheek. "He loved *me*. I wasn't ashamed, Gramma...not of him." He closed his eyes, hoping that would stop the squeezing in his throat. Opening his heavy lids, tears streamed wildly, streaking his face. Dorian choked, "He tried hard to hold onto me...and then he let me go."

"I know." Her voice cracked. "At last he let go of you."

"He was happy, Grandmother. He went up with a smile on his face." His sobs went unchecked.

They held each other for a long time.

R & R

Like air blasted in. Pressurized vacuum. Squeezing.
That's what it feels like inside my brain.

I've had a headache all day. Maybe it's because I can't wait
to leave this ant colony and get to the beach to relax. I'm on 50
approaching Cambridge; at least an hour to Ocean City,
Maryland.

Earlier this morning, sitting at the wheel of my car, I read
the newspaper from front to back while traffic inched along
like a footless centipede wriggling behind a snail. In town,
people lined up at street corners waiting for the light to change,
crossing like a herd of elephants, faces set tight. Determined.
They rushed. Pushed. Ambled in the crosswalk even when I
had the light, then banged on my car's hood, screaming,
"Pedestrians have the right of way!"

Drivers were no better; they aimed their cars. I saw a man in
a three piece suit close his eyes, ram his foot to the gas pedal,
and pull out in front of me.

Did you ever hear the bells on the ice cream man's truck?
Their incessant ring tells neighborhood children there's
Klondikes and ice cream sandwiches. That's what my office
phone sounds like. One call after another. I'm an insurance
agent. A client called to ask if he could insure his balls. I almost
fell off my chair. He then explained he was a juggler and had
specially made balls that audience members somehow swiped
during his act.

At lunch in Arby's I ended up in a line where a guy was
buying twenty roast beef sandwiches to go, each with different
ingredients, and he wanted each made fresh. I can almost recite

his order; he had to repeat it at least ten times. We all clapped when he left. Then I had to stand and eat because every god-blessed seat was taken.

Walking back to my office, elbows impaled me as mobs hustled and bustled, dressed too warmly in skirts or jackets and ties, lugging expensive briefcases. Shoving open revolving doors. Forcing space in tight elevators. Twice, doors were shut in my face.

Subways roared under my feet, taxi drivers screamed at pedestrians and each other, and shoppers jaywalked all over the city.

After work, I took my family to the mall, and the shoppers were like caged animals released at playtime—chaos, everyone scampering up and down corridors, wanting to be first for everything. At dinner we waited forever to get through the line at Bonanza restaurant, and then we waited some more until our food came. I've had it with city hassles.

That's why I always make sure we get away from the city at least every six months, like we're doing now. Don't get me wrong. Ocean City gets about 350,000 people every weekend in the summer, and more during their festivals and special events, but once you get on the sand and watch surfers and boats skip the rolling waves, it's worth the maddening crowds and the all the barkers on the boardwalk.

We got on the road around four today. I had to work later than I wanted because I know trips to the ocean get backed up at the toll booths.

"Oh, cripes," I mumble to my wife. "Look at this!" I point ahead. Cars look like beads strung closely together on a long necklace.

"It's 5:00pm, Friday. The worst time to try to get to Ocean City. What do you expect? You know that. Everyone goes to the shore," Martha says matter-of-factly. I hate when she uses that tone.

"Why didn't you remind me?"

"We did, Dad," my daughter Mandy says. "But you said you had to work later today. Why didn't you just leave work earlier like you promised?"

She sounds like her mother. Women, any age, have a way of

putting men in their places just by a look or a series of words connected in such a way they make you feel like hell.

Is that smoke coming from my car? I peer over the wheel. "Joe! The car's on fire!"

Immediately I swerve off the road and onto the berm. Horns blare.

Car's overheating, so I put on the heater. It's an old trick.

"You're roasting my toes," Martha gripes ten minutes later, back in the cooled off car and crawling towards the Ocean.

"Dad, I'm sweating," son Alex says.

Mandy chimes in, panting for effect.

They make me pull off the road again and walk in search of water. Now I've got to get my car back in line, only to wait some more.

Minutes later, everyone in the car is laughing, telling jokes. I can see the bridge ahead with lines of cars motoring around the toll booths. Boy! I can't wait to get to my feet in the water!

* * *

Well, seems there's a minor back-up. Ah, here we go. Not bad. Just twenty minutes to pass to Tanger shopping center, and another two hours to get to the famous sign on the bridge that states, "3000 MILES TO CALIFORNIA," or something like that. Looks like every lodging spot is occupied.

"Martha, where's our hotel?"

"80th."

"Clear up there?"

"Why?"

"Look at the traffic!"

"Careful, Joe. There's some kids on the street!"

Isn't that a helluva thing—people buried by blankets, crossing streets with beach umbrellas, surf boards, towels, and covered with greasy ointment and dark sunglasses? I wait almost a full minute for them to cross illegally, and then wait again at a red light not more than 100 feet past that.

It's seven o'clock when I arrive at the hotel. I'm smiling because I know within the hour, I'll be in my room, popping open a beer, changing into trunks, and sitting on the balcony while Martha cooks up dinner. Or maybe we'll go out for a nice relaxing meal.

The clerk at the office takes forty-five minutes to correct some error in our reservation. Then hands me a key.

* * *

The room is a mess, I notice, as soon as I swing open the door. My wife screeches at the naked man who dashes into a closet.

"Hell, man! What're you doing here?" I yell, dropping the heavy

Samsonite on my foot, hopping around, yet trying to seem dignified.

He says from behind a louvered door, "I live here. I've rented this suite for two weeks."

"Cripes." I run my hand across my mouth as if checking the smoothness of my day-old beard. "They gave us the wrong room."

Back in the office the clerk says, "Sorry. Mix-up. It's the only room we have available."

"But someone's already in it!" I wanted to yell, 'you moron!' but I held my tongue.

"I made the reservation and this is the place they gave me." My wife actually banged her fist on the counter.

"Sometimes the reservation people screw up."

She banged it louder this time, and I swung her around and headed out the door, with my kids in the background muttering under their breaths. We return to our car, drive all around in search of a suite, bucking speeding motorists, jaywalkers, and left-turners. I go to Harbor House motel on the boardwalk. This time my whole family, eyes wild, accompanies me to the front desk.

I lean against the counter. Waiting. Fidgeting with my car keys. Hoping I can a room here. My kids dramatically sigh in the background. My wife groans emphatically. A half-hour passes before we're handed a key to an expensive suite—the only available lodging that will cost me a fortune. It's 8:30 when we're finally calmed, unpacked, and headed for dinner.

* * *

Like a hornet's nest, the boardwalk is jammed shoulder to shoulder. A cyclist pedals right through my wife's and my hand-holding. "Hey!" I yell like a crazy man. "You're not allowed to ride bikes on the boardwalk now."

He gives me the finger.

Ten feet farther down the boardwalk, another bicycle catches the heel of my shoe as I dive for the sidelines where I collide with a baby buggy and a dog. The dog goes sprawling, somersaulting into the sand. Quickly it recovers, leaps back on the Boardwalk like a tightly wound coil, snarls, and snatches my pants, ripping the cuff. I squeal. Everyone stops and looks at me.

"Watch what you're doing, Joe," Martha scolds, looking embarrassed.

"Me? It's all these lunatics!"

* * *

By the people lolling on the restaurant's porch and straddling the steps, I should have figured the eatery was packed inside. When our turn finally comes, the hostess puts us in the only available seats—the smoking section. I think my wife's grinding her teeth to powder as we sit here. She can't stand the smell of smoke and everyone around us is puffing away like factory smokestacks.

I have no idea how long it has taken to get waited on but I think it might be over an hour. This I gauge from Martha's foot tapping and the kids' spoon fight. The food's cold when it arrives, and our waitress, who looks harried and like she might cry, has dropped our food off and disappeared into the nether world of "severland."

It seems I have a knack for picking the longest line, the busiest clerk, and the most crowded restaurants. I can tell my wife's ready to explode. Her breathing's heavy, jaw tensed, lips pressed—lips that look like they've been sewn together—and her glaring eyes. I feel needles running through me, fearful of what she'll turn into if one more thing goes wrong.

"How about a walk on the beach?" I suggest, trying to redeem myself after asking for my check five times. I shepherd the family through the throng.

You'd think the wide Boardwalk would be big enough to allow me to walk with my family. But no...the three of them are moseying along side by side while I'm relegated to following them like some outcast.

"I wanna swim," grumbles Alex.

"Read the sign. No swimming at Night."

"Then why'd we come here?" Mandy crosses her arms on her chest just like my wife does when she's disgusted.

"To relax," I snap.

The beach walk doesn't last long because my wife gets cold and my son wants to get back on the Boardwalk. At twelve, he's discovering girls; at forty, I'm still trying to please them.

Inside the hotel room the sliding door to the balcony doesn't close all the way, so I know I'm in for a night of my wife whining, "Joe, it's cold in here." Then after I manage to seal the door, she'll say, "Joe, it's hot in here." The best solution is to get her to bed and under the covers. One of the reasons I demand two-bedroom accommodations is to spend time with her, you know what I mean? But I fall asleep on the sofa by nine o'clock. She leaves me lying there, uncovered, all night. I think she's mad I conked out on her.

I wake up early this morning to the T.V blaring. I struggle off the sofa, eager to get some java into me, and head for the beach. I love Ocean City sunrises. I think God does something special with them.

It's raining.

I cuss as I step into the shower. Then I scream. The water's so hot I get third degree burns. My kids laugh as I enter the kitchenette.

"Funny huh? Your old man gets hot wax poured on him and you laugh. Wait 'til you get sunburned, then see who laughs."

"There's no sun, Dad," says Mandy. "It's pouring. Rained all day yesterday, and here it is Sunday, and raining again."

"I know the days of the week." I leer at her. "Where's the bacon? eggs?"

"No breakfast; Mom's sleeping."

"Sleeping? On vacation? That's a helluva thing. Why didn't you make breakfast?"

"I wasn't hungry."

I throw my hands up and rifle through the cabinets. "Did

you think about making coffee?"

"Yeah. I thought about it." There's this long silence while she watches *CBS Sunday Morning*. If I were bald like the TV host, she wouldn't even admit I was her father. Then she says to me as an after-thought: "But the stove's all icky."

"Icky?"

"Messy, Dad."

"It's not supposed to be messy. These rooms are well taken care of." They both shrug disinterestedly. They're not the ones paying the bill.

I groan, search for my summer jacket among the opened and disarranged suitcases, scattered sandals, swimming paraphernalia, and books. I wonder why my kids brought books; they never even do their homework. I pick up one lying near Alex's surfboard: *The Art of Ogling Women and Looking Cool about It*. I promise myself to take that to the bathroom on my next reading session.

Even on a soggy, gloomy morning, every diner and donut shop I go to is packed. Finally, I order a dozen cream and glazed, two coffees, two large milks, and grab the morning paper on my way out.

A few hours later, in the Convention Center, at this arts and crafts function my wife has dragged us to, my kids take most of my money to buy popcorn, soda, and junk. I dig up enough coins for a cup of coffee. I hold the Styrofoam cup and walk around the booths with my wife, sipping away, wondering if the sun has come out yet. In a few hours it will be time to drive back across the Chesapeake Bay Bridge to home.

Most of my coffee is on me. Every time someone passes, they bump me, sloshing my drink all over my sweatshirt. I give up and ditch my cup into an overflowing trash can, getting something sticky on my fingers. Doesn't management believe in emptying those "icky" things?

I can't wait to leave, to be back in Baltimore, in my own bed, away from this hassle, eating my own food.

The Chesapeake Bay Bridge is in front of me. Did you know it sways? I know this because of the number of times I've gotten stuck on it...like now. I live less than forty minutes from the Bridge's other side, then I'll be back in home sweet home.

And up for work the next morning, where the crowds kamikaze my body, cars beep, and busses roar, and the phone rings like stuck church bells.

A car swerves in front of me. I hit the brakes and pound the horn. "You jerk!" I scream out the window. "Don't you know how to drive!"

I just got another headache.

I don't think I'll wait six months to return to the beach.

AT THE END OF THE REINS

Maxine watched her husband Ken bounce his pick-up across the dirt road leading to their 30-acre farm with its overshadowing three-story, white house, white silo, white three-car garage, and big, old red barn holding forklifts, plows, and other strange equipment. A diminutive figure sat next to him looking out the passenger's window.

Max waved to Ken and the child as he whirled the truck up to the garage and jumped out, grabbing suitcases from the back. Maxine only hoped this summer's house guest—a foster child—behaved more gratefully that last year's. She put her hand over her eyebrows to block the sun, and then glanced down at her daughter Katie whose oval face had a perennial scrunched up look from paralyzed nerves.

When Maxine stepped forward to welcome the visitor, she was surprised at how tiny the twelve-year-old was. "You must be Antonia."

"Anto-knee-a," the guest corrected, "But everyone calls me Toni."

"That's Italian, isn't it?"

"I wouldn't know."

Max pulled back; then, pointing to her daughter, she said, "This is Katie who's nine."

Toni leaned on the girl's wheelchair arm rests. "So what happened to you, kid?"

Strained, Ken said, "Our daughter hurt her spinal cord when riding horses. She can't walk or talk, just can't communicate. She used to be lively and -"

"Ken, stop, please." Maxine lowered her eyes.

"You ever gonna walk, kid?" Toni yelled.

"Antonia!" Maxine flashed a cross expression. "She's unable to speak, not deaf."

Toni laughed. "Not deaf like old people." She turned back around and asked Katie in a normal voice, "So, you ever milk cows?"

"Have you?" Maxine shot at her.

Antonia napped back, "And how many times have you ridden the subway at midnight?"

Maxine's lips tightened; yet she was glad that Antonia seemed relaxed with her daughter. She followed the two girls into the house, noticing Antonia's thin frame reminded her of a tiny Twiggy. And her red hair makes her look like 'Annie' even more. The child has had a rough life, all right. Her father had left his wife and child when Antonia was believed to have been maybe six years old—left for another woman who didn't even love him. Months after his mistress rejected him and he jumped off a bridge and was instantly killed. So did he cut the child and scar her face before he left? Max didn't think her scar would be the bad. Likely that's way she hasn't been adopted.

Neither Maxine nor Ken had any details on the youngster because the foster agency said Antonia never talked about her parents, life with them or life without them; in fact, said the agency supervisor, "The kid never talks much anyway, except for biting sarcasm." What have I gotten my family into? Another child who can't, won't communicate?

Maxine recalled from having read Antonia's bio that when Toni was about six, the mother had taken her own life shortly after the father had also committed suicide, and then the state had taken the child. She had been in an out of foster homes for about the last six years. Everything seemed to have had happened when the child was only six. So unfair!

"Is it just your precious Katie who I'll be sharing a room with? Oh what the heck. It can't be as bad as the six beds in one room in the orphanage where I stayed."

"You'll have your own room."

"Oh, at least I don't have to sleep with the mute and crippled kid."

Maxine wanted to slap Antonia, and slap her hard. She was rude and cruel. This would be a long summer, and nearly a repeat of last year. "Didn't your mother ever teach you manners?"

"Never trust mothers." She turned back to Katie. "You have a bedroom downstairs and a ramp in and out of the house. Ever do wheelies?"

Katie tried grinning.

"I told you, you have your own room upstairs. You can walk, you know." Maxine snapped. "My daughter can't." When Ken gave her cutting look, Maxine toned down her derision. "Katie can visit you in your room. We had an elevator put in."

"Cool! I guess I can get through it here. Why don't you ever keep any of the kids you foster in the summer?" Antonia had a challenging look. "Or do you scare them all off?" She glared at Maxine.

"Maybe it's just that we haven't found the right one yet," smiled Ken.

"Well, I sure the hell ain't it," The girl threw her head back and laughed as she headed for the house.

* * *

Maxine looked up when Toni, yawning, trotted into the kitchen, the flip-flop of her slippers against the old hardwood floors resounding throughout the house. "At last, you're up. It's almost eight, Antonia. The cows are milked, chickens fed, and Mr. Peri's already out in the field, and Mrs. Peri is putting the produce together to sale at our stand. Once you're settled, you'll get used to rising at five and doing your chores."

"Five? No way!"

"Sit at the table." Maxine set a bowl, fresh milk and a box of Cheerios before Antonia. "You will rise early to do chores or we can drive you right back to the state home."

Toni crossed her arms. "You're a damn drill sergeant."

"We don't talk like that here. If you want to stay with us, Antonia, you must obey rules."

Toni sighed loudly enough to blow all the oxygen out of her lungs. "I don't wanna eat." She pushed the bowl away from her.

Trying, she's going to be trying. This was Maxine's fifth summer of taking in orphaned girls in hopes of giving them a sense of "home" and a sense of sister-ship to Katie, but this Antonia seemed to be more challenging than the others, though not as wild. "Fine," Maxine snorted. She put the bowl back into the cupboard. "But you won't eat now until lunch. Get dressed and start your chores in the greenhouse, then do the crops."

"I said no." She spun around to Maxine and spit out. "I don't know what the hell to do with green homes or crops!"

"Stop swearing! We are Christians in this house! Get yourself to Mrs. Peri for help in the greenhouse and the crops." Maxine pivoted around and pointed her finger at Antonia. "Let's get something straight: In our home, you do as we say. We're the parents; not you."

"I don't have parents; I don't trust parents."

"For the summer, you do have parents."

Maxine saw the muscles in Antonia's jaw flex, and then heard her say, "I'll get dressed but I want to see Katie first."

"When she wakes from her nap."

"Oh, I see; 'cause she's an invalid, she gets to sleep in but I have to get up at five."

"Katie was up doing chores before five-thirty, and in spite of your rudeness in saying she's an 'invalid,' she, too, is expected to do her share of the work."

"You are a drill sergeant."

Maxine caught the hoarseness in Toni's voice. "Are you allergic to dust and plants?"

"It's the horse shit here,"

"Antonia!"

"Call me Toni, I said."

"Did you have an allergy check?"

"You gotta be kidding.' The orphanage is short help, food's bad, rooms have roaches, and unless we're spreading Bubonic Plague, we don't get medical care. Look, if you're trying to ask me in a nice way if my scar can be fixed, forget it!"

I wasn't. But let's talk about it." Maxine pulled out a chair for Antonia.

"No."

"What did you fall on?"

"I didn't," Max corrected.

"Whatever!" Toni stood with arms crossed. "I know it's ugly, but you didn't have to bring it up."

"Yet you feel my daughter's an invalid, mute and deaf, isn't that what you said?"

"Oh, I see. You're not asking about the scar to make me feel wanted better but you're criticizing it to get back at me."

"Antonia—"

"Look, that was mean of me to say that about Katie, but I was kidding around. I wouldn't hurt Katie on purpose. I always wanted a sister."

"Did someone cut you, Antonia?"

"Mind your own damn business."

"You are my business now!"

"I said I was wrong about what I said about Katie; what else do you want?"

Maxine went to her and touched her arms, whispering, "I'm sorry."

Antonia angrily pulled away from Max. She turned and stomped out of the room.

"Don't forget your chores!" Darn. I shouldn't have said that just because she rejected me, but I can tell she doesn't like me. Seems okay with Ken and Katie.

Maxine rolled her eyes, smirking as she watched Antonia sneakily jump into Katie's elevator and sing all the way up to the second floor.

* * *

When Friday night arrived, Max mentally registered that it had made two weeks Toni had been there. And at every turn, it seemed, the child undermined the rules. One time Toni refused to help Katie do dinner dishes; another time she tested Maxine on her rule that Sundays were to be reserved for church-going, prayer and quiet time, by riding an antsy bronco, nearly maiming herself and traumatizing the horse. Every time Max turned around, she was scolding Antonia; then she felt guilty for doing it.

So this Friday night, Max and the family sat around a booth—with Katie's wheelchair at the end of the table—at Carson's

Grill, ordering burgers and fries from ketchup-stained menus.
Antonia bounced chaotically to the music in the next room,
with Katie laughing; that pleased Antonia

When the waitress left, Toni jumped up, "Let's do the Juke."
She had Katie's wheelchair whirled around and headed out to
the bar where the jukebox blared, coins jingling in her jean
pockets.

"Wait...the bar-"

"Let them go, honey," Ken whispered. "They're just going
to play music." He grabbed Maxine's hand. "Besides, she's good
for Katie, pays her lots of attention and doesn't treat her like
she's slow or an invalid."

"I guess I have been hard on Antonia. I think she gets on
with Katie because she too is physically scarred."

"And emotionally."

Maxine nodded.

"You can handle her. You love kids, Max, even though you've
withdrawn after Katie's accident."

"It was my fault—"

"Max, stop. We've been over all this before. It was not your
fault."

"I should have paid closer attention to her saddling that new
quarter horse."

Ken squeezed her hand.

"Besides, Antonia's different: rebellious, hard." Maxine
watched the waitress set steaming burgers and fries on the table.

"And she shouldn't be at that terrible orphanage."

"I know it's hellish there but it keeps the kids off the streets."

"Does it?" Maxine couldn't help sounding critical. "This
is an institution that claimed innocence to its in-house chaos,
ongoing illicit acts—even rapes—as well as having dozens
of its children running off or roaming the streets." She was
glad her family lived in the country where neighbors knew
and trusted one another and were there for each other if
need be. Nothing else compared to the fresh aroma of
country air, the lingering bouquet of lilacs and roses in
bloom, the earthiness of virgin loam fertilizing gardens and
fields, the feel of a bracing breeze cutting across the face on
a dazzling sunny morning.

On their spread, with the crops, greenhouse, animals, coops, Maxine felt alive and relished every minute of living. The city made her feel closed in, and it smelled like rotten garbage, with litter lying everywhere, and impersonal inhabitants interested only in their own needs. Nope, she would never go to the city. Besides, driving in its traffic scared her. "Where are our girls? Lunch is here." She rose to collect the girls. She hadn't gone to the bar before; rather, she and Ken and Katie and whomever was their guest would lunch in the diner area, so her daughter and Antonia being in the bar area entirely unnerved her.

In the barroom, near the jukebox, Max saw Antonia hunched over a pool table, a cue stick pointed at a white ball, and an innocent Katie looking mesmerized. "What do you think you're doing!" She whipped Antonia around to face her.

"She said I could take a shot." Toni pointed to an overly made-up woman standing nearby with hands on hips, puffing on a cigarette, bright red lipstick on fat lips, and her skirt jacked up to wide thighs. She cracked her gum so loud that Maxine wanted to pluck it out of the woman's mouth and smack it and the cigarette atop the woman's nose.

"Only twelve, and shooting pool in a bar with my daughter.

"So that's it...worried that I'll corrupt your darling?"

It happened so fast that Maxine had realized that the loud, sharp clap made the child nearly reel backward. Antonia stood, head down, rubbing her sore cheek. The loud gasps behind Antonia coming from those in the bar brought Maxine back to the present. The slap resonated through the smoke-filled air as she hauled Antonia into the other room, Katie wheeling alongside. The four ate dinner in silence with Toni staring at her plate. Another day ending in failure. Max feared that because she was failing, she'd have to send Antonia back.

* * *

Over the weeks, Antonia defied Maxine at every turn. One time she sneaked out of her bedroom around 4:30am but farmhands Mrs. and Mr.Peri were up early having coffee before they started chores. Mrs. Peri glanced out the small kitchen window in their little rancher on the property. There, running across the back of the farm was Antonia. Mr. Peri retrieved her and commandeered her to Max's front step.

Shortly after, Toni hid in the corner of one of the barns, smoking a joint. Katie wheeled upon her. They stated at each other. "You know what this is?" Toni pointed to the weed.

Katie nodded.

"Cripes! You'll run and tell your nasty mother. Go away!"

Another time, Maxine glimpsed Antonia standing in front of her bedroom mirror, running her fingers down her scar, tears wetting her cheeks. Maxine had gone to her and hugged her. Antonia pushed her away. "Don't act like you care, like you understand. You're not ugly like I am, and it gets worse as I get older. Even your kid is prettier than I'll ever be. Just leave me alone."

Maxine murmured, "Just know you are wanted here."

"F you!"

"Antonia!" Maxine was sure she screamed it.

"What? The pure mother bear never heard that word before?" She shook her head. "You silly prim and proper church-going woman who knows little about life. I know more than you. I know the hate out there; I know all about parents who hurt their kids, who don't lov-"

"Who hurt you, Antonia?" she paused. "Your father scarred you, didn't he? Is that why you hate him so much? He loved another woman than your mother, than you?"

"*Stop It!*" She covered her ears with her hands.

"It must hurt knowing that he abused you and your mother." She tried to reach out to the child but Antonia backed away.

"You don't know nuthin!" She was screaming. "My dad was a saint. He had a girlfriend because my mother was drunk all the time. Did you hear me? *All* the time. Especially the time she took a knife and carved my face and then killed herself because she was drunk and mad at my father for killing himself. She made him do that. You know nuthin about life, about love and hate." She broke into sobs so loud and shook so hard that Maxine thought the child would collapse.

"Oh my god!" Maxine gasped. "I am so, so sorry." She choked up so much that her tears spilled over her cheeks. "I understand now, and I am so so sorry." Maxine went silent as

177

the child cried hysterically. She yanked the child into her breast and held her as Antonia shook and wept.

"You won't get hurt here, Antonia. And that scar, we can find a doctor—"

"You don't get it! It's not the ugliness as it so much that my parents—especially my mother—didn't love me enough *not* to ever hurt me." She bawled louder.

Suddenly she wrenched herself out of Maxine's embrace. "Go away! Just go away! I hate you!" Antonia stood straight as a board, hands crossed, as her tears spilled over her arms.

Maxine stood firm, but Antonia threw herself on her bed, and crawled into a position to ward off any attention. Maxine left the bedroom.

* * *

Maxine was collecting eggs for the market. Her mind was on Antonia, recalling two nights ago when Ken heard noises in the house around 4:00am. With a baseball bat, he tip-toed in the dark, sneaking around corners to find the threatening source. He heard it again, past Katie's bedroom. He threw open the door, hit the light, and positioned his body in karate form with the bat poised. There sat Katie and Antonia giggling under the covers, looking at Playgirl with a flashlight. Ken forcefully led Antonia to her own bedroom upstairs and gave her a good dressing-down the next morning.

"It's no use, Ken," Maxine said after Ken yelled at Antonia and sent her to her room. "The child hates us."

"We're not quitters, Max."

* * *

It was mid-summer when Katie came down with an agonizing sore throat and temperature. Maxine was running ragged, between doing her farm chores, making meals, keeping her eyes on Antonia, and taking care of her 10-year-old.

Having just checked dinner in the Crockpot, the aroma of fresh beef, home-grown potatoes, and carrots permeating the air, Maxine, looking haggard, stooped at the kitchen sink, tried to peel potatoes for dinner, cut green peppers and onions, and there were the chickens to feed yet, too. But right now, Katie wanted—needed—her. Max knew she had to drop everything to go up and sit with her ailing child, get her temperature down, and just good ol hugging and loving.

"What's up with you?" Antonia came from Katie's room. "Katie and I did some drawing but she got tired real quick. I think she needs you."

"And I only have two hands. There's the chickens, and these potatoes, and the onions and green—"

"Chill. If we don't get dinner, you can like buy us MacDonalds."

"Like no!" Maxine washed her hands, grabbed ice water, cold washes cloth and carried the hot chicken soup to Katie's room.

It was about one-and-a-half hours later when Katie dozed off, that Maxine went back to the kitchen to finish her dinner tasks, and try to remedy the likely over-cooked beef. When she went to the sink, she froze, stared. All the potatoes were peeled, onions diced, green peppers sliced, and the Crockpot turned down to medium. *That child; always full of surprises.* Maxine grinned.

* * *

Several hours later, Maxine and Ken sat at the dinner table, waiting for Antonia who, to Maxine's thinking, was likely outside playing. She wasn't yet late for supper but in ten minutes she would be.

Maxine commented, "One minute she wonderfully surprises me; the next, she's stubborn and undisciplined." She looked at her watch. "I was hoping we would be eating by now. I have to get dinner to Katie yet."

The screen door banged behind them. "You're nearly late, "Maxine sighed, not turning around to look at Antonia.

Ken sniffed the air. "Baaaok, bok, bok, baababok."

Maxine spun around. She gasped.

"Next time you want to help by feeding the chicks, get a face mask from me." Ken winked. "Shower quick, so we can eat together like a family."

When Antonia dashed upstairs towards the shower, Maxine sat stunned and mute. Then she muttered. "Not only did she do the chickens for me but she peeled potatoes and cut up pepper and onions. She even knew enough to turn down the Crockpot a few hours before dinner."

* * *

The next few weeks, Antonia swayed like a pendulum: one second, almost angelic; the next, rude, defying, disobedient. Maxine re-read all her books on foster care children. Usually, the literature indicated, foster children were traumatized by being shifted from one household to the next, not counting the conflict imposed on them by having had to deal with parents who gave them up. Those children, Maxine continued to read, who acted out frequently, rudely and even violently were often behaving rebelliously due to some major event in their lives before and while going in and out of foster care.

Maxine reached over for the typed sheets that came from the agency that placed children in foster homes. The information included Antonia's name, age, and parents' names, her schooling (not rocket scientist material) and her health state, which briefly stated:

Appears child has received all vaccinations. Traumatized by her parents' absence. Appears was rushed to hospital once for cuts on face. Likely incurred severe strain and PTSD, resulting in anti-social behavior. Seems to bore easily in class when not truant. Rebellious at agency and in all foster homes; hence, not a viable prospect for adoption. Has few friends. Undernourished.

Why doesn't it detail her mother's role in scarring her? And no wonder she's anti-social! It's surprising she's as together as she is for a kid who's gone through what she has! Maxine was a bit surprised at herself that she wanted to protect Antonia.

In fact, sometimes she found herself enjoying Antonia's spunk, how she made a room sparkle when she entered, and how her laughter infected everyone. Her eyes—something about them made Maxine want to hold the child because in them she could see vulnerability.

* * *

180

The morning glared bright and promising. Maxine relished in this rare moment of enjoying a freshly made cup of coffee before continuing with the chores. Yawning, Max headed up to Antonia's bedroom to get her moving. In the upstairs hallway, she heard Katie squealing with glee and Antonia's voice dovetailing it. She walked into Katie's room where the two sat head to head at the desk, facing the window, chatting and giggling as though at a slumber party. Neither looked up nor turned around; they were too engrossed in sketching on construction paper.

From behind them, Max could see characters drawn on the paper that resembled herself, and Ken's angular, muscular body. She was shocked at Antonia's talent.

"Okay, Kate," Toni began while guiding Katie's hand, "You gotta shade the left side of the drawing because of the sun's direction. And see, we use the gray crayon to give your mom's hair the right color. And we have to make her larger to keep her in proportion 'specially since she's like the 'adominal' snowman."

Katie howled intermixed with gurgling sounds.

"Oh, you've seen them giants, huh? Not that your mom's an Amazon but she could carry me around as easy as she does one of her chickens."

Maxine smiled at that, and Katie snorted louder when Antonia added: "Let me move your hand to get your mom's mouth right. Yeah, that's it. Put a smile there because she ain't really all that mean."

Toni responded to Katie's murmur. "Sure, I like her, but, man. she's one tough cookie. I bet you don't let loose with her around. I can just see it, Kate: You flying through city streets in your chair, burning rubber, skirt blowing, and you tooting your chair's horn at all the cute guys, and your mother racing after you like Bugs Bunny."

They both whooped.

As Katie slouched over with laughter, Maxine quietly backed out of the bedroom, a smile on her face much like the one Antonia had drawn.

* * *

In mid-July's dawn, the sun winked at Maxine as she made a pot of coffee before heading to the barn. It wasn't quite five, so she figured the girls were still in bed. Ken was already up and about. She prepared herself for another humid day that would sap everyone of their energy. Maybe it's this heat's that taming Antonia, Max thought; she was beginning to dread the next six weeks when Antonia would have to return to the orphanage until another foster home opened. She looked over when she heard the back screen door open. "Antonia, what are you doing up so early?"

"I keep having to tell you to call me Toni. Sheesh!"

"Where were you this early in the morning?" Maxine reached for a mug.

"Couldn't sleep so I went out and did my chores."

"Good for you." Pouring herself another cup of coffee, Max stole glances at the child's pasty appearance. "You okay?"

"It's the heat. Cripes, it's like two-thousand degrees out there."

"Nap until breakfast and then take a cool shower to cool off." Maxine watched Antonia climb the stairs.

* * *

Toni leaned against the corral's wooden fencing watching the bronco stomp proudly around, whinnying and throwing its head back. She liked how the horse moved confidently, as if in control of its destiny. But the bronco continually shook its head, pranced angrily around and whinnied and snorted loudly.

"Grrrgh," resonated behind her.

Toni turned. "You did super maneuvering your wheelchair on the dirt path. I thought you weren't allowed out here after...you know, because...."

Katie managed a nod.

"Well, don't get too close. Suki don't seem so calm; acting up."

On the drawing pad Katie had started carrying around, she scrawled a girl in a cowboy hat, chaps and spurs, and underneath it was a big question mark. She banged her charcoal pencil against it for Toni to look.

"Ha! I'm an expert rider, all right." Toni thumped her index finger against Katie's cheek, and both giggled.

The bronco trotted around, antsy, irritated. Toni felt uneasy about its behavior since it had never done that in the months she had been there. Suki, the wild stallions was a part of the ranch for years. Toni's heart sped when it broke into a canter, erratically galloping from one end of the corral to the other. She turned to Katie. "I'll push you back to the house."

Out of the corner of Toni's eye, she glimpsed the bronco charging in their direction. Quickly she grabbed the wheelchair's arm to push Katie out of the way. Terror mounted in her bile.

Too late!

Suki rose on his back legs, towering over the two, kicking, grunting. Katie let loose with a gargled scream but Suki neighed louder. Then, in one swift movement, he kicked the fence, collapsing the old wood with a loud wallop and knocking the girls to the ground; the chair's wheels spun wildly.

"Oh my god!" Toni jumped to her feet. Frenzied, she tried backing Suki away from Katie, only to catch again his left foot across the ridge of her eye. White hot pain zinged through her head but her thoughts centered only on getting Katie out of there before Suki trampled her to death. Knowing she couldn't chase him away and couldn't lift Katie, Toni started screaming. But Suki loped even closer to the paralyzed girl. In a flash, Toni threw herself on Katie, covering her head and body with hers.

Sounds of fast-moving feet and Mrs. Peri's squeals reached Toni. She opened her swollen eye to see both Mrs. and Mr. Peri and a couple of ranch hands steering Suki back into a corral, and then she felt Maxine gruffly pulling her off Katie who was immediately snuggled into her mother's breast, with Maxine, running her hands, up and down her daughter's body, checking for injuries.

"Are you hurt, honey? Tell Mama. Are you okay, Katie?" Maxine calmed a second. "Thank God nothing's broken." She turned to Antonia, her face red, eyes narrowed, voice strident. "How could you do this! How dare you bring my daughter here? Are you trying to kill her? That's it! I've had it with you! Pack your stuff now. I want you out of here within the hour!"

"Maxine," Mr. Peri cautioned.

"Never trust mothers," Antonia screamed, then bolted faster than Suki had, and was at the farmhouse's front door and upstairs, packing.

* * *

In the kitchen, Maxine sat still, shaken, watching Ken wash the dirt off Katie's face. So jolted by what had happened, Maxine knew she had over-reacted, but how dare Antonia risk Katie's life? Was she that jealous?

"Max," she heard Ken say. "Come here. Katie's drawing a picture."

"Later; I'm upset."

"You need to see this now," he insisted over Katie's "Grrghs" and rapping the pencil against the paper.

Maxine studied the crude but apparent rendition of what represented Katie lying on the ground, and a figure—probably Antonia—trying to shoo Suki away. Below that sketch was Antonia in motion toward Katie. And below that was a sketch in the shape of Antonia throwing herself on top of Katie.

"Oh sweet Lord," Maxine said. "How could I—"

"Oh my oh my!"

"You were upset, honey, but you better go to her. Looks like she saved our daughter's life...as well as taught her how to communicate." Ken examined the drawing. He kissed Katie on the top of her head. "Did Toni wheel you down to the corral?"

By Katie's attempt to shake her head, Maxine knew, and her understanding was confirmed when Mr. and Mrs. Peri came to the house to check on the girls. They told their bosses that Katie wheeled herself down the path; Antonia hadn't encouraged her in any way.

Maxine swallowed the knot rising in her throat. *How could I have been so mean to Antonia? Hurt her like that? Will she ever forgive me?* She quickly swiped at tears and took the stairs two at a time.

Max opened Antonia's bedroom door, and took in the bed piled high with clothes and a suitcase next to it. When Antonia turned to the sound of the door opening, Maxine gasped. *How*

184

could I have missed that? She rushed to the bathroom medicine cabinet, returning minutes later with mercurochrome and a bandage.

"Ow!" squealed Antonia as Max cleaned and dabbed at the clotted cuts above the eye.

"Suki got you good." Maxine looked into the child's eyes. "It's not going to be another scar, Antonia."

"I keep telling you! My name's Toni! And leave me alone. Go back to your darling daughter!"

"You have every reason to be angry with me. I judged you unfairly, didn't even give you a chance. Then I learned you saved my daughter's life by risking yours." Max's voice cracked. "It's just that...." She swallowed hard. "Well, I mean, with another horse having tramp-"

"I understand" was all Antonia said lowly.

Maxine stared at her, grateful for being spared. That a child of twelve—one who Max had believed was too self-centered to care about others—passed up the chance to berate her. That made her care about Antonia even more. "Thank you," she whispered.

Maxine's lips trembled. Impetuously she grabbed Antonia by the shoulders and pulled her into her chest. They stood that way for long minutes. Maxine whispered, "We love you, Antonia. I...I love you."

Antonia quickly swiped at tears on her cheek, turned away from looking at Maxine,

"Would you...would you please let me be your mother? Pleas, be a member of our family? I know you can't trust mothers or ever call me Mom, but I want to be your mother."

This time Antonia broke down, wept so hard that Maxine had to seat her on the edge of the bed, hold her.

When Maxine slightly turned, she glimpsed Ken and Katie in the door frame, Ken smiling wide, Katie trying to nod.

Antonia collected herself when Katie rolled into the room and went to Toni to try to hug her. They clung to each other.

"What was wrong with Suki?" Antonia then looked at Maxine.

Maxine pressed the piece of adhesive tape to the gauze and checked the child's bruises. "I think the heat got him." She removed the clothes and luggage from the bed. "I want you to lie here for awhile; you took a nasty kick to your head." Maxine studied Toni's eyes. "But your pupils are normal. Still I want you to rest."

"I am tired." Toni's eyes closed.

"But you must stay awake."

Ken kissed Toni's forehead. "Welcome to the family." Then he and Katie left.

"I'll stay awake. You don't have to be here with me."

Maxine remained sitting on the bed's edge as Antonia lay quietly.

Silence

Antonia's voice cracked. She wet her lips. "I guess I can trust mothers after all." She wet her lips again. "Well, at least one." Her eyes flitted to Maxine who smiled.

"And I guess I'll get used to having an active girl around the house."

"Yeah, you better be ready, mama bear."

"I am, Toni. I am."

THE MISSING LINK

I think my life has been rocky because of my birth: I was born in rough waters. My aunt—we call her—Zia Maria, helped deliver me on the boat coming to America from Sicily. Zia tells me my mother, her sister, lived only long enough to give birth and name me Ernesta.

I married Antony, a bricklayer from Abruzzi, when I was twenty-two; we settled in the Erie area—a little town made up of ethnic groups like Italians. Pollocks, Irish, and Jews. Antony and I had a daughter we named Cara-Laura but she Americanized it to Courtney. Some Italian name. Eh!

She's here now, visiting under the pretense of the celebration of her birthday. We need a pretense to see each other. She sits before me, drinking coffee, in my kitchen with its old black stove and badly humming fridge. She lives in San Marcos now; looks like a Californian, too—tall, blond-haired (she dyes it; Antony and I blessed her with rich black hair; no California sun could have bleached it that much!). Kind of atypical for a good ol' Italian girl.

If Cara-Laura is anything, it's all-American. Yesterday she said, "Ma," (she says it like it rhymes with 'la'). "Let me make you a nice homemade lunch." I expected the likes of an antipasto steeped with olives, cheeses, eggs, prosciutto, Genoa salami, and lots of seasoning, and maybe a dish of pasta alla lenticchia or something that took a little skill and lots of love.

What I got was a mug of Lipton's chicken noodle soup—the kind in a packet you dump into water boiling from the microwave—and a sandwich she said she labored over: two slices of mortadellai and Provolone cheese stuck inside a ranch

187

roll. To my only child, meals must come in boxes, packages, frozen, or zipped.

So now you see the difference between us: she's unmarried, childless, I was a family woman; she's college-educated, I quit in eighth grade; she's a career woman, I'm a homemaker; she's self-sufficient, Antony cared for me until he died six years ago; she's big-city, cosmopolitan; I'm sheltered.

Although she would never agree, I think she tries to get away from her roots; she believes a lot of our relatives act pazzo. I can tell that just by the smirk on her face, as she sits there listening to me.

I make small talk; over the years we've lost the natural gift of conversation between us we once had. "So, you're thirty. What do they call you? One of those yetis?"

"Yuppi, Ma. Not yeti. A yeti is an abominal snowman."

"You believe in those animals?"

Cara grins, crosses her arms at her chest like a big shot. "Well, our high-technology has managed to detect a missing link in our evolutionary process. In the Himalayas particularly, tracks of big-footed cave-like humanoids have been found."

"What?" I paid for her to go to college and she only comes home to make me feel guilty for being so stupid. But I get the gist of her message. If there's any missing link, it's between my girl and me. "High-technology, you say; and yet it can't even cure cancer. This modern world is falling apart because of high, schmihg technology. Look at all the drugs, the crime.... Things were better in the old days."

"And so unscientific." Cara leans forward. "With your old folklore, wizardry, charms, curses, and whatnot, it's a wonder we've progressed at all from the Dark Ages."

"Don't laugh. Those things are real...simple and dark, but real, not like today where everything is complicated. Look at Zia," I say, pulling the conversation back to the topic of my concern.

"All right, Ma. Tell me what happened; I know you want to talk about it."

She's switched into her "professional" role now—another stranger to me. I suppose she feels she must listen to me because she is a counselor. I watch her shake Romano cheese into her

188

dried chicken soup saturated with water. I taught her that—cheese in soup. It's an old Italian custom.

"Some mortadella?" I push the lunch meat resting in wax paper toward her.

"Too salty."

"You picked it out for lunch."

"Only because I knew you wanted 'Italian.' Turkey would have been healthier."

When Cara-Laura wasn't so weight conscious she ate that stuff. I think she's anorexic. She tells me all the girls are slim today; it's fashionable. So is clap fashionable, but who the hell wants it? I tear off a piece of the lunch meat sitting next to the Provolone and say, "When I tell you what went on, you'll laugh. How can you be a counselor if you laugh at people's problems?"

"Psychologist, Ma, not counselor. I'm a doctor of psychology."

"What's the difference? Head doctors all the same."

Impatiently she asks, "So, Zia Maria is sick?"

"Cursed."

Cara sets her soup spoon down, looks at me. Wets her lips. I can tell she's going to laugh. But she manages to say, "Cursed? Like in the Exorcist?"

I lean over my coffee cup. "Her neighbor claims that the minute Zia picked a tomato, her whole garden turned to seed."

"Zia's garden?"

"No. Her neighbor's."

"Zia's neighbor?"

"Her garden."

"Ma!" She slams her hand on the table. "Stop using pronouns. Use names. I hate when you do that."

My smart daughter can't even follow a simple conversation, and yet she can "dialogue," as she says," with computers and patients all day. "Last spring, Zia walked next door to Cinconi's garden. You follow?"

Cara nods.

"Flavia Cinconi's from the old country—she's as old as her Palermo—and knows things like witchcraft. Old native-Italians know that stuff."

Cara frowns, like she's terribly confused. For her, there must be order and logic. One thing must sensibly flow from another. She says, "What does age have to do with anything? Zia's old, too."

"She gets around, does for herself. I should look so good when I'm eighty-seven." I wave her off, sip my coffee. "Anyway, Zia said to Flavia, in Italian," (I'm talking with my hands. I try not to do that too much around Cara.) "Zia said, 'Flavia, how do you do this? Grow such biggy tomatoes?' And Zia picked one. Flavia began screaming, 'Bruta bestia—'"

"Ma, you are the youngest of your siblings and born in America; why must you still use Italian?"

"You know my parents and brothers and sisters came over on the boat and knew only Italian, so Italian was my native language until I learned English in school. Hey! Bi-lingual is popular you know. Whadya want from me. Mama mia!"

"Back to the tomato."

"So Flavia yells at your zia, 'How dare you picka my fruita! Go to hell!' And Flavia made a fist, then pointed her index and pinky fingers at Zia. She put a maloccia, the evil eye, on her."

Cara busts out laughing.

"It's not funny. Zia goes around swearing, screaming, spitting."

"You've seen her do that? Spit? Swear?"

I nod. "But if the doorbell rings, she straightens out and acts normal. I told Zia's daughter Gina this but Gina does nothing. She claims that every time she goes to her mother's house, her mother is normal."

Cara lights a long skinny cigarette—long and skinny like herself. She takes a puff and says, "So what you're saying, Ma, is that Zia acts like that only around you?"

I nod.

"Were you there when Zia picked the tomato?"

"Yes"

"Then why didn't that lady, what's her name? Flavia? Why didn't she curse you?"

I smack my hand to my breast. "I didn't pick a tomato!"

"But you were with Zia when she picked the tomato?"

I shake my head up and down.

"Well, did Flavia say anything to you?"

"Eh! It meant nothing. She said, 'You too, Ernesta. I curse you, too!'"

"I don't understand. Then why don't you think you're cursed?"

Kids today understand nothing about the old ways. "How can I be cursed if I didn't pick the fruit?"

Cara crosses her eyes. It makes me smile. She rises, pours more coffee. "There's no scientific or rational proof for curses, Ma. We're a post-modernistic, high-tech society that requires proof and logic—particularly computerized-"

"I know cursed when I see it, damnit! I know about such things, modern day or not. And don't make fun of me, missy!"

She gracefully and sophisticated-like slides back into my kitchen chair. "Ma, this is the contemporary world, not the old country. No one believes in that voodoo."

"Voodoo!" I take a sip of her chicken soup—it's terrible. Like drinking wet saw dust. I wave my hand. "I'm not talking about voodoo-smoodoo! *Maloccia* is real and bad. If you're cursed, your life is no longer yours." I'm quiet now, knowing my silence will force Cara to my side. Guilt is a powerful weapon and I. like any mother. am an expert marksman.

"Okay, Ma. What do you want me to do?" She sets her cup inside my orange-streaked once-white porcelain sink.

"Come with me to Zia's. See for yourself."

"Maybe I should. Could be some medical cause."

Medical cause?" What excuses modern world uses for the unknown.

* * *

We're in the foyer of Zia's two-story Victorian. I tell my old sister a hundred times, "Maria! Lock the doors!' but she thinks she's living back fifty years in a tiny Sicilian village where everyone knew everyone, and all were likely related.

Cara calls out, "Zia Maria? It's me. Courtney."

I smack my daughter across her shoulder blades. "Courtney bullshit! Zia's like your grandmother. Show respect!"

"Zia," She calls again. "It's me. Cara-Laura."

"Better," I snort.

From upstairs, loudly come the words, " *Aspetta perfavore*

uno momento"; then the sound of floppy shoes on the landing, followed by, " qua!"

"She's coming," I translate for my daughter.

"So I figured."

From the corner of my eyes I see Zia descending the stairs, looking the way she'll always remain in my mind: curly hair brushed with gray; she's short and bosomy with the old but clean polka-dotted bib-apron almost covering a below-the-knees pastel flowered dress. In my fifty-eight years I have never seen my Palermo-born, oldest sister in slacks. For such an old woman her skin is soft and nearly smooth. It gives me hope.

Immediately Zia swarms over Cara, kissing her, cupping the young face in her old hands, gently pushing Cara backwards to get a full-length view. I watch my sister's cataract eyes roam her niece's features. With authority she pronounces, "Cara, you losa more weighta." How can my sister live in this country over fifty years and still speak broken English?

Cara doesn't understand or speak Italian. We didn't talk to her in Italian when she was little because she didn't want her friends to ridicule her. I remember how she used to chastise her father and me for being so ethnic.

I hear Zia saying, "Bella! Bella!" She hugs Cara again. "Qual è il nome del luogo in cui vivi? Chi?"

Cara cuts her eyes at me. I answer for her, "San Marcos. Dove; non chi. It's a place in southern California." How many times have I told my sister what and where San Marcos is!

Zia shepherds Cara to the kitchen table where she promptly pulls out chicken from the refrigerator and magically has steaming left-over rigatoni on its way to the table. She points to the chicken and says, "Mangia. Pollo fritto."

I smile as Cara tries to tell Zia that she's not hungry, but I taught my daughter well and, out of respect, she'll sample the food and tell her aunt what a great cook she still is.

Zia expertly throws a salad together and sets it in front of Cara. "Insalata. Mangia, mangia."

Zia and I watch Cara pick at a breaded chicken cutlet, eat a few tablespoons of pasta, but finish off the salad—enough to satisfy her aunt that she ate something, so Zia says nothing. Maybe my daughter's taking something to make her skinny. I shrug, knowing that my daughter isn't interested in sharing that with me. Is it because we are so different in such a different world? Or is it because after Antony died I was busy trying to make a living for the two of us, earn enough money to send her to college, meet the bills. As a seamstress I did okay but not anywhere near being rich. I only hope that in California—somewhere—Cara has found someone who loves her as much as I do but has more time for her than I have given, someone who can substitute for me, someone who's "modern." Our relationship is what she terms "alienated"—that we love each other but aren't close.

I watch her, so charming and poised, fold her napkin and kiss Zia on the cheek, thanking her for the lunch, telling her, as I expected, what an excellent cook she still is. Zia laughs, kisses her back. They chit-chat, about the weather, Cara's work, how Zia's been feeling. Cara has learned over the years to interpret most of her aunt's broken English, though I play translator a lot.

I had made it clear to Cara that she was to say nothing about the curse.

Carrying her plate to the sink, Cara asks, "So, Zia, how's Mrs. Cinconi?"

I gasp. Behind Cara's back Zia shoots daggers at me with her dark eyes.

"Since her marito morire last-a month-a," answers Zia, still looking at me, "she gonna mov-a to-a Pittsburgh-a, liv-a witha son." Zia's arm makes a wide sweep to indicate the move.

"You said her husband died?" asks Cara, surprising me she understood her aunt. "How did he die?"

"tings happen som-a time."

Silence.

Cara quietly studies her aunt, then walks back to her chair, looking at Zia. My daughter persists, "But you and Mrs. Cinconi are still good friends?"

"Basta!" Zia eyes me, and then says to Cara. "Talky 'bout some ting else-a. We no amici no more, Flavia and me."

Cara feigns surprise. "Oh why?"

My aunt waves her arms like she's swatting a fly. "We talky 'bout some ting else-a." Zia crosses her arms at her chest. The matriarch has spoken.

We change the subject and talk about the health of relatives, how the plumbing needs updated in Zia's old house, and when and how Cara's going back to California.

I rise and say, "C'mon, Cara. We've got to go." Zia and Cara manage the expected farewells with hugging and kissing and "I love you's" and "keep in touches". I lean over and kiss my sister while saying, "Cara, start the car. I'll only be a minute."

My daughter obeys.

Zia and I stand face to face. "I'm sorry," I say.

Zia's eyes blacken, pupils widen.

A chill rushes through me.

She turns her back on me, walks away, saying in a hiss, "She ask-a about-a Flavia. Your-a silly idea? Stupido!"

"Maria, tell Cara because she can help you," I say in Italian. Her words come speedily, disjointed, but I understand her message; her finger goes up and down at me as she yells, "Some-a old-y lady say-a she curse us, and-a you believe-a!"

In one swift movement Zia spins around, inhales intensely, rapidly, then spits on me. Suddenly I'm in a whirlwind of vulgarity, screaming, spitting, howling, hands smacking counters, feet kicking walls, oven. Her face grotesquely distorts into an elongated twisted shape, her tongue rolls out.

Shivers run down my arms.

"Maria Stop!" I yell. I'm afraid to go to her, touch her. "*smettere!*" I'm shouting. "**Perfavore...basta!**"

Then comes the sudden and quick sound of shoes smacking concrete, closer now, up the porch steps. Zia and I both turn to look.

Cara's standing in the kitchen, her face cotton white, her mouth moving: "I heard voices. Yelling. Everything okay?"

Calmly, her eyes soften; her face angelic, Zia walks to Cara, squeezes her shoulder. "Fine. You-a mama and me, a fight-a we have-a. Buono. Every ting justa fine." And then she winks at my daughter.

I shake my head, walk out the door.

* * *

194

Cara says nothing to me during the drive back home. I wonder what she's thinking. Minutes pass before I finally say, "You heard her. Do you believe me now?"

"Ma, I heard nothing; just Italian. Voices raised. A fight between sisters. How can I tell if she was in a curse?" No use. Only the sound of her car engine breaks the silence. It's a long, awkward quiet between us. I want to fling my hand out and smack her fingers on the steering wheel.

She clears her throat; the silence makes her uncomfortable. Softly she says, "Ma, did you ever think that it's just your perception that's off?"

"My perception? You know, Cara, there are things in this complex world that man doesn't understand, things that the mind and all your great computers don't have explanations for."

"Don't you think I know? Who's the psychologist here?"

She stops at a red light. Her face is frontward, her gaze out the windshield. She doesn't turn to look at me when she says, "You know, Ma, maybe you're cursed after all, and your curse is having to be the only one to see Zia like that."

She doesn't believe; yet this is the psychologist who thinks "missing links" leave tracks in the world.

195

Added Note

"So You Want to Know if You're Cursed?"

"Maloccio," the "Evil Eye" or "Jettura" has been around for centuries, before Egyptian times. Italians claim Evil Eye-doers (witches called strega) resulted from some misfortune, or being born on Christmas Eve, or to a mother who did something wrong while pregnant, like turning around in church just as the Host was lifted. Italians use articles like amulets (the horn), garlic, salt, statues of saints and symbols of knives, scissors, and fish, to ward off the Evil Eye. Pointing the forefinger and pinky and spitting three times at a potential evil-doer could also deflect a curse.

The numbers 1 and 7, particularly as 17 are very unlucky, while 3 or 13 are considered good luck,

Those with eyebrows joined in an unbroken line were recognized as being a witch. Saying such praises as "You're beautiful" would immediately label you as having a curse.

Birds in the house, in any form, even as pets, is bad luck, especially if the bird(s) are black and fly through a window or down the chimney and are frittering around your home.

If you move to a new house, evil from the former owners must be destroyed. Italians do this with a broom and salt, to sweep away anything sinister left by the former inhabitants, and the salt for cleansing away the curse...

Upside-down bread means you are cursed. This dates back to the peasants in Europe who relied on bread as their major sustenance.

If your world seems to be collapsing lately, it could be that you're cursed and, thus, doomed. Most methods of destroying a curse have never been written down but rather passed on only through word-of-mouth.

A few of the known curse-nullifiers (all of which involve the muttering of some kind of incantation, with In nomine patris, et filii et spiritus sanctum, being the most common) are:

The Oil and Water Test:

Go to a charm-worker (one presumably able to break curses) who places a basin of water on the table. The charm-worker holds a tablespoon of oil over the basin, where, using the thumb, she/he allows it to fall drop by drop into the water. If the oil stays amassed, you're cursed. The charm-worker must say the incantation and cut the floating oil with a knife or pair of scissors in order to break the curse.

Cupping:

Don't tell your old Grandma straight from Italy that you're not feeling so hot. She'll think you're cursed and turn a cup upside down on your body, usually on your stomach or back. She'll place a match held by some makeshift device underneath the cup and light it. The flame will eat up the remaining oxygen in the overturned cup and create a suction that will pull your flesh into the cup, and supposedly draw the sickness out. It's not a good idea to rub yourself with anything flammable before doing this.

Bleeding:

Chances are if Grandma doesn't use the cupping method, she'll go for "bleeding." In the olden days, it was a barber who usually performed this. He would cover the ailing body with leeches to suck out the blood and, hence, get rid of the sickness. If leeches couldn't be found, he would lance the skin everywhere. If he wasn't too busy cutting hair, he could open abscesses, cauterize, and perform surgery.

Sacrificing:

Of all the different ways to cure a curse, sacrificing was the worst. This takes little imagination to figure out what the charm-worker would do. Usually small animals were used but stories circulate that humans, especially children, were also killed.

So if you think you're cursed, keep it to yourself. The cure is worse than the illness. Besides, in today's modern world where high-tech offers answers to everything being cursed is not a popular affliction. Contemporaries will think you're crazy and institutionalize you, which might be a lot safer than cupping or bleeding.

Often the charm-worker would advise the sick person that it took two weeks for the charm to work. In reality, the body naturally rids itself of minor illnesses within fourteen days.

PADDED MIND

My husband is trying to make me crazy.

I'm sure it's his way of getting rid of me just so he can get the money my mother left me—quite a sum at that, enough to buy that yacht he's been talking about, or that super sports car he's had his eye on...neither of which I want.

Today was the climax of his little game.

I woke up to what I thought was an ordinary day. After showering and patting on moisturizer, I headed out the bedroom door. I could hear him talking to our five-year-old and seven-year-old daughters:

"Remember, Girls, don't make any noise. Mummie's not right up here."

I caught him pointing to his temple when I walked into the kitchen.

I reached to kiss my girls—just the way Sally had in my story—and they shied away from me. Sally's an older woman, forty-three, who's lost her desire in life for everything but her painting; she's possessed by her painting. I'm a writer, you see, spending much of my time split between living real life and designing imaginary life. I do tend to get confused at times but so do all artists.

"Don't!" my husband Frank shouted at me, as I set the coffee pot under the spigot. "Can't you see I already made coffee?"

I looked over. "I guess I wasn't thinking."

"That's your problem lately, Mandy; you just don't think. You're so busy making paper-people and pulp-style crises, you just don't know the difference anymore between realty and fiction. Why, I'm afraid to leave you alone with the girls these days."

"You're ridiculous. Why would you be that way? I love my daughters."

"Yes, but you're so...so...absent-minded. What if there was an accident, a fire...."

"Knock it off, Frank! You're making me out like I'm crazy. I'm preoccupied, that's all."

"Preoccupied! Get serious! Your head's in plots and characters, and not dinner, laundry, or making the beds. I think you need a long vacation."

I sat at the brown Formica kitchen table, head bent in arms. I was soooo tired, that was true. Writing was soooo demanding, and I was losing track, writing, re-writing, writing, re-writing.

Frank was going on. "Yesterday you called the neighbors and said I beat you-"

"You lie!"

"Just like in your story with...what's her name...Sally something or another-"

"You're a liar, Frank!"

I saw the girls shrink in fear at our yelling, and I felt terrible; yet I couldn't stop countering his lies.

"The day before you took all our groceries, put them in paper bags, and set them out on the curb like garbage-"

I jumped up, shouting, "That's not true!"

"I bet Sally did that too."

"You're making all this up! Why? Why would you d-"

"Last week you slept eighteen hours straight! Don't tell me normal people do that!"

"I was tired, Frank. I work hard all day writing, taking care of you and the kids, all the household chores-"

"All women take care of their homes, Mandy. You're no different. But most normal women don't tell people their husbands beat them, or put a $150 worth of groceries out on the curb-"

"None of this is true..."

"Not true? Not true? Well, let me cite some other loony-tunes things you've done-"

And on and on he went, fabricating things that should have made him the writer and I the CPA, and not reversed. And he said all those ugly untrue things in front of my little girls. He's since come to me and apologized for saying them with the girls present, but not for saying them.

When he comes to me I act like I don't know him. I find some spot and stare while he talks.

As a matter of fact, I'm so fed up with everything—what he calls the 'real world'—that I just don't talk at all...period, with a capital 'P'. That tends to irk everyone, and they shake their heads while I go back to my story-making, which pleases me to no end. My writing, you know, is my life.

Hold up a minute; someone's at my door.

"Yes?" I say to him. He's tall, wearing white top, brown pants, glasses, and snapping gum loudly. He's half-way in my room and half-way out in the hallway.

He's telling me, "It's okay, it's time to leave. You can't stay in this padded room forever."

...but you can stay nestled in your mind.

Part 4:
Fall

There is a harmony in autumn, and a luster in
its sky, which through the is not heard or seen, As
if it could not be, as if it had not been!"
—*Percy Bysshe Shelley*

A HALLOWEEN MEETING

Skull and crossbones, black cats, ghosts all hang in storefront windows. It's Halloween. Cold, sleeting.

I stand over a steaming street vent for warmth, watching a grisly-looking tramp approach me. He's big, unshaven, and smells like a backed up sewer. He eyes me eating a hamburger I found in a fast-food dumpster.

He's next to me now; I can feel his looming, stinking body. Suddenly, in one quick movement, he kicks me in the knee and grabs my sandwich. "Hey you! That's my food!" I scream at him.

He kicks me again.

Stop crying, I tell myself. I move on.

* * *

Gosh, I need a bath. What I hate most about living on the streets is feeling grimy, smelling like a sweat factory. All this is my mom's fault; if she hadn't fought with me, things would be different.

I'm starved. I'd give anything to feel a hot bagel between my hands. I walk along litter-lined Broadway, searching for food. My money's gone and so is my dignity. Street life is new to me, so I'm not sure where the safe spots are to sleep. Seems like every place I've picked, I've had to move on because someone bigger than me wanted it. I stay awake most nights making sure rats as large as squirrels don't crawl all over me, and roaches don't get into my hair. I try to find park benches or hiding places in bus and train stations; usually I get thrown out.

But living day-to-day on the streets is better than going back to mean Mom. Besides she doesn't want me anyway. I remember how she screamed like a crazy woman: "So help me, Samantha, if you leave, don't come back!" I ran down the sidewalk, yelling back over my shoulder, "I won't come back. EVER!"

New York City is where I am, several hours from home—a big city so unlike my sheltered little town of Hampton where everything stays clean, and thieves, rapists, bums are hardly heard of. It's been four days I've been here: Four days of sneaking baths in public fountains, struggling to stay out of fights where my eyes could get ripped out or my throat sliced open, and crunching hunger pains eased only by an occasional soup wagon where homeless males try touching me while I wait in line.

I'm thinking about going back to my warm bed with its crisp sheets and soft, clean pillows. But Mom doesn't want me. I'm not that bad a kid. I used to be on honor roll, had a paper route, too.

And then Dad just up and left.

Mom's been mourning so long she's forgotten about me. Why does she even care about a man who would leave his wife and child? I remember him but I constantly try to put him in my past; that's where he belongs.

I walk Park Avenue, my eyes darting from building to building, alert for any danger. Mom didn't have to embarrass me in from of my friends who she caught smoking in my bedroom, although I was thinking about trying the pot myself. She went bonkers, shrieking, crying. For days after, we fought, yelled, slammed doors. When she said I was grounded for a month, I had had it. I packed a few things and hit the road.

And here I am.

I run my fingers through my hair. I'm filthy from the tips of my curls to the bottoms of my worn out feet. Oh to be home where there's food, water for bathing, and warm, clean clothes. And Mom's reassuring words. Maybe I do miss her...a little.

But she told me if I left to never come back.

I've got to admit, she had tried. When I skipped school, she sat down and talked to me, and when I got caught looking at someone's test paper, she talked to me then, too. Mom had been understanding...until that pot-in-the-bedroom incident. Then she didn't want to hear that I never even tried it.

So okay, what if I promised never to mess around like that again, and to not skip school, or cheat—would she take me back? Probably not. She was real mad that day. But the bum did kick me and steal my last bite. I need food. I'm tired, weak, and grubby. There aren't many choices for a homeless teenager in a big city. Staying awake all night, constantly being on guard of my belongings...and my life...is not how I want to live the rest of my life. I could call home just to see if Mom maybe isn't mad anymore. If I get her answering machine I'll leave a message; this way we won't have to exchange words.

A pay phone isn't more than ten feet away. My hands tremble as I deposit a quarter, my last and only emergency coin. Then using Mom's phone card, I punch in the numbers. My knees quiver as the other end rings. On the sixth ring, the machine connects. I wait for the beep and then speak rapidly: "Mom...Mom...it's me, Sam. I wanna come home. I know you're real mad at me, and never want to see me again, but please let me come home. Give me some sign that it's okay between us. Put a pumpkin on the porch. Anything, just so I know it's okay between us. If there's no pumpkin out, I won't come in; I swear, I won't bother you anymore." The answering machine disconnects. I hang up with a clink and quickly wipe tears away. I guess I'm not so tough.

Now to get home. No money for transportation. I walk over to the curb and stick out my thumb. I know this isn't safe but I've gotta get home just in case Mom does put the pumpkin out. I wouldn't want her to change her mind if I don't get home in time.

* * *

The driver is a well-dressed, middle-aged woman wearing a white skirt, white blouse, and something looking like a white cape—maybe she's a nurse. She has a special smile that makes me feel okay being with her. She's telling me that she has "compassion" for young kids like me who live in the streets and risk hitch-hiking. "The Lord loves youngsters," she says, making me think she's a religious fanatic, and then she goes on saying, "And since you seemed harmless enough standing there in the street, thumbing, I thought I'd stop and give you a ride."

"Me? I was afraid of you." Shifting uneasily in my seat, I entertain more fully the idea that she might be a weirdo. I take a deep breath and cower next to the door.

* * *

Hours pass with her and me not saying much. And when I do say something about my mom, she acts as though she knows all about it. Imagine how difficult it must be living with somebody like her.

She breaks into my thoughts: "How close is your house from here?"

I keep looking out the windshield, watching the sky darken, telling me winter's coming. "Sixty miles, maybe, down the Interstate. Maybe an hour or so."

"I'm going to drive you right up to you door; it's getting dark and it looks like it might snow."

"I'm grateful enough for the lift; you don't have to go into town."

It's dangerous out there these days; someone needs to watch over you." The classy lady smiles, then asks, "You hungry?"

My cheeks sink in. I picture a steaming roast beef sandwich with melted cheese on a roll, sitting next to a pile of hot fries.

"Make you a deal," the lady says. "I'll buy you the best meal you've had in a while if you let me drive you to your front door."

I shake my head. People aren't usually this nice to strangers. "You a nut or something?"

She chuckles. "How about an angel?"

"Oh, sure. Tell me another. Angels, witches, ghosts — all make-believe."

"Witches and ghosts are from the underworld."

"Oh, and I suppose you're from heaven." She is crazy, I decide. "Where every time a bell rings, an angel gets wings, right? Give me a break, will ya."

"If you're hearing bells and thinking wings, you're the one who's the nut." She winks at me and turns down the exit ramp to a gas-food service area. In the street lights, I see how soiled my clothes are, and I know I'll be an embarrassment to her. I must have lost five pounds, too.

The diner's a truck stop, so I don't think I embarrassed her too much. Just as our meal arrives twenty minutes later, she says, "I want you to know there's more to life than a big, frightening city, or meeting up with bums-"

"I was one of those bums."

The lady looked over at me. "And God loves them too."

Yep, she's a fruitcake, all right.

"You believe in God, don't you?" She stands, pushes her chair in. "Maybe if you turned to Him for guidance, you and your mother would get through your dad's absence a little easier."

I shrug as if tossing off goose bumps. I don't remember saying anything to her about my father abandoning us...or did I? Creepy, is what she is. Suddenly I notice a pin on her white collar. "What is that—an angel pin?"

"You didn't think I'd be wearing a 'human' pin, did you?"

I bust out laughing.

* * *

A half-hour later, back in the car, the lady says, "You told me awhile ago that you're hoping your mother will welcome you home, that she'll forgive you...but have you forgiven her? After all, you're the one who's angry because she supposedly accused you of doing something you say you hadn't done, and that she had made a big scene in front of your friends-"

"I'm no scaredy-cat; I woulda tried the pot if Mom hadn't walked in."

The lady takes her eyes off the road to look at me. "I don't think so."

"How would you know? You never even met me before."

"Your mother reacted naturally. But you're still holding a grudge."

"Am not."

"Ask yourself why all of a sudden you want to go home."

"It's not all of a sudden. I'm hungry, cold, tired. It's a bad rap out there on the streets, you know."

"So you want to go home to make things better for yourself." The lady turns the car radio down "Maybe you ought to go home to make things better for your mother."

We ride in silence. I steal glimpses of the woman, wondering if she was right. Mom has been so lonely since Dad left; he had been her best friend until he just up and went away, without an explanation, without a reason. Gosh. That's a double loss for Mom.

"This is your exit." says the woman softly, looking straight ahead.

I say nothing. What if we get to my house and Mom hasn't put out a measly pumpkin? I would know then, wouldn't I? My stomach flip-flops. Sighing, I give in. "Look, I'll let you take me to my house but you got to promise to keep driving unless I tell you to stop."

I feel her eyes on me.

Just as I open my mouth to give her directions, she says in a melodic voice, "Okay, then, off we go to 412 Chainey Court."

"Yep," I agree. And then it hits me. "Hey! How did you know my address?"

She beams that sweet smile while saying, "It's snowing."

* * *

Two streets away and my stomach's jitterbugging. I chew my nails. Oh, man, what if Mom didn't put out a pumpkin? It would mean she's stopped loving me. I see where street lights illuminate yellow hydrants brushed white with powder—a snow that has stopped now.

And my heart will stop too if Mom doesn't have even one pumpkin out...just one. One silly little pumpkin will tell me that she's at least willing to let me back into the house, and from there, maybe we could talk out our problems. But I know her all too well: Stubborn, strict, and inflexible. What if she just forgot to put out the pumpkin? Or what if she doesn't even know I called because the answering machine broke or something?

My heart's thumping.

I brace myself as we near my street, bite down on my lip. In the lighted avenues and porches, I see little kids dressed in costumes going door-to-door with treat bags. I remember doing that, my dad holding my hand, walking me to the neighbors, saying to everyone how cute I looked as a ballerina...a ghost another year...Cinderella the next year...a clown...Snoopy... Elmo...Cookie Monster.....

In the full moon's light, I make out the little Gibson girls costumed as witches—one all in black with a pointed hat, the other in white. I mumble, "Look at that—a white witch."

"White witches are supposed to be the good ones who watch out for the lost, but witches are witches."

It dawns on me then. "Aha! You're a white witch. You're dressed all in white, and you know these things about me that—"

"Over there," interrupts the lady while pointing at Susie Horne who's in a white gown with cardboard wings attached to her back, and a circular wire rising above her head like a halo. "That little girl is who I am."

I giggle. Susie Horne was far from being angelic. Last year, in tenth grade, she averaged three days per week in detention, and just this past year, she was suspended twice for writing on the girls' bathroom walls with maroon lipstick...writing things that would embarrass even a trollop—a word my mom told me about and I had laughed at. Trollops. Witches, angels, and spirits. Love it!

Well, I'm a block away from home now. One pumpkin could change my life forever.

I see that Mrs. Carver has dressed her outside lantern into the shape of a ghost, and that she has drawings of black's cats on her windows....And a pumpkin on her front stoop; another in her yard. I shift nervously in my seat, never taking my eyes off the road and the surrounding houses.

Eight houses away.

Mom was pretty mad at me, and she never goes back on her word. I ought to prepare myself for the worst—a totally dark house with no pumpkin outside, no Mom inside. Fact is fact. I should be old enough now to handle rejection. My dad taught me that. Here one day; gone the next. No one ever said they saw him again. Maybe he was with a trollop.

We pass Mr. Cella's place. He has construction paper pumpkins in his windows; real ones in his yard. And next to his house is Old

Lady Matthew's, and she even has pumpkins in her driveway, and she seldom even talks to people...just to herself.

Seven houses away.

I see Mrs. Hartley has a scarecrow tied to her lantern, with straw all around it, and on the straw are pumpkins, some piled on top of each other. You would think that with all the neighbors putting pumpkins out, that my mom could have at least one...for me.

Five houses away now.

"Look," I say aloud to the lady, forgoing my reserve. "Mr. Shanahan has pumpkins all around his veranda, even on the brick fence. And there are more in the next neighbor's yard!"

And in the next: ten, fifteen, all carved and lit up setting on a light blanket of snow.

And the house after that, and the house after that...fifty, sixty, a hundred pumpkins everywhere! Each ablaze, shoulder to shoulder, from one yard to the next. My whole neighborhood glows with smiling orange balls.

And then a brilliant illumination magnetizes my vision: Every light in my home is on, upstairs, downstairs, outside. "There's my house!" I shout. And lining the sidewalks, on the porch, even on the roof, are pumpkins everywhere! In my yard stands my Mom standing at the end of the long line of houses with lighted pumpkins. She's holding a huge jack-o-lantern with the biggest carved grin I've ever seen. "Mom!" I scream as I throw open the car door as the lady starts to slow down.

Dropping my backpack in the snow, I'm out of the car just as it pulls into our well-lit driveway. I run, run, jumping over pumpkins, tears blurring my vision. And then I run harder and right into Mom's arms. Her body wraps around me; I bury my head into her chest. I'm blubbering all over her and she's sobbing just as much.

"Mom," I manage after awhile, wiping my dirty jacket sleeve across my eyes. "I want you to meet this lady who drove me home." I turn around to wave the stranger over but her car is gone. I lope back to the driveway.

There are no tire tracks in the fresh cover of snow. Twinkling on my backpack is a gold pin shaped into a tiny guardian angel.

GOOD MORNING...AMERICA

It's Election Day and only in this shore town would a garbage man have to work.

Getting into the black truck's passenger side, I say to Bobby, "This doing the same stuff every day is gettin' to me." I shake my head, look out the windshield. It's early morning, my favorite time of the day, because sometimes I'm lucky enough to be in the right place to watch that big orange-yellow globe slide up ocean side.

I hate collecting garbage. You oughta see the stuff people throw away—some of it the likes of things I'd have in my apartment. I grunt. "This is boring, Bob. Same-o same-ol', day after day, and no one appreciates me. Sheesh. What a life."

Bobby pushes the stick up to second gear. He's my partner—the color of our truck—and the best friend a man could ever want. I can see a tiny smile playing at the corner of his mouth as he says, "Harry, your problem is you don't read. Life's not so dull. Learn to sit quietly, maybe read a good book, and enjoy life. Why, in the morning paper it said Camarata's coming up in the presidential polls."

"And a woman to boot!"

Bobby takes his eyes off the road, looks at me. I know what he's gonna say. And he does: "You racist."

We both laugh.

He lights up one of those god-awful pipes, saying, "Camarata might even win."

"What's important, Bobby, is that she's somebody. Everyone knows and appreciates her, even if she is a woman."

He sighs. Goes back to driving. Bobby always drives. He's the best driver in the whole company. I watch him move the steering wheel in wide sweeps while at the same time smokin' his pipe. I never could do that amphibious stuff.

Out of nowhere, he says, "I think this is the year."

"Ain't never no year for a woman president."

"No. I mean the business."

"Think we can make it? We'd have to compete with this company, and others. And things are gettin' mechanized today, you know."

"We can do it, Harry. And so what if automation's taking over—we'll just have to make sure that we keep up with technology. Get us one of those trucks with the mechanical arms that lifts the trash container; then we won't need as much manpower. The timing is right, and we've got seed money."

For over a year now we've been talking about starting our own garbage collection company. We both got money saved and he can get one of those minority loans. He tells me doing that would make us administrators instead of laborers. What's the difference? Garbage is garbage. I rest my back against the torn seat, prop my arm on the open window well, watch as our truck glides past trees, houses, and sidewalks that feature dark trash containers, some of them on carts that roll.

We're at the Kellery Condos; I hate it the most. There's gotta be at least a hundred trash cans. My company told Kellery to get dumpsters for his building, but he's tight. Instead, he made his tenants go out and buy bigger trash cans. Some renters use three, four of those suckers. I spend half my morning just on this complex alone. And what those rich tenants don't throw away: unopened food boxes, steaks hardly eaten. Hell, they could feed the whole planet!

Hot mornings like today are the worst because of the odor steaming up from the garbage—a smell like manure mixed in with rotted eggs. I'm on the twenty-third can—I always count cans to keep my mind off what I'm doing in life—and I can see I got a long way to go. Bobby's out of the truck helpin' but even with both of us doing it, we ain't gonna get done much before noon.

Removing my gloves, I wipe the sweat from my brow. Water beads cling to my beard, muttonchops. So does the smell. I can understand why Marcie left me. She got tired of sleepin' every night with the stink of decay.

Look at this! Sealed boxes of frozen foods. What a waste. Settin' out next to the garbage cans is a good-lookin' chair and an expensive lamp. Jeeze! Everything's disposable today.

Thirty-fourth trashes can. Put gloves back on. Flex at knees. Grasp. Lift. I groan. I must be gettin' out of shape. I hear tell that a county trash collector dropped dead last month while in the middle of lifting a container. Slumped right over into the garbage. That quick he went. Ticker broke. Helluva way to die.

I look down the row of hoddy-toddy townhouses, shake my head. I'll be here forever. Why did I ever take this job? Bend, lift, balance container on my shoulder, and toss. I took the stinkin' job 'cause I can't do nuthin else. Only Bobby knows I can't read. Well, can't read much. I know the road signs and can figure out anything written below a fourth grade level. On this job, I don't got to do nuthin' but bend my arms and legs.

Maybe Bobby's right—start our own business....

Thirty-eighth can. What's this? A kid's blanket. Pink. My little girl used to have a blanket, too. Called it her blankie. Never went anywhere without it. Never to bed unless her little face was layin' next to it. Now her face lies next to a man's—who ain't her husband.

Why'd anyone throw out a kid's blanket? Look at it. It's in great shape. I can get a good penny for that. High fa'lutin people do stupid things like that—throw away valuable stuff. Last year I found a color, portable TV in the trash. Costly little sucker. I fiddled with it awhile, got it to work. It sits in my bedroom now. If someone like me could figure out how to make it work, surely these rich over-educated snobs here could, too. For them, it's easier to buy new than maintain or fix old. Hell, they oughta have to live in my shoes for a week.

The pink blanket looks like it might wash up real nice. Maybe I'll get fifteen for it—fifteen would buy some of my groceries for the week. I slip my big gloves off again; lightly touch the pretty pink fluffy material, accidentally smacking my hand against the garbage. What a difference! One's dainty and pure, the other rough and spoiled. I shrug, undecided as to whether I want to mess with the blanket. It would cost me about the same to advertise it; I wouldn't make money on it.

I bend my knees to lift the can, my eyes on the blanket, as though it's gonna tell me what to do: sell or toss. I groan again as I lift the container to my left shoulder and walk balancing it to the truck. Cripes, I'm panting. Maybe I'm gonna go the route of the broken ticker. I set the can down; inhale deeply. Only a few yards to the truck. I need a breather.

"What's matter, ol' man? Want to put in for disability?" Bobby snickers, lowers his can to the ground after tossing a heavy load into the truck as though it was filled with feathers.

"Lose some weight," he tells me. "Then you won't huff and puff like a panting dog."

I throw him a dirty look.

He laughs, strolls on over to where I stand, dragging the can behind him.

I say, "Tell me what you think this is worth." I point to the blanket sitting atop the can.

"Going into a new line of work, Harry?" He eyes the blanket. "Maybe five bucks."

"Five bucks! Feel it, for petes sakes, Bobby. It's pure cotton. Expensive, too."

Bobby sighs like he's real irritated with me. Then to satisfy me, he runs his hand up and down the blanket while saying, "What's in here?"

I stare at him, blinking. Then I trail my hand all over the cotton. It's lumpy. Don't tell me some lady threw the kid out with the blanket! You know how many times I would have liked to have done that with my kid? I lay my hands under the blanket and lift the lumpy thing out of the can. Wouldn't it be wonderful if there was wads of stolen money in it! I ain't above keepin' it.

I throw open a flap of the blanket. Suddenly, my heart races. "JesusGodAlmighty!"

Bobby's eyes get big, wide, like a doe's eyes. "Is it breathin'? Is it breathin'?"

Big man like me and I'm trembling. My legs quiver as I hold the tiny bundle of flesh.

"Put your mouth on it. Breathe, Harry! Quick!"
I see his hands out ready to grab this tiny, wrinkled grayish baby from me. The fuzz on her head is dark.
"Breathe!" He's screaming.
I can't move.
"Start the truck, damnit! We've got to get her to the hospital!" he yells at me.
His mouth almost covers her entire little face. He's puffing into her as I run to the truck, jump in it and rev the engine. But I'm shaking so bad, I can't drive. I get in on the passenger side and before I know it, Bobby's handing the baby to me, and then runs around to the driver's side. I just can't do nuthin right.

* * *

I'm home, trying to rest a little. The minute the emergency doctors took Pumpkin (that's what Bobby and I named her) from my arms, everything blurred together. Out of the cracks in the walls came the police, television and radio crews, reporters, my company's boss, and Bobby's wife Maxine. I don't remember nuthin but pops of light going off in my eyes and black microphones shoved into my face. "How did you find her, Mr. Druitt? Was she alive?" On and on the questions went. Bobby said nuthin. Just leaned his spine against the waiting room wall, his arms crossed at his chest, his lips tight together.
The whole time we sat in the emergency waiting room, I thought about that baby, wondering how any parent could just...trash...their own blood like it was a piece of junk. I tried picturing Pumpkin's parents, imagining their faces, guessing that maybe they were young, scared. My skin crawled whenever I'd envision one or both of them walking to the trash can, holding the cute, squirming, warm baby in their arms, and then plunging it into the garbage. It'd upset me so much, I'd have to get up out of the hardback chair and pace around the waiting room.
It seemed, then, that it took hours before the short, grim-faced doctor came out and said Pumpkin was gonna live but he didn't know yet if there had been any brain damage because he weren't sure how long she ain't been breathing. "Poor baby,"

I mumbled as the doctor retreated from the waiting room, with reporters at his heel, while Bobby and I were left standing there.

Bobby looked at me. "But not 'Poor Harry,' right?" he said. "Everything's going your way."

"What're you talkin' about? Hell, I feel just as bad about the kid as you do." It's the first time I'd ever seen Bobby look at me so ugly.

"You wanted this, to be famous." He looked me. "This morning you said you wanted to be 'known' like that Camarata woman. You took all the credit, Harry, when all you did was hold the baby in the truck. If you didn't wanna give me some, you coulda at least given some to Pumpkin who's been fighting so damn hard." He walked out of the room full of vinyl sofas and high-back chairs. I heard his footfall fade.

I hung around, talked to the news people. Told them over and over how I pulled Pumpkin out of the trash can and saved her life. Never got tired of hearing myself. Everyone said how quick-thinking I was. How heroic. It was good that Bobby wasn't there then.

But that was hours ago; it's over now. Bobby hasn't even called. So I'm gonna sit here in my armchair—or did my ex call it a club chair?—watch the news and go to bed. Tomorrow's the same ol' stuff. I just hope Bobby overlooks it all and we get back to normal. It's hell working with a teed-off person.

I fasten my eyes on the TV. The curly-haired anchorman says, "Good evening, and welcome to the eleven o-clock news." Here comes the news about the presidential election. I heard it all day, about how that Camarata lady come zinging up in the polls...her picture splattered all over the screen, her voice on all the radio stations.

The college-smart, clean-cut lookin' newsman says, "Tonight's news-breaking story is about a garbage man, Harry Druitt—"

I jump up. Screech in my empty apartment, "I beat out the damn election!"

* * *

I haven't seen Bobby in two weeks. It all happened so fast. One day it was Tuesday, and the next I was on the morning, noon, six and eleven p.m. news. Thursday my phone rang like a broken blaring horn—hot-shot city PR agencies calling to represent me. Men coming in three-piece suits saying they can make me a star. Hell, I'm already one.

Everywhere, I'm in demand to speak: at clubs, colleges, organizations; and they pay me good money to get up in front of them, brag about how courageous I was. I love that stuff, just as much as I love seeing my photo in all the dailies, as well as the Washington post, New York Times, Newsweek, Time, and a bushelful of other mags and newspapers. Someone at a publishing house in Manhattan wanted to talk to me about writing a book on my heroism. I told him, nope; I wasn't going to say that this baby rescuer can't read. He mentioned something about a ghost writer but I don't need no guest to tell me how fantastic I am. I already know. Damn! I'm good!

I got scheduled to be the Grand Marshall in the upcoming Fourth of July Parade, and I was visited by The Committee for Electing City Council Candidates.

Went out bought me a pair of Gucci shoes, box of expensive cigars, and a dark designer suit—three-piece job just like those ad men wear. I quit collecting garbage, too. Hired me a secretary. She does all my PR crap; got to keep me in front of the public. And she's helping me write that book since I told her I was too busy to do it and a publisher wanted an outline and chapters, and I would give her a percentage of my earnings. I love sitting down, telling her all about my childhood, my school friends, prom dates, on and on...most of it embellishment. I mean, think about it. If I didn't stretch the truth some who would want to read about a garbage collector who can't put two sentences together in proper grammar.

So, now, weeks later, I'm wondering why I feel like something's eatin' at my craw. This is everything I could ever want. Maybe it's because I don't see Bobby no more. It's his fault; he could have had all of this. He's a poor loser.

Maybe, too, I'm bothered 'cause I haven't seen Pumpkin since that day we rushed her to the hospital. I hear she's still there, not doing well, but alive. What's the point of me going to see her?

There goes the damn phone again.

"What?" It's some fast-talkin' New Yorker—I can tell by the accent. He repeats himself much slower, as if he's talkin' to a ridge-runner. My stomach's somersaulting'. The city-slicker's saying he's a producer from GOOD MORNING AMERICA, and wants me to appear on it day after tomorrow for a human interest segment. All expenses paid.

A grin's stuck on my hairy mug. Can you believe it? I look around my apartment. Seems to me this hell hole is all behind me now. On my way to fame and fortune, just like Bobby said. Why couldn't we've shared it? He's a jealous son-of-a-gun. He's the one who didn't wanna talk to the reporters. It was his choice. So, I did it.

* * *

Bobby's driving me to the airport. I called and told him all about me going to The Big Apple and how GMA wanted me. He offered to see me off, knowing I don't have no family here to do it and I don't wanna pay a decade's salary at the airport parking lot. I said that much to him, and he said he'd take me; that's what best friends do.

"Don't you look like the star!" He whistles, his eyes soaking in my expensive navy-blue pants, vest, and jacket. He looks out the window, occasionally checking his rear-view mirror, puffin' on his pipe. With precision, he sets the meerschaum in the ashtray, then says, "I quit my job, Harry. Got to move on in life. Pumpkin taught me that."

He's gonna go mushy on me. "So, man, what're you gonna do to make a living?"

"Oh, I'm lookin', Harry. Thinkin' about opening that business we used to talk about." He turns his head, eyes me.

My laugh sounds nervous. "Who the hell would want to do something like that?"

"You did...at one time. You're behaving like an ass, Harry. You're going to get hurt." He sighs. "No matter how mad I am with you right now, I made a point of driving you to the airport so I can tell you to stop before you get hurt."

"You're just jealous."

"No, I'm just your friend."

His stare makes me jittery. I go back to looking out the passenger window.

"Harry," he starts soft like. "Where you gonna be in six months...a year?"

Stupid question. "Where I'm at now. A star." I turn back to face him. "Where you gonna be, pal? Same old two-bit, foul-smelling trash man."

He gets a look on his face that I remember he had the same day I told him Marcie left me.

"Just as I thought," I grumble.

He prods me: "You've never once gone down to see Pumpkin."

"She's my past." I look back out the window. "I can't do nuthin for her now."

"And what did you do for her before, Harry?"

That stung. He knows I know he really saved Pumpkin, but I'm the one who found her before she got tossed into the compactor.

Bobby shifts gear. He's the best damn driver I know. He says, "If pumpkin's your past, then I guess I am, too."

I look at him. "I guess you are."

We're at the airport. Bobby pulls himself out of the car, stands waiting for me to get my suitcase. His king-size hands are crossed at his chest. He's a tall mother, not heavy and big like me, just tall. But most of what he is, is the greatest friend I ever had. So why's he so jealous!

He says, "I wish you luck on TV"

"I'm gonna be someone important. Rich. Filthy rich; filthy like the garbage we haul."

"Fame goes away, Harry. It's not forever. In a short while, everyone's gonna forget about you and Pumpkin. You got to remember, buddy, that heroes like you are once a week."

"Hell! I went from garbage man to star!"

He just shook his head from side to side. I ain't never seen him so envious. His look eats at me. I can feel myself tightening inside, ready to explode. "You're mad, Bobby, cause I got all the attention. Tough shit."

"You hogged it all. Worse, Harry is that in all this, you never even cared about Pumpkin... or me; it was always yourself you looked out for." He looked away. "Besides, the fame means nothing to me. Our friendship meant everything."

"Don't go soupy on me." I study him. "You are jealous, Bobby Dixon. If you wanted any of it, you never showed it. How was I to know?"

"You're missing the point. I'm not jealous, just really mad that our friendship didn't matter that much to you, that you'd blow me off just for fame. Is that all Pumpkin meant to you?"

"What a low blow, Bobby." I'm tryin' to slow down my breathin', I'm so angry.

"Where's that put us?" His hand swings back and forth from him to me, as his eyes settle on me like laser beams cuttin' into my heart.

I look at him; it's his choice, though, to be left in the dust; he's makin' me out like a bad guy. I might not be able to read no textbook, but I can read the situation here. We're sayin' good-bye...permanently.

Nervous like, I shrug and head for the terminal. I don't bother to turn around and wave. No use. He thinks I'm doing wrong. What's he? A lowly middle-aged guy trying to start his own business? Big deal! I'm the one going on Good Morning America!

* * *

I'm backstage in some tiny room off a big, wide studio. In thirty seconds I'll be sitting in a chair across from Diane Sawyer, telling about how brave I was. People really suck up to that shit.

My palms are damp; could grow moss in them, like some of the garbage I used to dump. Kinda miss the job. This—being here in New York City in a national television studio—don't seem natural. Don't seem like the Harry Druitt I know belongs here. My stomach's rollin' like I ate lox and bagels before going on a merry-go-round. But I'm flyin.' Soaring, high, high, High!

Boy! I look good! Got on that fancy Botany three-piece suit, wearin' my Gucci shoes, the whole shemeal. Even a top hat. The audience is gonna love me. Before I know it, I'll be on other shows, do a movie, have my picture on posters; maybe they'll even make a Harry-Doll. What a wonderful life!

"Mr. Druitt?"

I turn around, see some squat bald fellow with funny-lookin' earphones on his head.

"There's been a change in plans." He clears his throat: "Mrs. Camarata, the presidential candidate, has agreed after all to appear on our show to discuss her loss. Things happen like that in this business. Got to go with whatever is hot at the moment. Of course, your return home is paid for."

He never even looks at me as he says all that. Never even steps near me. Just mouths it outside the doorway of this small room, then quickly moves on. He does it all so fast that it takes me 'till the end of his message to understand what he tells me.

Camarata lost, for god's sake! A loser. And they take her over me....

Impulsively I yell out to him as he crosses the back of the studio towards some camera man, "Hey!"

He stops, turns, his face holding a look of impatience.

"Want me to come back?"

By his expression and the way his mouth moves, I think he's swearing. When he speaks, it seems as if he's saying it too loud; everyone in the studio turns and looks. "No. No. You're old news now."

I shut the light out behind me.

Good-bye...America.

* * *

They got her in a special rig so she can breathe and all. I watch her from the window. She's so little and pale. They don't let nobody in to see her.

"She's a fighter," a voice says from behind me.

I spin around. Seeing Bobby makes me feel good inside again, almost of some value. I swallow, mumble, "What're you doin' here?"

"I come every day." He looks at me, smiles. He doesn't make me feel bad by staring into my eyes. Instead he returns his gaze to the glass window. "You okay, Harry?"

I say nothun. I know he'll throw it up to me that I wasn't on the TV show, and that all that I was scheduled to do, cancelled me, that the fame is gone, just like he said. Heroes like me are once a week.

"You're looking good." He nods at the window.

My throat's tightening. This man is acting like ain't nothun bad ever happened between us. Why doesn't he just mock me and get it over with?

"I've been worried about you. I'm glad you're back," he says softly.

Oh, sweet Jesus, don't let me get teary. He's lettin' me know we're still friends and that he's forgiven me. I couldn't have done that. I swallow my pride, cough a little, and ask, looking at his profile, "You still got room for a partner?" I can hear the thinness in my wobbly voice.

He don't look at me. Instead, he stays standing, unmoving, staring into the glass, allowing me my dignity.

I sense he's gonna forgive me. I don't deserve it.

Slowly he turns and meets my gaze. Stares.

And he's smiling. Nope, ain't no way I deserve him. He has a right to humiliate me but he won't because he's my best friend. I'm reading the signs here, and I feel him forgiving me for being such a jerk. How will I ever pay him back?

"Harry," he starts, and then stops; his eyes take in the room, as though different thoughts keep poppin' up into his head. And he grins real wide. He's gonna tease me. That's okay. I've got to give him some revenge. I won't make no big deal about him gettin' my goat. I'll just laugh at whatever he says. I wait patiently for him to say something. As I look at him, then back through the glass, I wonder what really happened to my life the last few weeks. Been like someone put me in a jar, shake me up real good, open the lid and I come sprawling out, eyes closed, dizzy, and lost.

I turn and study Bobby's face. All the years we've been together. Like brothers. He's the best damn driver there ever was. I guess I did screw him and I'm real sorry for it.

At last Bobby shifts. Focuses his eyes back on me.

My mind hears the sounds of sirens nearby, the hustle-bustle of hospital activity, and I look at little Pumpkin fighting to get on with living. I wonder what I've invested in the last twenty years of my life. A job? An honest job...a damn good friend...and now I got nothun.

But Bobby's gonna fix that for me. We'll start our business together and I'll have Bobby back and a job again. And I'll have my dignity back, too.

"Harry," he repeats, his voice a tiny bit hoarse. He turns his body to fully face me and says, "F-off." He smiles real pretty for me, and then walks away.

Speechless, I stand here, watching him walk down the hall. I guess I really don't read so good.

BRICKS

Danielle stood waiting in downtown Oakland in Toledo. Her father hovered nearby, immersed in the bus schedule. She wished she had parted on better terms with her brother; as twins, they had always been close. She thought back to a few months ago when she made her announcement. Her father had looked up from the newspaper, nodded. Her brother argued with her all the way up to yesterday, saying, "Dani, don't do that; find another career. You're always so impetuous."

"Impetuous," she thought, waiting on a busy street corner. "The bus is here." She told her father, zipping her jacket.

He handed her the bus schedule. "If traffic's good, you'll be there in an hour. Are you sure you don't want me to drive you there?" He shoved her suitcase into a compartment on the side of the bus, then turned and embraced her.

"No, I have to start doing things for myself." She smiled but the corners of her mouth deceived her and quivered, but she was determined not to cry."Take care of Robby. I love you, Daddy."

She felt him release her and then watched him head down Fifth Avenue, with the wind behind him kicking up litter, and steam puffing from street vents. He stopped walking and spun around to blow her a kiss.

Instantly her throat knotted and tears sprang to her eyes. She wanted her brother to come walking along to say goodbye but there was no sight of him. He had said nothing at breakfast, and he'd left in a huff. That was how they ended their eighteen-year relationship.

The second she stepped into the bus and found a seat, she dozed off.

* * *

It was only when the ride came to a stop that she knew she had arrived at her destination in Hyattown-about an hour from the heart of Toledo. Looking up at the knoll where a huge, stately, red brick building sat surrounded by cast iron fencing, she wondered if she had made the right decision. Red and yellow leaves danced onto the circular tree-lined drive and over a dark, domed entrance made of solid grooved double doors with curved handles. Hurricane lamps—originating in the 1900's and looking, like she had seen on the old T.V. classics— shone eerily on each side of the doors.

She took a deep breath and started up the sidewalk. What if they end up not liking me? She lugged her suitcase. What if I don't like them; that would make my brother right. What if I'm just not cut out for this? She considered turning around and getting on a bus to home. No, I've been wanting this since I was a kid and I'm going to do it.

She remembered the second she had said "Yes!" to her life's dream. She had gone to career day in her high school gym where students hustled about, chatting with career experts. At one booth, Dani had talked for forty-five minutes with a woman—with short hair, and wearing dressy slacks and a white blouse. The woman reinforced that dream.

And now Dani stood eyeing the menacing-looking brick building that was to be her home. She ran a hand through her long hair, and rang the bell.

The heavy steel doors creaked open; an old woman dressed in black and white stood before her.

Dani felt her heart rip off its stem to bang around inside her chest. The lady at the booth lied to me! She had said things had changed, and that now they were "modern." Dani felt her body shake like a strummed bow.

She dropped her suitcase and sprinted down the driveway, her hair blowing behind her. Darting into a phone booth, her hand shaking as she dialed the number and listened to the rings on the other end, she cried into the mouthpiece, "Robby, come get me!"

Seconds later, she ambled the back streets of Hyattown, sat under a lemon-colored leafed oak tree and composed herself. After she returned to the brick structure and gathered her suitcase, she plopped down on a bench near the brick building's doorway to wait for her brother.

Oh boy, what if I change my mind again and decide to stay? I really wanted this. I'm so confused! No, they lied to me on career day; I can't stay here.

A door shut, footsteps sounded, and then: "I see you're back."

Dani looked, recognized the woman dressed in slacks and a sweater similar the one she had met on career day. "You lied to me. Nothing's changed. You live in old place just like back in the Dark Ages and the women wear-"

"I didn't lie to you; it's the younger women like me who are more modern. Some of the older ones wear them because they feel more secure in them." The woman sat next to Dani. "As I promised, we are sending you to college to become a nurse and you can work anywhere in our province. I didn't lie to you. But you judged us based on an old brick building with an elderly woman answering the door. For your information, inside our building is a very modern home, with brass and glass and wide airy rooms and long windows off the back. And the women living here are marvelous."

Dani stared at the barren trees.

"I guess I didn't give you a chance. I judged you by the old bricks of the building."

"Like the cover of a book."

Dani was thoughtful before asking, "Could you introduce me to the director so I could apologize?"

"You're looking at her," the woman grinned.

Just then Robby drove up. He walked over to the bench as autumn leaves swooped down around him.

Gathering courage, Dani rose. "I'm staying, Robby. But I wanted you here to do this." She hugged him hard. At first she felt no response but when his big arms went around her, she squeezed him tighter.

He stepped back. "Are you sure?" He hugged her again. "I'll miss you but will always be there for you."

"I'm sure. I used to talk to Mommy about it."

"So what will you call yourself?"

"Sister Roberta, after you."

"Be happy." He climbed behind the Buick's wheel. Suddenly he called out the open window, "I love you, little Sister," and he drove off.

Dani studied her shoes. "Why do I have to be such a big baby?"

"You'll make a good nun and nurse," said Sister Benedict. "You're sensitive and compassionate." She patted Dani's hand. "You have a roomful of Sisters waiting at the front door, ready for you to join us."

Dani smiled. "And so am I."

HEART BLOCK

I knew I was going to die that day, five years ago. And at that moment nothing else was as important as my hanging on until help came. It hit me then that my life at age thirty-six was over.

* * *

For the last fifteen years, the most important thing to me, as a college English professor, was becoming a "blockbuster author"—one of those writers whose work turned to gold the second they touched paper. I could just envision myself moving through throngs at autograph-signing parties; chatting with my doting agent; writing my signature on a $5 mollion dollar book contract. This is what I had always wanted and didn't think anything else mattered in life. But, boy, was I ever in for a shock! I suddenly had gotten sick.

* * *

The doctor had said it was double pneumonia and threw me into the hospital. I had been in for over nine days when the wheezing and breathlessness got worse, making it difficult to ambulate when not sleeping or out cold from medications. What bothered me the most—a cardinal sign of the disaster that was about to happen—was having to call nurses to get off the toilet. I just didn't have the energy or bodily power to lift myself. It was not only embarrassing but frightening as well.

Getting out of bed and struggling to the shower was akin to climbing Mt. Everest. I was so sick that I begged to be covered with blankets from head to toe, and left to fade away. And thinking about all the work I had to do, how behind I was in my assignments, how my students were being taught by a substitute, and how helpless my family was with me in the hospital, made me feel worse. I was too preoccupied with these worries to turn to God.

"I can't even get off the toilet without the nurses' help," I repeatedly told each physician who examined me, from cardiologists, lung specialists, infectious disease doctors, to nephrologists, dieticians, and my family intern.

"It's because you have pneumonia and an irregular heartbeat," they answered.

I had had rheumatic fever several times which left me with a bum ticker and weak kidneys.

"But this has never happened before," I protested.

They'd pat my shoulder, nod their heads, and go off to see other patients.

* * *

Around two in the morning, I woke restless. I dragged myself out of the hospital bed and shuffled into the bathroom, holding on to furniture along the way. I was so exhausted that I couldn't wait to get back into bed.

I had managed to get myself off the commode, wash my hands at the sink, turn and shuffle back out of the bathroom. Actually, I started feeling better about my health since I didn't need to call a nurse to help me that time.

But then half-way across the room, I felt as if I had smacked into a brick wall. I gasped as though suffocating, struggling for deep breaths full of oxygen. No matter how much air I gulped, none of it seemed to enter my body. Somewhere in the back of my mind, I understood that my lungs and heart had stopped working right. I fell across the bed, panting, and, with the grace of God, managed to grope for and hit the nurses' button.

From there, I can't say for sure what happened because I sank into unconsciousness. The only time I woke was when a bevy of nurses stood around my bed, shaking their heads. I heard one say, "Pulse and BP are too weak; can't get a reading." Minutes later, I felt myself being laid on a gurney, whisked out of my room, and rushed through the halls to CCU where a nurse screamed, "Move it! Rate's only eighteen beats. She's in complete heart block!"

I didn't know a lot about medicine but I knew I was dying. My heart was shutting down, and with it—one by one—all my organs. This was a state that, unless handled with a high-degree of expertise and blessed with a huge miracle, always ended in rapid death. I sensed medical personnel hustling about me, attaching this and that machine to my chest.

The next time my eyes opened was hours later. I took in, with much surprise and confusion, my husband and daughters, mother and uncle, standing around my bed, crying. "They called us at three a.m. and told us to get here right away, that you wouldn't make it until morning," my mother wailed.

My husband and pre-teen boys cried, "We love you. Please fight."

A nurse hurried into my room, ushered out my family, and went to my I.V. while saying, "You came this close to dying," and she pressed her forefinger against her thumb, leaving a slit between.

It was many hours later before I could utter anything coherent, and then several days before I was moved to a step-down unit, and then finally back into a regular hospital room. Nearly two weeks more passed before I was discharged.

* * *

A month later—with a permanent pacemaker implanted—I was home and walking from one room of our house to the next when realization clobbered me like an electrical shock. I had almost died! Died! At my age...gone from this earth, never again to see my mother, brother, husband, children, aunt; never again to smell the sweetness of lilacs in Spring, hear a catchy tune, lunch with friends, watch lightning zig-zag through the sky, work on writing another book, laugh at my girls gleefully opening Christmas gifts, or touch my husband's face.

When my eyes closed in the hospital as my heart slowed to nothing, my end should have been then—an existence having gone to blackness in an instant. Later, "they" would have said wonderful things about me, mourned over how young I was, how sad for it to have happened.

None of it would have changed the fact that while my family would have gone on, I wouldn't have.

The thought struck me so hard that at that moment, right where I stood, I leaned against the wall, cast my eyes heavenward, and whimpered, "Oh, Lord, thank you! Thank you, Father, for holding my hand through this, for breathing life into me, for finding me worthy of going on. However you want me to serve you, I will. I owe you big time. I shouldn't be here right now."

I stood in that position for long minutes, thinking how it could have been, how I could have not found the nurses' button, how the CCU staff could have not done all the right things, how I could have fallen into the abyss of darkness and not have been standing there, a month later, holding on to that wall. Wow! So close. I wanted to find God, jump into His arms, and kiss Him.

* * *

Things haven't gotten any easier since then. The pacemaker has given me trouble, I picked up a heart infection, my cardiac stamina has greatly decreased, and no longer can I teach. But, hey, I'm alive, and I thank God for that. I might not be able to race my kids to the end of the block, shop with them for any length of time, attend all their school functions, but I can watch them dress up for the prom, receive awards on "Honors Day," feel their soft wet lips against my cheek, hear them giggle over a funny show, or smell their freshly shampooed hair. And I still have the presence of mind to write in spite of not becoming a blockbuster author; the Lord allowed me to keep that gift.

For these things, I will be eternally grateful.

Part Four:
Summer

> *That beautiful season the summer! Filled was the air with a dreamy and magical light; and the landscape Lay as if new created in all the freshness of childhood.*
> *— Henry Wadsworth Longfellow*

CHITTER, CHATTER, BANG, BANG

I really like margaritas but I drink martinis because they're more manly.

The lady before me in her calf-length sequined dress is still babbling about artists to this denim clad, bearded fellow whom I'm sure is a painter. I couldn't care about painting; I'm not an artsy type fellow.

Anyway, this broad's saying, "Renoir was by far the most accomplished." Her lips part and she asks, "Wouldn't you agree, Clay? You're the expert." She runs a long finger around the inside rim of her glass.

Both are standing in my circle but neither is looking at me. I drain my drink and look around for the roving waiter.

This guy Clay looks at her from creased eyebrows, sips a concoction reminding me of Maalox, and says, "That depends on what criteria are used in the comparison."

Sounds like BS to me.

Clay asks in a pitch louder so I'll hear him over the clink of glasses and outbreaks of laughter, "What'd you say your name was again?"

Events like this are so noisy and superficial that you don't really get to know anyone. This is a fundraiser for a hot-shot who is shooting for the senate; we are waiting for this politician. I'm hoping I'll find out quick enough who this secret guest is; I hate surprises. But I especially hate politicians; I used to be married to one. I'm only here because I like Gloria's style and looks; she's the hostess and I think down the road a short piece, I can make it with her.

GIANNI DeVINCENTI HAYES

"Les Barnard," I answer the artist, chewing my ice and spitting the big chunks back into the glass. The prim woman rolls her eyes when I do that.

"What do you do?" Clay asks almost nonchalantly.

"You mean how much money do I make?" He looks taken aback, but he deserves that. "I'm a real estate broker."

"Oh," they both say on cue.

"I own several offices and have 200 or so agents working for me."

"My oh my," says the woman, now impressed. I'm enjoying the change in her behavior. She doesn't know how I bled my guts to get where I am today. I light a cigarette. Our circle widens to admit a redhead and a fancy-suited gentleman. Suddenly I have the floor as I offer property investment tips. I'm enjoying the attention. Before, my politician spouse always gobbled up the limelight for both of us.

My investment secrets spark a bevy of flying comments on whether property will appreciate as fast as CD's or mutual funds or gold, which is actually performing better than anything. Everyone's out-talking and out-drinking each other. I laugh at them...people are such animals at cocktail parties.

"Hey, Les," greets Gloria, running her hand across my chest, fondling my starched collar, my dark tie; teasingly she slides her hand inside my belt. "Can I get you a refill? Lots of people here want to meet you. They've heard about that 400-apartment village complex you're developing. It will make you a rich man."

"I'm already rich."

"Everyone knows that too." Her hand is back at my chest, gliding over my shirt. "I love the way you're built."

In a husky voice, I say, "And I would love to see your personal real estate."

She giggles, escalates her flirting with me.

Alcohol has a way of loosening inhibitions; rumor has it that Gloria hasn't been to bed with a man since she lost both breasts to cancer. But I still think she's beautiful and want her warmth lying next to me.

"Really, Les. You're so fine."

I smile. My trip abroad was worth it.

236

"Oh, and you just returned from overseas, didn't you?"

"I did, and maybe next time you'll go with me. Europe has lots of good deals." I egg her on.

"Well then, deal me in."

"He's here! He's here!" The chorus of shouts grows louder as guests break into applause and scramble after him. My hostess squeezes my arm, looks in the direction of the doorway where this messiah is apparently standing. "Our honored guest has arrived. I've got to go, Les."

Try as I might I can't get a glimpse of this wunderkind. I crane my neck. Hordes of people are around him. His voice is booming, just like a politician.

He soft-shoes into my periphery. I freeze. Holy shit! Ohmigod! I spin around, shaking my head. Can't be him!

It is him. I can tell. I may have been abroad for awhile, but this guy hasn't changed any. It's impossible for me to hate anyone as much as I hate him.

Nauseous, I stagger over to the bar. "Double martini," I tell the red-vested bartender. "No. Triple." He looks at me with lifted brows.

Sensing movement next to me, I turn. It's the hostess and the guest. "Keegan, I want you to meet Les Barnard. Les, this is Keegan Maxwell, our guest of honor."

He eyes me quizzically but sticks out his hand.

I chug my drink, chew my ice.

Burned, he pulls back his hand and shrugs at the hostess. "Man doesn't shake hands, or what?"

"Man doesn't shake Keegan Maxwell's hand," I say a bit too loud. "Another triple." I see the hostess wince. "Gloria," my voice is raspy as I talk to her yet remain focused on the bartender, "if you had told me this bastard was going to be here for this fundraiser—even worse, the guest of honor—I'd have stayed home."

"Hey, buddy, what do you have against me?"

He's trying to come off like he's the good guy and I'm the lunatic. I can only hope he doesn't remember me, because if he does, I've got to expose him...and me too.

"Forget it." I wave him off. It's best if I set my newly filled drink on the bar, bid my lovely hostess a goodnight, and get my ass out of here.

He's staring at me. Studying my eyes. "You look familiar. Have we met?"

I ignore him

"Too much to drink, ol' boy?"

I hate when he needles me. I hate it. "Forget it," I offer again. "Look, fellow, you started in on me when I walked in to this room, and now you want me to forget it. I think you ought to apologize in front of my 'constituents' here." He chuckles a politician's chuckle. Slaps me on the back. A crowd has gathered.

I turn around and look him right in the eye. "I'll never apologize to you."

The crowd gawks. Mutters.

Shut up, Les. But I can't help myself.

"Hey, Barnard! You got a problem?" He's scrutinizing me now.

"Gentlemen. Please." Gloria is in between the two of us.

Maxwell's gently shoving her aside. His dark eyes inspect me. "Barnard, I know you from somewhere." Grabbing his silk handkerchief from his three-piece suit pocket, he wipes his brow. A nervous habit he always had. "Well. Speak your piece. You've got something to say to me, say it now!"

Making decisions on several martinis, in a stuffy room full of stuffy people, and with an abhorrence so thick it clogs up the brain, is not a healthy thing to do. But I owe this creep. I could ruin him now.

"Oh, nothing to say, Barnard? Hot air, are you? How dare you treat me like this? Do you know who I am? I bust my rear from morning till night working for my voters, helping to make this a better country!"

"Yeahs" resound in the room.

I stand, light a cigarette, walk over to him, and blow smoke into his face. He reddens. The multitude hisses at me. "I can tell your constituents who you really are," I goad him.

I like how the room gets very quiet, subdued, wanting to catch my every word.

"Barnard, I know you, don't I? Something about you. Can't put my finger on it. Did I do a number on you somewhere? And now you're getting back at me? Did you get jerked around?

Play hardball and lose? C'mon, Barnard. That's the name of the game in politics."

"None of those, Maxwell." I am amazed at how calm I am. Forever I have waited for this minute, and now that it's here, I'm not even trembling. Yet my heart's speeding as fast as a gerbil on his toy wheel. "Remember 1972? You worked hard at campaigning and brought in a lot of money? Only you reported less than half of your campaign funds."

Maxwell catches his breath. "You're a liar!"

The crowd murmurs.

"You told the blacks you were on their side, but then behind closed doors you said -"

"Stop it!" He turns to our hostess. "Gloria, get him the hell out of here." Under his breath I hear him say, "The man's going to ruin me." He spins back around to me. "Lies. How would you know such things?"

"And your children, Keegan. Remember them? How you abused them. Demeaned them. Told your daughter she had no friends because she wasn't pretty; told your son that he had no talent for sports or hobbies. Neglected your children. And your wife. It was always more important to you to ingratiate yourself to the press, to forget your obligation to your family who sacrificed so much for you. How many times did your son ask you to go fishing? To a baseball game? Father-son banquet? And each time you shooed him away, saying, 'Not now, Tommy. I have more important things to do.' And the poor ten-year old would turn on his heels, wipe tears from his eyes, and walk away."

"This is preposterous!"

On a roll, I push on. "Your wife was talented, and in love with you, but you treated her no better than a whore. Kicked her around, demanded she serve you. And you tore her apart, called her ugly, useless, that she was homelier than a man. That she should have been a man!"

He flinches, steps back, blinking in surprise, then takes in the growing crowds. "This man's a liar. There's no way he'd know those things about my family."

I ignore him pointing at me. "You never allowed your daughter to have friends in the house because they interfered with your day, never let her dress the way other kids did because she had to uphold your image. You never let her live like a normal kid, until at seventeen, she had a nervous breakdown. Still in an institution, isn't she, or don't you care enough to look into her well-being?"

He moans; the room whispers with oh's and grumbling.

Feeling good inside myself, on a high from the martinis, floating with the joy of revenge, I challenge him, "Are you still mentally sick? And what about all those one-night stands in every city you campaigned in? How do you think your wife felt?"

He goes to take a swing at me but quickly others restrain him. I'm almost done with him. One more thing his "constituents" ought to know before they vote him into high office. "I'll never forget the day you told your wife how you felt about your son's death. Remember that? You had been driving drunk, hit a telephone pole. He died immediately. Days later you were released from the hospital, after your staff fixed the police report. Instead of consoling your mourning wife, you shut off your bedroom light, leaned back on your bed, and said, 'I feel bad about the kid, but at least now he won't be bothering me about doing this and doing that.'"

The crowd gasps. Maxwell drops his head. I'm done with him now. I return to the bar, motion to the barman to refill my glass, and I light another cigarette.

"You're not going to get away with this, Barnard. Making all these stories up. Slandering me. You yourself said these things happened behind 'closed doors.' There'd be no way you would know anything about me; you're fabricating all this to make me look bad. Who are you—someone from my opposition's camp?"

A hush forms over the large group encircling us. He thinks he has discredited me. I take a drag on my Marlboro and say, "I just know."

The crowd snickers.

I guess I'm going to have to tell my secret in order to damage him. I can't allow him to become the victor once more.

He's laughing with them. "See, gang? What'd I tell you? This man's a fraud."

They're nodding in agreement.

I have to tell them, or he might actually win the election. If any powerful bloc of people can put him in high office it's this group here tonight. Likewise, if any bloc can squash him smoothly and quickly, it is also this group.

I stomp out my cigarette and turn to him, interrupting his back-slapping, his chuckling, "Maxwell, you don't remember me, do you?" A silence falls; once more I've got their attention. "You should. I went to bed with you."

Loud gasps and squeals, hands up to their mouths in total shock.

Keegan Maxwell's face is the color of Elmer's Glue.

"Never! Never have I gone to bed with...a man!"

This time I laugh. "Only because the gays are far too good for you." His jaw tightens like a winch. "Your wife...her name was Leslie Barnes...she certainly could testify as to the veracity of my accounts, couldn't she?"

Out of the corner of my eye, I can see the crowd nodding their heads yes to my question. "Then let me explain that I, Les Barnard, was Leslie Barnes. When I left you after years of torment and ridicule, I did what you said I should do...become a man. The Swedes have the operation perfected, don't you think, Keegan?"

He's blubbering, his eyes glazing over. I'm the one chuckling now.

Someone is leading him to the doorway. He looks profoundly weak. Within minutes the room is emptied. Emptied so quietly that its process should be entered into a Guiness World Record.

Only Gloria the Hostess and I are left. She's standing at the end of the bar, watching me, her hands on her hips. I think she's trying to discern through my clothes any flaws in my surgery.

"Another martini," I tell the shocked bartender.

He isn't moving. Instead he looks over at Gloria for some kind of sign.

I flip him a quarter, wink at Gloria, and say while departing, "Never mind. I always did like margaritas better."

FLYER TYLER

From the shiny gym floor, Tyler saw Mr. Jenkins leaving the bleachers as the fog horn sounded to signal the end of the game. With him was that couple again. Mr. Jenkins waved him over. Sweaty and panting, Tyler stood with them at the sidelines. "You remember Mr. and Mrs. Gale. They've taken quite an interest in you."

A thrill rushed through Tyler. He shook their hands, then looked at the hardwood floor while listening to the hum of the spectators chatting as they met up with their sons, congratulated other fathers and mothers, hushed little brothers and sisters who ran out on the gym floor. He looked up when he heard Mr. Gale talk to him.

"That was some game you played, son. You really fly down the court! You're going to go far in this sport. Have any big plans?"

Tyler grinned, his cheeks sinking in where dimples formed. He pushed his short, straight falling lemon-colored hair off his face. "I'm only gonna be a sophomore now but next year I plan on applying to colleges."

"You'll get sports scholarship offers, for sure. They'll call you Flyer Tyler because you're so fast." Mr. Gale slapped him on the back.

"Scholarship...oh how nice," Mrs. Gale cooed, and immediately Tyler could tell she knew nothing about sports.

"Nebraska has a great program", said the man. "I always wanted an athletic son."

Tyler looked at him. Maybe they were serious. At last he would get out of the hell-hole he lived in. "I...I've got to go.

My ride back to the orphanage will be waiting and I have to hit the shower and change."

"The Gales want to spend the day with you tomorrow," advised Mr. Jenkins, the orphanage director who brought the couple to the school.

"Sure." He seldom had any plans on Saturdays. "Good seeing you again." He shook their hands yet another time and then dashed across the court into the locker room. The smile remained stuck on his face even when he climbed into the bunk that night.

* * *

He donned his best blue jeans—nothing expensive or designer-made, since the orphanage didn't allow for them— and a Yale sweatshirt that one of the other orphans had given to him in exchange for a basketball the Coach had honored him with. He washed his face twice that morning in the common bathroom of the boys' dorm, making sure no ugly zits raised red flags, and he dabbed some cologne on just to smell sweet for Mrs. Gale, who might become his mother. With the few moments he had before they were due to arrive, he pulled out his notebook hidden between his mattresses and began to write:

> *Cathedral High came down hard on us. Being*
> *tall and slender, I got the jump ball and tapped it*
> *over to McConley who dribbled it to Robarts*
> *where a screen was set up. I went in, laid-up, and*
> *plop, down it dropped, and we were up by two.*
> *Dirkson rebounded, beat out Cathedral to mid-*
> *court, tossed to me, and I pivoted, wound up,*
> *dashed off in a fast break, and galloped down*
> *court, pitched it at the net, and whoossh, in it*
> *went. Today the Gales stopped by again. I like*
> *them but they want a son's who an athlete. I want*
> *to be an engineer and not play sports in college.*
> *Mr. Gale thinks I'll get a college scholarship but I*
> *only play for fun, not for competitions. They*
> *probably want a different kid.*

He quit writing when he heard Mr. Jenkins call him to announce the Gales.

Tyler stooped as he climbed into the back of their BMW where he sat next to the window and said very little, though he politely answered all their questions. He wished he could get over his shyness, become more out-going, like a lot of the other kids who managed to get adopted. But he wasn't like that, and so he ended up being one of the oldest kids still residing in the home. In another three years, he'd be eighteen and then could leave of his own accord. But he so badly wanted to be part of a family, even if he was fifteen. He worried though what the motive was for the Gales' interest in him. Most couples wanted babies...not teenagers.

"So, let's talk basketball, Tyler," Mr. Gale veered into Minneapolis's huge zoo. He shut the car engine off. "Eric, our son, played basketball, too...was all set to go to Nebraska...when the accident happened."

Mrs. Gale turned her head away and looked out the car window. Tyler went mute, fearful of saying something that might upset her even more.

"I told him a hundred times not to get into a car with a drunk driver." And his words faded. Suddenly, he turned and looked at Tyler. "You don't drink, do you?"

"No sir."

"Good boy."

The zoo displayed some of the most exotic animals Tyler ever saw. They took their time going from one cage to the next, all the while Mr. Gale giving some background on each animal while Mrs. Gale clucked over the baby polar bears, little chimps, and cheetah cubs. She asked Tyler about school, what his favorite subjects were, what he hoped to major in, in college, if he had a girlfriend, and all kinds of questions that he didn't mind answering. *At least she doesn't get on me about sports.*

At lunch in the new Minneapolis mall the size of the sun, Tyler ordered a bacon cheeseburger, double fries, and a vanilla shake. After he wolfed it all down, he noticed Mrs. Gale was still daintily cutting her lettuce. *Gosh!* He hoped he hadn't blown his chance with them by eating like a slob. He sat quietly while they finished eating, trying to tune into Mr. Gale who was again rambling about basketball.

At the movie, he laughed all the way through *Sister Act*, and then when he looked at Mrs. Gale, he laughed even harder because she kept wiping tears from her eyes. Mr. Gale howled at the plot when he wasn't up getting Tyler a colossal bag of buttered popcorn, a jumbo Coke, and a candy bar the size of a briefcase. He just wanted the man to sit still and enjoy the movie.

The night was topped off with dinner at a seafood restaurant. Having never eaten Lobster before, he closely watched the Gales, copying their every move, setting his napkin on his lap, removing his elbows from the table, and picking up the proper fork to dissemble the lobster's shell.

Neither mentioned adopting him and he didn't say anything either, but he kept hoping they would, even if it meant listening all day to Mr. Gale's plans for Tyler's future as a professional ballplayer.

When they returned him to the orphanage, he thanked them and went back to his room where he again wrote in his journal. His last line read, "Well, I think I could be happy with them, but I sure hope I don't disappoint Mr. Gale; I don't think he'd want me as his son if I couldn't play sports on a scholarship."

* * *

For the next two months, the Gales saw Tyler nearly every day, seeing the sights in the city, having him over for dinner, going on short jaunts. What Tyler liked best was Mrs. Gale's homemade lasagna, and her prime rib roast with scalloped potatoes. The nights he went to their house, they played Trivial Pursuit, Monopoly, shot pool in their finished basement, or took walks, rode bikes, or played some lame video games, and just watched television, allowing him to pick the shows, something he seldom got the chance to do at the orphanage

On Saturdays, Mr. Gale took him to see some type of ballgame. When he managed to get tickets, he picked Tyler up at the orphanage on Sundays to see a national football game, hockey event, or any other sport that was going on within driving long distances; and those that were, they watched on

T.V.. He even made a point of scrutinizing Tyler at his practices for basketball, football, soccer, or whatever was going on. And afterward, when he was back in his dorm room at night, when all the other boys were sleeping, Tyler made sure he recorded everything in his journal.

On Friday night of the third month of seeing the Gales, Tyler—as directed by them—put on his best slacks, white shirt, tie, and navy blue blazer. He figured he was going to church; instead, he was to meet the rest of the Gale family.

As soon as he and the Gales walked into the fancy restaurant, twenty-some other people crowded around him, introducing themselves: Aunts, cousins, grandparents, uncles, close friends. Tyler loved being the center of attention.

"Did you enjoy our families?" Mr. Gale asked as he pulled the car into the orphanage's circular driveway.

"For sure." He knew if they took him in, it would be a good life, with Mr. Gale's job as a bank president, and Mrs. Gale owning her own interior design business where she worked only the hours she wanted. In time, he might even allow himself to come to love these people as his mother and father.

"Good," Mrs. Gale said, smiling.

* * *

The next morning, around 10:00 a.m., Tyler was called into Mr. Jenkin's office where he saw the Gales were sitting, grinning.

"Sit down, Tyler," Jenkins began. "Mr. and Mrs. Gale want to talk to you."

They asked him questions about his goals, if he liked living in Minneapolis, whether he had any memories of his very early childhood and his real parents, and on and on. Then Mrs. Gale said, "I'm sure you know that we can't have children of our own now, so you wouldn't have any brothers or sisters to play with, but still we'd like you to come live with us, Tyler.

He remained unmoving, understanding this was a trial basis even though the actual words were never said. But Tyler remembered what happened with some of the other kids in the orphanage who were to be adopted. After a few months of living with their new families, they were sent back to the home because of "incompatibility," so Tyler refused to get his hopes up.

"Go pack your stuff, Ty." Mr. Jenkins added, "Mr. and Mrs. Gale need to sign the necessary papers."

"All of it?" he asked hopefully.

"If need be, we can always come back later to get what you left behind," Mr. Gale winked.

Tyler's worst fears were confirmed: This was meant to be only a trial period.

"I always wanted a son who played sports." Mr. Gale patted Tyler's shoulder.

* * *

The first month flew by even though it took some adjusting on Tyler's part: Eating with a napkin in his lap, detailing his daily activities at the dinner table, meeting new kids at the private high school, attending formal affairs, and doing chores. But there were the awesome benefits, too: Earning weekly chore money—more money than he imagined possible for taking out the garbage, carrying groceries into the house for Mrs. Gale, helping Mister paint or seed the lawn or trim the hedges; Tyler knew Mr. Gale piddled around in the yard only because he liked it, as he had a regular lawn crew and landscaper. But the greatest perk, Tyler thought, was belonging to someone...to a family. He could handle living like this, but what he couldn't handle was calling them "Mom" and "Dad," even though he knew how much it meant to them.

By the second month, he started feeling as though they were his real parents. He easily grew accustomed to the large bedroom Mrs. Gale had designed for him, with various college pennants hanging from the ceiling, and colorful racing stripes brushed across the walls. He gave it his own finishing touches by setting his bats in the corner, his mitt on the desk, basketballs under and on the bed, model airplanes and cars on the floor and on his headboard. On his dresser lay paints and screwdrivers, pieces of paper with notes on them, rabbit's fur keychain, something from an Erector set, ticket stubs from baseball games.

It pleased Tyler that Mr. Gale never missed one of his games, no matter how busy he was. And usually on the ride home, he'd say, "Tyler, son, have you given any thought to the college you want to attend? Now's the time to start thinking about sports scholarships. You're so good; you could even become another Michael Jordan of national fame."

"Aw, Gee. I just play the game 'cause I like it, Mr. Gale."

"Dad, call me Dad."

But Tyler couldn't...at least not until he was sure they really wanted to be his parents because they loved him, not because they wanted a famous son...someone to replace the one they lost.

"My boy would have made the Bullets or the 49'ers, for sure."

Sure, sure, Tyler thought, feeling used and nothing more than a substitute son.

That night, in his journal, Tyler wrote:

I really like and care about Mr. and Mrs. Gale, but they don't really care about me. Mr. Gale just wants a son who will become famous and replace his dead one, and Mrs. Gale just wants a son...period. She'll take me because her kid died.

Writing in his journal was the one thing Tyler felt good about, as though he could unleash his inner feelings. Sometimes, though, he just wrote about anything. One time it was on trees, another time on how political sports were, and yet another time, on what he thought was the difference between good and bad.

Over time, Tyler became ensconced into his new life, though he still couldn't call Mr. and Mrs. Gale, Mom and Dad. Yet, they treated him much they would have treated their own son, Tyler was certain about that. And they encouraged him to not forget his friends from the orphanage, who they welcomed into their home, and invited to Tyler's birthday party and swimming in the backyard pool, along with his teammate from his old high school, as well as those from his new private high school. Pop, cake, and ice cream flowed, and men and women dressed in black and white served hot dogs wrapped in dough, and some fancy kinds of appetizer. They shot pool, listened to CD's, danced in the huge finished basement, played video games on the arcade machines the Gales had bought Tyler, and watched a hired magic show.

"This has to be every kid's dream," Tyler told his closest

friend from the orphanage that night, in the homey basement, among the noise, music, clink of ice, and clang of billiard balls. "You got it made, Ty, but remember what happened to Mike: Everything went fine until his parents-to-be learned he was a mild epileptic and returned him to the orphanage."

"That's because those people were ignorant."

"But still, you never know how people think, or why they want to adopt a kid...especially older kids, like us teens."

Tyler narrowed his brows. "Yeah, but nothing like that can happen to me."

* * *

Not more than four days after Tyler's sixteenth birthday, he and the Gales were having breakfast when the doorbell rang. The housekeeper brought the guest into the kitchen.

Mr. Gale rose. "What are you doing here?"

The scraggly-looking man with an unshaven beard, and a light blue shirt with dark blue pants, wet his lips, stared at Tyler.

Mr. Gale moved forward, putting his wife and Tyler behind him.

"Do you have some business with my family here, Mr.—-?"

"Hendy. Mr. Hendy."The man continued staring at Tyler.

Mr. Gale beckoned to the housekeeper to call the police.

"Hendy. My name is Samuel Hendy." He looked at Tyler. "Does that mean anything to you, boy?"

Tyler looked quizzically at Mr. and Mrs. Gale. "No sir."

"'Sir' huh? That's fancy talk for a feller living in a fancy house."

"It's time for you to leave, Mr. Hendy. We have no business with you."

Hendy pointed at Tyler. "He does. 'Member me? Must be hard, living the life style you're living. I'm your father, Sammy."

Complete silence.

Mrs. Gale went to stand in front of Tyler. "His name is Tyler, not Sammy. You have the wrong party." Mrs. Gale's voice was sharp, annoyed.

"Nope. *You* got the wrong party. This boy here is my son and his name is Samuel Hendy, Jr. He was two when they took him away from me." He shuffled his feet. "But, hey, if you want to keep him, I'm reasonable...couple grand, maybe ten. A kid's gotta be worth that, doncha think?"

The tension in the Gales thickened.

They all turned at the whirl of a police siren. The second the police stepped into the room, chaos reigned, with the Gales insisting the police take the stranger away, that they put the schemer, blackmailer, scam artist in jail. The stranger shouted back that they had stolen his son.

* * *

Later that night, the Gales and Tyler sat in the living room, reciting everything that happened at the morning breakfast table, to the so-called father being taken to the station, to the Gales pressing charges of blackmail.

"Don't you worry, Tyler. This is probably some expert con man who goes after families who have adopted kids, falsely claiming that the kid is his and offering settlement through a pay-off. We'll take care of him." Mr. Gale made a steeple with his hands.

"But why would the orphanage give out adoption information?" Mrs. Gale pressed. "And why would that man make up a name?"

Silence.

Then Mrs. Gale softly asked, "Tyler, didn't you say you didn't remember your parents? Your father? The biography on you states that your mother died in childbirth and your father gave you up at age two." Her voice surprisingly but notably trembled.

"No I don't remember him... or anything! The authorities are going to take me away!"

"All right, calm down, son." Mr. Gale paced around the room. "Right now he's in a holding cell but he may be let go because it got down to his words against ours and the housekeeper. His offering pay-off money is only verbal, so we have no real proof."

"Did anybody ever call you 'Sam' or 'Sammy'?" Mrs. Gale persisted.

"No, I said. An older cousin kept me after my dad died and

over time—maybe a year or so—I began being placed in homes of other distant relative or friends, and then I was in and out of foster homes for years, and finally ended up at the orphanage when I was eleven and been there ever since."

"Well, you're home now." Mr. Gale said.

"Am I? It's always something. All those other foster homes either didn't want me or I didn't want them, and when I'd get real close to being taken in by a family—permanently—something would go wrong...like now."

"You are not going anywhere, Tyler. You home is here." Mrs. Gale glanced at her husband. He chimed in with support. She picked up a file folder and re-read it. "Nowhere here does this ever talk about someone named Samuel Hendy. I think the man was trying to scam us." She sighed. "But you're sure no one has ever said you had a father still alive?"

Tyler threw his hands up in the air and stomped up to his bedroom. Lying across his bed, he could hear hollowed whispering downstairs, with Mrs. Gale saying something like, "That man might be able to take Tyler from us." And Mr. Gale worriedly adding, "I'm going to call Jenkins again because if Hendy can prove he's the father, then we have trouble. And why could he not be? Maybe the orphanage or the kid's relatives or the foster homes didn't call him by his correct name and it ended up in all his records as Tyler."

"But...but...we can pay him so we can keep Tyler," she pleaded.

"That's the last thing we should do. One payment leads to another, and then another, each getting larger and costing us more. We will never feel safe if we have to pay to keep a son." Mr. Gale tightened his lips, stared at his crushed wife.

Tyler muffled the pillow around the back of his head. "nonononono," he moaned into the pillow.

* * *

Tyler woke the next morning, after a night of tossing and turning, to voices downstairs. The housekeeper knocked on his door and told him to rise, dress, and go downstairs.

There stood two police officers, Mr. Hendy, and Mr. and Mrs. Gale.

"We made copies of the birth certificate for you," said one officer as he handed the copy to the Gales. "It's a computerized version set by the state capital. Read it. Look at the names: Samuel Hendy, Jr., the date he was born, his parents' names, " the officer pointed at a line, "and the father's name...Mr. Hendy who's standing right here. This kid," he pointed to Tyler, "belongs to Mr. Hendy. Pack your stuff, young man. You're leaving with your father.

Mrs. Gale let loose with a loud sob.

"And just who sent this?" Mr. Gale scrutinized the form.

"I told you, the state capital where birth records are."

"And they sent it by computer, without a seal on it?"

"You can see the seal at the bottom." The officer pushed his cap up with one finger.

"I see an image of a seal, not a real seal. That only comes in the printed copy when the clerk embosses it."

"There was no time for a snail-mailed copy. Look here," started the other policeman, "if you want an original, you can get one which can take months, but until then, the boy goes with his father."

"No no no!" cried Tyler.

Mrs. Gale went to him and put her arm around him, trying to stop her own weeping.

"You said it was sent by computer, but who asked for it?"

"Only Mr. Hendy has the authority to request a copy of his son's birth certificate. Now get that kid to pack his clothes. We all have to get back to protecting the public." The officer looked a bit smug.

"And protecting this young man who we've adopted as our son is a job you should be doing. This certificate if flawed. It means nothing."

"Mr. Gale, we've looked into the boy's records. Mr. Hendy came to us days ago, so when you called us, we already knew he was going to come here to retrieve his child. We had done all the investigation before we let Mr. Hendy come to your home."

"Oh no," Tyler muttered again.

"The orphanage said the adoption papers haven't yet been finalized, so you have no legal recourse."

"We'll let my attorneys make that decision."

"Very well, but we've already made ours, and the boy goes with his legal father."

Silence

Then Mr. Hendy said to the police officers, "Look, do you mind waiting outside a minute? I know how hard this must be for these people."

The officers stood on the veranda, waiting.

Tyler watched Hendy look at Mr. Gale who stood perfectly erect with his arms crossed at his chest—just like a bank president, he thought. Mrs. Gale wiped at her tears. Tyler felt it was hopeless.

"Look," said Hendy softly, almost kindly, "I know you got used to my boy and that you want him, so my offer still stands, but I want $25,000, now that the proof is out. You should have taken my original offer."

"You shaman!" sneered Mr. Gales.

Tyler leaped forward, nearly weeping, "No! No! You will not pay him!"

"Tyler, I didn't say I would."

Tyler looked at Mr. Gale, a questioning, quizzical look on his face. The knife cut deeply into him.

"I want our Tyler. Pay the man," screamed Mrs. Gale at her husband.

Hendy snickered, "He's my son...not yours."

Mr. Gale stood, staring at the man, then he would glance back at the paper handed him, then back at the man, and then at Tyler.

"Make a decision, Mr. Gale, or I walk out with my kid and you'll never see him again."

Mrs. Gale, dropped to a dining table chair, and wept.

Suddenly, Tyler turned and walked out the door, his father behind him.

Mr. Gale went to the window and watched.

* * *

Weeks passed, and every day the Gales were silent, wondering what was happing to Tyler and where he was. Mr. Gale seemed to come home late from work on a regular basis.

Mrs. Gale lived in a deep sullenness, seldom speaking or sitting with Mr. Gale. It seemed like time had stopped, just suspended itself in the air. Another 10 days and the official trial period of the adoption would have been over and Tyler would have legally been hers.

Ten days, she thought.

"Honey," Mr. Gale would say, "don't lose hope; something might break."

"You let him go!"' She would sniffle and yell, "You let our son go! You could have paid and we—"

"It would never end. The father would have constantly harassed us for more money and more money and—"

"Then give it to him! Is your money more important than a son—that son, *our son*? I love him!"

Another week passed and Mrs. Gale entirely stopped going down to the dinner table. She ignored her husband who seemed to be gone, not only during the weekdays, but also at night and weekends, staying out later and later. She despised that her husband didn't fight for their son.

At bedtime one night, she told her husband, "I'm leaving in the morning."

"Leaving! Where? Why?"

"Don't worry about 'where,' and you know 'why.'"

He went up to her, swept her into his arms, and she bawled into his chest, cried so hard that she trembled as his arms tightened around her.

Minutes later, he shuffled her over to the edge of the bed, and held her even longer. Then they sat there in the quiet, darkened room.

Then he whispered, "Don't lose hope, honey. Please. Trust me."

* * *

It was a bleak, rainy Saturday morning when Mr. Gale received his mail. Again, it was there, the damned letter from Samuel Hendy asking for money from him in order to get Tyler back. For weeks, Hendy had written him or called him at work making deals so that Tyler would be returned to him, but Mr. Gale refused. And he refused to tell his wife about the constant harassment—the very kind he wanted to avoid if he had paid the "ransom." Nonetheless, Tyler still was not back with them, but Mr. Gale continued working on it.

The phone's shrill ring woke both Gales from their reverie. Mrs. Gale heard her husband say into the phone, "Where? When?" His voice sounded fearful.

Tyler! He must be hurt or sick or worse! "What is it what is it!" she squealed.

"Get in the car. It was the orphanage, said he's missing."

"What! Why did the orphanage call now? Missing? Is he okay, what—"

"Let's just get there and see."

* * *

Rain gushed in sheets, wind howled menacingly when the Gales pulled into the circular drive of the orphanage. They saw Mr. Jenkins run out to the car, soaked.

"What happened?" Mr. Gale asked.

"He was delivered here but then in an instant, he was gone! The housemothers and others are watching the others kids while some of my staff and I are out here, scouring the area for Tyler."

Mr. Gale jumped out of the car, telling his wife to stay inside.

Not listening, she was out, combing the area with the rest of them, confused over everything. She turned when the police roared in, their siren nearly faded in the torrents and gusts.

It must have been twenty minutes later when they came upon Tyler standing behind a building, trying to scrunch into the bricks so as not to be found or continue to get drenched.

The Gales sprinted over to him, pulled him into their arms.

"C'mon, son, let's get inside."

"Leave me alone! Why would you even care?" Lightning streaked through the sky and thunder cracked so loud that all three jumped. Through tears and rain on his cheeks, he sniffled, "You let me go! You don't love me! You don't even want me! You never wanted me."

Mrs. Gale wiped the tears and downpour from his face with her dress.

"We'll talk inside." Mr. Gale led Tyler with a strong arm back inside the orphanage, where he, his wife, Mr. Jenkins, some of the staff, the police and a stranger stood, water dripping from them.

Tyler screamed, "I told you, leave me alone! All of you!"

Through sobs, Mrs. Gale objected, repeating how much she loved him, trying, in some way, to hold and hug him.

"Sit down, kid," ordered a police officer from another precinct. "Mr. Gale told us about the man coming to your home to take you away unless they paid for you."

Stunned, Mrs. Gale stopped sobbing, pulled back and looked at her husband. She dabbed her eyes with her handkerchief.

The officer continued, "So he took you with him, and the police disappeared, but what happened to you? Did you stay with the man?"

"Disappeared?" Tyler rubbed his eyes to hide his tears.

"Hendy hired them and put them in police uniforms. That man was a fraud."

"He's my father, not 'that man.' But he was awful. He ignored me, even hit me...but he's my father."

"He's not." Mr. Gale wiped his soaked face with his hanky. "Ever since this Hendy guy came to the house, I suspected something was wrong. I had hired investigators"—Mr. Gale pointed to the stranger who led his team of PIs—"who learned where Hendy kept you, and then I got the police involved. It took awhile for us to get this far, but—"

The other officer stepped in. "We had to spend time getting all our ducks in the row to arrest him. We only could do it with the investigators' help and Mr. Gale's persistence. Hendy's in jail, awaiting arraignment for fraud."

"Fraud!" Mrs. Gale and Tyler said simultaneously.

The officer continued, "There's a large band of men and women, all across the country, and maybe even worldwide, who check out orphanages and track kids, learn if they've been adopted, and then go to the adoptive parents' home, and claim they're the biological parents who would 'reluctantly' forego their parenthood for a price. Usually they try to get younger children because the older ones would get out on their own sooner. The Hendy guy—not his real name, and not yours either—and the two men from the gang dressed as police officers been on police blotters everywhere but no one has been able to pin them down until Mr. Gale here. They are a sophisticated group, hacking computers, cracking sealed orphanage and foster home files, creating false birth certificates, passports, driver's licenses, and anything else needed to blackmail parents. Can't even begin to figure out how much money they made. No one wants to give up a kid they picked out."

Tyler glanced at Mrs. Gale.

Mr. Gale jumped in, "When I watched you and Hendy— whatever his name is—and the so-called police leave the house with you, I noticed the car wasn't a cruiser, and the license wasn't a government plate. It took an agonizing week after week after week, but I worked with the police, the investigator and Mr. Jenkins."

"That's right," said Jenkins. "The police dropped you off here, Tyler, until Mr. and Mrs. Gale could be called to get you. We were preparing your papers when you ran away."

"Oh my!" is all Mrs. Gale uttered.

Mr. Gale said to everyone in the room. "If you don't mind, my wife and I would like to be with our son."

They began to file out when the investigator turned around and said, "You know, kid, it's pretty special to be picked by someone who loves you when there are so many others to choose from, and you ought to be damn proud of your new dad for what he did to make sure you got back to him and his wife. I've had colleagues in other states called in on these cases but only Mr. Gale endured day after day. I wish happiness for all of you."

The room went quiet. Mrs. Gale reached for her husband and kissed and hugged him, saying, "Thank you" over and over.

Tyler stared, made no sound, no movement.

"Let's go home, son." Mr. Gale headed for the door. He turned when he realized Tyler hadn't moved. "Tyler?"

Mrs. Gale strode back to him.

"I'm staying here."

"Tyler!"

He looked at Mr. Gale. "You don't really want me." He jumped to his feet, his face red, his lip quivering. "You left me with that man. He was mean, beat me, and seldom gave me something to eat. Every day I thought you were going to rescue me, but you didn't!"

"Tyler," Mr. Gale began softly. "I wanted you badly enough to hire investigators, paying richly for them and every worth every penny of it. I would do it again and again until I went bankrupt, if it meant that I would get you back. You have no idea how hard it was on my wife and me. She wept all the time, blamed me, wouldn't even talk to me. We fought, and all along I was living in my own private hell, wringing my hands, praying the police, FBI, the investigators would find you. I couldn't bear the thought of not having you."

Mrs. Gale gushed, "Tyler, we picked you because we love you. We wanted you to feel that you were home. That's why I did that entire bedroom decorating and thinking, 'What would my new son like?' My husband and I loved you the minute we first met you, and our love only grew for you over time. You make us laugh, you're handsome and thoughtful, sweet and kind, and everything we want in a child. We talked about a future with you, about you—"

Tyler walked away from the Gales calling him.

Mr. Jenkins heard them in the other room and walked over to them.

"What's going on? Did Tyler go up to say good-bye to his friends here?"

Raspy, Mr. Gale said, "He's not coming with us."

Jenkins snapped his heels and stepped up the stairs in seconds.

It wasn't even ten minutes later when Jenkins returned. "He's not talking. He left me to meet his orphanage friends in the rec room." He handed Mr. Gale multiple sheets of paper, as Mrs. Gale, wiping tears, rose to read them.

"Oh no, no." She looked at her husband. "Do something please!"

"I intend to. Mr. Jenkins, can you send Tyler back in here?"

* * *

Tyler sat on an over-sized leather chair, across from the Gales who sat on the sofa.

Mr. Gale said, "You don't want to come live with us as our

son because you think I didn't want to give those crooks money?" Tyler stared.

"You think we want a son who's a basketball player?" Mrs. Gale looked at Tyler's papers in her hand. "You wrote that here." He jumped to his feet. "Who took my diary!" His face turned beet red.

"Calm down, son. Mr. Jenkins gave us these when you walked out on us. We're trying to understand why you don't what us as your parents," Mrs. Gale sniffled.

"I know that Mr. Gale wants a flyer Tyler, a son who flies down the court, making baskets. You two want someone to replace your son, someone w—"

"Tyler!" Mr. Gale stood stiffed-back. "Look at me. Look at me now."

Tyler's eyes locked with Mr. Gale's.

"You cannot ever replace our son. Ever! Get that straight now. And my wife and I would not want you to replace him, to take away his specialness any more than we would want someone to take away yours. And you are special to us."

"I don't want to play sports. And that's what you want."

"Oh no, honey," cried Mrs. Gale.

"We realize that now. I've read it in these papers. You could have told us that anytime. I only talked about sports with you to try to find common ground with you, to show you I am interested in you, that I want you as my son." Mr. Gale gently pushed Tyler onto the sofa. "I can only tell you that you're wrong and that we love you for whom you are."

He buried his head and in hands and whimpered. "I loved you!"

Mrs. gasped. "And we love you. Let's go home, please."

In the thunderstorm, the wind roared high and rain soaked deep.

The Gales stood, waited.

Tyler did not rise.

"Tyler, honey, please," whimpered Mrs. Gale.

Mr. Gale folded his arms across his chest. Waited.

Silence

"If you love us, then why can't you join our family?" Mrs. Gale was dabbing her nose with a Kleenix.

259

Slowly Tyler stood. His voice quivered. "When I ended up living with that man who made me think he was my father, who treated me like I was no more than a bothersome roach, I began to understand even more what love is because you gave me that joy of comparison. You showed me love; he showed me hate; you showed me patience; he showed me intolerance; you showed me integrity; he showed me dishonesty. You showed me an honorable work ethic; he showed me sleazy, shameful manipulations. You showed me how wealth can help and save others; he showed me how money can be used to destroy others. You showed me everything that is right and wonderful, and what a fantastic life I could have with you."

"So?" both Gales chimed

Tyler inhaled deeply, ran his hand through his hair. "But you don't get it. I do love you, both of you." He breathed deeply again. "But I love my friends here at the orphanage, too, many who have experienced in foster homes what I went through living with that Hendy guy. Sure, I could go with you—want to go with you—but I would know in my heart that the people I love here will never know the love and gifts you showered me with. I would be abandoning them after living with most of them for the last five years."

"You can always bring them over to the house, Tyler." Mrs. Gale's voice was weak.

Tyler walked over to her and hugged her. "I know but it won't be the same. I would be living a life of luxury while the kids here would here would live in austerity. The staff is nice here but there is no luxury here, no real love here, no freedoms and privileges...just a day by day existence, waiting to either run away or get adopted."

"And we've offered you the latter; yet you reject us, reject our love, and deny us our happiness." Mr. Gale turned to leave, tugging on his wife's arm.

"Good-bye," Tyler whispered. "I'm sorry."

Mr. Gale walked straight for the door, never looking back. Mrs. Gale halted, turned around, tears in her eyes and watched Tyler mouth:

"I'll visit you."

A Living Death

My hex is that I'm adopted. I don't know my real parents. I was adopted as a child by my current family.

After my adoptive father died, I'd get out of bed to a silent alarm, then shower, dress, and hurry off to catch my ride to Sacred Heart while my adoptive mother slept. When I got back home, there'd be no water boiling for macaroni, no meat frying. I'd find her still sleeping in the same clothes she wore the day before. In two weeks I had lost eight pounds.

Sometimes I'd wake up in the middle of the night to strange noises. I would find my mother standing, facing a wall, her fists—scraped and bleeding—pounding plaster. Other times I would find her roaming the house, smoking, when she had never touched a cigarette before. Twice. she had been standing talking to me, her speech slurred, her eyes at half-mast, when she slid to the floor. A neighbor got her into bed where she slept uninterrupted for days, unaware I lived and breathed inside the same house. I passed time staring out the window at falling snow, waiting for my mother to recover.

Since my dad had always handled our finances, Mom never learned to write a check. I stood over her one day, directed, "On the first line, write the date. Always remember to sign your checks...." My mother was not a willing student.

The incident that eats away inside me even today happened a month after Daddy had died. I had been in class listening to the civics teacher recount Nixon and Agnew's inauguration when, like a thunderclap on a perfectly clear day, chills rocked my body so hard I tried curling into a fetal position at my desk. Must be that flu, I told myself.

Sister Nightingale, as students called her, with her black habit down to the floor and sleeves that hid the tips of her fingers, stood over me in the infirmary angling a long thermometer near my mouth. "You're shaking so hard, Lisa, the thermometer wiggles," I heard her say in my fever-fog. Somewhere beyond the infirmary's concrete walls a buzzer sounded, hundreds of shoes marched on tiled floors, and then the halls went silent again.

Knowing my mother didn't drive, Nightingale had the gym teacher drive me home. In my boiling brain, I insisted she remain in the car, convinced her through my insistence that I was fine and just had a cold. I didn't want her to see my mother staring at some imaginary spot on the wall. When I weakly neared the front door, the gym teacher slowly drove off.

On the front stoop of my brownstone, where I hung on to the storm door steadying myself, my joints glowed hot as a fission reaction. Like crossing a desert, I stumbled from one piece of furniture to the next to get to the kitchen. I felt the fever drying out my eyes, steaming my blood. A cold glass of water imprinted itself on my brain, and it was the only impetus that kept me on my feet. I drank and drank from the largest glass we had.

Where was my mother? It was her place to be with me. Is it because I'm adopted that she doesn't care about me?

When I finally was able to construct two complete consecutive thoughts, I made my way to the stairs. My joints throbbed read as I limped up the carpeted stairs, one step at a time, past my parents' bedroom where my mother had stopped sleeping, past the guest room where she sat on the bed crinkling and smoothing out a piece of tin foil, and into my bedroom. I lay on the bed until the sun had set and then risen again.

Over the next few days, I suffered through a sore throat that felt like someone had punctured my larynx with skewers. I vacillated between freezing and burning up. The joint pain in my heels and ankles travelled to my fingers, wrists, and elbows. Everything ached and my body felt like it would crumble any time like a sand castle.

Not once did my mother get out of bed and search the house for her daughter who had gone to school days before and not been seen since. Even today as I stand in a hospital waiting room, I find it hard to believe she could have done that to me, but then the better part of my ego forgives her, empathizing with her hurt and pain over my father's death.

By the beginning of the second week I managed to get through the day. And on the morning I was well enough to return to school, my mother walked into the kitchen, said, "I've been in my room alone for over a week and you never bothered to see how I was. What kind of a daughter, are you, Lisa Marie!"

"And I had a severe case of the flu! Where were you?"

We stared at one another in a stalemate.

She turned, and with a toss of her head, mumbled, "I'm *your* mother...even if not your biological mother. You're obligated to respect me."

My eyes rolled as she disappeared around the corner. "Obligated?" Since when is a child "obligated" to love a parent who discards the child?

* * *

When the second anniversary of Dad's death rolled around, my mother stood watching me trim our artificial tree. I asked, "Did you take your anti-depressants?"

She smiled, said, "Of course I took them." She finished her cup of freshly made coffee, and laughed as I buried the tree in mounds of garland. I loved the sound of her laughter, like thousands of bubbles popping all at once, and how her eyes danced, and her dimples made her face look young and joyful.

And in the next second she swooned and collapsed in a heap, her body functions shutting down one by one. It was the first of her suicide attempts.

In my senior year of high school, I had been offered an all-paid college scholarship for academic achievement. I had a good roommate...my very wealthy roomie who often didn't understand how we commoners lived. When she'd take me on an expensive shopping spree for her designer clothes, or anything she wanted, I usually heard myself saying to her, "Terri, we poor people of the middle-class don't do that." Then she'd laugh.

While my roommate's family visited her for holidays, birthdays, and special events, my mother thought nothing of allowing months to pass without even a phone call. I made excuses for her. Sometimes, of my own initiative, I returned home to see if that old familiar mother had somehow managed to overtake the demons inside her and transform her to the mother I knew and loved before my father died. Other times I raced home to respond to another of her death attempts, pacing outside the emergency room while they pumped her stomach or sewed up her wrists.

I often found her incomprehensible, drugged, sleeping, smoking, and staring. Probably it was the tenth or thirtieth time I called her doctor, who said, "Look, every time she tries suicide, she goes to the mental health ward, stays awhile, and promises to not do it again, but it happens over and over."

"What do you expect from me? What can *I* do?" He was gruff and annoyed.

"What you can do is stop prescribing narcotics for her!"

"She's so depressed, that if I do that, she'll never function."

"Oh, and you think she's functioning now?" I yelled back.

As usual, he hung up on me.

My scholarship paid for everything school-related but I received no stipend, so I had to work two side jobs to make sure I had money to send home to Mom so that she ate well. I paid a neighbor to go in every day, make sure she bathed, make her meals, and return at night time to put her in bed. The neighbor told me that over the few years she had taken care of my mom when I wasn't home from school—I stayed with her all summer—that she wavered between being lucid and cognitive, even talkative and acute, to being in a fog, rambling, and refusing food.

For three years, I continually pleaded with God to please heal her, or at least let me find my real mother. Now that I think about that, maybe my adoptive mother felt that I had wanted that all along. My adoptive parents never reminded me that I was adopted, and not of their blood. I did ask them questions about my real parents but they had little to no information. I came from some agency that has long been out of business.

What I wanted more than anything was to have Mom back— the mother who shopped with me, lunched with me, watched me play softball, laughed on our family vacations, served as den mother to my Scout and Brownie troops, protected me, supported me, and cooked every meal—beef, chicken, pork, soups, pasta—to perfection, with side dishes galore and extravagant desserts. She used to love cooking for my father and me, and nine out of ten times, the three of us would laugh at something over dinner.

And then my father died in a plane crash. The police came to the door that day to tell us. My mother answered it, listened to them, and then fainted, an officer breaking her fall.

Inside me, I knew my life was forever changed. They never did find all of his body parts. And my mother never did find the will to go on; the will to do for herself what my father had always done for her, or even the will to be my mother again.

Sometimes I screamed at her for being so drugged and falling asleep with a lit cigarette (she never smoked when Dad was alive); other times, I beseeched her to please get help; still other times, I just ignored her. Mainly, I was hurt and pissed off. The resentment festered deep inside of me to the point I didn't want to ever be around her. I knew that as soon as I graduated from college, I would disappear from her life, yet still send money to a care-giver. But her behavior, her giving up, her refusal to try to get through a day, left such a bitter taste in my mouth that I had a knee-jerk reaction to spit her out. How could she do this to me?

* * *

A week before graduation, my roommate's family came down to take her out to dinner. I didn't have the money for a car to go out or even the drive-through at McDonalds, so they always tried to include me in their activities.

The restaurant that night was one of those with fine linen table cloths, fancy silverware, and fancy napkins folded into designs that I didn't know there was any geometric model for. Someone named "concierge" —or maybe he was a maitre'D— floated around, making sure everyone was happy. Our waiter was dressed black-tie style and had a French accent, almost as great of an accent that was placed on the prices.

My roommate and her parents ordered strange sounding appetizers like caviar, pates, risotto, and dishes with names like tenderloin au jus, twice-baked potatoes, tapenade, French rolls, and some vegetables I didn't even know existed.

My roomie went for French onion soup and—something she later spelled for me—Tarte au pistou (a quiche-something, she said) with Chips de Citrouille, which she explained were pumpkin chips, like an upgrade of French fries. Who knew!

My turn came. "Bacon cheeseburger."

The maître'd, our waiter, our table, and those all around us snickered.

"You have had French cuisine?" smiled Terri's mother.

"Oh no, I'm not queasy."

Again, laughter...louder.

* * *

Over desert, I continued listening to their summer plans at their beach house, the Tennessee Walker my roomie rode and owned, the new car the father was going to have custom-ordered, some king of BMW, I think, and the big graduation party Terri's Mom and Pop were having for her.

"You're coming, aren't you, Lisa?" the mother asked me, again with that great smile.

"No ma'am. I have to return home to work."

"But our daughter tells us you were awarded a two-year, all-expense paid scholarship to Brown for your master degree, in conjunction with that big energy corporation...what's the name of it? But surely you want to take a break from work before starting your graduate studies, and my sincere congratulations to you for not only getting into such an Ivy League school, but also for also being awarded an academic scholarship." She sipped her tea. "Our daughter tells us that you're very smart, and you make great decisions, and after you earn your masters, you're going on for your Ph.D."

"Thank you. That corporation you mention gave me a shared endowment between Brown and ISALEC." She looked at me quizzically. I clarified. "ISALEC is the International Solar and Land Energy Corporation."

"I can see why my daughter claims everyone thinks you're very bright."

"Thank you." I repeated, playing with my dessert— something called Mascarpone and Strawberry Trifle, and a crème broulee setting next to it. I learned that it's pronounced like krem, not cream.

The dad cleared his throat, and reading the label on the wine, he held the bottle up to pour, asking me, "Now that you're twenty-one, would you like some de Venoge Cordon Bleu Brut Sélect Champagne?" I had to ask my roommate later on what the name was and how the hell it was spelled.

"No thank you, sir. I don't drink."

"That's because you're still new to alcohol," said Terri who knew I had skipped two grades in elementary school and the other in middle school, so I was the young one.

"That's because I don't want to ever be drunk or drugged out."

The three of them stole quick glances at each other. I'm a private person and I tell no one anything about my life, so only the Lord knew what they were thinking.

The mother smiled at me. "You parents taught you admirable manners."

I stared, recalling how insistent Mom and Dad were about etiquette and manners.

The dad made a toast to my roomie and me. Terri was going to Harvard, so she was no slouch either.

The mom said to my roomie, "Your sister's coming in from Sarah Lawrence this summer, so I thought the three of us would hit Saks, and then Tiffany's for some new jewelry, and finish the late morning with lunch at the Grande Mira Vista. I love all the girl talk we have, and how we end up giggling so loud that people turn and look at us, and—"

"And the girlee secrets we have," squealed Terri.

The father looked uneasy, interjecting, while looking at me, "I bet, Lisa, you and your mother do the same things."

Inhaling, I said, barely audible, "Not anymore, not for a few years."

The mother quickly jumped in: "Oooooh! It would be wonderful to make a foursome with you."

I managed a smile. "Thank you kindly, but I have to work."

"She even worked while in college," said my roommate.

"What kind of work do you do," the mother asked.

"In the summers, during the day, I work at a large Laundromat, and at night I waitress at a dive."

No sounds at all.

Minutes passed when Terri said, "But now that you're going to Brown, you won't have to do that."

"Yes, I do. I need money to send home to my mother."

They all knew my father had died a few years ago, so they didn't pressure me about that, but the mother praised, "What a good daughter you are! Any mother would be proud of you!"

I said nothing. Every mother but my mother would have been proud.

* * *

By the middle of my first semester at Brown University, I felt reinvigorated. I was establishing a reputation of brains and a degree of cuteness (not glamour), as well as wit, which I hadn't used in years. Of late, it's been more cynicism than any wit. Unfortunately, my professors often used me as an example of how to get A's, which alienated some from me.

A T.A. (teaching assistant) for biology would always bump into me when I was at the coffee shop, sipping a mocha while on my laptop, working on an essay dealing with analyses of fracking—I was an "energy engineer" or geek. It seemed miraculous that he knew when I would be there, but after many weeks of "meeting" that way, he told me, "I fell in love with you the moment I saw you talking to one of my students."

"Aw, you're full of it." I laughed. So as we neared the end of the first semester, we had become more than "friends." We started doing everything together, talking a lot about our future after grad school.

Both he and I received a lot of ribbons and awards, and numerous letters from corporations wanting us, paying outrageous salaries, plus sign-on bonuses. We figured the two of us would get through the next three and a half or four years for our doctorate barely bruised or damaged. Our future shone brilliantly.

"Listen," he began in that soft but manly voice, "I want to thank you again for pulling strings for me at ISALEC. Now I'll always be with the woman I love. Nothing will ever stop me from being at your side. When we enter our doctoral studies next year, we'll be together; when we graduate, we'll be together; when we go to work at ISALEC, we'll be together; when we have kids, we'll all be together. Forever I will be at your side; nothing will ever come between us."

I teased, "Just remember, Mr. Biologist—expert on fossil fuel—you'll be working under me."

"And I know you enjoy being under me." He chuckled.

* * *

I was in an international business class when my professor was called to the door. He turned and motioned to me to come forward. I was ordered to the office of my department chair.

"You need to get home ASAP. Your mother is very ill. I'm sure you can find transportation: Bus, subway, even plane...whatever can get you there as soon as possible." He hustled me to the door.

* * *

On the subway, I thought only of my mother and how ill she must have been. I feared she was at death's door; yet, a part of me—shamefully I admit this—kind of hoped for that. After all, never a month went by without my being called home, or my boyfriend pushing me to go home and get my mom settled down so our lives wouldn't always be in a state of confusion, or the doctor telling me she was in the hospital again. Each time I returned home, I went through hell, trying to calm my hysterical mother or fighting to wake her, or yelling at her to quit the drugs and to stop ruining both of their lives.

I often missed classes when I had to stay for days to make sure my mother was lucid—at least for awhile—and that the caregiver would be there to tend to her when discharged. I was physically and emotionally drained from my mother's antics. Financially, I kept her secure though I knew the money I sent her would likely go to drugs, cigarettes and alcohol.

This time would be no different than the others. The medical staff and I would work with her in the psych ward, clean her up, sober her up, and then they would discharge her under my care; during the school year, I was in charge of her by proxy of a hired caregiver. Again, dollars flew out of my fingers while more emotions burned and charred and frazzled, and then it would take a week to get myself back into the school-mind-mode until Mom repeated the scenario.

I looked up as the doctor entered the room, saying, "Sit."

"You're still giving her the narcotics?" I watched his shifty eyes.

"She's on medication for her state of mind."

"You mean the craziness, the heartlessness, the grogginess, the nastiness and spitefulness, the inconsideration and suicidal—"

"I mean," he began with heaviness, "for a complete nervous breakdown and near collapse of several of her vital organs."

I stood unmoving, speechless.

"It's different this time. Between her poor physical condition and erratic mental state, I don't know how much longer she'll make it."

"And we have you to thank for this!"

"Pay attention to your mother instead of accusing me. You may very well lose her."

Stop! I ordered myself, upset for that momentary leap of happiness over my mother being out of my life. Stop it! Don't think like that! But, but, then, I wouldn't be living a life with an albatross around my neck. Stop it! She's your mother!

The doctor rose. "It's up to you."

"What's up to me? Going through the same old crap with her? If you hadn't given her narcotics whenever she wanted them, she wouldn't be the way she is. It's your fault."

"You listen here! Your mother has been emotionally destroyed over your father's death. The pills helped calm her and let her sleep."

"You should have stopped two years ago when I told you that you were addicting her!"

"You just heed me! Your mother may very well die before she gets out of this hospital. They've pumped her stomach, gave her blood for her deeply slit wrists, and her rationale is gone. She has no will to live. She looks aged and deathly ill."

"And that's my fault?"

"You're heartless! I know she's made your life a living hell, but she's always loved you, always told me how proud she was of you, and of how sorry she is over making your life miserable. She's only 48. Someone needs to be with her, help her turn her life around, support her, love her."

"Gawd! Here we go again." I looked the doctor in the eye. "You want me to give up my scholarship, my opportunity for endowment to doctoral studies, a high-paying, long-term job that leads to my being a vice-president, and with a guy I love?"

"Are all those things more important than the one who gave you a life when you were a child? Who raised you? Who stood by you year after year when school was trying, or kids were mean, or when you were sick, or sad, or hurt? Your mother wasn't always like this. What's it been—two, three years since you dad died so young? You are the only one who can bring your mother back around, make her look 48 again, and cause her to laugh and love. It's all your decision." He walked away.

Holy shit! It's always me who has to give things up. But, I mulled over, my boyfriend would be with me. He said he'd never leave my side.

I dialed his cell phone number.

"Hey, babe," he cooed. "I've been trying to reach you for hours."

I explained everything to him. "So she's still in the hospital here and—"

"That old hag has made your life miserable, so why would you want to stay with her. You have a promising future ahead, Lisa, we both do."

"She's not a hag, for Pete's sake! And she's not old either! She is *my* mother."

He was mute.

"It would just mean that we get a later start. We get her back to good health, and then we finish our masters in months, and begin our doctorate. We can always get other jobs if ISALEC doesn't hold our positions for us. I mean, we should be with my mother until she gets better."

"The only thing she'll get better at is drugging."

I froze.

Then I heard his throaty voice, almost harsh sounding. "You don't expect me to give up my masters, doctorate, and a six-figured job just for your nutty old mother, do you?"

I gulped. "You promised we would always be together, side by side. You told me you loved me, that we had a future together."

"Things are different now. A screwball mother is more than anyone wants to deal with. Maybe if she were my mother and loony, I would deal with it, but she's your maniacal mother."

"You're doing it for me, not her, but you should do it for her if you really love me."

"Oh for god's sake! Get real," he huffed, puffed. "Good luck with your hopeless life. I'm taking care of mine." He clicked the phone.

I stood in the waiting room, peering off but not really seeing anything. Go or stay? Go or stay? She's my mother!"

A nurse came up behind me. "Excuse me. You should go see your mother."

She is my mother, always has been since my real mother didn't want me.....

But then there's my future; just snap fingers and it's all gone. I could turn around and walk out of this waiting room, off this ward, out of the hospital and only come back to bury her. My future would remain intact.

But he really isn't, hasn't, and won't be at my side. And my mother always had been.

I turned to the nurse. "Let's go to my mother, help her" loony, screwy and all. But my mother.

LIFE'S ABRUPT END

I knew I was going to die that day, five years ago. And at that moment nothing else was as important as my hanging on until help came. It hit me then, that my life at age thirty-six was over.

* * *

For the last fifteen years, the most important thing to me, as a college professor, was becoming a "blockbuster author" — one of those writers whose work turned to gold the second pen touched paper. I could just envision myself moving through throngs at autograph-signing parties; chatting with my doting agent; writing my signature on a 5-million-dollar book contract. This is what I had always wanted and didn't think anything else mattered in life. But, boy, was I ever in for a shock! I suddenly had gotten sick.

* * *

The doctor had said it was double pneumonia and threw me into the hospital. I had been in for over nine days when the wheezing and breathlessness got worse, making it difficult to ambulate when not sleeping or out cold from medications. What bothered me the most—a cardinal sign of the disaster that was about to happen—was having to call nurses to get off the toilet. I just didn't have the energy or bodily power to lift myself. It was not only embarrassing but frightening as well.

Getting out of bed and struggling to the shower was akin to climbing Mt. Everest. I was so sick that I begged to be covered with blankets from head to toe, and left to fade away. And thinking about all the work I had to do, how behind I was in my assignments, how my students were being taught by a substitute, and how helpless my family was with me in the hospital, made me feel worse. I was too preoccupied with these worries to turn to God.

"I can't even get off the toilet without the nurse's help," I repeatedly told each physician who examined me, from cardiologists, lung specialists, infectious disease doctors, to nephrologists, dieticians, and my family intern.

"It's because you have pneumonia and an irregular heartbeat," they answered.

I had had rheumatic fever several times which left me with a bum ticker and weak kidneys.

"But this has never happened before," I protested.

They'd pat my shoulder, nod their heads, and go off to see other patients.

* * *

Around two in the morning, I woke restless. I dragged myself out of the hospital bed and shuffled into the bathroom, holding on to furniture along the way. I was so exhausted that I couldn't wait to get back into bed.

I had managed to get myself off the commode, wash my hands at the sink, turn and shuffle back out of the bathroom. Actually, I started feeling better about my health since I hadn't needed to call a nurse to help me that time.

But then half-way across the room, I felt as if I had smacked into a brick wall. I gasped as though suffocating, struggling for deep breaths full of oxygen. No matter how much air I gulped, none of it seemed to enter my body. Somewhere in the back of my mind, I understood that my lungs and heart had stopped working right. I fell across the bed, panting, and, with the grace of God, managed to grope for and hit the nurses' button.

From there, I can't say for sure what happened because I sank into unconsciousness.

The only time I woke was when a bevy of nurses stood around my bed, shaking their heads. I heard one say, "Pulse and BP are too weak; can't get a reading."

Minutes later, I felt myself being laid on a gurney, whisked out of my room, and rushed through the halls to CCU where a nurse screamed, "Move it! Rate's only eighteen beats. She's in complete heart block!"

I didn't know a lot about medicine but I knew I was dying. My heart was shutting down, and with it—one by one—all my organs. This was a state that, unless handled with a high-degree of expertise and blessed with a huge miracle, always ended in rapid death. I sensed medical personnel hustling about me, attaching this and that machine to my chest.

The next time my eyes opened was many hours later. I took in, with much surprise and confusion, my husband and daughters, mother and uncle, standing around my bed, crying. "They called us at three a.m. and told us to get here right away, that you weren't going to make it," my mother wailed.

My husband and pre-teen daughters cried, "We love you. Please fight."

A nurse hurried into my room, ushered out my family, and went to my I.V. while saying, "You came this close to dying," and she pressed her forefinger against her thumb, leaving a slit between.

It was much, much later before I could utter anything coherent, and then several days before I was moved to a step-down unit, and then finally back into a regular hospital room. Nearly two weeks more passed before I was discharged.

* * *

A month later—with a permanent pacemaker implanted— I was home and walking from one room of our house to the next when realization clobbered me like an electrical shock. I had almost died! Died! At my age...gone from this earth, never again to see my mother, brother, husband, children,; never again to smell the sweetness of lilacs in Spring, hear a catchy tune, lunch with friends, watch lightning zigzag through the sky, work on writing another book, laugh at my girls gleefully opening Christmas gifts, or touch my husband's face.

When my eyes closed in the hospital as my heart slowed to nothing, my end should have been then—an existence having gone to blackness in an instant. Later, "they" would have said wonderful things about me, mourned over how young I was, how sad for it to have happened.

None of it would have changed the fact that while my family would have gone on, I wouldn't have.

The thought struck me so hard that at that moment, right where I stood, I leaned against the wall, cast my eyes heavenward, and whimpered, "Oh, Lord, thank you! Thank you, Father, for holding my hand through this, for breathing life back into me, for finding me worthy of going on. However you want me to serve you, I will. I owe you big time. I shouldn't be here right now."

I stood in that position for long minutes, thinking how it could have been, how I could have not found the nurses' button, how the CCU staff could have not done all the right things, how I could have fallen into the abyss of darkness and not have been standing there, a month later, holding on to that wall. Wow! So close. I wanted to find God, jump into His arms, and kiss Him.

* * *

Things haven't gotten much easier since then. The pacemaker has given me trouble, I picked up a heart infection, my cardiac stamina has greatly decreased, and no longer can I teach. But, hey, I'm alive, and I thank God for that. I might not be able to bike with my husband anymore, or race my kids to the end of the block, shop with them for any length of time, attend all their school functions, but I can watch them dress up for the prom, receive awards on "Honors Day," feel their soft wet lips against my cheek, hear them giggle over a funny show, or smell their freshly shampooed hair. And I still have the presence of mind to write in spite of not becoming a blockbuster author; the Lord allowed me to keep that gift. For these things, I will be eternally grateful.

So, for me, there isn't a morning that I don't begin it with, "Thank you, Lord, for this day. I give it all up to you."

But, you know, it could happen again tomorrow and maybe I won't be so lucky.

What about you?

276

EPILOGUE

I've written these stories over a period of about thirty years. If you read closely, you will see what I see: how my style has changed, how my writing has matured, how I delved into different topics, particularly more sophisticated ones, than those with which I initially began...and how much I have changed.

Over time, some of my altruistic ideology transformed into a semi-cynical philosophy, as well as a more observational position than a participatory one.

The alteration of my Weltanschauung or world view comes through in each account, even though the book is not arranged by the dates of writing of each story. That no doubt has come through all the same once you finished the book and got to this part.

You may have also noticed that the topics I wrote about over time changed, and a healthy skepticism crept into my writing and my thinking. "Trust," as identified in this Post-Modern world has metamorphosized into disbelieving everything until truth and trust are established.

Much of this has to do with the social media that has affected every author's writing, allowing him or her to be somewhere where they are not, as well as tainting their Weltanschauung via television, radio and all the relatively new high-technology systems: Facebook, Twitter, Linked-In, Ipods, droids, i-Pads, and so many other gadgets and formats.

It is my hope that you have read each story with a tongue-in-cheek attitude, not projecting the story onto my private life, which is the fear of every writer. Authors tend to dribble parts of their real lives—small, often irrelevant, chunks of their past—in their stories from which they build a façade, a fake set much like a Hollywood backdrop, that they strive to strike up for you the reader, and not they, the writers. So not everything an author writes is about him or her, but rather it's about the characters who "people" their lives.

Still, inklings here and there give some insight to the curses and blessings of the stories' creator, but the most important element that any reader should be concentrating on is the story itself and how it affects you, maybe changes you, maybe has you re-thinking your life, your philosophy.

Paramount to all of this is that you, the reader, enjoy this imaginary life away from your real life.

About Dr.
Gianni DeVincenti Hayes

Besides working as a university adjunct teaching, she served as a college department chair and associate professor in 1989. She is also a recognized author with over thirty years of writing experience, and 21-published books, hundreds of articles, and multiple anthologies.

Dr. Hayes earned her Ph.D *Summa cum Laude* in from the University of Maryland College Park, both her masters from Duquesne University, one, *summa cum* laude, and the other, with high honors. Her bachelor's degree is from Gannon University, where she was honored with *The Distinguished Alumni Award*. Her bachelor's degree and two masters' degrees were in scientific research and education. Additionally, she attended the University of Pittsburgh for two years where she earned *A Letter of Highest Commendation,* and has been endowed to the University of Rochester's writing program for five summers, as well as to Middlebury College's prestigious Bread Loaf Program. Being uniquely both left brain/right brain oriented, she handles logistical data and the creative arts equally well, giving her an edge in brainstorming as well as constructing logical, sequential and unique processes in problem-solving.

Hayes's expertise is in research design, development, and methodologies, as well as in organizational systems and leadership, along with technical, nonfiction, and fiction writing, and other genres. Some of her studies included Hegelian Dialectics, charismatic and transformational/ transactional leadership, as well as the political, educational, and corporate arenas. Her strong scientific background gives her unique insight into research processes, methodologies, instrumentation, and strategies. Her corporate, educational, religious, organizational skills, coupled with her international public appearances make her an asset in investigative projects, models, patterns and constructs.

In the past, she has also worked as a correspondence instructor for a company, taught AP science students, served as a college department chair and professor of communications, and taught education courses. Currently, she is employed as a university teacher/committee chair and member of doctoral students in organizational leadership, which requires both on-site and online attendance.

Additionally, she has authored over 100 articles and short stories, has been published in major newspapers and religious and national magazines such as *Woman's Day, Redbook, US, People, Brides, Parade, Writers Digest,* and many others, including books published by royalty houses. As a researcher, she conducts extensive literature review and countless articles to create all-encompassing papers, including biographies and topics on current events, globalism, and the American educational system. Too, besides her natural byline, she writes under various pen names, and has appeared on dozens of national radio and television shows, including *A & E Biography,* and in country-wide newspapers and magazines. Recently, she completed her 50th radio/TV station interviews on the subject of "media & globalism." She also was interviewed on Pennsylvania Cable Network TV, with 145 stations statewide, and nine million viewers.

An internationally recognized researcher, recipient of many tributes, former college professor and department chair, and author of five novels (one of which had been optioned for book-to-film project) and 16 nonfiction books, including two grammar supplementary textbooks, Hayes also writes screenplays, one of which has been optioned by a movie company. Besides her media appearances, she does book tours, seminars, signings, public speaking, authors' receptions, and readings of her work.

She has online columns syndicated nationally and internationally. Her novels appear in both print and digital formats, and she travels the world on cruises, speaking about politics, education, writing and the topics of "communications in a global world," as well as "globalism and the media."

In addition, she is the host of her own live radio show on AVR—The American Voice Station: www.theamericanvoice.com on Wednesday evenings from 8 to10 p.m. EST, which attracts a worldwide listenership.

Hayes also has expertise in eschatology, which combines religion, science, politics, communications, philosophy and history with Bible prophecy. She has been the honored guest at many authors' receptions. She has been featured in *Contemporary Authors* encyclopedia and has been invited (several times) for listing in numerous biographical marquees. She has been asked to donate all her writings to the Libraries of the University of Maryland College Park for a permanent collection, in her name, for their archives on her writing and university teaching.

Hayes was also nominated for the Governor's Award of Writing by a state senator, a state delegate, an area council president, and several high-profile people, and was honored at her undergraduate college for *Women's History Month* 2003 where she gave a campus-wide presentation. She also has been unanimously voted into her high school *Hall of Fame Award for Distinguished Alumni* where she flew to Pittsburgh to be inducted in September 2003. Dr. Hayes also served as Special Assistant to the University of Maryland Eastern Shore Chancellor.

When not writing, Dr. Hayes enjoys university teaching, oil painting, and listening to classical music, along with spending time with her husband and daughters.

Experience Summary

Author of 21 published royalty books

Author of major articles and short stories in worldwide publications

Author of two screenplays (formerly optioned)

Author of a book-to-film deal (formerly optioned)

Online columnist for several publications

Founded the 20-year-old writers' organization, The Writers Bloc, Inc

Former college department chair, and associate professor

Recipient of two "Distinguished Alumni" Awards

International radio show host

International speaker

Former regional TV show host on writing, and radio show on Access TV

Director of writers' workshops and conferences

Recipient of numerous writing and academic awards

Former high school and college plays director/producer

OTHER BOOKS BY THE AUTHOR

Jacob's Demon: A Novel of Alternative Reality
Lucifer's Legion
Heartbroken love
Rough Water
22 Friar Street
Zambelli: The First Family of Fireworks
Wicomico County; Images of America: Maryland
Move It: A Guide to Relocating Family, Pets and Plants
Ocean City, Vol. 1 (Images of America: Maryland)
Ocean City, Vol. 2 (Images of America: Maryland)
Chincoteague and Assateague Islands (MD & VA)...
Wallops Island (Images of America: Virginia)
Rehoboth Beach in Vintage Postcards (Postcard History: Delaware)
Grammar & Diagramming Sentences (Advanced Straight Forward English Series)
Troublesome Grammar (GP-019) (Advanced Straight Forward English Series)
The Last of the Wallendas
Salisbury: Picturing the Crossroads of Delmarva
Drugs and Your Teen

And many anthologies.